Strands of Fire

A Tale of Magic in the Great War

The Shards of Lafayette
Book 2

Kenneth A. Baldwin

EBURNEAN
BOOKS

Strands of Fire

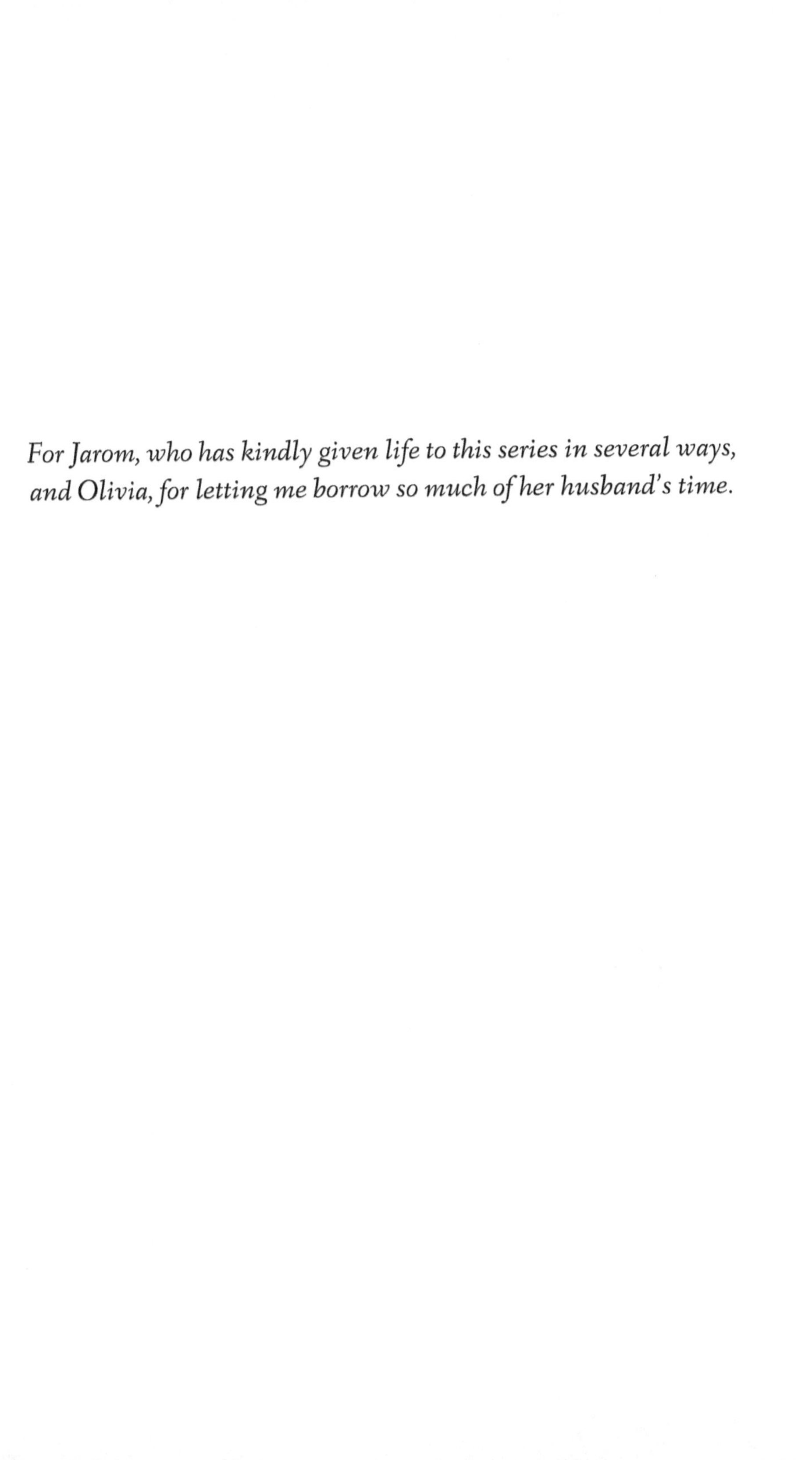

For Jarom, who has kindly given life to this series in several ways, and Olivia, for letting me borrow so much of her husband's time.

Chapter 1
The Magic of War
Jane

That woman's days were spent
In ignorant good-will,
Her nights in argument
Until her voice grew shrill.
What voice more sweet than hers
When, young and beautiful,
She rode to harriers?
-William Butler Yeats-

The wind rushed loudly by, the night closed in around us, and the two machine guns at my side whispered dark promises only I could hear.

The first time I'd pulled the trigger on a pair of Lewis guns was nothing but an experiment. I'd been thrown into a gunner's bay with hardly a moment's notice before my best friend, Marcus, flew us on a secret assignment. We were to track down a magical device at an airfield near Dunkirk. As we glided through the air, safely far behind the Allied side of the front lines, I had sighted a wispy cloud and ripped it apart with hot lead.

Even though it was nothing but a cloud, the violent outburst from the guns changed me, even if I hadn't realized in the moment. All the theories of diplomacy and dining room strategy I'd been so ready to debate at a distance became more complicated, perhaps laughably simplistic, even.

That was before the Blue Flyer had tried to kill us.

War found me, and despite all of my reservations, once it had ripped me from my hiding place, nothing in the world seemed to promise safety the way those Lewis guns did.

Now, my teeth chattered from the cold, and my hands shook as I gripped the handles of those ring-mounted guns. They swiveled around to give me ample space to twist their sights at enemy pilots. German pilots.

A couple of years earlier, the thought of German bomber planes swooping in at night to drop explosives from the sky was ludicrous. Now, it was routine misery.

Thousands of feet below my gunner's bay, the peripheries of Paris sprawled out like electric wires.

The world called Paris the City of Light. But now that the German advance threatened only fifty miles from its borders, the city's nightlife had muffled its enthusiasm.

Only days before, Germany had rained hell itself down on London in the nightmarish guise of thirty heavy bombers. Gothas. The repercussions rattled through the Allied lines.

And though, technically, our assignment tonight had nothing to do with German bombers, I scanned the sky for them anxiously. I had my Lewis guns. And it was not common for fighters to escort the bombers in the dark of night. If I saw one, I would take it.

"Anything?" Marcus yelled from the pilot's seat in front of me. He sailed us through the air, his engine presently switched off to facilitate communication. But even without its roar, it was hard to hear him through the dark wind.

"Nothing," I called out to him, flexing the glove on my right hand.

The glove was our mission tonight. It was much too large for me. Though my hands had grown strong from my time repairing planes since joining the service. Given my belief in the arcane, I'd developed a reputation for hex-like miraculous repairs on aircraft. I winced at such a reputation now. I knew nothing about magic. Magic could devour me whole and I'd be none the wiser.

"Did they say what that glove is supposed to do?" Marcus asked.

I gritted my teeth.

"You are fully aware they did not."

"Where'd they get it, again?"

Marcus didn't know how much his questions ate at me. He was only trying to comfort me with some pilot chatter. But he'd grown critical of Command in an unbecoming way. If they did not divulge every detail on a mission, he assumed they purposefully left us in the dark. Some clawing nerve clamped at my throat.

Marcus continued with a shake of his head. "I'm surprised they let us know what we were testing at all!"

His joke was laced with sarcasm, but even I had to admit it wasn't far off the mark. That was the way of it when you worked for secret units kept far away from the history books. I'd not have been surprised if they'd sent us into the air with an unmarked box. What did we know about our current assignment?

It was a leather glove. Classification? Possible arcane artifact. Magical effect?

That was for us to discover.

"We should turn back," he called.

"A little longer," I replied. My eyes narrowed as I squinted into the surrounding dark.

"Come on. I'm freezing!"

"Not yet!" It was hard to keep the edge from my voice when I was yelling over the wind. Marcus bobbed his head side to side in a gesture of disappointment. He was hesitant to fly at all, now. He'd changed so much since we'd come back from Ghent—since Lufbery's last flight. We both had.

I scanned the night sky. Weaves of clouds masked the stars above and despite how I strained my eyes, I'd noticed no hint of magic from the glove on my hand. Still, I squinted to find something in the dark. We'd been flying for an hour and a half, to no effect. Marcus was right. If the glove had any enchantment, it would not be revealed by another hour of peaceful travel.

I let out a breath of disappointment and was about to concede we should head home when something caught my eye.

"Hang on," I said, peering far beneath our wings. For just a moment, a shadow obscured the gray of a cloud below. "Did you see that?"

The wind howled knowingly before he responded.

"We don't have to engage him," he said. I scoffed.

"We have to test the glove."

He shook his head again.

"It's our mission," I insisted.

"To hell with the mission. Even without an escort, those bombers have teeth."

Even as he said it, I heard the defeat in his voice. I didn't need to remind him that Lufbery, his great hero, would have engaged any enemy plane at any time. Nor did I need to remind him of what similar bombers had done to London.

Lufbery had trained him to be a good pilot, even if he was a reluctant one.

From the city below, we heard a faint explosion. I peered over the edge of our fuselage to see a cloud rising from a concentration of buildings on the ground. The flashes of anti-air guns blazed to life, streaking hot tracer rounds into the sky.

It was a night raid then, not some solo reconnaissance plane.

Sweat beaded underneath my oversized flight suit as my thoughts raced to England, to the Gothas that had bludgeoned the English capital, a city that had rested safely behind a channel guarded by the best Naval Force in the world for centuries. The magic of aerial warfare had laid waste to a millennium of wartime strategy.

When news of the attack on London came, I'd clutched a tattered photograph of my parents and cried the night through, praying that they were safe in Gloucestershire.

Marcus's shoulders slumped, and I knew with only a small push I could have my way.

"Our allies might fire on us," he said. "No one knows we're up here. Top secret, remember?"

"The Germans don't know we're up here, either," I said.

Reluctantly, he hit the top wing of our Salmson with his fist.

"I hate this," he said. It barely reached my ears.

"You fly, I fire," I replied, trying to mask the relief in my voice.

I double checked my harness. My breath raced, heart pounded, and in the moment of calm before the dive, I wondered if I was afraid or excited.

Marcus barreled us over into a plunge, reversing our direction and chasing after the shadow beneath us. He'd likely seen the enemy plane even before I had. He had much more practice spotting enemies from his cockpit. My stomach twisted as we pummeled downward, and I locked my arms against the ring mount of my Lewis guns to brace myself. The shakes came, knees wobbling like an unbalanced step stool.

Smoothly, and quietly, he evened us out. The French anti-air guns streaked dazzling fire into the sky. Their tracers poked holes in the spotlights, searching the sky. Against the racing light of their rounds, I noted the silhouette of our enemy plane. It was no Gotha. In the dark, I could not distinguish its model, but from the size of its fuselage, I supposed it to be a two-seater, perhaps a light bomber.

In the daylight, pilots preferred to attack from above with the sun behind them because the sun's glare offered the best cloaking cover imaginable. But the moon provided no concealing glare to advantage our approach. Instead, Marcus had settled us in beneath and behind. I craned my neck to face the enemy above our nose. My guns did not swivel that far. He would have the first shot.

I bit my lip. The first shot was not Marcus's strong suit. But then, he earned his first victory on our way back from Ghent, unofficial though the victory was. And although we'd flown several missions to investigate suspected artifacts since then, he'd yet to have much opportunity to pull the trigger again.

The plane sailed on ahead of us, doubtlessly distracted by the anti-air fire reaching up from its target below. I breathed shallowly to preserve the quiet, then laughed at myself for such an inane concern—as if they could hear my breathing amidst the howling wind, percussive battery of the guns, and the roar of their engine.

My eyes settled on Marcus, watching his shoulders heave up and down, the way a man might breathe in preparation to lift a couch.

Perhaps this was a poor idea, after all.

But just as I contemplated our chances of slipping away into the dark undetected, our nose peaked up suddenly, and the single Vickers gun on the front of our plane blazed to life.

For a prolonged instant, the night sky around us moved in strobed slow motion. The German plane jerked to the side, sliding then banking, before the flashes revealed the panicked gunner in the back seat.

Marcus had hardly fired off any rounds at all.

"I'm jammed!" Marcus shouted to me.

Now we were truly in danger. Despite the moon waning as brightly as it did, night was no time for dogfighting. Even if we managed to keep the enemy engaged, visibility was too poor, and we were liable to crash into them by accident.

So I swung my body, locked my elbows, planted my feet firmly against the bottom of my gunner's bay, and let holy fire rain.

My guns screamed and thrashed on their mount, but I did not let off the trigger.

Marcus's shot sent them scrambling by instinct, and the pilot made a terrible error. He veered into my sight lines and had exposed his belly to us, cutting off his gunner from making any reply to our attack.

I splintered the fuselage to bits.

The fire from my guns laid siege to my dark-adjusted eyes. The enemy gunner tried in vain to return a volley, but they shot in any direction but ours, and soon their aircraft burst into flame.

I followed the light with my arms, welcomed the vibrations of the guns through my shoulders, into my ribcage, and waited for it to shake something loose in my heart.

Marcus had gone two years before his first victory, and all the while I'd lectured him about peace and the futility of war. But when my first kills came along, the guilt never came with them. I'd waited and waited for the grief, braced myself for the crushing remorse, the disgust—at least some moral solemnity about the value of human life.

It never came. Something else did. Something dark.

Marcus screamed at me. I did not hear him amidst the wind and roaring guns. The enemy plane had already fallen, but I could not pull off the trigger.

This plane would not hurt Marcus. It would not hurt my family in England. It would not hurt anyone ever again. I'd seen to that. There was finicky magic about it.

Suddenly, I lurched to the side. Marcus pulled us into a steep and diving bank. The force of it flung me to the edge of my gunner's bay. He climbed upward steeply and pinned me to the back of my seat.

We flew directly toward the moon before the engine cylinders gave way, and we turned back over, weightless. Marcus barreled us three times over until I wanted to vomit, then finally evened us out.

"Jane, what was that? What is the matter with you?" he shouted.

He didn't need to understand. He was an excellent pilot, but a terrible soldier. And that was all right. I could accept that burden.

He flies, I fire.

Our quarry plummeted to the ground in a strand of flames against the dark night sky.

I could keep him safe.

The spotlights searched the sky and illuminated other bombers heading toward Paris. I reached for my guns again.

I could be the guardian.

They were far off, and I knew Marcus would not engage these others. We'd tested the glove in combat, discovered it had no effect. We'd done our duty. We could run back home.

But he didn't understand like I did.

There was no outrunning the magic of war.

Chapter 2
Sinn Feiners
Marcus

Jane squeezed my hand tightly. Her fingers interlaced with mine as we walked down a crowded street in Dublin. Her other hand gripped my arm between bicep and elbow.

"You nervous?" I asked.

"I'm playing the part," she said as she skirted a pothole filled with muddy water.

"I think we're already in with these folks. It's been a couple weeks already. If they thought we were spies, we'd have sensed it by now."

"I'm not nervous," she whispered.

"It's natural to look nervous on a night like this. They told us they were sharing something big tonight. We should be a little nervous. It'd be weird to look too confident, in fact."

"Marcus, you're the nervous one. Clearly. Your knees are practically wobbling."

I sighed. It wasn't only the meeting wobbling my knees. It didn't matter how many evenings we'd already gone out pretending to be married, it weirded me out.

I tried not to think about how many times we'd held hands before this trip to Ireland. In the past, there was never any danger of it coming across as romantic. Whenever we'd huddled close or wrapped up in an embrace, it was for comfort and support. No more questions needed.

But for this mission, a prolonged one at that, we needed to be in love, a convincing kind of love, or things might go sideways. I knew it was pretend, but we'd never needed to pretend like this before, and she had no qualms about leaning into the bit. She was a good actress. It was weird.

So despite all of Dublin's many fascinating sights, sounds, and smells, all I managed to concentrate on was whether I was crushing the fingers she laced between mine.

The sun had already set, and lights from pubs and night clubs illuminated the streets around us. Above, the tall, dark facades of buildings on our left and right made me a little claustrophobic. They stared like angry faces that knew who we really were—not deserters and separatist sympathizers, but Marcus and Jane, the only flying members of what Dupont had decided to call the Arcane Escadrille. Atkins hadn't liked that much. After all, we were supposed to be confidential, and usually confidential units didn't have flashy nicknames.

"Why are you so stiff?" Jane protested. "Please. There is nervous and there is petrified."

"I'm just getting into the character. If I were really a deserter, I would be petrified."

"Not deserters," she said.

"Right. Worse. Defectors."

"Yes," she replied as she put my arm around her waist. We were getting closer to our destination. Ahead, light from the pub we sought spilled out into the street, and patrons caroused at tables of different heights just outside. "It's not like we're meeting the President of Sinn Fein tonight or anything. You know Cillian well, by now. He likes you."

I tried hard not to let the weight of my wrist and arm settle on her hip and considered how awkward an arrangement it was to walk while having your arm draped around someone like this in the first place. Her waist shifted and moved as she walked, and the only natural way to rest my hand was to settle it on the groove of her side. As soon as I managed that, the movement came easier.

"Is this all right?" I asked, a little embarrassed. Before she rolled her eyes or cocked her eyebrow to suggest the question was stupid, a warmth had washed over her expression.

Or was that just the streetlights of Dublin casting her in a strange light?

"Marcus, I know this is uncomfortable. It will be less uncomfortable if you stop treating me like a dangerous animal," she said.

I laughed.

"Maybe a lion cub," I said, memories tugging at my mind. A long while back, the Lafayette Escadrille had adopted two lion cubs as their mascot. The lions made themselves at home on the airbase and behaved more like dogs than wild animals. They had taken a particular liking to my best friend, Raoul Lufbery.

The thought of him nearly stopped me in place. With my free hand, I reached for the machine gun round in my pocket. The casing was perfectly polished by Luf's own hand before he—

Jane squeezed my torso.

"Sorry. I didn't mean to bring up Lufbery," she whispered. I must have looked confused. "You always stare at the ground like that when you think about him."

"You didn't. I did," I replied without warmth.

Luf was my hero. I idolized him like an older brother. He meant everything to me. And he was gone. He went after a German recon plane and never came back.

I'd been at war since I was young, since the war was young. I'd lost a lot of friends. I'd never been angry at one before.

His death was still fresh. His loss had changed Jane and me as individuals and as a partnership. We were scared to talk about him. It was like watching a squad member go out of formation to engage someone on his own. I had no way of communicating what I knew, and she had no way to do the same. I didn't know how either of us would look by the time we were done processing the grief. Sometimes, it popped up in scary ways, like how she'd succumbed to a fit of violence a few nights previous when pumping rounds into a dead German pilot and his dead gunner.

I shook my head to rid myself of the gloom. We were Marcus and Jane. We'd gone through hell and made it back. I wouldn't fail her now.

We sauntered into the pub and pushed our way through a mass of drinkers. It was a small place with a big bar. Around us, all types mingled on the worn wooden booths and polished counter. Amputees, rough old men with leathery skin, young women done up in curls and makeup to accentuate their beauty, widows done up in curls and makeup to cover their age. Most of the men between ages eighteen and thirty were either injured, crazy, or absent altogether.

I made my way toward a stool by the bar, recently made vacant by a young woman running off after her group friends that headed out the door.

"It looks like Mr. Ryan is occupied," I said to Jane. "Here. Have a seat."

"What? So you can hover over me like a bodyguard? I don't think so."

I glanced around. Amidst the crowded room, Mr. Ryan, the

bartender of the pub and the keeper of the door behind the counter, was busy tossing out a disorderly veteran who'd had a pint too many.

"I don't think another is going to open up."

She rolled her eyes again before putting both of her arms around my neck and tugging me onto the stool. When I was firmly planted, she took a seat on my lap and leaned playfully into my chest.

Suddenly, I considered it would be easier to unjam a mounted Lewis gun than to act natural. But I tried.

"Put your arms around me," Jane said through smiling teeth.

"What?"

"Can you please pretend to be enjoying yourself?"

"Oh, right," I said, trying to smile. I wrapped my arms around Jane's waist again, and she laughed. I laughed, too. What else was there to do with my awkward energy, let it sweat out of my palms?

Jane played the part well, rocking back and forth, saying silly things just loud enough for the people beside us to hear, things like, "It's so nice having you home" and "You didn't dally with any of those French girls, did you?"

After a few minutes of this, when I was convinced she was really about to plant a big wet kiss on my lips to sell the bit, Mr. Ryan returned behind the counter. I raised my hand to call him over.

"Mr. Ryan, we're here for—"

"Two?" he replied, cutting me off.

"Oh right," I stuttered. We weren't supposed to know him personally, even if we'd been coming here each night for the past few weeks. He turned his back to me and started pouring something from a bottle into two shot glasses. He turned back around, planted them on the bar. His fingernails had grime wedged under them, and he was missing a tooth. He grinned.

Each evening, he tested us again with two shots and false conversation that sounded a little too sincere.

"She's a beauty," he said, nodding at Jane. She beamed and pretended to be shy. I looked at her.

We'd been teased a lot since meeting. Other guys on base had batted their eyelashes at me plenty of times or told me she was beautiful with a mocking lilt. They'd shared no small number of crass jokes at our expense. At first, I'd fought it. Then I realized the more I let others know it bothered me, the stronger it came on.

But Mr. Ryan was sincere. And he was right. Painted as some of the other young women in the bar, with rosy cheeks, cherry lips, and darkly painted eyes, she might have had her pick of the men in the room.

"Don't remind me," I told him.

"With a beauty like that on my lap, I'd look a bit more happy if I were you," he said. I couldn't tell if he was being playful or casting doubt on our cover. I forced a laugh.

"How affectionate do you want me?" I asked, then burrowed my nose into Jane's hair. The panic still grew. Whenever anyone asked questions about our marriage, my heart started racing for fear of being discovered. I wasn't an operative. I was a pilot. I had no business pretending to be someone I wasn't.

"You going to drink?" he said. Jane's hair was perfumed.

"What?" I asked, pulling myself back to his attention.

"You going to drink?" he asked again solemnly, pointing at the glasses on the bar. I hesitated. He knew I didn't drink. I didn't do it to calm my nerves on a flight, and I certainly couldn't now when I needed all my social wits to keep from blowing our mission. Besides, I had no idea what was in the glasses. For all I knew, Mr. Ryan had found out we were with the government and poisoned the—

Jane swooped forward, grabbed them, and downed one after the other. I stared in shock. She winced and shook her head from side to side before holding one glass above her head and slamming them back down on the bar. A couple of women to our right clapped. One of them mouthed the word "wow."

"I want to dance!" Jane said, slipping off my lap. It was the first time I'd noticed the fiddle playing from the corner of the room.

"In a minute, darling," I said as I pulled her back toward me. I turned back to the barkeep. "Say, we're supposed to be meeting a friend here. Maybe you've seen them."

He shrugged. He shrugged every night we rehearsed this script. I knew what he'd say next.

"What's the name?"

"Casement," I said, repeating the code word we'd been provided. He paused, then whispered.

"That was last night's friend," he said.

"There's a new friend tonight?" I asked.

"There's a new friend."

"I don't know the new friend."

"Then I can't let you through the door."

Jane's plastered-on smile faltered. She took the reins again, tossed her curls, and pouted.

"New friend?" she asked. "That's odd. Margaret didn't mention any new—"

At mention of the name Margaret, the man relaxed.

"Keep your voice down," he said. "Everyone's spooked right now. They arrested over a hundred of the Feiners only a little bit ago. The new word is Eamon. Come on, then."

We followed him to a darkly lacquered door in the corner of the room. He cracked it and went back to polishing his glassware, leaving us to slip inside. The sounds of the pub muffled in an instant as we closed it behind us.

Inside, we navigated a dark, creaking stairwell up a few flights before light peeked out from under a door. We knocked three times slowly and waited.

After a hushed shuffling of feet, the door opened.

"Well, there you two are."

Margaret's worried face appeared in the crack between the frame and the door.

"Sorry, Margaret," I said. "You know Jane, always fussing about her hair."

Jane jabbed me in the side. She didn't hold back any, either, and I doubled over.

"I'll never do it for you again if you keep up like that," Jane said. Margaret ushered us inside and locked the door behind us. The apartment was shabby, dilapidated, downright broken, but I loved it. We'd only been meeting with the Irish nationalists for a couple of weeks, but something about them felt homey and welcoming. It'd been a long time since I'd experienced such a thing. Even my tenure at the Lafayette, which was full of congeniality and friendship, had undertones of transience. But here... These folks would have kept you forever if you wanted.

Unless, secretly, you were betraying them, that is. I pushed the thought to the back of my mind.

We sat in a small group of what were by now familiar faces. Margaret stood near the kitchen, while her cousin Beth and her friend Grace conversed on two rickety chairs by the door. Cillian, the sole man I'd met so far in connection to this unit of the Sinn Feiners, wore a tortured expression at rest but couldn't help himself throwing a welcoming arm around you. I had taken an instant liking to him, and the affection had only grown from there.

"You'll be all right while the men talk over here?" I asked Jane before bracing for another poke. She shook her head at me and broke off to speak with Margaret and the others.

"Be careful, Markie," said Cillian. "Or that Jane of yours will have you sleeping alone tonight."

I laughed and joined him by the window. He offered me the

second half of the cigarette he'd been smoking. I waved it off but smiled as I sat beside him.

"Look at them," he said, nodding toward the women. "They were born for this type of thing. You see how animated and excited they all are? Have you ever paused to think, Markie, what a war of women would look like?"

I cocked my head and wondered. Once, I'd have said there'd be no such war. My mother and Jane shaped my understanding of women. My mother was relentlessly sweet, and Jane had challenged my perceptions of violence since our early days together.

But then, lately, Jane had been changing. The girl in front of me now was not the girl I met in Gengoult. Had a man's war affected her, or did she have the soldier's fury in her all along?

"I don't want to think about that," I replied.

"Nor do I," he said. "I think that's why men fight the wars. Men are treacherous, and bloodthirsty, yes. But if women ran the wars, I don't know if I'd ever trust a peace treaty. They know something we don't."

I furrowed my eyebrows, snorted, and turned to him.

"You been drinking, Cillian?" I asked.

"Doesn't mean I'm wrong," he said.

Margaret waved us over to a torn and battered couch.

"Get over here, you," she called. "There's news."

Cillian put an arm around my shoulders, a gesture half-rooted in affection, half in a desire for support. He had only one leg—a gift from his time serving the King at the front lines. When he'd had a little too much, the one leg counted for half. But he wore sympathy well, and his hardships rendered him all the more likable.

"You've just cut off an important conversation," he told Margaret as I helped him onto the couch. I sat down beside him and pulled Jane onto my lap.

"Oh, I heard your conversation," said Grace. "Philosophy at its finest."

"Did you forget how to whisper during your time at the front?" asked Beth.

"Hush now, all of you!" Margaret said, batting the air again as though to swat away a pesky fly. She owned the gesture for how often she used it. It would always remind me of her, the same way a half-hearted shrug would always remind me of Luf.

I caught Jane performing that half-hearted shrug from time to time.

A rat scurried across the room, but we paid no heed of it. Rats were co-tenants with the Dubliners, I'd learned, and it was best to ignore them. There was no beating them.

But despite the busted furniture, the bare rugs, and the rodents running wild, a warmth spread over me. I wanted to live in these moments, now. I squeezed Jane tighter, and she turned to me in concern. I shook my head to let her know nothing was wrong, but I didn't let up.

I could live this life, if fate would allow it. It was not optimal, but it would do. By now, I wasn't too picky.

"There are rumors coming down from the top," Margaret said.

"What kind of rumors?" asked Grace.

"There's a shipment that's come in," she went on.

"Not more weapons," Cillian's voice droned in disappointment. "I won't believe that—not after the failed smuggling that was meant to support our boys and girls in the Rising."

"It's a weapon, but it's no gun," Margaret said. "And they're only telling a few of us about it. Don't want it getting out that the leaders of the Feiners have gone crazy."

This was what we'd come for this evening. Our task was to infiltrate this branch of the Sinn Fein movement and discover if there were seeds of another uprising, like the one that had happened two years prior.

Or at least, that's what I thought the assignment was.

"Does this weapon concern my husband and me?" Jane asked. I let go of her, confused. What did she mean?

"Aye," Margaret replied.

"What's that supposed to mean?" asked Grace. Cillian and Margaret shared a troubled glance. It wasn't lost on the others in the room.

"No, Margaret. You'd told us you'd given those beliefs up," Beth whined. "Really? A magic weapon?"

My heart sank. I hadn't asked many questions about why we'd be stationed in Dublin so far from any aerial action. Truth be told, the assignment came on the tail of a frank conversation I'd had with Smith about getting Jane away from combat. When they gave me the vague directions of cozying up to Irish nationalists, I thought it was Smith making good on his word.

But he wasn't. We were still playing the same game. I stared at the woman sitting in my lap. Had Jane known the truth?

"Why shouldn't I?" Margaret replied, voice turning sharp.

"There's no magic out there." Beth stood and crossed to the window. "It's all a bunch of stories and tall tales to keep children from misbehaving. I wondered why you two brought these outsiders in so quickly."

"They're not just stories, Beth. Tell them, Cillian! Tell them what you've seen."

"Cillian's drunk. And even when he's sober you can't trust half of what he says!"

"I resent that!" Cillian replied.

I pulled Jane closer to my mouth while they argued.

"You knew about this?" I whispered. She set her jaw and tried to pull away, but I held her fast. "Why didn't you tell me we were here for magic?"

"We can't all get lost in our grief," she replied. "And besides, I shouldn't have needed to tell you."

"What's wrong with you two?" asked Margaret when she noticed our quiet back and forth.

"Nothing," Jane replied. "Just nervous."

Everyone turned to me. Jane squeezed my hand tightly, not in support, in warning. My head reeled, and all my blood was rushing to my face. She shouldn't have needed to tell me. That was true, but that wasn't all of it. Smith, Atkins, Dupont, Jane... I hadn't been shy about voicing my complaints when we didn't get all the details on an assignment. Maybe they'd given up on me.

"Darling?" Jane asked. I coughed out some guttural disbelief. Darling. Here I'd been enjoying our play acting. I was embarrassed for that, too. Yes, I knew it was pretend, but I didn't know it was pretend this way. I thought it was pretend the other way. "Are you well, darling?"

I turned my gaze on Margaret.

"You mean to tell me that you think Sinn Fein has received a shipment of magical weapons?"

Margaret took my question as encouragement. She tried to hide her smile.

"I don't know the details, but I think it's just one."

Jane hadn't eased her grip on my hand. She sensed my volatility, had realized the extent of my ignorance. My feelings were stupid. She was right. I should have known. I wasn't a child. I wouldn't blow our cover.

I only needed a moment to reconcile that I hadn't found us some cozy assignment. Jane was in danger. Again.

"I don't want to," I said quietly. Cillian put a knowing hand on my back.

"Look at that, Beth." His voice was solemn and respectful. "You don't have to believe a drunk old amputee. But I recognize that face. I see it in the morning after nightmares that I've been called back to the front. If the magic weren't real, why would he fear so at its mention?"

Grace and Beth quieted. Maybe they weren't convinced about the magic, but they might be convinced that whatever had come in this new shipment carried its fair share of danger.

"We all have our demons," Margaret said. "I don't pretend to know what you've seen or done, but you came to us with your hands outstretched. We doubted the letters, but now with you here, I've found myself hoping in a way I haven't since the Rising."

"Maybe it's a false alarm," I said.

"No," she replied. "The British government arrested one hundred and fifty Sinn Feiners a week ago with little pretense. They said Joseph Dowling was set ashore in County Clare by the Germans. He said that the Germans were planning military action in Ireland. So they locked up one hundred and fifty of us! But we know the truth. When Dowling came ashore, he had time before they found him, time enough to set the wheels in motion."

"You mean he smuggled the weapon in and stowed it somewhere?" Jane asked.

"He gave it to the right people, but we've been fooled before. The failed weapons shipment before the Rising was a disaster. There are many who believe it was a set up. We want to be thorough. When word got round that we had two new recruits with an alleged reputation for magical information, not many believed it. But I did. And now, it's time for us to prove ourselves."

Jane put her hand in my hair and leaned my head against hers.

"How do you know we're not the set up?" I asked.

Margaret paused, but Cillian laughed.

"Oh, please, look at you. Look at how you reacted when you heard the words 'magic weapon.' And besides, I can tell. You don't want their war. We're the same, you and I."

My superiors' masterstroke landed with Cillian's vote of confidence. By keeping me in the dark, they preserved the horror of this discovery. Smith wanted me to believe he'd got us a safe assignment hundreds of miles from the front so that this moment would be sincere.

Meanwhile, Atkins had lined up our search for the next great magical artifact all while landing a devastating blow to the Irish movement for Independence. My stomach churned as I looked at the hopeful faces in the room. I'd been hiding here, but their war was now. Their battle was not in a trench. It was everywhere.

"We will help," Jane said. "We want to help."

But one of us could not decide, and everyone there knew it. Again, all eyes turned on me. I swallowed.

"Can you give me a day to think about it?"

Chapter 3
Bit of a Domestic
Jane

Marcus kept quiet during the walk back to our flat. We followed our usual precautions to ensure no one had followed us, and I held his hand far longer than necessary. He didn't pull it away.

At length, we arrived at our tenement building, where we'd been holding out as a married couple. Our unit was close to the ground level. We could come and go quickly without navigating many flights of stairs. Not only that, but Atkins had arranged for some Unionist supporters to alter one of our walls so that it connected to the adjacent flat, which faced the direction opposite ours and had easy egress to the alleyway behind the building.

We waited to take that route now, knowing that it was best traversed after midnight if we didn't care to be noticed.

"What is it, Marcus?," I asked, breaking the silence. He sat on a chair across the room, picking at Lufbery's old polished round absent-mindedly.

"Just a little embarrassed, I guess."

"Don't be so hard on yourself. You've been grieving," I said.

"I thought Smith was doing us a favor and giving us some time away from everything to cope with everything."

"Well, we're not being shot at while suspended thousands of feet in the air.

"No," Marcus replied, "we're just lying to a bunch of Irish nationalists, all of whom were involved in a violent uprising a couple of years ago."

I pursed my lips, and he continued.

"Answer me this, did you all depend on me not knowing? So my reaction would genuine?"

I rolled my head to the side.

"You're being paranoid. Doesn't that seem a little drastic, withholding mission details so that a reaction to some pre-supposed revelation would come across sincere?"

"Then why?" he asked. "Just so I'd cooperate? Have I become that obnoxious?"

I stuffed my hands into the pockets of my coat.

"Your emotional state has been somewhat volatile lately," I confessed.

"And yours hasn't?" he responded. I shrugged.

"I'm sorry."

"You had orders to keep it from me."

I nodded sheepishly.

"I get it, Jane. We've got an assignment. They didn't think I could do my part if I knew about the magic. So Smith made me believe it was about something else."

They were stinging words. I'd always fancied myself Marcus's greatest supporter. Knowing that I'd knocked his self-confidence like this made my next protest sound weak even to my ears.

"You could have. I just doubted you would have."

"I didn't really get a choice, did I?"

"Come now, Marcus," I replied. "The truth of it is you're not a good soldier."

"This again?"

"What I mean is you don't follow orders well."

"Not when they're crazy!"

"You're accustomed to a very high amount of input. Lufbery listened to your feedback in a way few other commanders would."

"Please, don't bring up Luf right now."

"And the fact of the matter is this war requires that men march to their deaths. Those are facts."

He shook his head in exasperation.

"That's right. We're at war. We follow orders. We fly the missions. We don't ask questions. And when it's our time to die, then it's our time."

"Marcus, come off it. That's not fair."

He stood up, stuffed his hands in his pockets, and crossed to the window.

"What time is it?" he asked.

"I was trying to take care of you, if you really want to know," I said.

"By keeping me in the dark?"

"Yes!" I jumped up. "Look back at our lives since Lufbery's passing. What wouldn't you have given for a week of peace? Yes, they've ordered us to chase after the magic again. But for a couple weeks, they allowed me to take care of you in a way that I'd never have managed if we were still flying missions near Paris."

I grabbed his arms and locked my eyes on his to entreat him.

"His death rattled us both—"

"I know that—"

"—and I spent the time since that horrid, horrid day holding your hand and hugging you close. Do you think that was make believe? That was me, Jane, wanting with all of my heart to take away the pain of that loss. I could only buy you a short window of time, but even if you hate me for it, I can't regret it."

His eyes, darting and evasive, finally rested on my face. In them swirled all of his confusion and humiliation, but they surrendered to me.

"I'm sorry, Jane," he mumbled. "I want to trust you. You're right. You've always taken care of me. I'm just scared."

"Of course you are. As am I. I've been reeling since Ghent, Marcus. Put yourself in my position. The magic is more dangerous than I ever imagined. I've always been known as the girl with the magic. But I knew nothing. What are you supposed to do when the ground you've always stood on gives way beneath you? I close my eyes at night and see the Blue Flyer shooting at us from his awful shape-shifting plane."

He squeezed my arm.

"Jane, I'm sorry."

"And you still wear that marble around your neck."

I laid my hand on his chest where the marble hung beneath his shirt. I'd had a pair of them made by my mother's best friend, my tutor in the ways of magic since I was a young girl. This adoptive aunt had brought me up with an education of every little secret and method she knew of manipulating the world's unseen forces. The marbles were meant to protect us. As we wore them, if one stayed safe, so did the other. One strand of my hair in his. One strand of his in mine.

And yet, mine had been stolen. The Flyer had ripped it from my neck in the crypt under St. Bavo's cathedral. How I had racked my brain and tortured my conscience for allowing such a thing to happen.

"I promised you I wouldn't take this thing off," he muttered, eyes darting down to my hand.

"But we don't know what you wearing it does. He has the other. I'm the one asking you to take it off."

"A promise is a promise."

"Promises are purposeful. And when the purpose serves, they should be adjusted," I said.

"Maybe I'm just scared of things changing."

His eyes flicked back up to mine as he said this, and suddenly, I was very conscious of my hand on his chest, of how close we were standing. How strange that noticing closeness changes it altogether.

In all our time posing as husband and wife, I hadn't kissed Marcus on the mouth. Amidst the necessity of the role-play, I had drawn an invisible line, and sworn never to cross it unless absolutely necessary. Despite all the reasons I'd rehearsed in my head for this, none of them explained why I was perfectly comfortable sitting on his lap, taking his arm, or nuzzling his hair, but not comfortable touching lips.

But in this room, now, his mouth was very close to mine.

I lowered my hand.

"What time is it?" I asked. He took a deep breath through his nose.

"Time to go."

The routine was familiar by now. We moved the cabinet that hid the door in the wall and slipped through, careful to replace it behind us. Then we scurried through the neighboring flat, checked for anyone looking in the hallway, rushed down a flight of steps and out the back door into the alley.

Our meeting place was a boarded up garage accessible by

means of an iron door. We skirted a nest of rats looking for scraps of food in a pile of garbage.

The door rested behind a tall pile of wooden crates. Marcus had turned up his collar. We did not hold hands on the way to meet with our superiors.

He knocked on the door in our covert pattern. One. One two. One.

Marcus had proposed it as a type of rhythmic version of the Nun Yunu Wi keyword we'd used for the Clairmarais cipher. It was simple, distinct, and worked well for our purposes. And for whatever reason, perhaps because it was uniquely American, it had stuck with Marcus uncommonly well. I often caught him muttering it to himself or reciting the cipher's displaced alphabet. So long as it kept his mind off of Lufbery, I couldn't fault him for it.

The door opened, and we scrambled inside.

Smith, Atkins, and Dupont waited for us in a dimly lit corner of a garage. The space reeked of old oil and cigarette smoke. The latter wafted off the orange glowing tip of Dupont's cigarette.

"Well?" asked Atkins when we arrived. "A few minutes late, this evening."

"I'm sorry," said Marcus. "I know you had tickets to the theater."

I winced. I disliked it when Marcus was sarcastic to the others. The practice bred disrespect and gave a rude impression.

"I see you've not lost that fighting spirit," Atkins replied.

"How is the honeymoon?" Dupont asked. I rolled my eyes. Since our team had settled on our cover, Dupont's jabs about our relationship came faster than rounds from a Spandau machine gun.

"Productive," I replied.

"Is that so?" asked Atkins.

"It's as you hoped," I went on. "The Irish believe that one of their own has smuggled a magical artifact out of Germany. They attribute it to Dowling, who they claimed stowed the artifact before his capture."

Atkins slapped his knee in triumph.

"Easy there, skippy," said Smith as he patted Atkins condescendingly on the back. "Do they know where it is?"

"I think so. But they haven't told us," I replied.

Atkins breathed deeply through his nose with a hissing sound.

"Vindication. This justifies the measures we took in arresting all those Sinn Fein leaders." His voice carried a good measure of relief, as though this information somehow exonerated him from an ethical burden. Smith scrunched up his eyebrows.

"You figure? Arresting a hundred fifty like-minded people because one man tried to smuggle something into the country?"

"I don't expect you to understand," Atkins said. "A magical device in the hands of the Irish poses a significant threat to the empire."

"You lost me at empire," said Smith.

"Oh, please. Don't pretend the *United States* are too holy for imperial pursuits. They'd never—"

Dupont inserted himself between them and slung his arms over their shoulders.

"You continue like this, I'm going to make you kiss," he said.

The very thought disgusted them both into silence.

"So what now?" I asked. "We try to retrieve the device?"

Atkins escaped Dupont's arm and double checked the lock on the door. His voice came out much lower than before.

"You've done well," he started. "And it's time I brief you in full. For this mission, the device is but a secondary objective."

Marcus spoke up.

"What are you talking about?"

"On your flight back from Ghent, you shot down the Blue Flyer," said Smith. "But, as you know, the Flyer's body was never recovered. We didn't accept that. So we went hunting."

"Two years ago, the Rising in Ireland hinged on a critical misstep. The rebels expected a shipment of weapons, ammunition and, possibly, a magical advantage. His Majesty's government dispatched agents to disrupt this shipment, and as a result, the weapons never arrived. The Rising was frustrated in Cork and Dublin. The Crown deemed this a success, but there are some who would have preferred a less invasive intervention, one that we might have teased out to discover all parties allied to Irish independence."

"What he's trying to say," Smith interrupted as he slumped back into his seat, "is he thinks the Blue Flyer helped the Irish uprising two years ago, and we think he's doing the same thing now."

It took a moment for the implication to set in. When it did, my whole body rejected the thought. I had associations with the Rising that I had yet to share with either Marcus or our superiors. I had a cousin serving in the Sherwood Foresters when they were called to quell the Irish uprising. The regiment was slaughtered in the streets of Dublin, my cousin among them.

I heard not long after I'd left home to volunteer. The news had crushed me, but I'd stuffed it away with the many other sorrows the war had brought me. I didn't care to share the news with anyone, especially after learning we'd be working as operatives in Dublin.

I had no wish for the others to deem me too emotionally invested, not when they already had so much doubt about Marcus's state of mind. But the thought of the Blue Flyer joining forces with them was a stroke too far.

"That is absolutely and utterly ridiculous," I said.

"Why?" Atkins asked.

"Because we shot down the Flyer," I stammered. "Even if he did survive, you're proposing that he crawled away from the wreckage, got himself sorted, and still had a hand in smuggling a magical artifact from Germany to Ireland by means of a U-boat? Tell me, did he make it home in time for dinner as well?"

Marcus put a hand on my arm.

"We didn't kill him," he said.

"Precisely," said Atkins. "And if he's not dead, he's still dangerous."

I couldn't find the words. It had been bad enough posing as a friend to the Sinn Feiners. I knew that Margaret and Beth and Grace and Cillian hadn't pulled the trigger on the shot that killed my cousin. Logically, that made sense. I might even manage to conjure some sympathy for their cause, but their reckless ambition to get hold of a magical weapon, to partner with a monster like the Blue Flyer.

I took a deep breath.

"What are you asking us to do?" Marcus asked carefully.

"If Joseph Dowling smuggled a magical device ashore," continued Smith, "the Blue Flyer will either want the device or he's helping the Irish cause. Either way, he's gonna be with that artifact, eventually." He leaned back in his chair. They were all grim-faced and solemn.

"We want you to capture him," Atkins said. "And if that's not possible, to kill him."

A dread silence settled in the room. I heard a skittering speed across the dark in the far corner. My voice came out in a whisper.

"Do you mean it, Atkins?"

He nodded, sending a shiver down my spine. A capture. A raid. Soldiers on the front did this all the time. And if not, then an assassination—an execution. What word suited for this?

"The honeymoon is over," said Dupont as he lit up another cigarette.

"No." Marcus shook his head back and forth. "No."

"Marcus, we haven't heard the details yet," I said.

"No," he repeated. "I'm not an assassin."

"You already shot him down once, kid," Smith started.

"That's different," Marcus protested. "That's combat. That's war. This is just killing behind closed doors."

"It shouldn't come to that," Atkins corrected. "Take him alive."

"I'd be fine with capture." Marcus put his hands on his head and laughed in disbelief. "But did you see what he did to us in Ghent?"

"You have the element of surprise this time," said Atkins.

"There's no surprising him."

"That's not entirely true," I said. "I surprised him under St. Bavo's. He didn't expect me to jump at him as I did. Marcus, if you'd been with me, surely we could have overpowered him."

Marcus stared at me in disbelief. Despite how I cared for him, it raised my hackles in defense.

"Then you're delusional. If you think this ends any other way than someone dying, you're kidding yourself."

"Then someone will die. Marcus—" I started.

"If this is about abducting the Flyer, why send only two of us? Don't you have a whole regiment stationed here, Atkins? We can help recon, then send in your boys to get him. Why the hell would you need to send Jane into such danger?"

Atkins's features exhibited no frustration.

"Such a move would be politically unwise," he said simply.

"So that's it." Marcus turned to Smith. "What about our deal?"

I folded my arms. It was a bold tactic. He already knew that Smith's alleged deal to keep us away out of danger for a bit was nothing but a ruse.

"I've done what I can," Smith said.

"Yeah, I'm sure you have," Marcus said. He started pacing.

"Hey kid," Smith said, irritated now. "There's still a war on."

"Yeah, over there," Marcus pointed dramatically. "Not here. This is a British problem. Not yours. Not ours."

"The magic is my problem," Smith said. "And guess what? Jane is British."

Marcus gripped the back of an empty wicker chair they'd set out for him and stared at me, his attention unwavering. He pleaded with me, silently, to see his way.

I couldn't. This had become personal. The Sinn Feiners were dangerous. The Blue Flyer was dangerous. I would not stand aside if there was something to be done.

"How certain are you the Blue Flyer is involved?" I asked.

"Hopefully, I'm wrong," said Atkins. "And if I am, go in there, confiscate the magic device, and we'll get you out of Ireland."

"What use do the Irish have with one of these things, anyway?" Marcus asked. "Did they have combat pilots in that Rising a couple of years ago?"

"Maybe this one doesn't have to do with flying," DuPont suggested.

"It's all been about flying," Marcus replied. "That's the point. They're all about pilots—the best pilots. And the war's best pilots aren't flying around Ireland."

He was right. Thus far, our only assignments had been tracking down artifacts left by aviators. But I knew, full well, that magic could spring from many sources. Arcane objects had a long history across many disciplines.

My gaze slid to Marcus's chest, where he still wore the glass marble I'd had made for him. Words from the Blue Flyer came back to me. The marbles sang differently, he'd said.

Yes. There were other powerful sources of magic.

"If you're right, Marcus, then what's the harm?" I asked.

"The harm is putting you at risk!"

All eyes settled on him. Since we'd returned, it had become harder to pretend that our welfare was not paramount to one another. But this was not the way to conduct military business. A blush crept into his cheeks. He shuffled his feet and hedged his words.

"The harm is risking the only person we've got that can unravel this magic problem facing the Allies."

Smith sighed and stood up.

"Look, kid, this is no request. I did what I could, but command has forced my hand."

I pulled my arms closer around me. Should it have bothered me I agreed with everyone in the room but the one I considered my friend?

"And if I refuse?" Marcus asked.

"I beg your pardon?" Atkins said putting down his glass. DuPont snickered from his chair.

"If I refuse?" Marcus jutted out his chin in defiance. Smith couldn't hold back a smile.

"Court martial. Dishonorable discharge. You could forget all your pay. Geez, kid, they could throw you in prison and forget about you the rest of your life."

"This is outrageous," Atkins started. "You're shell shocked! You're a—."

"A coward?" Marcus asked. He smiled, knowingly. "Wasn't that in my file, Atkins?"

"He's principled," DuPont countered, if only to cut the tension. "It's a good thing."

I rested my hand on Marcus's arm. He turned toward me, his shoulders drooping.

"I think we could both use some sleep. We don't need to decide anything tonight."

"It's already decided," Atkins started. I cut him off with a vicious glare. There was no need to pile on. A begrudging soldier was a commander's worst nightmare.

"We're the ones on the ground, and I'm sure you'd agree that our insight has great tactical worth," I went on. "Let us ruminate on everything and meet in two days."

"Very reasonable," said Dupont. "It is the spy that hurries at the wrong time who gets caught."

I bristled at the term *spy*, but nodded.

The others grunted their approval, and soon, we headed back to our flat, Marcus steaming the whole way.

But I had great trouble ahead of me. I had a mind to agree with Atkins. Since the Blue Flyer had demonstrated that my knowledge of magic was nothing but a child's understanding, I shrank from what I once considered a passion. As dark as it sounded, his death gave me great comfort. But now?

Perhaps we could capture him, but if we failed, the Blue Flyer could not be left at large, or I'd never feel safe again.

Chapter 4
The Veteran
Marcus

He, too, has resigned his part
In the casual comedy;
He, too, has been changed in his turn,
Transformed utterly:
A terrible beauty is born.
-William Butler Yeats-

"You should have seen it, Mark," said Cillian as he looked out over the street. We sat at a small table outside one of Dublin's countless pubs. I could smell the fumes of his drink from where I sat. He'd offered me one as well, but I opted for something less pungent. "The whole damn city stood still. No one worked. It was a strike to scare the King."

His voice was full of gravel, and he smacked his lips as he put back his liquor. My eyes rested on the dirt beneath his fingernails. It wouldn't surprise me if the grime came from his service in the trenches from months before, stubbornly refusing to go away despite the occasional wash. I didn't like thinking about how strenuous life must be for him. He hobbled around on a crutch. But the wound from his amputation, despite scabbing and scarring over, he still carried like a new psychological burden. He wasn't a one-legged man yet. In his mind, he still had two legs. One was just missing. I noticed this presumption in his movements. His first instinct was not to reach for a crutch.

"It must have been a sight," I said pushing my hands deep into my pockets. The evening was crisp. We were so close to the sea that the air reached right through my coat. The smell reminded me of home in California.

"Help me up," he said. "Let's take a walk."

I did as he asked and spared a glance toward Jane. She sat inside, conversing with Margaret and Grace. Beth's shift at the munitions factory had gone long, so it was just the two of them.

Jane offered a weak smile. We hadn't spoken much since the night before. I didn't have words yet, still embarrassed from how I'd come to understand that the rest of the team didn't trust me with all the details. I should have suspected our assignment here was still connected to the magic devices and the Blue Flyer, but I hadn't. Jane helped me pretend that was just a dream. She suspended the illusion. She said she wanted to protect me, and I believed her. That's what she always wanted.

I could accept all that from her.

But the way she seemed ready to accept her assignment to kill the Blue Flyer... I wasn't a child. I understood that war required ugly realities. It was the change in her that scared the hell out of me.

"You've got a great woman there, Mark," Cillian said, grinning. His smile was white, but missing a tooth. "She's fierce."

I sighed.

"Yeah. She knows how to look after herself, that's for sure."

"Where'd you meet again?"

"She was a mechanic at Villeneuve-les-Vertus. I'd just finished working with the Lafayette Escadrille, and they pegged my friend as the commander of the first US aero squadron."

"You're pulling my leg, Mark."

I winced.

"The Lafayette?" he asked.

"Yeah. You heard of it?"

"Everyone's heard of it. A bunch of American pilots volunteering to fly in Europe's war... Word gets around."

I smiled, remembering how the newspapers inflated all of my old friends' accomplishments.

"You can't believe everything you read in the papers," I said. He grunted.

"You can't believe anything you read in the papers." We settled into an uncomfortable pause. His breathing staggered more than it should have for the gentle pace we kept down the street. He didn't sit on his discomfort long before spitting out his thoughts. "Can't believe anything you read anywhere. That's why we were so hesitant when your letters came in."

I nodded.

"I'd be suspicious, too."

"You don't understand, Mark. We are well aware of English spies trying to infiltrate the IRA, Sinn Fein, even the Brotherhood. When we got wind of a young couple trying to escape military service, looking for a place to hide out... Well, safe houses we have. Deserters we despise. But then we heard whisperings about your reputation."

My foot caught on an uneven cobblestone, but I corrected myself before stumbling.

"My reputation?"

"We've got spies too, you see. And though we protest Conscription, it's at war that many Irelanders convert to independence. Those boys hear whispers, hushed conversations about magic, pilots, women firing machine guns, the whole lot."

I wondered if these rumors had dispersed organically or if Atkins and Smith had engineered their spread to reach the correct ears. Either option hardly surprised me. At the start of our mission, secrecy was paramount. But too many peeping eyes had seen our curious deeds.

"And speaking of magic, convenience of conveniences, the two of you happened to be stationed in Dublin. And not long after? We hear about a magical import in the wake of a shoddy arrest job of hundreds of Sinn Feiners. I'm willing to believe a lot of things, Mark, but I don't fancy myself a stupid man."

A large knot worked its way into my throat. I swallowed and tried to keep my voice calm.

"It does seem like funny timing, doesn't it?"

"Aye."

We hobbled along down the street in silence. Cillian let the implication he'd made go to work on me. I tried not to panic. At first, I wanted to run. Was he accusing me outright of being a spy? Were we headed into an ambush? Was Jane safe with Margaret?

But if that were the case, why would he wait until we were alone? He was newly crippled, and I figured I could overpower him in a pinch.

"I like you too much, Mark," he said suddenly. "That's one of my problems."

"One of your problems?"

"You and that wife of yours aren't just trying to desert the army, are you?" he asked.

I set my jaw and spoke carefully.

"Not exactly."

"I suspected. But I also suspect that there's something your wife doesn't know either."

I kept quiet, but shook my head. He was right. There were things, mostly thoughts and desires, I was keeping from Jane. They weren't insignificant either.

"You sound like you have something specific you want to say to me," I said.

"I do." He stopped walking and glanced around, checking if anyone might overhear us. "I don't care if you're a spy. I don't think you're happy with Allied leadership."

I laughed.

"Are you trying to baptize me a Sinn Feiner?" I asked.

"The Feiners." He rolled his eyes. "No. I'm appealing to a brother in the fraternity of freedom."

I was surprised by how hard his words hit me. They stirred something that had lain dormant since joining the Lafayette.

"Fraternity of freedom? Did you come up with that?"

"I did. Just now." He grinned, setting my racing pulse at ease.

"Do you care to elaborate?"

"We want a free Ireland. And no one seems to agree on how to go about it. But I'm sure you can appreciate the desire to make our own decisions. They conscript us. They send us to fight a war that has little to do with us. You chose of your own accord to fight, didn't you?"

"With whatever accord a teenager can have," I replied.

"Our teenagers are not extended that luxury."

"You're talking a lot, Cillian."

"Margaret, Beth, and Gwen don't know what they've walked into. Sinn Fein aren't the only ones interested in the magical shipment that came in up north."

"You don't want them to get the device do you? You're not with Sinn Fein?"

"Sinn Fein. The Citizens Army. The Irish Republican Brotherhood. They're all words. You find it odd that a man named Eamon de Valera is President of more than one of these organizations?"

I shrugged.

"If I'm being honest, I'm woefully uninformed about Irish politics."

"There's a movement in a movement in a movement. And now, I appeal to you because I think you know that the people who really make a difference in any conflict are the ones whose names are never written down."

His words reminded me of Smith and Atkins's insistence on our absolute discretion when they'd first asked us to go artifact hunting. They wanted us and our deeds to disappear from history entirely.

"What do you want?" I asked.

"I want you to meet one of my friends. They have a proposal, one you might not want to tell your wife about." He grinned when he said the word "wife," as if he saw right through our cover.

"How do you know I won't simply turn you in to the British?"

He smiled even more broadly and started back toward the pub.

"I don't. But I think you'll be wise." He raised his voice and spoke past me. "Isn't that right, Harry?"

Leaning against a stone entry to a tall building on the street, stood a tall, lean man with a curious face. He picked his teeth in a cracked handheld mirror. When he heard Cillian, he turned toward us with a mischievous smile hid behind his cheeks in a contagiously conspiratorial way.

I liked him immediately.

"We're finished," said Jane. She paced furiously back and forth across our small apartment. "We need to pull out."

I sat in a well-worn rut in the old sofa that lined one wall in our flat. I'd expected a reaction like this.

"Let's just talk through it first," I said.

"Talk through it?" She came to a stop and gaped at me. "Cillian knows the truth about us. In what world is that a sign post that says move forward?"

"He didn't shut us down yet," I said with a shrug.

"Well, we haven't acted contrary to his interests yet, either," said Jane.

"And maybe we won't. We're here for information about the magic, aren't we? We're after the devices. So is he. And he knows things we don't about what's really happening behind closed doors on the Irish side."

"So do Margaret and Beth and Grace—"

"—not just the group that those three are signed up for. He was talking about the Irish Volunteers, the Citizens Army, the Brotherhood. Jane! I think we may have found a source in Cillian that Atkins never anticipated. This guy is connected."

"All the more reason we cut our lines and run. I'm not going to have you shot or stabbed on some back street in Dublin, Marcus. I won't."

"That's not going to happen. I'll be careful. I'm not a child."

"You're not a soldier, either! You fly. I fire. Remember?"

She folded her arms, and an immovable plaster seemed to fall across her features. The sentiment behind her arguments came from her affection for me, but she refused to budge. She was granite. But her words stung me. I'd been classified, not only by Jane, but by the rest of our team, too. Even Luf knew I didn't have the soldier's mettle in me.

But Luf was gone. Whatever conclusions he'd come to, it didn't win him the war, and it didn't keep him safe, either.

I hadn't told Jane I'd already met with a man named Harry. I'd been too afraid it would blow up. Instead, I told her Cillian wanted me to meet some contacts of his that didn't mix well with the Sinn Fein women we knew.

"So what's your plan, then?" I asked. "Are you going to keep me in a box until you can ship me out of the war?"

"If I could."

"Then why don't we just leave? Aren't you fed up with all of this? They don't care about us." I stretched my hand out toward the wall, motioning vaguely toward our rendezvous spot with our superiors. "Do you think any of them give a damn about our lives beyond what we can do for them, whether we can accomplish their missions?"

"What we can do for our countries, Marcus. We can't simply desert. Where would we go? We'd never get a chance to see our families again. They'd lock us up, or worse."

I stood.

"You think continuing on is the best way to see our families again? If we keep going like this one or both of us won't be going home."

"There's no other way though," she cried. "We have to play their game."

"Stop, Jane. Just stop. This isn't you." I put my hands on my head and turned toward the wall to let out a slow breath. She had Jane's face, she had Jane's voice, but it was like I didn't even recognize her sometimes. "You were the one who sat me down after they killed the Baron and explained that war is to be endured, not celebrated."

"I am enduring it," she muttered.

"Are you? Or is it an itch, now?"

"That is not fair. Don't blame me for believing the same things that all of your other friends and heroes did. Did Lufbery have this itch?"

"He did. And he's dead, Jane."

"I miss him, too! But every time I mention his name, you seem, somehow, I don't know. Perhaps angry with him."

"I am furious with him!" I had found myself on my feet, breathing hard. Jane stared at me with pity and disbelief.

"What?" she asked.

I stared at the cracked plaster and struggled to understand why I cared so much about Cillian's offer. Yesterday, I'd been the one digging my heels in against this assignment. Why not just admit defeat and go back to our superior for new instructions?

I'd sat with Cillian and Harry for hours yesterday, and I drank deep from the philosophies they shared. They'd had me in the palm of their hand. They could have crushed me, outed Jane and me as spies—even been justified in making us disappear. But they didn't. They extended a hand of friendship in my direction.

Talking with those two yesterday woke something up I hadn't felt since I'd met Luf and Kiffin and Prince and all those other boys in the Lafayette Escadrille. I was fluent in idealism, and that gave us another option. Maybe rather than turn Jane into an executioner, we could explore this other byroad.

If only she'd let us take it.

I stuffed my hands into my pockets and tried to relax. My hand found the familiar metal of Luf's old machine gun round. To me, it was a sacred relic I was burdened to carry. His obsessive mechanical maintenance extended to polishing his machine bullets one by one, inspecting them by hand, doing all he could to ensure they didn't jam his gun. When he went down, he was in a machine that was not his own. He didn't have his polished rounds. His gun had jammed. His plane caught fire.

I squeezed my eyes shut. I ground my teeth willing the scene from my memory. It came to me though, in dreams and at the most inconvenient times.

"We still haven't talked about it," I said before turning back to Jane.

"About Lufbery?" she asked, her tone softening.

I shook my head. "About your first kills."

The air seemed to go out of the room as her face darkened. The softness she'd just put on for my vulnerability vanished in an instant.

"What's there to talk about?" she asked, busying her hands in her own coat pockets.

"Come on. You're going to pretend like it was nothing? No big deal, just filling two men full of hot lead?"

"They were shooting at us," she said coldly.

"That doesn't make it easier."

"It made it necessary."

"And I've seen those necessary evils haunt a lot of soldiers. Those guys walked around and just bottled it all up. And I get that because—"

"You don't get it, though. You haven't killed men. Have you?" she said darkly, throwing my record in my face. Once that might have bothered me. I was a pilot without a kill count. The closest I came was my blind barrage toward the Blue Flyer. I'd downed his plane, but they never found a body among the wreckage.

"This isn't about me. You've always been there at my darkest. I know you. I'm here. I want to help you. What you did is huge. You might have guilt or grief or—"

"I feel nothing!" Her voice wheezed out of her, half shout, half whisper. I took a step back. "I felt nothing. Is that what you're so interested in hearing? You're right. I killed two men. I remember it clearly—their faces, their uniforms. They were about our age. They looked scared, and I shot them because I had to."

I struggled for words. What did she mean she felt nothing? How was that possible?

"I've waited. I don't know where the remorse is meant to come from but I'm afraid it's broken. I'm afraid I'm broken. Or maybe God has taken this part of me and given it to you twice over. I don't know. Maybe I've found a way to bury it so deep that it's become a part of me, as natural as the soil in the earth."

She opened her mouth to go on, but then shook her head, as though she changed her mind on what she wanted to say.

"But maybe it's for the best. Maybe this is how I keep you alive."

My heart twisted in my chest.

"By leaning in?" I asked.

"By doing whatever is necessary."

"How do you know what is necessary, by listening to Atkins?"

"Atkins and Smith are our commanding officers and our best hope right now." She took her hands out of her pockets and smoothed them on her skirts.

"Best hope at what?"

"To get a handle on the magic that's affecting the war. If the Blue Flyer is still out there, then he must be eliminated. He has my marble. He has an interest in us."

"Then why not let me follow through with Cillian's lead?"

"Because it's too dangerous!"

I sank back onto the couch and let my face fall into my hands. Jane took a moment to collect herself before sitting beside me.

"Please, don't treat me like I'm a monster," she said. "I'm trying to protect you."

"You're not," I said. I lifted my face and looked her in the eyes. "And that's what scares me. You're not protecting me. You're only making yourself feel like you're protecting me."

Her mouth twitched and twisted, but she smothered the hurt and forced a calm tone.

"What do you propose, Marcus?" she asked.

"I'm not saying we should go against orders. I just want to see where this trail leads before Atkins and Smith can tell us what to do with it. They weren't there when we had to navigate our curve-balls in Ghent. My gut is telling me there's something here. Come on. You keep saying I'm not a soldier. Let me be useful here."

She took a deep breath and faced forward. It gave me a chance to appreciate what looked like traces of wrinkles at the corner of her eyes. I'd never noticed them before.

"Promise me that after you meet Cillian's contact we will inform our uppers and get the support we need to do this right," she said.

"I promise."

"And promise me you'll be careful because I can't lose you, Marcus. You're, I mean, we're..."

"We're what?"

She didn't have an answer. I didn't either. But her bringing it up broke some type of silent code we'd established. Asking her to continue after such a slip up was cruel.

"You promise me something, too," I said.

"I might have known it would go two ways."

"Promise me you won't let this thing inside of you win. I think you're right. I think you've buried your darkness deep, deep down, and if it's not time to dig it up, that's fine. But please, don't let soldiering ruin who you are."

She put her head on my shoulder and sighed.

"That hardly seems fair. Your promise is a simple to-do item, and mine is a lifelong commitment."

"Do you promise?" I asked.

She didn't respond right away, and I heard laughing and shouting through our shuttered window from the pub across the street.

"I'll try."

Chapter 5
Layers
Jane

The soil of Ireland throbs and glows
With life that knows the hour is here
To strike again like Irishmen
For that which Irishmen hold dear.
-Joyce Kilmer-

I couldn't quit Marcus's accusation.

He was acting like an ungrateful idiot. He didn't have the benefit of an outside point of view, and frankly, since Lufbery's fatal crash, keeping Marcus semi-coherent had been like dragging an unconscious body through a crater-torn battlefield.

How had he expected me to ward off the wills of a British, American, and French superior officer while he was busy grieving? It was all well and good to accuse me of keeping things from him, and of that I was guilty, but the greater part of his ignorance was because he suffered episodes of blankness. On one occasion, I did all but slap him across the face to get him to focus and pay attention in one of our briefings.

"Jane?" asked Margaret. "Are you with us?"

I snapped to attention.

"Yes? Oh, right. Of course. I'm sorry."

"Poor lass," said Grace. "You were just somewhere dark and ugly in your head, weren't you?"

"Never you mind that," I said. We all busied ourselves wiping tables down in the pub beneath Margaret's flat. It was a common bit of work we set ourselves to while discussing confidential business. They exchanged this labor for Mr. Ryan letting them hold meetings above his pub. But while we worked, we spoke quite freely. Cleaning women were all but invisible, and there was no one in the pub that morning. "Tell me the plan once more."

Margaret put down her rag and wiped her brow with her shoulder.

"I need to know that you're taking this seriously, Jane," she said with a bother. "It's not every day an opportunity like this comes up. You've gone on at length about needing to escape the Allied forces with your husband. Well, you do this correctly, and you'll be a hero to us. They'll build a way for you."

"I know," I said. "I'm grateful, and I'm eager to help."

"Good. Because it's not easy convincing others that this business is real, let alone that we have a woman who knows her way around it—a woman who's not daft, that is. But you're my chance to prove it. I'm taking a big risk on you. The powers that be want you to examine the shipment that's come in and determine if all is as claimed."

"You mean if it's magical," I said.

"Not so loudly, now," Grace said, glancing around.

"Yes, Jane," said Margaret. "Precisely that. Can you do it?"

I considered the question. My Aunt Luella had taught me myriad ways to detect magic, but I never got a knack for it. When I'd asked her clarifying questions, she'd always admitted that different magics have different markers. But, I'd thought of this days prior and had already requested that Atkins release Boelcke's goggles to me. They should do the trick. And what a lovely excuse to get the goggles back in my possession, even if it were for only a little while.

"Quite confident, though it may take some time," I admitted.

"How much time?"

"A day or two. Is that manageable?"

"It will have to be," said Margaret. "To be true, I'm not sure how many other options they have. It's not as if we have a magical research division. They'll want to treat it like any other weapon."

"That's been my experience with the English as well," I said. "It's one of my many grievances against them."

"In a couple of days, Cillian and I will drive you and Marcus to a special meeting."

"Where?" I asked.

"Can't say. The fewer who know, the better. After this, though, if you can prove your worth, they'll be more liberal with you. And I'd be so happy about it. Truly. It's all terribly exciting. My mother always told me that the world was full of magic, even if ours wasn't."

I nodded. I'd grown up a believer, and it was always sobering to witness someone's first interaction with the inexplicable. I remembered when Marcus finally gave in and started believing. It had nearly undone his concept of reality. I supposed it still threatened as much.

"Do you think it will be enough?" asked Grace. "To finally rid ourselves of the English, I mean."

I cast a pitying look in her direction, and her face reddened. I didn't mean to stamp out her childlike faith in the paranormal, but I shuddered to think what arcane force would have the power to reconfigure, summarily, national claims of sovereignty.

"It can only help," I said.

· · ·

That night, I was a wreck waiting for Marcus to return to the flat. Cillian had followed through with his plans to introduce him to a mysterious contact from deep within Irish radical circles. We still had a busy evening planned checking-in with the Allied officers.

Already, though, I was exhausted, and my fingernails were bitten to pieces in the waiting.

At long last, he shuffled in and hung up his coat.

"There you are," I said, jumping up from my spot on the old sofa. "Where have you been?"

"Talking," he said. "And talking and talking. I'd never seen Cillian like that. He's so sleepy around the others, but today was totally different."

"I wouldn't bother with those." I hovered over him as he took off his shoes. "We're going out again in just an hour. Who did you meet with?"

"Just an hour? With who?"

"Who do you think?" I replied.

He groaned, but stopped untying his laces. I rolled my eyes.

"Yes, I'm sure your lot is very rough. Now tell me. How did it go?"

His eyes took on a shade of contentment, as though I asked him about a pleasant date with friends.

"I think we've got something," he said. "The contact's name is Harry. He's as excitable about the idea of freedom as a man can get. Though, I can't place his accent. I'm not sure it's strongly Irish —at least, not to my ears."

"I appreciate your sense of humility regarding these matters," I said.

"Well, as you know, regional dialect appreciation isn't my strong suit."

"What did Harry want? Did Cillian tell him about us?"

Marcus cocked his head back and forth in consideration.

"Maybe," he said. "If he did, Harry didn't seem to care two cents. We talked about the Rising a lot, the same way you might talk about a ball game. They were bothered the Rising didn't achieve its purpose, but they also gave the impression that this was because of logistical execution, not a failure of planning. They even talked about the other team the way ball fans talk. You heard of the Sherwood Foresters?"

I swallowed hard. This was a chance to tell him about my personal grievance with the revolutionaries, to share the burden of my cousin's death. But we'd been fighting so much lately. I didn't want him to think that vengeance had anything to do with our mission, not when he already had accused me of giving myself in to the darkness of war.

"Of course, I have. They were butchered in these streets."

Marcus raised his eyebrows.

"Well, the way they talk about it, it's the Foresters who were the butchers, and their replacements. Jane, I had no idea. It's like you're in a war and you think there can't be more hell than what you experience. You're so close to it the idea that other people, somewhere outside the conflict, want a piece of the violence is crazy. But it goes on."

I closed my eyes. Normally, I'd be pleased that Marcus took such a keen interest in the world around him. But it was not easy watching him fall victim to such a one-sided indoctrination. I resisted the urge to set things right. That's not what was needful now. With my nerves strung so tightly, I needed information or I might snap.

"Why did Cillian want you to meet Harry?" I asked.

"The magic, of course." Marcus stood up and rummaged through the cupboards in our kitchen. We didn't keep food in the flat, though, and he knew it. The rats were too bold. He must have been nervous, looking for something to do. "He, uh, wanted my help dealing with the magic. They're planning something."

"Something?"

"They don't want Sinn Fein to have the device," Marcus said without looking at me.

A weight fell in my chest.

"What are you talking about?"

Marcus shrugged and closed a cabinet door.

"They said Sinn Fein doesn't have the backbone to use it the right way. They think that if the cause has arcane power to wield, it should be in bolder hands."

The hopeful faces of Margaret and Grace sprung to mind. They considered the magic as their opportunity to make a name for themselves in the Separatist community. If the opportunity was stolen from them, they'd be crushed. And crushed hopes made for unpredictable choices.

"So it is a weapon?" I asked. "We haven't found a weapon yet."

"Either a weapon or something like Richthofen's scarf that will make their ammunition bite harder. Harry wasn't sure. But they sounded eager. I don't know, Jane. It was hard not to catch their enthusiasm a little bit."

I gaped. Now that he mentioned the word enthusiasm, I recognized it in his face. He guarded it, as if he was afraid to show me, but it animated him. I hadn't seen him this way in a long time.

And that frightened me.

"Enthusiasm for what?" I asked.

"For their cause," he said with a shrug. "I don't know. Maybe it's an American thing, but you say enough about self-representation and natural born liberty and suddenly I get all riled up."

"Might I remind you, you haven't finished the last war you volunteered for because you got all 'riled up?'" I said, trying not to let my annoyance come through. The urge to lock the door and tell Atkins the game was up came on strongly. Cillian had his claws in Marcus. How had I let that happen? Perhaps it was wrong not to be more clear about our assignment from the outset. He'd developed a sincere attachment to the cripple. He'd forgotten our purpose.

Something about the Irish had ensnared both of us. The longer it took to get away, the more twisted that snare would become.

We needed to complete our mission here in Dublin, quickly.

"Well, I'll be," said Smith with a whistle. "You have yourself a multi-layered coup on your hands."

True to Marcus's word, we informed the officers about Cillian's new contact and with no further complaints or convincing on my part. I appreciated that, as I didn't want to come across as any more difficult to Marcus than I already had.

Atkins, who had just been leaning toward Dupont for a light to his cigarette, bristled.

"That there are more than one Irish radical group is not news to His Majesty's Government." He took a slow drag in thought. "Though I must admit, it is troubling to know how many players are now at the table hunting the magic devices. It makes our job more difficult."

"More difficult?" I echoed. "How's that?"

"It's simple to take something from one interested party," he replied. "Either you get it, or they get it. But if the Irish Republican Brotherhood is already planning to steal the device out from the nose of Sinn Fein, then it's doubly complicated to come out on top."

"The same way one plane can pit two of its enemies against each other in a dogfight," said Marcus.

"To us they're two enemies," said Dupont. "But for them, it's one ally secretly split into two enemies."

"Not exactly," Marcus replied. "Cillian knows that Jane and I are working both sides. Right now, I think he considers Jane loyal to the Allies and immovable. But he's willing to take a chance on me. I'm not sure what he's told Harry. But if Harry knew I was a spy, that didn't stop his zeal for collaborating. And I'm more sure than ever that Margaret and the others don't know about Cillian's secret allegiance to the IRB."

"What a mess," said Smith as he rubbed his neck. "Might be time to pay the check and get out of here."

"I couldn't agree more," I added. "We can't keep up the lies for much longer. The mission is collapsing."

We all quieted as a loud group of men passed through the alley outside. Their voices were raised, angry, and public. It was a tone I'd become accustomed to in the streets of Dublin, but it shot shivers through my spine all the same.

Atkins blew out a stream of smoke and broke the silence with a whisper.

"We need not continue much longer. I understand they will bring the device to you for inspection soon?"

I nodded.

"Under great scrutiny. I wouldn't be surprised if Margaret had a pistol in her coat pocket trained on me for two straight days. What will we do with her when we return to our flat with our objective in hand?"

Atkins, Smith, and Dupont exchanged a sheepish look. My heart jumped.

"Oh, come on," Marcus protested, louder than what was prudent. "You can't mean you intend to kill her. I don't want to sound prudish but you can't just kill everybody that's a problem to you."

"No, we don't intend to kill her," Atkins said. "But we will have no choice but to imprison her."

"Under what charges?" asked Marcus. He unfolded his arms and leaned forward.

"Under the charges of securing a deadly weapon to further armed insurrection. And that is gentler than the word treason."

I clenched my jaw. Thus far, largely due to the initial overzealous backlash by His Majesty's army to the Rising, the government had been lenient sentencing Irish nationalists.

"She's just interested in the magic," Marcus said. "She doesn't know what it is. None of them do. She's peaceful. If you lock her up, you might as well say you have cause to lock up her entire political movement."

"Why do you think we arrested so many Sinn Fein leaders?" Atkins asked, an edge in his voice. His response silenced Marcus, but even in the dim light, I recognized traces of disgust on my friend's face. "We will do what is necessary with Margaret. But the orders remain. You must retrieve the device. And if he shows himself, you must capture or eliminate the Blue Flyer. If anyone, or anything, attempts to interfere, you must do whatever is necessary to accomplish these objectives. Have I made myself clear?"

I swallowed and nodded. The mood in the air shifted. We had entered a new phase of our assignment, and it was as palpable in the room as the cigarette smoke. Already, I noticed the change in my body. The adrenaline had started pumping slowly, attuning my senses.

"Have I made myself clear?" Atkins asked again, his voice sharpening in irritation.

"Sergeant?" Marcus asked Smith. We all turned to the American officer.

"Oh, stop being so squeamish, Marcus. I'm tired of babying you. Just get it done right and no one will get hurt."

Marcus's nodded without a hint of letting Smith's tone affect him.

"Are we done here, sir?" he asked.

"Dismissed," said Smith. Marcus spun on his heel and went straight to the door. Before I could catch up with him, Atkins had me by the arm.

"I mean it, private," he said. "If anything threatens this

mission, eliminate it. We suspect this device may dwarf the power of all the others."

Atkins handed me a small pistol.

"Conceal this somewhere within reach. Use it well."

The thought of magic as strong as he suggested made my knees tremble. My thoughts raced to my parents, my relatives and friends back home, and most of all to visions of Marcus being hunted relentlessly by a merciless Blue Flyer.

I took the gun.

"Understood."

"Oh, and I received your request. Please return these intact."

I looked down and a curious relief flooded my chest. In his hand were Boelcke's magic goggles.

Chapter 6
Howth
Marcus

And when I came, she stood alone—
A woman, turned to stone:
And, though no word at all she said,
I knew that all was known.
-Wilfrid Wilson Gibson-

Jane and I walked arm in arm across Dublin to the Stag's Head pub, a different bar than our usual haunt. We were to meet Cillian and Margaret there before they led us to a secret rendezvous location set by Sinn Fein leadership. Once arrived, a contact named Bridget would drop off the device if she was satisfied that nothing smelled fishy about the situation.

My head swam with competing ideas.

I'd met with Cillian and Harry twice now. I'd told Jane about only one of those meetings. Maybe it was the secrecy of those meet ups, or maybe something about the philosophies those two spouted when we met, but a part of me wished I could jump at their invitation to join their movement.

I wasn't sure when it had happened, but Cillian had

entrenched himself in my affection. I recognized in him the bravery I'd known in so many fallen soldiers, and it took me back. There was a type of brotherhood I couldn't expect to share with anyone who had not paid the price that he had. First, he'd won my respect through his sheer knack to carry on despite any hardship. Then, he won my friendship with his warmth and eager smile.

But he'd won my heart when he decided to take a chance on me instead of turning me in as a spy. He said he sensed a courage and passion in my spirit.

I thought that spirit had died, killed by the war, buried beside Luf.

In our meetings with Harry, Cillian spoke lively, vibrantly, filled with passion, energy, and drive.

His passion painted a stark contrast to the backroom, underhanded ethics that Atkins and Smith currently trafficked in. When compared to Atkins's holier-than-thou morality, who wouldn't be seduced by such blatant sincerity?

And Harry? Harry was a vision.

He had been instantly magnetic. He spoke quietly, but with a hint of a smile around his lips at all times—and not a smile that demeaned or condescended. His eyes lit up with so much joy being among like-minded men that he might have burst out with laughter at any moment.

The way they talked about the Irish cause breathed new life into me. The way they talked about magic sang with hope and opportunity, not the dismal fear that Jane adopted for the subject.

And why shouldn't it be a joyful thing? If magic existed, didn't that fill everything with meaning? I missed the way Jane used to light up when she explained how she used paradox to fix wing fabric to planes better. She used to love magic.

But I had to check my emotional momentum before it carried me away to mutiny.

Something Jane said troubled me: maybe I was just grieving for Luf. Grief distorts everything, so I'd heard.

Dublin sprawled in every direction, its black, coal-infused mud staining every corner of the city. Our flat stood somewhere near the docks off the River Liffey. To our left, on the other side of the river, the tall spire of Trinity College loomed. It cut through the sky, filling me again with awe of Europe's architecture. It never got old. Despite the filth and disease in the streets, beauty stretched overhead.

We cut south into the city. Margaret's instructions had been clear enough. We took a left across McConnell Bridge and continued along the river before turning east, where we'd meet beneath a mounted timepiece known as Taylor's Clock at the Stag's Head pub.

"Are you ready?" I asked Jane.

"Of course," she said. Her mouth was set firmly, and her shoulders were rigid and tense.

"We'll be all right. No one needs to get hurt. We'll follow the plan, and once we have the device, we can figure out our next steps."

"You mean leading Margaret into captivity without her shooting us?" she asked.

I shook my head.

"We might find a way to set her free," I said.

"She won't leave the artifact," Jane replied. "She's been assigned to it. How could she ever show her face to the movement again if they knew she'd let it slip through her fingers?"

"Then maybe we find a way to make her less culpable. I bet Harry and Cillian would be willing to stage something."

"Yes, but that would require giving the device to them, wouldn't it?"

As we crossed an intersection, and the tall facades of Irish housing gave way, I noticed a dark castle tower off to the south.

"Maybe we can stall, and our resourceful officers can fashion a decoy. Then, Cillian and Harry are happy, Margaret isn't culpable, and the Allies get the magic."

Jane stopped walking.

"Marcus, that might be the best idea you've had in weeks."

I smiled.

"Well, I'm not all ideals and passion. I've got at least a few problem-solving skills. I probably got them from hanging around you so much."

She took a breath, and I saw at least some of the weight of our task slide off her shoulders. A moment ago, she had the resolution of a killer, preparing herself mentally and emotionally to carry out dark orders. But a small sliver of hope chased some of that out of her. It was beautiful.

"There it is," she said with a nod.

Three narrow roads stretching in starkly different directions lay in the crossroads before us. On the corner sat a crowded pub with a fashioned stag's head protruding above the door and a large clock with the word Taylor splayed across its face.

"You know," I whispered. "Taylor's Clock isn't the most creative name in the world."

Before we could get any closer, Jane fished Boelcke's goggles from her bag and put them to her eyes. The sight of those goggles stirred a swell of mixed feelings in my gut. Excitement, fear, trauma, empowerment, and a bunch of other sensations all jockeyed to have my full attention.

"What do you see?" I asked. She took her time responding.

"Nothing. If they have the device, it's not here."

The pavement rounded the corner on the side of the pub, and small standing tables lined both edges of the building. Small clusters of men and women congregated at these tables, drinks in hand, rowdy already in the early evening. We got closer and searched for our friends, sidestepping a couple in an amorous exchange against the Stag's Head's brick wall. I didn't look too closely. Some of the passion in their kisses made me blush.

"Oy," one of them whispered.

I did a double take. It was Margaret and Cillian.

"There you two are," Margaret clamored and pulled Jane in for an embrace. Cillian let out a good chuckle.

"Not the worst cover in the world," he said to me in a hushed voice. "But you'll know about that."

I shushed him immediately.

"Where should we go to get our present?" I asked. I craned my neck to evaluate a few nearby pockets of revelers.

Cillian produced a cigarette and struck a match. The night was dark enough for the little flame to cast a striking effect on his boyish features. Then, he took a pocket watch from his vest and glanced at it.

"We're slightly ahead of schedule," he said, sliding his arm around Margaret's waist and pulling her closer. Margaret laughed.

"You two look like tax collectors," she said out of the corner of her mouth. "Try to act at least a little more natural. Here, have a drink."

She pushed a cup toward us on the little table. I glanced at it, then up at Cillian. He wore a bemused and sly smile. The little cup struck me the wrong way, and I pulled Jane into my own arms.

"Jane's all I need to relax," I said. The tension in her shoulders made holding her awkward. Slowly, she eased herself into my chest. It didn't bode well for the evening that she couldn't hide her apprehension from even Margaret.

"All right," said Cillian. "Let's take a walk, then."

We sauntered down the street past the wanderers and loiterers and drinkers and peddlers. We walked for several minutes before Cillian broke the silence.

"The city's boiling since the arrests," he said. "It's preparing for something. You can almost taste it in the air."

"We'll be ready," said Margaret. "And you two will be there with us."

I pulled Jane a little closer. She squeezed my arm, fearful.

Cillian unlatched a small iron gate and led us into a cramped courtyard nestled between a pair of tall buildings. He flicked the remains of his cigarette into the street before stepping into a shadowed corner and pulling a canvas sheet off of a large, hulking shape. He backpedaled toward us, both hands in his pockets, proud as a peacock.

"This is Betty," he said, noting an unveiled automobile. It was a simple car. The four of us would stress the motor if we ran it too long.

"It's a Ford," Jane blurted out.

"Right she is," Cillian said. I inspected it, tracing the wheel covers and headlights with my fingers. Touching one gave me a rush of nostalgia.

"I used to work on these in the United States when I was a kid," I said. For a second, I was back home in California, finishing up a shift at the mechanic's shop, waiting to go home for a dinner of shepherd's pie. "That must have been—" My nostalgia came crashing down. "—three years ago."

I looked toward Jane and knew she understood my disappointment. War had aged us a lifetime. Remembering what came before was harder every day.

"It's not cheap maintaining a car like this," Cillian said. "But this is a special night, and we're the lucky benefactors."

"How far are we going?" I asked.

Cillian laughed. "Do you have other plans?"

Jane's expression betrayed her concern. We'd shared our rendezvous location with our Allied officers so they could keep an eye on us. There was safety in knowing the cavalry would come to our aid, if push came to shove. But maybe we were naïve to assume that we'd continue by foot.

If we went in that car, there was no telling where we'd end up.

But I trusted Cillian, and I didn't think Margaret wished Jane any harm either.

We all piled into the car. It was cozy, with the Irish in the front and Jane and me in the rear.

The Ford had no more than twenty horsepower, and with all four of us, we'd be unlikely to hit any commendable speed. So I settled in and pretended to be brave for Jane, who pretended to be brave for me.

Time stretched as we drove through the streets of Dublin. Cillian was ready on the horn to clear out pedestrians, but he also exchanged his fair share of waves and salutations with some small gatherings at pubs or on street corners as we passed by. And many of his acquaintances gave scrutinizing glances toward me and Jane in the back.

Moving at a clip like this, I noticed how right he was about the discontent. We were driving through a powder keg of anti-English zeal. Between the strikes, the activity on the streets, and the general hushed excitement coursing through the night air, it was a small wonder to me that Atkins had Ireland top of mind.

We passed over the river and headed north for a half hour. Eventually, the dense clusters of buildings in the heart of Dublin eased somewhat. We were leaving the city proper. Soon, water stretched to our right, and a beautiful view of Dublin by night graced us from across a small bay.

The smell of the sea overwhelmed me. Riding in the Model T like this, so close to the ocean, took me right back to younger years again. We'd tested our customers' cars after tuning them up. On some evenings, though we couldn't see the ocean from the streets we drove on, the air was thick of it, like drinking milk instead of water.

I had fond memories of the sea, building sand castles with mom and dad, letting the waves chase me up the beach...

Memories like those were strong enough to break a man.

Cillian drove us through a narrow stretch of road into winding, mountainous coastline before finally pulling into a sleepy village just a stone's throw from the water. It was dark now, but we were nearing a full moon, and flashes of its reflection on the waves shone brightly.

We turned away from the shore, though, toward a set of dark brick buildings.

"There's our rendezvous," said Cillian dryly.

I elbowed Jane. She bit her lip and tried to calm what I knew was a terrible excitement bubbling up inside her. Looking around the car, I noticed it in Margaret and Cillian as well. All were eager to find the truth about this fabled shipment, at last.

Cillian pulled the Ford through two old wooden gates into a shadowed courtyard and cut the engine.

"This is where we get out," he said. "Ladies, stand there against that wall for a moment. Marcus, if you'd give me a hand."

He hobbled to his work as we covered the Model T.

"Why so much secrecy with the car?" I asked.

"Since the war broke out, and more since the Rising, they track everything. I don't want it to go missing from wandering authoritative eyes. This way."

He extended a hand and motioned for us to follow him inside. Jane grabbed my arm with something akin to a vice grip. I all but heard her heart hammering beneath her coat, and suddenly I was concerned about how little influence I had over the simmering energy beneath her stone exterior.

She was afraid and desperate. I'd seen that look in scared pilots before. Many didn't return from flights when they went up with such a mentality.

I'd been so occupied by Cillian, my grief about Luf, and my reservations about our superiors that I hadn't properly considered her welfare. Now that I saw her this way, my more basic instincts had a better grip on my emotions. This was my Jane. I protected her.

Shame reddened my cheeks.

We followed Cillian through a heavy door set on the side of one of the brick buildings.

"Are any of you afraid of the dark?" Margaret asked.

"What?"

"It'll just be for a second while I find the light," she said. "We've boarded up the windows in this place. Keeps wandering eyes out."

We entered, and she shut the door behind us, plunging the room in total darkness.

An old instinct brought my hand to my neck to grasp at the marble fastened there, reaching for the protective magic Jane had made for me.

Margaret and Cillian started down the hallway. I stepped forward to follow, but now Jane resisted. I guessed she didn't appreciate the feeling of being trapped inside this boarded up building either.

"Any problems?" Cillian asked when he noted our hesitation.

"Sorry," I said. "You all right, Jane?"

"The gravity of all this hit me only now," Jane replied. "That's all. I need but a moment."

"You're not having second thoughts, are you?" Margaret asked. Jane struggled to reply.

"You must understand," I cut in. "The Allies used her for her magical capabilities the same way you might use a horse. They didn't care much about the strain it put on her. It might feel like we're walking into a similar situation."

Margaret's hand settled on her shoulder.

"All the more reason to show them they can't control everything all the time," she said.

"Thank you," said Jane. "I'm quite all right."

"That's good," said Cillian. "Because you've come too far to turn back now."

I grunted.

"You two mix ideals and practical reality pretty well," I said.

"Exactly that, lad," he said. "We're not anarchists. We're republicans who believe in self rule. You've seen one of our better hideouts. We can't let you walk away without assurances you'll keep that information to yourself."

As we walked forward, a faint light came from down the hallway, and I noticed for the first time that Cillian carried a Webley revolver. The Webley had a loud bark and a powerful bite for its size. It said a lot about the man who carried it and the neighborhood within earshot.

I took Jane's hand in mine and looked her right in the face.

"My knees aren't wobbling," I whispered to her. Her wide eyes turned to me.

"Mine are."

Cillian ushered us forward, now walking behind us with pistol drawn. His actions tinted everything about the situation in a sinister hue, as if we'd all been pretending to be friends, but tonight the latent distrust would be reconciled at last. I nearly laughed at the absurdity. Our group comprised two spies and two concurring revolutionaries, every person with their own agenda.

Finally, we reached the end of the hall, and I pushed the door open.

Inside, at a table amidst sets of stacked crates and barrels, illuminated by a flickering lightbulb, sat a woman in a tweed vest and skirt. Beside her stood Harry. His wiry figure leaned against the wall, an aquiline nose directing the curious tilt of his head.

His charming air put me at ease instantly, and we exchanged a smile. But my comfort caught at my lips. I didn't realize Harry would be here. If he were here, why did Cillian need Jane and me?

After noting the two figures, my eyes flicked to the object

sitting on the table. It was an empty ammo drum, like the kind we used to load atop our Lewis machine guns in the old Nieuport biplanes.

But I couldn't study it long. Jane nearly fell over, gripping my arm with a claw to keep from collapsing in the doorframe. I attended her immediately.

"What is it?" I asked. Her face was white. Her breath labored. She pointed at Harry.

"That's Harry," I said. "Cillian introduced me to him. He's all right."

"It's him," she gasped in my ear.

Chapter 7
Burning Bridges
Jane

We planned to shake the world together, you and I
Being young, and very wise;
Now in the light of the green shaded lamp
Almost I see your eyes
Light with the old gay laughter.
-May Wedderburn Cannan-

The Blue Flyer.

He looked different. I first saw him wearing flight goggles when he almost shot our Salmson from the sky near Clairmarais. Then, he etched his visage into my mind as he pursued me relentlessly in Ghent and under St. Bavo's cathedral. His nose had changed, likely from where I smashed it against a stone column when he stole my marble, but it was his face.

He'd chased us by plane out of Belgium. He shot gaping holes in our fuselage, but Marcus shot him down. I watched the plane spiral to the ground and catch fire. They'd told me no one found a body, but I wanted to believe he was dead.

No one should have survived such a crash.

How could Marcus ask me what was wrong? Didn't he recognize our enemy?

The gun in my waistcoat burned. It begged me to draw it and finish what Marcus had started in the air, for if the Flyer was here, he was here to harm us.

"Here we are, Bridget," said Margaret as she strode confidently into the dark room. "This is Jane and Marcus, the ones you've heard so much about."

The woman at the table stood, her hand resting on the butt of a pistol holstered around her torso.

"I've looked forward to meeting you," she said. "It's my understanding that you're willing to peddle your expertise in exchange for our protection."

Marcus swallowed. My utterance about the Flyer had rattled him, and his eyes darted back and forth between all present in the room.

"Yes," he stammered. "We're tired of serving a war machine in a conflict that will never end. I've spoken with Cillian at length, and maybe it's the American in me, but I'm enamored with your cause."

I nodded along, but my eyes were locked on the Flyer without hope of escape.

Capture or kill. Our orders echoed in my ears.

The woman folded her arms. The hanging lightbulb cast her body in shadow.

"Those are charming words, and I want to believe them. You may doubt our military strength, but don't believe for a second we are helpless. There are whisperings that even England's great traitor Joseph Dowling, despite conspiring with the German government, will escape the noose. They don't want another uprising on their hands, you see. We're a political movement. And we have political power."

Marcus had not let go of me since I'd stumbled over.

"Has Jane had a shock? Is she surprised to find a woman in charge here?" she asked with a smile. "You wouldn't see that in the Allied forces, I'm sure."

I stared at the Flyer. His slender, plaintive features did not twist into malice or chagrin upon seeing me. He looked back peacefully. His coolness filled me with anger and desperation, the same way it had as he so calmly negotiated with me in St. Bavo's.

"She's fine," Marcus said. He squeezed my shoulders and forcibly turned me toward him. "It's all right. We're still alive. Everything is still fine."

I tried to breathe and realized he was right. The woman at the table didn't speak as though she'd trapped us in some snare. And the Blue Flyer had not pounced on us. I did not yet grasp the full picture of this meeting.

Still, I struggled to foresee any detail that would make peace between us. The Flyer had tried to kill us on several occasions. He had stolen my marble.

Should I really have been surprised that when a magical device surfaced, he did as well?

"Please," Marcus said to me. As the shock of seeing our enemy wore off, he probably came to the same realizations I had. With his "please," he begged me to wait.

I nodded but didn't leave the door frame.

"Are you sure she can handle this?" the woman asked Margaret.

"Wouldn't have brought her here if she couldn't." Margaret replied.

The gun in my waistcoat itched. What would Atkins want me to do in this situation? Our orders were clear. Capture the Flyer or kill him. At present, capturing him seemed an impossibility with three other Irish radicals on his side. What did Marcus mean that the Flyer was Harry? That meant he wasn't just the courier of the magic item. It meant the Flyer had infiltrated the Irish infrastructure. Or, perhaps, the Flyer was always a member of the Irish revolt.

"Cillian?" asked the woman. "Can you vouch for her?"

"Don't vouch for much of anyone, anymore," said Cillian. "But I've found no one else similarly capable. If we're trying to figure out what this shipment is, if it's a weapon we can use against the English, Jane is your best option."

"She can do it," said the Flyer at last. His voice was sonorous, and it filled the room even though he didn't speak loudly. The sound of it took me right back to Ghent, though I remembered it in a lower tone. "I have first-hand experience."

"Do you now?" asked the woman.

"Yes." Harry's confession seemed to puzzle Cillian and Margaret. They glanced between us several times. "She is much more capable than she looks. If I'm not mistaken, she's brought something with her for an initial diagnostic."

My hand had reached for the goggles in my pocket before my instincts stopped me. This was a trap. And yet, something whispered that the others didn't know the truth of the Flyer, either. Perhaps that was an advantage.

"This man tried to kill us," I said. "Several times."

"Of course, I did," the Flyer replied. "We were after the same thing in a time of war, fighting for different sides."

"What side is that, then?" I asked.

"Look around. I'd have thought it'd be obvious by now."

I turned to the woman at the table and addressed her directly for the first time.

"Can you verify this? Is Sinn Fein in the practice of sending agents treasure hunting across the front line?"

"Sinn Fein?" Cillian broke in. "No, I wouldn't think so. They don't like to get their hands too dirty. They still believe they can talk their way to independence. But there are bolder, more noble sects of the Irish movement, and we're not afraid of doing what it takes to get the job done."

Margaret turned toward Cillian with surprise, even hurt.

"Cillian? Are you a volunteer?"

"Sorry, Marge. We're all after the same thing, just under different names and methods."

The woman at the table grabbed her gun, but she was too slow. Cillian already had his pistol drawn. Marcus put an arm across my front to shield me from danger. He didn't know I carried the danger with me.

"You're with the Brotherhood, aren't you?" Bridget asked, staring down the barrel of the pistol. "You didn't trust us to do this?"

"Some of us lost faith after all the arrests," Cillian replied. "Did you think Sinn Fein could keep the magic safe? You're too open. Your secrets run in the streets."

He stepped forward and took the woman's gun from her holster. Then, he turned it on the Flyer.

"You didn't tell me you knew her, Harry," he said, eyes flicking back and forth between the hostile parties in the room. My gun was all but screaming at me. If only I could reach it without drawing attention to myself.

"He knows me well enough. He chased us across France," I spat.

"Marcus, too?" Cillian asked the Flyer. Suspicion and paranoia flashed across his eyes. No one had touched the ammo drum sitting on the table.

"Oh, yes," said the Flyer with all the ease in the world. "In fact, I was surprised when Marcus did not recognize me. I suppose our interactions were often at a distance, and I was usually in disguise."

"So am I the fool, then?" asked Cillian.

"No, my friend," said the Flyer. "We all have secrets, every one of us. Surely, you must have known that our infrequent meetings did not make up the whole of my assignments. And you have done fine work in bringing Marcus along. He all but begged to join the Brotherhood when we met the other day."

I gripped Marcus's arm and turned on him.

"You did what?" I asked, breathless.

"I didn't beg," Marcus stammered. "And I didn't say as much as that, either. Jane, don't listen to him."

"Not with your mouth," said the Flyer. "But I can feel it in you."

His words sent a chill down my spine, eerily similar as they were to what he told me in Ghent. Hadn't he said he could smell dark magic on me?

"You're not even Irish," I cried.

"Nor are you," said the Flyer. "But, as Marcus might know from history classes as a boy, every revolution requires assistance from beyond its borders. Was it not the legacy of a Frenchman that inspired him and other early boys from the United States to come and volunteer for the Allied effort?"

"What are you then?" I asked.

"Late, at present." He put a hand up. "Cillian, lower your gun. Just as you said, we're all on the same side here. Sinn Fein, Brotherhood, Irish Republican Army, it doesn't matter, for I am the device's custodian. It was the deal I struck with Dowling."

Cillian obeyed, and Margaret let out a sigh of relief.

"Damn it all, Cillian. You might have warned me instead of making me out to be such a daft fool!"

"No one mentioned this to me," said Bridget.

"You couldn't know," said the Flyer. "None of you could."

"What's changed now?" asked Marcus. The Flyer laughed. The sound was strange and tired.

"Cillian was pointing a gun at me," he replied. "You'll be

shocked at how quickly a morsel of truth can grow a bridge. Now, Jane, please, can you verify the device?"

"Why not do it yourself?" I asked. I didn't trust him, nor could I forgive him for his attempts on our lives.

"Now that we've established, quite clearly, that you despise the sight of me, if you and I both insist the object is magical, that's quite the endorsement, wouldn't you say?"

"Come on, Jane," Marcus whispered. Even this small whisper stabbed my heart like a bayonet. He was siding with the Flyer. Yes, in just a small way, but this man was our enemy, and Marcus was siding with him. "I won't let them take the goggles from you."

I didn't understand how he planned on defending me against four other people, one of whom had bested our combined efforts on several occasions. But I had little choice.

I reached into my pocket and produced the goggles.

The ammo drum was a flat, hollow cylinder. It lay solidly on the table. It had been weeks since the last time I'd seen magic through the goggles, but now, the ammo drum lit up my view like a lightbulb. The unearthly blue-hued haze that had marked instances of magic through all our terrible ordeals shone anew. The dangerous beauty, combined with my swelling fear, took my breath away.

"What is it, Jane?" asked Margaret.

"It's real," I said in a gasp.

"Well done," said the Flyer. "Do you know what it does?"

I shook my head.

"Not yet. I'll need time to study it. A couple of days, maybe more."

Margaret jumped in.

"Just as I told you, Bridget. I will accompany her and make sure nothing happens to it. I'll stake my life on it."

"I'm afraid that won't be possible," said Cillian.

"Why not?" I asked.

"You and Marcus will go with Harry," he continued. "He will supply you with everything necessary to study the device."

Many voices in the room broke out in protest all at once, but I was most interested in what Marcus had to say. He had visited with Cillian and Harry in private. What had he chosen not to tell me?

"That wasn't what we decided," Marcus said, chin jutting forward in defiance.

"I'm sorry, lad," Cillian replied. "I couldn't tell you everything. But you'll have to trust me that this is best."

"I'll go along, too," said Margaret, who tried, quickly, to process her disappointment in being cut out of so important an endeavor.

"That won't be necessary," said the Flyer.

"Now, wait a minute," Bridget cut in. "Like hell I'm about to let you three non-Irelanders walk away with this device, not after everything it took to get it here. I'm sworn as its custodian as well, and it's too important to our cause."

Cillian reacted strongly to this, as did Margaret, and even Marcus. The four of them dissolved into unintelligible arguing about who should bear the honor and responsibility of leaving with the magic, and where it ought to go.

The Flyer, though, stayed quiet, watching me intently from his place across the room. Two orders. Capture him or kill him. Capture looked less and less likely the more the meeting broke down. And there he was, goading me, smiling at me, calmly waiting as though I had nothing in the world with which to threaten him.

Could he read my thoughts? Did he know my orders? Or was it an obvious presumption that I hated him?

Just as he had across the chapel at St. Bavo's, where he so easily coaxed me from coming out from behind the choir balcony, he watched and tried to speak with his gaze.

It happened all at once.

He grabbed the ammo drum off the table, elegant and quick as lightning. At the same time, I pulled the gun from my waistcoat.

It shut up the argument right quick.

"Jane, what are you doing?" Marcus cried.

"Jane, lovely, let's talk through this," said Margaret.

But the gun was out, and suddenly I had power. The Irelanders had frozen like lifeless shadows of the movement that killed my cousin. The Flyer stood on one end of the room, ammo drum in hand. I stood on the other, finger itching on my trigger. Even now, he smiled his maddening grin.

"Everyone is so quick to point a gun when they don't understand something," he said.

Cillian and Bridget's hands inched toward their firearms.

"No one move," I shouted.

"This was a mistake, Marcus," Cillian said.

"I didn't think she'd do this."

"I should have known better. You can only turn one. Turning two is much harder."

"What are you going on about?" asked Bridget.

"They're spies," Cillian said. "Both of them. Marcus was ready to leave it all behind. Probably still is. But he had too much trust in this one." He nodded toward me in disgust.

"She just—she's trying to get her head around everything," stammered Marcus. "I needed more time to talk to her."

More time to talk to me? This mission was dangerous, but the chasm between us must have grown wider than I suspected if Marcus was as far gone as Cillian suggested. When had I lost him?

"Give me the ammo drum," I said icily.

"Or else what?" asked the Flyer.

"You don't think I'll use this?" I jammed the gun forward to drive my point.

"I certainly don't know what you'll do after," he replied.

"Jane, please, this isn't the way," Marcus pleaded.

My patience eroded at last.

"What is the way, Marcus? You're lost. Plain and simple. You're hurt and you're searching for something. But you don't know how dangerous this man or that device is. It's not just the war. It's the future! First, it was machine guns. Then it was artillery. Then airplanes. Now tanks. But this? All of those are nothing if this falls into the wrong hands."

"You know where the right hands are then, do you?" asked Bridget.

"My hands are the right hands," I said through clenched teeth.

"Jane," started the Flyer.

BAM!

The sound shattered the quiet dark of the room, but the shot sailed into the wall beside my enemy. Cillian, Bridget, and Margaret ducked for cover instinctively.

"Jane! Stop! This is out of hand!"

"The ammo drum," I repeated.

"Let's not be rash, now," the Flyer said. His eyes stretched wide in surprise for the first time. "Here." He stepped forward slowly and put the drum on the table.

"Marcus, pick it up," I said.

"Jane, please, no." Margaret was crying in the corner, the ambitious revolutionary laid low.

"This is what the war does to us!" shouted Cillian. "It turns even beautiful young women into monsters."

Marcus set his jaw tightly, and I knew the wheels turned in his mind. The heart of these people moved him, the same way that the Lafayette Escadrille had. They were idealists willing to risk all for their cause.

Heat climbed the back of my neck, prickling up each vertebra in itchy dread. I was losing him. I refused to accept it. We carried an implicit promise not to be separated, and I was not about to let them seduce him by some dream of Irish honor.

"Marcus, quickly," I repeated.

He was tender. Lufbery had warned me about that. It was a miracle someone so tender had lasted so long at war. But he was worth protecting, and I would not let him be hijacked to repeat the cycle he had survived once already. No more starting afresh for a new noble cause.

But he stalled as he dumbly struggled over what to do.

"Capture is still on the table," he replied.

His response should not have shocked me, but it hurt. I needed him behind me, and he was busy waffling.

"Marcus?" I repeated, voice choking. "Please."

In the corner of my eye, movement caught my attention. Margaret, with all her dreams of being a hero of the people, lunged for the ammo drum.

BAM!

I fired the gun on reflex. Its rounds went into the table, just shy of her reaching hands. She retreated instantly, but it set off a chain reaction, an outbreak of foolhardy bravery. The others tried to get the device as well. So I kept firing to keep them at bay. The gun kicked wildly in my hand, jerking at my wrist and trying to escape my grip. I didn't try to hit the Irelanders. I wanted only to keep them pinned down.

But when the Flyer moved for the device, as well. Now that was different.

He crept forward, and I wheeled on him.

Capture had been a fantasy. It had always been a fantasy. I closed one eye and pulled the trigger.

"Jane!" screamed Marcus.

I hadn't seen the cripple. Nor had I taken into account the genuine belief he had in his cause. In a pathetic, stumbling leap, he had tried to knock the Flyer out of the way.

They both lay on the ground. Only one had red fluid coming out of his chest.

It broke the reality we'd constructed in that room. This wasn't a battleground. We were a group of people who knew one another, if only in part.

Margaret was the first to tend to him.

"Cillian," she hiccuped. "Cillian, please."

She tore at his shirt and clamped her hands over the wound. It did little to help. Bridget rounded on me like a wolf.

"You damned witch!" she shouted. I held up the gun again, defensively. "You killed him! English pig! You killed him!"

"Jane, what have you done?" Marcus stuttered. His gaze haunted me, debased me as a demon, a devil. It was entirely unfair. If I were Lufbery or any other member of his beloved Lafayette squadron, he would not be so disgusted. If we were in an airplane, he would not be so disgusted.

We had orders from our commanding officers. We were on a mission to retrieve the device and eliminate the Flyer.

I looked away from Cillian and Marcus.

"The Flyer," I said, whirling around. "Where is he?"

Like a maniac, I moved through the room, checking behind the crates and barrels. Impossibly, the Flyer had vanished.

"Marcus, he's gone."

Marcus lay limply against the wall. The mission had gone to pieces.

I grabbed the ammo drum from the table.

"Let's go," I muttered.

He was crying now. Quiet tears ran down his cheeks. In my state of heady control, I refused to acknowledge the nobility of his tears. There would be time to evaluate everything later. Now, we needed to get away from these people.

I put the ammo drum in his hands.

"Carry this."

I stepped across the room, keeping Bridget on the other end of my Starr pistol. Margaret was a mess and posed no resistance. She was no soldier. I tried not to look at Cillian's blank stare as I fished the keys to the Ford out of his pocket. I took his Webley revolver, as well.

"Go on and loot the dead!" shouted Margaret. "That's all you're good for. We'll find you, Jane. We'll find your family. This isn't the end."

I pushed Marcus through the door, shut it behind us, and slid the deadbolt to lock them inside.

"He was a British subject," Marcus said as soon as I'd turned. I marched past him down the hallway toward the door leading to the courtyard. He hurried behind me. "He was a veteran. Your countryman."

"He was planning a treasonous uprising."

"This is Johann all over again." Johann. My memory raced to that nightmarish episode in Nancy when Marcus and I had first learned about the rogue flyers and their pursuit of magical artifacts. Johann was the pilot who tried to bomb our meeting location. Mustermann, a fellow German, shot him in the middle of the night to keep him from being questioned by American military forces.

That night made me sick. This was so different. I whirled on Marcus.

"We swore an oath to obey orders," I said. "Don't you remember? Or do you believe yourself exempt from your word?"

"Who ordered you to shoot Cillian?"

"They got in your head, Marcus."

"I was being strategic. We could have used my position to our advantage."

"You mean you could have used it to your advantage!" I stuck a pointed finger right into the space below his chin. I realized my chest was heaving and my jaw was sore for how I'd set it in defiance.

A moment before, Marcus had looked at me in disgust. I couldn't imagine what might be worse.

But it was this. He stared at me as though I were nothing but a dangerous stranger.

"Why'd you shoot him?"

I put Cillian's revolver in Marcus's hand and took a deep breath.

"I didn't want to—" I whispered.

We heard a thump on the locked door we'd come through.

"Time to go," I said.

Chapter 8
Escape
Marcus

My stomach churned.

All of my fears for Jane had come true. I'd seen combat take her as early as her first flights. It took her again at Ghent when she had to put down those machine gunners. And again when she shot down that bomber over Paris and couldn't let off the trigger.

But this was different.

We weren't in a vehicle. We weren't in the heat of battle. She'd shot the man like an executioner. No. Like a good soldier. Atkins had ordered her to capture or kill the Flyer, but I knew her well enough to understand what had happened. The Flyer scared her. He had wronged her. It made the orders easier to accept.

There was the great and important distinction. Atkins's orders were permission to take justice, perhaps vengeance, into her own hands.

That wasn't Jane. If she saw it like that, she'd be horrified. But that was the danger and the reason why what we had was so important. She couldn't see herself, the same way I couldn't see myself until I shared my burdens with her. It only worked if we kept going back to some quiet place to divulge, unload, even confess.

But as it was, the truth was an artillery shell. I hadn't protected Jane at all. She'd become a soldier so my hands could stay clean.

And Cillian...

We crossed the courtyard in the dark back in the Model T. We didn't know this part of Dublin, but the road off of the little peninsula wouldn't be too hard to find. We hadn't passed many turns in either direction, and we should at least be able to get back to the mainland. From there, we could find the river and limp our way back to the garage, back to our commanders.

But for what?

Cillian kept saying I was ready to leave. I never corrected him. After all, the only reason he hadn't blown up my cover earlier is because he thought he could turn me.

Maybe I'd pretended too well—well enough to fool myself a little.

Cillian's conviction, enthusiasm, and warmth had intoxicated me. And Harry, the Blue Flyer—how hadn't I recognized him? He was our enemy.

But maybe the way he'd come after us wasn't personal. War was war. I'd enjoyed countless stories of pilots treating their downed enemies like civil guests until they could be taken to a prison camp or exchanged back across front lines.

Sometimes, it wasn't personal.

Sometimes, it was.

"Get me started?" Jane asked.

She opened the carburetor under the hood while I hurried to the crankshaft at the front of the car. I placed the empty ammo drum and the revolver on the ground beside me.

"I'm ready up here. Go quickly. I don't know how long that door will hold," she said.

"There's gotta be another way out," I said as I primed the cylinders. "If Harry made it out—"

"His name's not Harry," said Jane sharply.

"You don't know what his name is."

She clenched her jaw and turned away.

"All right, turn on the ignition," I said. "Start it."

She nodded. Despite the strenuous circumstances, or maybe because of them, the actions of getting this Model T started calmed my nerves. It was muscle memory from that garage in California. This step of the startup procedure was always the moment of truth. Would the engine start or not?

It didn't.

I pulled the crank lever back, but the engine didn't respond.

"Come on, now" I muttered between grinding teeth.

I tried again and again, but nothing.

"Good thing we're mechanics," I said. Jane hopped out of her seat, and we opened the hood. It was too dark to see much.

My hand slipped along the engine, feeling its way along the familiar surface.

I froze.

"What is it?" Jane asked.

"The spark plugs are all gone," I replied. "And the cords and belt are cut. It's like someone really, really, did not want this car to go anywhere."

"But we only just rode it in," Jane said. "It's been sitting here idle for no more than fifteen or twenty minutes. No one even knew we were here."

"At least four others knew," I said. "One is dead. Two we locked inside. And Harry?"

Jane became very still. I couldn't see well in the dark, but I knew her enough to guess that the color had just drained from her face.

"I thought he'd—"

"Vanished into thin air?" I finished for her. I shut the hood with a loud clang.

"I don't know what he can and can't do!" she protested. "He survived that crash. He followed me all through Ghent without even breaking a sweat."

"He's flesh and blood," I said.

"I'm not sure he is!"

I took a deep breath to steady myself.

"Until we prove otherwise, I think it's safe to say there's another way out of that room. We can't start this thing unless we find spare parts. Do you think you can shoot our way out of this problem somehow?"

My comment was unkind, and regret struck me immediately after it left my lips. I picked the revolver back up. Jane put her hand to her mouth to nibble at a fingernail. Her other arm crossed her body, and for a moment, goggles slung around her neck and a gun dangling from her hand, she came across as that soft-hearted woman I'd met in Villeneuve-les-Vertus. She was the one who had taught me to dance the Grizzly Bear and looked the other way when I tried, badly, to cheat my way to winning a round of Crown and Anchor.

"We need to get this back to our officers," she said. Her eyes glossed over, but her voice was strong. She kicked the ammo drum without much force.

"Right," I nodded. "Well, despite the rising Irish tide, England is still the regulating force over here, right? Which means, if we're lucky, no one should come shooting at us in broad daylight."

She ruefully rolled her head to one side.

"That would be of great comfort if it weren't the middle of the night."

I crouched down and collected the ammo drum.

"If only we knew what this thing did," I said. "Maybe it could help. Do the goggles offer any clues?" I asked.

She slipped the goggles up over her eyes and examined the ammo drum, but her face fell.

"What?" I asked.

"It's just—I don't understand."

"What?"

"It's not shining blue anymore."

The sound of rifle fire snapped me back into focus and set my heart racing. It pinged off the metal hood of the Model T with an empty thud. We both jumped for cover.

"Where did that come from?" Jane asked. She held her arm cocked at ninety degrees, pistol at the ready and surveyed our surroundings.

"Jane, you've got two shots left in that thing at best."

"Did you see the muzzle flare?"

"No. But it must have come from that direction, seeing where it hit the car." I pointed out of the courtyard to the street. There didn't appear to be anything there other than a few sleepy buildings. The shot could have come from any window in any of them.

"We have to move. Let's make our way toward the coast. With any luck, we can find a port or harbor. I'd hope the English still have control of those at least. Then we can get in contact with Atkins and Smith."

Her shoulders fell in relief

"Oh, come on," I said. "Did you really believe I was trying to desert? Let's go."

Jane sprung from her hiding spot, bending over at the waist as she ran across the clearing. Another shot rang out, but it went wide and ricocheted off the iron railing topping the walls of the courtyard.

We hurried along the side of the building. To our relief, there was a small gate in the fence on the opposite side of the yard. We ran across the road, roaming shadow to shadow. I was grateful for our recent experience flying at night, as it had forced me to learn the basics of navigating by the stars. It was just clear enough to find Polaris, and I knew there was sea to the north.

The town was small, named Howth by the roadsigns. Before long, we found ourselves by a church that was small by Ghent standards but enormous compared to any church we had back home.

Home. I shook the thought off. The word had been coming up too often, lately.

I wasn't sure whether we should be tiptoeing around the town or sprinting through open streets. I wish I knew how deep and how structured the Irish movements were or who had just taken a shot at us.

Maybe it wasn't the Irish at all. During our escape from Ghent, we escaped enchanted shots from enchanted rifles, firing from innumerable windows.

With the church to our back, we soon caught a grasp of the land just in time to find the sea. A pair of street signs pointed us to the harbor.

Jane nearly sprinted across the street to a guarded outpost. I jogged to keep up behind her and sized up the young guard on duty. He was too slender for his uniform. Blonde hair poked out from under his helmet.

"Please!" she launched her appeal at the young man instantly. "You have to help—"

"Hold!" the guard screamed and leveled his rifle at Jane. He flicked the muzzle back and forth between the two of us. In an instant, a second guard appeared on his hip, his own rifle drawn.

"What are you doing?" Jane asked, bewildered. "We need to make contact with Lieutenant Atkins."

"Put your weapon on the ground and take two steps back!"

The guards were just kids, and they were jumpy. After all I had learned about the Rising, I could hardly blame them. Paranoia would spread like fleas in an environment like this.

"Jane, your gun," I said, putting my own revolver on the ground and kicking it toward the guard. "Put down your weapon!" the guard cried again. The gears worked behind Jane's resolute face. We had the device with us. We didn't know who could be trusted.

But these were problems we should have debated before walking up on rifle-bearing guards.

"Come on, Jane. They'll shoot you, and then what?" I muttered.

Carefully, she put her gun on the ground and kicked it forward. The guards immediately lowered their weapons.

"Bloomin' heavens!" the blonde guard started.

"What's the matter with you lot? Why would you run up to an armed outpost with weapons drawn in the middle of the night like that?" added his partner. He was rounder and freckled. The blonde one raised his hand.

"I'm shaking like I've had three pints already!"

"I could use a pint myself," the other said as he picked our guns off the ground.

Evidently, our fears that these young men were Sinn Feiners or members of the Brotherhood were unfounded. I'd become fluent in the language of young conscripted soldiers eager to get into action. Every new recruit spoke it, regardless of what country they hailed from.

"What's going on out here?" a more judicious, older voice hailed from behind the fence. A lance corporal came strutting out, both hands behind his back. He wore a patchy mustache, and a unit commendation medal labeled him as a major general.

I glanced at Jane. Both of our hands were raised in submission, but she rolled her eyes. We felt safe from all but the bludgeoning bureaucratic pedantry of His Majesty's army.

"These two came running up like they were charging a line, sir. Pistols drawn. Ammo drum in one hand."

"We were coming for help," Jane said. "We're just trying to contact Lieutenant—"

"And beg pardon, but how do we know you're not Irish radicals?" the Lance Corporal stroked his mustache.

"This is ridiculous," I said. "We're on assignment."

"A yank?" the freckly guard said. His blonde companion abandoned his attempt at lighting a cigarette. "Well, now I'm suspicious all over again."

"Suspicious of what? We're allies, aren't we?" I said.

"No, no. It is unusual. And unusual business on the streets of Dublin must be treated with every ounce of—"

CRACK!

A rifle shot wailed from the dark behind us. I dove immediately for cover behind a military truck parked beside the outpost. Jane dove the other way behind a barrier of concrete block. The guards lost any sense of composure.

In a moment they had dug in behind the barricades erected around their outpost, sturdy structures Frankensteined together with concrete blocks, rubble, and household furniture.

"Very suspicious, indeed!" the Lance Corporal shouted.

"This is what we're running from!" Jane called back. I tried to shimmy forward.

"Stay where you are!" the blonde guard screamed, pivoting his rifle in my direction.

"Stop pointing your rifles at him!" Jane cried. "He didn't shoot at you—he's been shot at, you dimwitted buffoon."

Another shot erupted from the buildings behind us. This time it sounded as though it came from somewhere else.

"Why didn't Atkins inform anyone in Dublin that we'd be here?" Jane called to me.

I had no answer. But now, I was pinned behind a truck afraid of being shot by a mysterious shooter or a trigger-happy English sentry. All Cillian's philosophizing about the absurdity of the war came calling.

"What do we do, sir?" the freckly private asked. "Do we fire?"

"How do you expect to fire if we can't see anything at which to fire?"

"Would you at least take us captive so we can have the protection of your custody?" asked Jane.

"We'd be happy to take you as a captive," he said after due consideration. "We have only to get you over here safely."

If our lives weren't on the line, this type of incompetency would be comical. But watching Jane convince this wanna-be aristocrat English officer that he should take us prisoner was maddening. The same way Luf getting shot down because some other pilot refused to engage an enemy plane himself was maddening. I was so tired of blind obedience to orders.

"She can just crawl over," I said, throwing my hands out in exasperation.

"And the mysterious gunman?" he asked.

"If you're that worried about him, lay down some covering fire, you idiot," I replied.

"But we don't know where he is—"

"The gunman doesn't know that!" I hissed loud enough that the shooter just might overhear.

"Ah yes, very clever. Together then, men. On the three—"

"No! You should stagger it to make it last long—"

"One, two, three!"

Both guards fired blindly into the night, and Jane sprinted past them behind the barricades. The rifle's discharge echoed into the town and met eery silence.

At least Jane was safe in their protection.

"Miss, you are officially a prisoner of His Majesty's armed forces. If you cooperate, you can expect to be dealt with civilly."

"You blasted idiot," Jane retorted, not so civilly. "I'm an enlisted member of His Majesty's armed forces."

I rested my head on the ground. The mission was all but over. Jane was in the hands of Allied forces, tucked away from the Brotherhood she had provoked.

She was safe.

But the mission was a failure. We hadn't captured or killed the Blue Flyer. And more importantly, at least from my point of view, the device was a dud. It had lost whatever enchantment painted it blue in Boelcke's goggles. We understood less about the magic than when we started.

This would only continue. There would be another mission for another artifact, and if we ever found anything, they'd whisk it off to some research facility and leave us in the dark.

And we hadn't even heard from Mustermann, Earnst, or Lina. If there was any activity on their side of the line, they'd send us out again. Our time at war wasn't done. The war would never be done. Even if we had killed the Flyer, the hunt for magical devices would continue. There would just be one less person after them.

"All right, now! Prospective prisoner two, are you ready to move?" called the corporal.

"Sure," I said after a pause.

"Very well, we are lining up–"

Another rifle shot fired from the dark. It ricocheted off the metal frame of the gate into the harbor. By instinct, I covered my head, praying that the pile of rubble was enough to obscure me from any real shot by the marksman.

"Did you see him, Tim?" the blonde soldier said.

"Right window, house on the left, Fred."

I took a deep breath and prepared myself to return and report our tepid success to Smith and Atkins, and beg them to sit Jane out of the next cycle somehow.

The image of Cillian bleeding on the floor shot through my mind and wracked my heart. With it came the sight of Luf's plane, streaking through the sky like a fireball. I shook my head back and forth. I didn't want to remember that. I didn't want that to be true.

"Even better, privates. Aim for that window."

I pulled myself to a low crouch. There was nothing else to do but go back. I wished there was something else. Anything else.

"One, two..."

"Marcus," called a soft voice behind me. I turned.

"Fire!"

Chapter 9
Friendly Fire
Jane

Can ye measure the grief of the tears I weep
Or compass the woe of the watch I keep?
Or the pride that thrills thro' my heart's despair
And the hope that comforts the anguish of prayer?
-Sarojini Naidu-

I covered my ears for their gunshots. Strangely, although I'd spent my fair share of time firing Lewis guns in the back of our airplane, hearing the rifles tonight, without the blanketing muffled aid of a passing slipstream, rattled my bones.

But loud noises aside, I took great comfort sitting behind the guards at the mouth of the harbor, protected from sight and blanketed by a hefty blockade.

After an echoing and deafening silence in the wake of their fire, the two sentries congratulated one another cheerily.

"Think I got him."

"Absolutely not. I got him."

"You didn't even see where he was. I did."

But I could not care less about their juvenile banter. Marcus hadn't come around the bend after their covering fire.

"Prisoner number two, you have failed to present yourself as agreed. We will provide one more round of covering fire. I order you to run to us immediately thereafter!"

"Another round? But we already shot the man, sir," said the blonde one.

"Better safe than dead," the corporal replied. "Ready, boys? One, two, fire!"

The shot was less uniform than before but more closely resembled a staggered volley that might serve as real covering fire.

Still, Marcus did not materialize in the aftermath.

"Marcus?" I called. Dread crept slowly up my body. My breathing staggered. Was he coming?

He wouldn't return to Margaret. He'd told me he'd fooled them. He'd said he was still with us.

He wouldn't desert, not without me. I refused to believe it.

"Marcus?" I tried his name again but met only silence.

"Proof is in the pudding, I'm afraid. The bugger has run off," said the corporal in an affected voice. But Marcus wouldn't. I lunged forward to see for myself, but he grabbed me. "Tim, Fred! She's trying to effect an escape as well!"

In a moment, the two soldiers had shouldered their rifles and had me by an arm a piece. I twisted and writhed to break free. Where was Marcus? Had he been shot while waiting to join me? If so, he may have fallen unconscious from blood loss.

"I need to find him!" I called out. My heart raced faster. "He might be just there and wounded."

"He's not there. He's gone, lass."

"Did you look?" I begged as I stopped my struggle against their grip. My sudden halt brought weight to my inquiry.

"If you insist, we can send a scout," the corporal replied.

"A scout? It's a matter of six feet over!"

"Now, now, miss. You may not be privy to this insensitive information, but I've seen men riddled to death by bullets for no more than three feet of progress on the front lines."

The idea of this man serving at the front in any capacity was ludicrous. Every second that slipped away from me was another second that Marcus's life might be running out a bullet hole in his body.

"Let me be the scout, then," I insisted. "It will take me three seconds."

"You'd like that, wouldn't you, prisoner?"

"Marcus!" I screamed into the night. But there was still no answer. He was slipping away. My eyes welled over and tears streamed down my cheeks. "Please."

Crying turned out to be the key necessary to unlock the corporal's cool demeanor. He softened instantly, likely hung up by inflated notions of gentlemanly etiquette.

"Now, miss, I think I see what has happened here," he said softly. "That man has disabused you. He is a rascal and talked you into some scheme of his, didn't he?"

My head sunk between my shoulders, face dropping to the pavement. My tears fell to the ground.

"Listen, if it means so much to you, I will check myself," the corporal said.

"But, sir, the shooter!"

"We may not have got him after all!"

"Honor calls, my lads. I will answer." He plucked up his courage, rounded the corner of our cover, and strode into the street. I watched him with suspended hope.

He walked back in, unharmed and accompanied by nothing but my disappointment.

"It's as I've said. The rascal has abandoned you."

The soldiers released my arms so I could bury my face in my hands.

Abandoned? Oh, any word but that one.

"Let me search for him," I said.

"Search where?" the corporal asked. All the humor and pomp had drained from his voice, resulting in a nauseating tone of pity. I didn't want his pity.

"In the nearby houses. The streets. Howth isn't large. He must be somewhere!"

The corporal's big melancholy eyes watched me without blinking as he nodded along.

"Fred, go wake George and Sam. They'll take your post. You two will conduct a search. I don't care if it takes all night. This woman needs answers."

Fred scurried off.

"Thank you," I said, though I hardly meant it. I wished I had my identification cards. I wished I knew how to get a hold of Atkins.

"Come now, how about a cuppa? Then, you can explain why it was you were brandishing a weapon at my soldiers."

H e forced me to have a cuppa at all but gunpoint. I burned my throat for how quickly I drank the tea, urgent to get on with the business of finding my lost friend. If only I could verify that this bumbling idiot hadn't missed him in the shadows somewhere.

We sat in a small outpost near the harbor. The corporal had draped a rough woolen blanket around my shoulders. My hands unconsciously traced the outline of the goggles hanging around my neck as I tried to piece the evening's events in proper order.

He alternated between showing me off and shooing his soldiers and orderlies away so I could have my peace.

He still did not believe I was involved with the Royal Flying Corps in any capacity, and when I would not deviate from these claims, he left me alone to call in my capture.

All the while, Marcus was... somewhere, not beside me.

Fred and Tim were still out searching. Perhaps they'd find him. It's not as though Marcus had transportation out of the city, and it was a long walk back to Dublin.

But in my heart, I feared something worse. Bridget and Margaret were out there, as was the Blue Flyer. One of them may have snatched him up or clubbed him, or...

There was so much I didn't know. And in that, I'd have preferred seeing him driven away by a German sentry into the heart of Ghent than this.

Atkins and Smith arrived after only half an hour. I heard the lieutenant before I saw him.

"You blithering moron! You arrested her?"

"She was brandishing a weapon at my unit."

"Brandishing a weapon? Did she point a gun at you? Threaten to shoot?"

"Well, no–"

"Then what did she do?"

Silence.

"Well, it was a very peculiar circumstance–"

"And the American?" That was Smith's voice.

"He ran off."

"What do you mean, ran off?" Smith's voice hardened into gravel.

"Just that. We laid down covering fire so he could run in–"

"Covering fire?" I could hear the vein in Atkins's neck bulge. "What the hell were you laying down covering fire for in Howth at 11 pm?"

"We were under attack, sir."

"Oh, shut up and go find the American."

A click of the heels.

"I have two men on it now, sir."

"Two men? I want ten, twenty, thirty, and I want every house searched if needs be. Get to it."

The corporal's footsteps made a hollow sound as he ran off, and a moment later, Smith and Atkins joined me.

"What happened?" Smith asked without ceremony.

"I'm fine, thank you," I replied.

"Drop the attitude," he said as he took a seat beside me. "Talk."

"He's gone," I said, helplessly. I stared at the space between their heads, still trying to come to grips with that reality.

"Where?"

"I don't know. I've been held prisoner here. The meeting went poorly. Someone pursued us from a meeting place nearby. We reached the outpost. Then, our pursuer fired a few rounds in our direction. The soldiers bunkered in, and Marcus and I jumped for cover outside the barricade. They laid covering fire while I ran in, then tried the same for Marcus, but he never came."

Smith folded his arms and tried to keep his composure, but I saw the muscle clench in his jaw as though he were biting a stick for an amputation.

"Defected. Deserted," Atkins said, pacing the room. "I told you, Smith. Dewar was compromised."

"You told me?" Smith rose. "I didn't want to send him to Ireland in the first place!"

"No. You'd have been happy keeping him busy playing pretend until the end of the war."

"I'd have been happy waiting until he was ready."

Atkins took off his hat and pinned it under his arm so he could smooth his hair with a hand.

"Wouldn't it be sporting if we could wait until all our soldiers were ready? Smith, you won't believe this, but we can't. Soldiers, by the very nature of war, must simply forget themselves and get on with the soldiering."

"We're not working with soldiers anymore. We're working with spies."

Atkins stopped pacing.

"That's not true."

"Wake up and smell the coffee, Atkins. Are you commanding a unit? A battalion? A squadron? The confidentiality has buried us alive. The damn kids can't even get help at our own outpost in some town in Ireland!" He slumped back down in the chair beside me and drained the corporal's teacup in one gulp.

"Why isn't this coffee?" he shouted. "Who was shooting at you?"

I shook my head.

"I'm not sure. Cillian and Margaret drove us to meet with a member of Sinn Fein to retrieve the device. When we arrived, they took us to a dark room where a woman named Bridget waited. This sat on his table." I nudged the empty ammo drum beside the teacup. "The goggles identified it."

Atkins pulled over a crate and sat down to inspect the drum.

"So you found it," he said in awe. "And how did you secure it?"

"Through blood," I said coldly. I waited, again, for the remorse to kick in. I was sorry about how it hurt Marcus. I was even sorry that Cillian had thrown himself where he ought not.

But when it came to conjuring remorse for taking a life, I came up empty.

"I see," Atkins replied. Smith studied me intently.

"The Flyer was there," I went on.

Atkins put down the ammo drum

"And?" he asked. "Is he eliminated?"

I shook my head, ruefully.

"Can you confirm he's working with the Brotherhood?" Smith asked.

"Yes," I replied and pulled my blanket closer.

"So it goes as deep as I suspected," Atkins whispered to himself. "How? If there were a clandestine aerodrome in Ireland, I think we'd know about it."

The more I ruminated on the issue, the more connections I found. Some were logical. Some were arcane.

Ireland had a long history of magic. The way the Blue Flyer spoke, the knowledge he possessed—it wouldn't surprise me at all to discover he'd established those roots in Irish soil. Part of me wanted to believe that he was made of the magic.

"Any idea as to what this thing does?" Smith asked, tapping the ammo drum with his finger. My heart sank lower.

"And there's the final piece." I sighed. "I think it's a dud."

Atkins scoffed and rapped his knuckles on the table.

"A dud?"

"After I shot Cillian, and we took the drum, it lit up blue in the goggles, just as every device we've seen before."

"So what's the problem?" Smith asked. I pulled the goggles from my neck and dropped them on the table.

"Take a look for yourself." Cautiously, Smith put the goggles to his own eyes, then lowered them. He repeated this several times before handing them back.

"Nothing," I concluded for him. "No shine at all."

"Could they have switched it out for a decoy?" Smith asked. I considered this. Could the Flyer have swapped it when I shot at the Irish? No. I'd have seen. The only time the drum wasn't in our possession was when Marcus set it down momentarily to assess the Model T.

"I don't think so," I said. "It never left our sight."

Atkins sat up straight and searched for his pipe.

"That's ridiculous. It's not as though it could simply stop being magical."

He lit a match to start his smoke and waved the fire out. Then, it hit me.

"Unless someone turned it off," I mused.

"What do you mean, Jane?" Smith asked.

"The Blue Flyer. What if he turned off the device? Or worse, turned on a device that wasn't on already."

Smith massaged his temples.

"I'll be damned. He laid a trap."

It took me but a moment to grasp his meaning. Perhaps this wasn't about the device at all. This was a regular, empty, worthless ammo drum. He was toying with us.

"But if he was luring us here, he must have done so for a purpose," I surmised.

"Any idea what that might be?" Smith asked.

My face paled. There was a reason, something that I had not yet disclosed to Smith or Atkins. It was an object the Blue Flyer had admitted he wanted more than any of the artifacts we sought, something I kept insisting Marcus not wear around his neck.

I was so stupid.

"It's Marcus," I choked. "He's after Marcus."

My mind seized on this epiphany. Marcus had not defected. He was at risk the moment we entered the country because he wore a marble with my hair in it around his neck.

"What are you talking about?" Atkins asked, smoke escaping his mouth.

"This mission was nothing but a distraction. And he's got him!" I stood abruptly. My chair scraped backwards and fell over.

"Slow down," Smith said.

"Smith! Marcus did not defect. The Flyer captured him, and I doubt he plans to stick around in Howth or even Dublin. We must find him, now."

"Poppycock," said Atkins. But Smith met my gaze and understood my urgency. We bolted for the door. "Where are you going?"

Smith called back over his shoulder. "Come on, Atkins, you slice of raisin toast."

We scrambled to find the corporal finishing a quick briefing with a small group of soldiers. They broke off into the town in every direction just as we approached. His face was flushed and humbled. When he spoke, it did not have the dogmatic tone he'd used so liberally before.

"We're combing the city, sir," he said to Atkins. "And I've sent word to the men near the inlet to keep an eye out. We'll find him."

"Nothing yet?" I asked.

"No, ma'am. But we won't stop until he is found."

He saluted and retreated a few paces to help a private whose rifle had jammed on loading.

"But why on Earth would the Flyer want your American pilot?" said Atkins. I chewed my tongue and debated divulging the truth about the marble Marcus wore or the Flyer's previous, successful attempts to steal my own.

Smith stuffed his hands in his pockets and cocked his head to the side to scrutinize me. He had deduced there was more than I let on.

But then Fred and Tim arrived, huffing and puffing as though they'd just competed in a school race. The corporal bounded back over.

"Well, lads?" he said. "Did you find him?"

"Absolutely not," said Tim as he gasped for air. He doubled over, his hand on his knees.

"Took a tour of the whole town, we did." Fred coughed.

"Looked about everywhere."

"All but interrogated anyone still out."

"No sign of the American prisoner."

Smith stepped forward and shook Tim by the shoulders.

"He's not a prisoner, kid!" Smith growled.

"Anything out of the ordinary?" asked Atkins.

"Well, yes, that's why we ran back." Fred put a hand on his side and winced. "One of the men along the shore said one of his rowboats had gone missing."

"When?" I asked, grabbing Fred by the lapels. His face retreated into his neck.

"I dunno! He said he had it this afternoon, but it was gone when he got in tonight."

I dropped Fred and bounded toward the harbor.

"Hey, I'll have to press this shirt now!" he called after. In a moment, Smith and Atkins were at my heels.

"He's trying to escape by sea," I said.

"Of course," Smith replied. "The corporal's sentries on the road won't be any help."

"Nor will the Flyer get far in a rowboat," added Atkins. "The harbor is defended. They can't simply row across the channel unnoticed."

We came to a stop on a wooden dock beside the sea.

"You'd hope not, especially with a near full moon," said Smith. "Do you see anything?"

The three of us stared out at the black water. The waves ebbed relentlessly, tirelessly against the shore. I put my hand above my eyes to will my vision further, more discerning. I didn't see a row boat anywhere.

"This is useless," Smith muttered. "Can't see a thing."

"I couldn't agree more," Atkins muttered. A thought hit me, and I slid Boelcke's goggles over my eyes and gasped.

I wasn't wrong when I had supposed Ireland to be a land of magic. As I squinted through them out toward the sea, small wisps of faint blue white danced above the water and through the sky in a subtle but dazzling show.

I had put on the goggles in an act of desperation, in a vague hope that somehow it would enhance my vision, magical or not.

But there, far out amidst the waves, one blue glow was brighter than the others. I pointed.

"There," I said. "Do you see anything?"

The corporal arrived at our side out of breath and offered a pair of binoculars. I took them but found only grief in their lenses.

Where I had seen the brightest blue, floating haphazardly amidst the waves, was an empty rowboat.

Chapter 10
The Flyers
Marcus

Terraced thousands died, shaking scythes at cannon.
The hillside blushed, soaked our broken wave.
They buried us without shroud of coffin
And in August... the barley grew up out of our grave.
-Seamus Heaney-

My head throbbed. The pain hugged the back of my skull and reached across my temples, finally coming to a point behind the space between my eyebrows. I'd heard about migraines before, but I had never known how debilitating they could be. Every movement of my neck sent a fresh wave of the smothering, dull stabbing into my crown.

I squinted through the pain. The light pricked at me like aggressive needles boring their way inside my head.

Fortunately, there wasn't much light in the submarine. Unfortunately, it turned out submarines were little hell pods.

Jane had made it to the safety of the barricaded outpost. The corporal ordered his soldiers to fire a volley to cover my retreat, or surrender as they viewed it. I'd been crouched, ready to run, and then I heard the voice. Harry had called my name. I don't know how he found us or if he'd collaborated with the shooter that had taken aim at us during our retreat to the shoreline, but when I turned, he motioned at me with a sad look of camaraderie. Cillian was dead, and somehow, in a single glance, Harry let me know that despite the cloak and dagger tactics, Cillian had been more than a contact to him. He'd been a friend.

We had that in common, and it made him trust me.

Suddenly, I saw an opportunity.

Maybe Jane and the others were right. I wasn't much of a soldier. But I'd done a much better job at being a spy than Jane so far. Atkins wanted him captured or dead. This might be even better, a chance to really learn about the magic and our enigmatic enemy who had bested at every turn.

So I went with him. Harry's preparations surprised and impressed me. We'd stolen away to a rowboat, and he took us out far off the coast. I would have never seen the surfaced submarine amidst the black waves. Another man helped us onboard. The hatch closed, and all was dark for a good while.

Now, metallic creaking assailed my ears as we floated in the underwater currents of the sea.

Questions swam around me.

Was Jane safe? Did she have the device? Had I really run off with the Blue Flyer?

"You'd better sit down," Harry said from behind me. I stooped in the small chamber, aimlessly walking back and forth across it for a long while. Rows of spider-like hammocks hung around the room. They reminded me of the sacks they used to transport the dead.

The walls creaked again, and a metallic hum reverberated beyond the metal to my right. The floor had grooves and stops as if to minimize slipping. There were no windows.

Harry took his own advice and sat in a hammock opposite me.

I followed suit. It made for an awkward chair, so I resorted to a type of slumped, leaning posture with my elbows on my knees. Between the changes in pressure, the industrial odors, and the quality of the air, my migraine was doing heavy work on me.

Harry had already changed. He wore a woolen coat lined with fur, similar to the coats my squad mates and I might wear for frigid flights. Another one lay beside him.

"Are you cold?" He asked, tossing it to me. I was. I'd hardly noticed. "It'll warm up very soon. But in the meantime..."

"We're in a submarine," I muttered. Harry stared at me with piercing blue eyes. His wavy hair swept up into a naval officer's hat that sat off kilter on his head.

"We are," he said.

I rubbed the back of my neck.

"Cillian's dead?" I asked. It was dumb to ask. I'd seen what happened. But something inside me hoped I was wrong. That was stupid of me, though. It was hope that hurt, hope in the impossible.

"He wouldn't have lived long. I think the bullet pierced his heart." Harry's voice softened in introspection. "He sacrificed himself for me."

"He believed in something," I said. I wanted to comfort Harry, even if just to keep my mind off the image of Jane shooting Cillian. "A free Ireland. The Brotherhood."

He shook his head, slowly.

"I'm afraid the Irish have a long way to go," he said.

"Longer without help," I replied. A wave of pain shot through my head. I winced and shut my eyes as it passed. "How long have you been working with the Brotherhood?"

"It'll be better to explain that when Dieter can join us."

"Dieter? You have a partner?"

Harry nodded and stuck his hands in his pockets so they rested on his legs.

"Dieter and I have worked together for a long time now."

"And here we thought there was only one of you," I said.

"What's that?"

"The Blue Flyer."

He perked up.

"The Blue Flyer?" he asked, eyes sparkling. My head throbbed, so I shut my eyes again just as the room creaked loudly.

"You shot us up near Clairmarais. You chased us from Ghent to Gengault. You—" I stopped myself before saying *magically transformed the model of your airplane from an Albatross to a Nieuport.* "You know about the magic, more about it than we do, anyway."

I stumbled over my words. It was strange speaking to Harry now that I knew who he was. I'd never had the opportunity to treat with an enemy pilot before. I thought talking cordially would come naturally, but the resentment rooted deep down, and it was different to speak with him without Cillian's soothing influence.

He didn't confirm my accusation, but a tugging at his lips gave me the impression he enjoyed that we'd given him a nickname.

"I'd like to say it wasn't personal. I've long been astounded that so many soldiers can commit such atrocities in so professional a manner. Where is the humanity in that? Such terrible things, and yet in the dark night, they repeat to themselves that it was not personal. They were fulfilling an oath. They were doing a job. They try to become inhuman."

His tone bordered on tickled curiosity, as though he were removed from such moral strain.

"Is that some kind of apology?" I asked with a disbelieving laugh.

He stood and took several slow steps toward me.

"You misunderstand. I'm trying to tell you it's all personal."

Up close, I noticed his eyes were wrong, off somehow. They still sparkled like a child's. I saw a remnant of this spark in the eyes of replacement soldiers still drunk on the propaganda of the

United States Press Office, but Harry's eyes went beyond even that. They practically hummed with a shine of their own, irises deep and bright despite the dark room. Why hadn't I noticed as much when I'd met with him and Cillian before?

"So what now?" I asked.

"Now, you help us pilot this vessel back to shore."

I scoffed.

"I don't know the first thing about operating a submarine," I said.

"You didn't know how to fly a plane either until you did. And that's a one person affair. Surely you can follow instructions well enough."

My eyes followed a stretch of pipe out of the room. I'd only heard rumors about life in these submerged vessels. The living conditions made an airy third line trench sound downright comfortable. But as a mechanic, I had to admit I harbored a deep curiosity about how they worked.

A thought hit me.

"Where's the rest of the crew?" I asked.

"What crew?" he replied. I blinked.

"You can't tell me you plan to operate a ship this size without a crew."

"The crew just increased by one."

"But you need—I mean this isn't a small U-boat. A full crew is bound to be—"

A second harder voice interrupted me.

"A captain, a pair of watch officers, a half dozen mechanics, another half dozen weapons operators, a few men to manage personnel, another handful for radio and communications, a doctor, a meteorologist—of course one must not forget the cook."

I turned my head to see another slender figure dressed in a workman's shirt and trousers and had to check twice.

At first, I thought it was Harry standing there all over again.

This man could easily have been his brother, maybe even a twin. But the initial impression wore off and I noticed the differences.

His hair was wild and waved, but his jaw was firm, his mouth a carving against a face like iron.

He made me afraid without so much as moving.

"But, if you break it all down," he went on, "it's easy to find redundancies and luxuries. We are the commanders and the officers. We have no need of weapons, nor doctors, nor cooks. Our provisions are simple, and our voyage but brief. All we need to do is fill the responsibilities of the machinists and engineers. Things going wrong is not a luxury we can afford. You may leave the helm duty and navigation duty to me."

He came to rest a pace or two from where I stooped in my hammock. His gaze swept over me slow and unafraid, committing my features to memory, until finally it rested on the marble around my neck.

My hand reached for it defensively. One of them had stolen Jane's marble. One of them, I realized. Jane identified Harry. But she could have been mistaken. This second man seemed more the type.

He produced a stool from a compartment by the door and sat down.

"Do you know what you have around your neck?" he asked.

"This? It's a good luck charm."

"We're on the same side now," he said coldly. "Tell me the truth." His cheekbones sat high on his face, and like his companion, his nose gave him an almost hawkish appearance, implacable and unyielding.

"You know full well what it is," I said, closing my eyes. "You know better than I do, don't you?"

Without turning his neck, he looked toward Harry with a smug curl of his lip.

"Are you willing to donate the marble to the cause?" asked

Harry. I scoffed, but they stared at me plainly. I promised Jane I wouldn't take this marble off. There was no way in hell I'd be forfeiting it without a fight.

I shook my head.

"Are you Dieter?" I asked.

The one in the work shirt stood.

"There is no need to mince words," he said. "We aren't friends. We're allies trying to get something done. In the present conditions, aboard this vessel, our only hope of survival is to cooperate so we may get back to land."

"And if a cruiser finds us?" I asked.

"Then we three die." Without another word, he turned and walked toward the front of the ship. When he was out of earshot, I turned to Harry.

"Well, he's good for company, isn't he?" I asked. Harry shrugged.

"He's seen a lot."

"So have I. But gee whiz, he's like a cold wind blowing through."

Harry suppressed a grin.

"Can I know where we're going?" I asked.

"Not yet. But our path is dangerous. We are not in remote waters. Bringing our vessel to the surface will almost always carry significant risk. Cruisers are on the lookout. Plus, we are beyond periscope depth because we hope to avoid any collisions with the vast landscape of mines laid in these waters."

I swallowed and put my hands to my head to massage my temples.

What had I gotten myself into? This must have been a dream. The pain in my head got worse as I realized that in an effort to prove my usefulness, I'd gone rogue, leaving behind not only the safety of the Allies, but abandoning Jane without so much as word.

No. Abandoned was the wrong word. This was part of the mission.

She would have tried to talk me out of it. She wouldn't have believed I had it in me. To her credit, this was insane. But their way wasn't working. It had failed us several times. It failed Luf.

Harry put his hands on my shoulders gently.

"It's all right. You're probably in shock right now. Take some time."

He crossed the room to rummage around in a satchel sitting in the corner. It was the first time I'd noticed the many sacks strewn on the floor in the neighboring compartments. I guessed they'd be the provisions Dieter mentioned. It must be possible to operate the submarine with three of us if they got it here with only two of them.

Two Blue Flyers...

We had originally expected an entire company of them, with the workload of managing a squadron of planes. Then, after Clairmarais, Ghent, and watching his aircraft shift models as it had, I'd assumed they were one.

Now, there were at least two.

Harry came back with a bottle filled with a clear liquid.

"Drink this," he said as he lifted it to my lips.

"What is it?"

"Water. It will help that pounding in your head. Drink."

I let him help me. The water was cool and clean, and once I started, I only wanted more. I hadn't drunk anything since before we headed out to the Stag's Head into Dublin. How long had it been?

I leaned forward and tried to climb out of the hammock. The water alleviated the pain in my head quickly, almost too quickly. He put out a hand and pushed me gently back down.

"Wait until it's done working its magic," he said.

Magic. It was a casual turn of phrase, easy enough to overlook, but it stuck in my ears coming from him. With our recent missions and the strict military rigor to the capture of the artifacts we hunted, magic had become just another force on the battlefield, as novel as any other innovative horror thought up by the enemy. I'd seen those technologies develop throughout the war. Long range artillery. Gas. Tanks. Airplanes.

But the results accomplished by the Blue Flyers, their ghost-like presence, and the uncanny events connected to my experiences with them so far all persuaded me that they understood a power we did not. And they understood it in a way even Jane resented jealously.

"Tell me one thing," I said, "or I can't agree to help run this ship."

He folded his hands patiently, unperturbed by my indolence.

"What do you insist on knowing?"

"Why Ireland?" I asked. "Why help them? Where are you from? Why are you chasing down artifacts and shooting down planes and blowing up ammo depots and all that for them?"

"That's more than one thing." He sat down on the stool left by his companion and crossed his legs. "It may surprise you to learn that Ireland is not the final outcome we pursue."

"You mean helping the Brotherhood is just part of something greater?"

He nodded carefully.

"In truth, I don't know how Ireland's situation will resolve. Our participation in their cause does not represent the entirety of our operations."

"How do you mean that?" My gut twisted uncomfortably. At first, I'd considered Harry's magnetism grounded in the same ideals Cillian espoused. They resonated with my own.

"We consider ourselves neutral parties," he replied, "at least to the armed conflict."

I scoffed.

"Most neutral parties don't go shooting down planes and supplying magical weapons to political militants."

"On the contrary, neutral does not mean non-participatory. It means only that we aim to treat sides equally—or at least with indifference to the allegiances they demand all take."

"So you call yourself neutral because you're attacking both sides? That sounds opportunistic. Are you trying to take advantage of those ground down by the war effort?"

He clicked his tongue.

"You know, people are so quick to recognize their own weaknesses in others. You assume that because you're ambitious, we too are ambitious."

"I'm not ambitious."

He let out a singular, musical laugh.

"You most definitely are, but we'll leave that for now. I was speaking about your people. We are not attempting to grab power."

"Then what?"

"Isn't it enough to be tired of the war? The slow grinding attrition? What started with economic blockades turned into deadlock in the trenches, and all sides are committed to bleeding the other slowly dry. What if there were ways to cut it all short before that happens?"

I puzzled over his comments. His implications scared me.

"You're trying to end the war?" I asked. "I didn't sign up to assassinate anyone, if that's your plan."

He laughed again.

"Assassinations don't end wars," he replied. "At best they weaken a side, at worst enrage it."

"Then, what?" I asked.

"Exactly. Then what." He stood up, smoothed his pants, and tilted his hat. "And why, too? They both matter. The how? Not as much."

This did nothing to help my hurting head. I reached to take another drink of water.

"What have I joined here?" I asked.

"A fellowship," he replied, putting a hand on my shoulder, "if you want it. You've joined others who think and reason as you do. We don't see value in wasting human life. We don't understand how some men deserve to control the destiny of so many others for the sake of gaining a hundred yards of ruined earth. We have lost faith in the command of both sides of the war and thus in war altogether."

I knit my eyebrows.

"Then why equip a violent Irish movement? England won't budge. It will have to end in violence."

"Working with Ireland was a gamble," he said. He looked at me with a funny sort of satisfied expression. "But I think it will pay off."

He tapped my ankle gently and walked out the door after Dieter.

Chapter 11
American Pilot
Jane

She carries magic in her streams,
She lifts our thoughts to higher themes,
She helps us realize our dreams;
The great resourceful smiling west.
-Emma Cowan Barber-

I stared at the plane in front of me. It was a Bristol F2B, of British design. I'd been working with Lufbery's unit for so long before our tangle with espionage that I'd nearly forgotten British engineering existed. The Americans flew French.

The F2B was the pride and joy of the Royal Air Force right alongside the Sopwith Camel. I could understand why. The Rolls-Royce Falcon engine added significant power and speed to an aerial battlefield that, at the time, was doing its best to recover from the proliferation of German Albatross pursuit planes.

I had been invited to help patch this one up, but it took all of two seconds to realize that was a task meant to keep me occupied and out of trouble. There was nothing at all wrong with the plane in front of me. I'd run some cursory inspections, examined the bolts and ailerons, opened up the engine to inspect the inline cylinders... The weapons were tight and oiled, both the Vickers on the front and the ring-mounted Lewis gun for the observer in the second seat.

My fixation on these mechanical details did little to distract me. Instead, I folded my arms across my chest, leaned back in my chair, and fumed.

We were at Baldonnel Aerodrome, just west of Dublin. Other than the flights British pilots flew over the countryside, Irish Sea, and English Channel to scout for submarines, it was one of the sleepiest aerodromes I'd ever seen. We'd hurried off to Baldonnel as soon as we realized that Marcus was no longer in Howth, and either abducted by sea plane, ship, or U-boat.

By the time we arrived, it was early morning, and Smith coaxed me into attempting sleep, insisting that they would work with the reconnaissance pilots at first light to sweep the seas for any sign of my friend. I spent the following hours acquainting myself with the ceiling of a private room in the officers' quarters. When I found Smith and Atkins in the morning, the latter did his best to cover up having no good news by suggesting I lend my efforts to assist the mechanics.

And the very notion that Atkins might keep my delicate sensibilities occupied while Marcus was missing in action was about the greatest insult he could have dealt me.

His suggestion had been no more or less than a *run and play while Mummy and Daddy are talking, won't you?*

So when I saw Atkins across the landing strip moving between the mess and the squadron headquarters with a cup of tea in his hand, I tossed my wrench into the toolbox and marched with all the furious speed of a German stormtrooper.

I bound through the door after him and slammed it behind me.

"Well?" I asked.

"Ah, Private Doe," Atkins said as he dipped some shortbread into his tea. "How were the planes? Fit for duty?"

"I won't be put away," I said. I planted my feet firmly and put my fists on my hips. "Marcus is out there somewhere, and I need to find him. He's my—well, he's—"

"He's Marcus Dewar," Smith finished to spare me any further awkwardness. "You two form a special unit. Peanuts and Cracker Jack."

I shook my head and pushed any thoughts about the categorization of my relationship with Marcus to the side. It hardly seemed important at present. Whatever it was, it was superseded by the fact that he was gone, and I needed him back. We needed him back. Not only had we lost a pilot and protector, his marble went with him.

And if it was the Blue Flyer that took him, that meant he had both marbles now.

"Has there been any news?" I asked as I massaged my temple with one hand.

"Nothing, I'm afraid," said Atkins.

"No news, but we made progress," Smith added.

"Namely?"

"We've been hard at work defining spheres of travel." He beckoned me over to a map on the table. "Look here. If Marcus got picked up by a ship, assuming they didn't burn out their engines trying to get away, by noon today they will be no farther than this line here."

He traced a line that extended near the southern tip of England and rounded in a large circle toward the very top of the Irish Sea. I choked.

"Is that supposed to make me feel better, sergeant?" I asked.

"Well, on a map, sure, it doesn't look great," he conceded. "But the thing is, it's much more likely they've had to take an indirect route to avoid detection, making the circle much smaller."

"But if he was taken by sea plane, we estimate around six hundred miles in any direction before they would need to land and refuel," said Atkins. He put down his teacup and rubbed any remaining crumbs off of his hands.

I took a deep breath.

"But even at the length of six hundred miles, they would still be in Allied territory," I surmised. "Unless, Sinn Fein or the Brotherhood have a hidden refueling station in the south of Ireland."

I closed my eyes and thought back to my first sortie with the Blue Flyer. We chased him out of Clairmarais on the northern coast of France near Dunkirk. He was headed northeast. If he had a home base, I had to assume it would be in that direction, or else why fly towards it after successfully stealing Baron von Richthofen's enchanted scarf?

But that meant a long voyage home, and Atkins was right. Short of some relic we didn't know about that might squeeze more mileage from their tank, landing for fuel to get all the way back there would be risky.

"Do you think they're traveling by sea?" I asked.

Smith leaned against his elbow on the table, belying a casual, perhaps fatigued, demeanor.

"Oh, Jane. I don't know," he said. "My brain says that they'd be flying, despite the risks of landing and refueling. All the man needs is a couple of well-positioned people on his side to get some fuel in the tank, and then he's got another full six hundreds miles to get wherever he needs to go. It's a risky landing, but it's just the one time. If he were at sea, it would take a lot longer to get anywhere."

"But—" I probed.

"But I think they're going by sea."

Atkins groaned.

"Preposterous," he said with a roll of the eyes. "How do you expect the rogue flyer to travel by sea? It requires a completely different set of skills than flying an airplane, to start. But what's more important, anything larger than a rowboat would require a crew. You and Marcus insisted it was one man after you saw his plane change forms in your sortie."

I bit my lip.

"You believed our report?" I asked. It was the first time he'd mentioned it with any deference.

"Believed it?" Atkins asked, gaping. "We've changed our entire working strategy based on it."

"Just because he can transform his plane doesn't mean he's operating alone," Smith argued, poking down on the desk with an adamant index finger. "You believe one man is responsible for all the damage we've chalked up to the Blue Flyer? The bombings. The downed planes. The misinformation campaigns. When's he supposed to sleep?"

"Even if he's not working alone, it would require more than a hastily trained comrade or two to operate a naval vessel," Atkins countered. His voice raised, and his face took on a pink tinge. "We've had no similar reports of naval attacks from rogue ships the way we have the rogue flyer."

"Forget the reports! We're in unprecedented territory—"

"Enough!" I shouted. Every impulse suggested I kick over a chair or rip the map off the desk or something else drastic, but I resisted. "Would you stop your bickering? You're like two school-children. And while you argue in circles, they get farther away."

They both quieted. Atkins sat back down, thoroughly put out, but Smith stared at the desk and snickered to himself.

"What's so funny?" I asked without warmth.

"Look at you," he said. His warm expression held no guile. "Dressing us down as if you were our commanding officer."

I ignored his comment and went on. If they wanted to act like subordinates, then I might as well give orders.

"If they've gone by plane, then there's nothing we can do. So,

I'm forced to hold out hope that they are traveling by sea. It's time you allow me to go on the reconnaissance sweeps looking for him."

Atkin raised his eyebrows, an unguarded reaction to the naivety of my suggestion.

"Oh, what is it, Atkins?" I asked, throwing my hands to my sides.

"What experience do you have in distinguishing a dreadnought from a light cruiser, let alone its country of origin from several thousand feet?"

"I'm not worried about that at all," I said, leaning back on the desk.

"And why's that?" Atkins asked.

In response, I held up Boelcke's goggles.

"You think you can rely on those?" asked Smith. "Didn't the Flyer demonstrate that he can manipulate how they perceive magic?"

"That might be true, but there may be a form of magic he doesn't have control over," I said. They both stared at me, puzzled. I took a steadying breath. "We didn't disclose everything in our report after Ghent."

Atkins looked up at the ceiling as if heaven itself could not spare him the grief I caused.

"I'm not going to like this am I?" Smith asked.

"A long time ago, after I met Marcus and he became a pilot, I wrote someone back home, someone who taught me all I know about magic, and begged her to craft a pair of protection marbles. She advised against it, in part because such magic is unreliable. But she sent them to me all the same. It's a simple reciprocation charm. So long as one marble stays intact, it will protect the person wearing the other. Marcus wore his, at first, at my insistence, but since he learned magic is as real as the science that allows flight, he's worn it with near religious fervor."

Atkins frowned with his whole body and fidgeted with the hem of his jacket.

"So all this time we were asking you track down magical artifacts, we've had two homemade ones you kept secret?" Smith asked. I wrung my hands as I went on.

"When we went to Clairmarais, and we survived the dogfight with the Blue Flyer, it was because of the marble."

Smith shrugged.

"So it was more reliable than you thought."

"No. Not like that. The Flyer had us dead in his crosshairs, ready to shoot us to the ground. But in a moment of desperation, I held my marble above my head. He was close enough that I saw his face. He was shocked, bewildered even. It gave us the moment we needed for Marcus to twist us away and LeBoutillier came to our rescue."

Smith sucked at the space between two molars as he took it in.

"Hell, Jane. If I'm being honest, I'd have been bewildered, too."

"It goes deeper," I continued. "In Ghent, the Flyer and I had an altercation in the tombs under St. Bavo's Cathedral. He told me that Ball's violin strings were of only nominal interest to him, but he demanded that I give him my marble. He said it *sang* differently than the other artifacts."

"You didn't give it over, did you?" Atkins asked. He sat at stony alert, his theatrical annoyance from before all but vanished.

"I tried to escape, and we grappled. I managed to pull his face into a stone column and make my getaway, but he must have grabbed it from me in the melee."

We heard the sound of a plane landing outside as they both quietly took in my story.

"But he still came after you," Smith said. "Was that just to get the other marble?"

I nodded.

"It's the only reason I can work out. He took great risk flying across Belgium and over the lines to pursue us, a risk that meant the loss of his aircraft and his discovery."

"What does he want with them? Is he just interested in the protection charm?" Smith scratched his jaw. He spoke aloud, but I suspected it was to help him think.

"Perhaps," I said.

"Interesting." He leaned forward pointedly in Atkins's direction. "That almost seems like more evidence that he's not working alone."

Atkins ignored him.

"Are you suggesting that your marble is visible in Boelcke's goggles?" Atkins asked.

"It wasn't before," I said. "But I think something has changed. The glow in the goggles is what led me to finding that empty row boat last night. Perhaps it will work again. It's better than me doing nothing here."

Smith stood up.

"She's right," he said. "But we can't have you paired up with some other pilot and risk widening our circle. If the press gets wind of you, just imagine. We'd never get a moment's peace again, and all chance of confidentiality would be shot to hell."

I furrowed my brows and stuck my hands in my pockets.

"I'm not sure what you mean, sir. Do you intend for me to pilot the plane myself?"

Smith looked like he just bit into a rancid tin of beef.

"Oh, absolutely not. Are you kidding? That'd be way too dangerous. I'm not about to risk you on flight school. Besides, we don't have the time. I'll take you up myself."

My mouth fell open.

"You're a pilot?" I asked.

He pulled a bit of chocolate out of his pocket and picked at the wrapper. I looked to Atkins. Had he known about this?

"These days, just about everybody seems to be a pilot. All they need is a good five hours in a cockpit. Isn't that right, Atkins?"

Atkins reddened and pursed his lips.

"Anyway, something like this, I think I can handle." He bit off a corner of his chocolate bar. "I hope you got that F2B in prime condition."

"It's... it will do fine." I still struggled to get over my surprise.

"Good. Atkins, make yourself useful in the meantime, won't you?"

Atkins cleared his throat.

"Indeed. I will see about questioning the Sinn Fein leaders we arrested a couple of weeks ago. If Joseph Dowling worked with the rogue flyer to bring this artifact to Ireland, someone is bound to know something."

Smith whistled.

"That's some good thinking, there, lieutenant. Come on, Jane. Wings up."

Smith strode confidently out the door. I again looked to Atkins, as if to ask whether it was wise to get into a plane with the American. Atkins nodded discreetly before picking up the telephone on the desk and getting to work.

Chapter 12
Underwater Navigation
Marcus

I was beginning to think there was something more than just water in that cup Harry gave me.

My migraine subsided unnaturally fast, and I jumped up, ready to move around before I'd even had a full chance to make heads or tails of his philosophizing about neutrality.

Harry's smile signaled only a hint of surprise when I hopped out of the hammock, and we got straight to work. In the hours that followed, he taught me all I would need to know about fulfilling my motley role on our tiny submarine crew.

My job boiled down to a few key responsibilities. One, I needed to monitor the ship's battery capacity. While on the surface, the U-boat used a gasoline-powered engine to move around. But trying to use gasoline powered combustion underwater proved impossible. Gas-powered engines need air, a precious commodity below the surface. The escaping fumes would kill all of us. But even if some engineers had managed to get oxygen through to fuel the combustion process, the engines were so loud and put out enough wasteful gas that any other boat with a pair of headphones would hear us or see the bubbles streaming up to the surface, defeating the whole point of a submarine.

That meant while we were submerged, we relied on a battery that the gas engine charged when we weren't submerged.

I learned quickly that Harry and Dieter valued secrecy above all else, so although we moved at a much more sluggish pace underwater than we would above, we spent as much time submerged as possible, popping up only at night to charge our battery.

Apart from battery work, it was my job to read a whole range of dials when prompted, and to adjust other wheels and levers as needed to help us surface or dive. This sounded much more simple than it was in practice, at least to start. There were hundreds of tangled pipes, dials, wheels, and switches crammed into every operable part of the vessel. Even with my mechanic's background, it took me a few days to get the swing of things. Dieter ran a tight ship, and when I had to ask for a reminder about the location of a specific dial, he made a show of stomping over to my spot and pointing it out as if I were a complete idiot.

In some ways, it reminded me of my early days working on planes with Luf. He wasn't quite as sharp as Dieter in pointing out my mistakes, but he was just as thorough.

Harry was kind, though, and with his help, I managed just fine.

But even with the learning curve and crew duties, I was surprised by how much downtime we had.

Dieter wasn't much for conversation, and during stretches of inactivity, he disappeared into a small, makeshift officer's quarters near one end of the submarine. I figured him to be the leader of their partnership, though they seemed to address each other with a lot of frankness and intimacy, the way I'd expect from family. I'd asked if they were brothers, once. Harry laughed and responded, "who knows?"

That was Harry, wildly different from Dieter. He was easy to talk to, eager to listen, and devilishly curious. He was quick to laugh, and happy to embrace any ideals he considered just and true. Many of his duties onboard coincided with mine, so even when we were working, we had ample time to chat.

"Can I know where we're going, now?" I asked as I double-checked the tubing on our bilge pump.

Harry shook his head.

"It doesn't matter how many times you ask, I cannot tell you," he said, arms folded. "Not yet."

"So you will tell me later?"

He smiled and adjusted the rudder gear before ducking his head and leaving the ship's central station. I followed, hand over hand, to make sure I didn't bump my knees on any metal fixtures, a lesson I had learned painfully over the past couple of days.

"I just don't get what harm it would do," I said. "Our telegraph apparatus doesn't work, and it's not like I've got anyone else to spill the secret to."

"It's important that you continue to cooperate."

"I see. If you told me where we're going, you're afraid I might not cooperate anymore. That it?"

"You're cooperating well. Why would I risk changing it by giving you new information?" he said with a shrug.

"What if you telling me that I'd be upset if I knew our destination *is* the new information that makes me discontinue my cooperation?"

He turned to me with a delighted smile, sly and triumphant. He loved witty paradoxes even more than Jane did. And she considered them magical. I wondered where she was. The last time we'd been separated like this, without knowledge of the other's whereabouts, was Ghent.

"Do you miss your friend?" he asked as he inspected his teeth in his cracked pocket mirror. "The one you used to fly with?"

How had he known that I was thinking about Jane? I set my jaw and tried not to show any emotion. Truthfully, I had made it a point, as much as possible, not to think about her. It was too painful and too messy.

Yes, I missed her. But in our brief time apart, I recognized that I had been missing her since before I'd left. What if I missed a version of Jane that wasn't there anymore?

It wasn't hard to blame myself for that. Sure, I hadn't been the one insisting we accept Smith's assignment from the get go, but secretly, I wanted the adventure. And for a long time before then, I'd droned on and on about the honor of flying, how great it'd be to get my first victory, how much I admired all those other pilots who shot down so many German planes.

When I broke, she propped me up. I had leaned on her without any regard for how much she could support. She took it upon herself to dive into the darkness so I wouldn't have to.

I didn't ask her to do that for me. But I let her.

Even in the confines of that hot, suffocating U-boat, that was what woke me up at night in a sweat.

"You're too easy to derail," Harry said with a chuckle, stuffing the mirror in his pocket. I glowered at him. "You should eat something."

"I'm not hungry."

"Are you certain?" he asked, nodding to the sacks of food tins and rations stashed on the floor. They must have planned for a long voyage because they didn't eat much, and when they did, it looked like torture unless it was chocolate bars or anything they could dip into a can of molasses.

Who knew how long they'd been living off these rations?

A steady rhythm of metallic footsteps caught my ears, and I turned to see Dieter blocking the passage to the conning tower.

"We're going up." He stared at me. I'd learned that these bald-faced statements were actually commands. In this case, he wanted me to bring the ship up by the rudder gear in the central station room. We had a dive control in the conning tower, but I suspected he wanted his space.

"Is it night already?" I asked.

"No. But we need to charge the battery cells again," he said. "We'll be using them all night."

"Why?"

Harry took in a deep breath.

"Mines?" he asked Dieter.

"Yes."

"Must we go through them?"

"Going around will take too long and too much gasoline, even with our modifications. We will rise and charge the batteries. And it will give me a chance to survey the sea."

Dieter turned and climbed back up into the tower. I furrowed my brows and looked at Harry.

"Survey the sea? What is he talking about? What does he hope to find in the sea?"

Harry put his index finger to one of the steel bolts in the wall.

"A way through."

I balked.

"You mean he hopes to travel through the mine field?"

"He has done it before, to get to Dublin. It is very taxing."

"Take us up!" Dieter's voice called down from the tower, impatient and heated.

I tripped over a raised barrier between compartments as I scurried to obey. Harry followed me.

"We're in a U-Boat. How the hell does he plan on navigating

anything when we're submerged? The whole point of mines is that you can't see them even when you're above the water. How are you supposed to get through when you're navigating with nothing more than a pen and paper?"

My heart started racing. But the answer came to me as I asked the question. I was traveling with two men who were obsessed with magical artifacts.

They knew how to transfigure a German Albatross pursuit plane into a French Nieuport fighter. They must have had something in this U-Boat that made the impossible possible. My mouth fell open. That was powerful magic, all right. And I wanted to hear them confirm it.

I clambered over to the rudder controls, unlocked the wheel, and spun it to take us up.

"What do you mean that it was taxing?" I asked amidst my effort.

Harry cocked his head as the lifting sensation started on us.

"Do you imagine navigating a minefield would not be taxing?" he asked.

"What do you fellas have onboard that lets you navigate a minefield?" I asked.

"I'm not sure what you mean."

"I think you do," I said, staring him down. "Come on. We have fought over these artifacts. I know you're not risking your life for collectors items. I've seen one of you change the make and model of your airplane mid-flight. What do you have onboard that lets you navigate a minefield?"

Harry's inciting smile slipped across his face again.

"We have Dieter."

He leaned against the panel beside the compass and made no sign of leaving. This emboldened me, and I took advantage of all the camaraderie we'd developed in our short but intense time together.

"What are you going to do with all these devices?" I asked. "One of you nearly shot us out of the sky for the Baron's scarf. It's got to be important."

He began to speak but stopped himself. Then, after reconsidering his thought, he tried again.

"What do you know about the items you are chasing?" he asked carefully. My heart skipped, and I tread carefully so as not to scare him off the trail.

"I know they once belonged to good pilots, maybe the best," I said. "And I know that when you're using them, some unexplainable things happen."

He cringed when I used the word *unexplainable* before ducking his head through the doorway and up toward the tower to check if Dieter was nearby. When satisfied that we were alone, he turned back to me.

"You only say unexplainable because you don't know how to explain it," he said. His explanation reminded me of Jane and teased an unconscious smile out of me.

"Well?" I asked. "Care to enlighten me?"

He took off his hat and put a hand through his hair.

"Some phenomena defy reason, or at least, reason as we know it. And such phenomena, under the proper circumstances, can be," he searched for the right word, "reduced into a physical manifestation ."

I scrunched my eyebrows.

"How?"

"Myriad methods, some more effective than others," he said with a vacant stare. He paused, distracted by some memory I didn't dare explore, at least not while he was so talkative. I urged him on with an insight I'd suspected since Luf.

"Death is one of them," I said. Harry nodded.

"Death is one of them," he confirmed.

"But death is everywhere. Millions have died. Why aren't there millions of magical devices?"

"How do you know there aren't?" he replied. I stuttered, wanting to say Smith, Atkins, or Dupont had us test several relics from soldiers alive and dead and we never found anything magical in them. But already I knew that our efforts to decode arcane powers were clumsy at best. The first time I'd looked through Boelcke's goggles and believed, really believed, the concept of our smallness smothered me.

"It's a question of degrees," Harry went on. "Degrees of power and fields of harmony. For example, if you turn on a radio, you don't instantly hear every frequency."

My eyes lit up.

"Is radio one of those phenomena you were talking about?"

He leaned his head back on the wall and stared reproachfully up at the ceiling.

"Oh, please, don't get me started on radio." He stretched a leg gingerly, touched the metal of the ship again, and closed his eyes as though he were downing a shot of whiskey. "Come along. I've said too much already."

I stopped our ascent at periscope depth before getting the all-clear from Dieter that no ships waited on the surface. That hardly surprised me. If we were on the edge of a minefield, I expected most warships would either be keeping their distance or at the bottom of the sea already.

When we surfaced, Harry and I switched over the engines and got our gas combustion going to charge the ship's battery. When I finally made it up through the top hatch, I was sweating and ready to gulp up every breath of fresh air on the sea. The water lapped against the side of our U-boat in moody swells, spraying white foam over the top. I welcomed it without a care that the salt would grime and stick later. With the electric battery and no ventilation, the air in the submarine was stifling.

The smell of the ocean took me back to my childhood. Suddenly, I was a kid again, building sand castles and scooping up sand crabs as the waves retreated from the beach.

I smiled to myself. Traveling under the water was so different from traveling in the sky. I stared up at the clouds and missed my plane and my gunner. The clouds didn't look friendly, though, reaching high into the sky with tall rain-making cumulus towers. Sometimes, on my way back from patrols, I'd get mixed up in a cloud and end up soaked. Luf always scolded me for that. He thought I wasn't paying attention or being careful.

But then, he was the one who took some other guy's plane and had to be a hero.

I glanced over and found Dieter leaning over the edge of the boat, a hand in the water, and staring across the surface to the southeast. The horizon misted out into an opaque fog, but I imagined that on a particularly clear day, we might have been able to see coastline in at least one direction. As I understood it, U-boats didn't travel very fast underwater, and with our skeleton crew, we did not push the limits of our machine.

If we'd headed south from Ireland, and gauging by how warm it was despite the clouds I was pretty sure we hadn't gone north, we should see the English coast to our port side or, if my perception of time and space had been distorted, the French coast to our starboard.

Beyond us lay the waiting and deadly expanse of an invisible maze of mines. The locations of such minefields were kept secret by the military power laying them, but for how large the seas were, it turned out to be pretty hard to do anything in total secrecy, and ship captains were always on the lookout for other ships that might be in the business of setting them.

"Mines," Harry said behind me with the shake of his head. "Huge metal balls of explosives, capable of utter devastation. Do you know the trigger mechanism for a mine?"

I shook my head.

"They are anchored to the bottom of the sea floor with measured chains so that they float at a pre-determined depth. Protruding from these iron spheres are rows and rows of glass tubes, delicate enough that improper handling of them by their setting crews might accidentally cause detonation." He stared at the stretch of water ahead of us and clicked his tongue. "It's just another technological monument to the bloodlust of human beings."

His voice dipped at the end of his speech into tones of disgust. I was surprised to find myself defensive over his comments.

"How else do you suggest they stop U-boats from sinking merchant ships?" I asked bitterly.

Harry turned on me with a stare so filled with intent it made my skin crawl.

"Ask them nicely," he said.

I snorted sheepishly.

"And if they refuse?"

He turned back to the sea, relieving me of his burning gaze.

"Then kill the commanders."

Dieter stood and walked across the deck to where we stood.

"What do you think?" Harry asked him. "Is it navigable?"

"We cross when the battery is ready," he replied, but I noticed bags under his eyes that weren't there before, and not only that. He'd unbuttoned his shirt to cool off. Resting around his neck was Jane's marble. The sight of it rattled with me with anger. I struggled to keep it under control.

"What are you looking at," Dieter snapped at me.

I turned away quickly.

"Nothing," I said. "You look a little tired is all. Why not let Harry drive for a bit?"

"*Shrink from no great work today,*" he recited with a poetic cadence. "I'm fine. We cross when the battery is ready," he said coldly.

"You might be fine, but we are not," called Harry.

Dieter and I turned to follow Harry's outstretched fingers. Far on the horizon was a warship, and by the looks of it, it was heading straight toward us.

"Get ready to dive," said Dieter. "The battery will have to do as it is."

Chapter 13
The Prisoner
Jane

I can see that field of clover
In the twilight softly falling.
Where the fireflies gleaming over—
Lanterns for the fairies' feet—
When the whip-poor-wills are calling
Through the darkness cool and sweet.
-Emma Cowan Barber-

We touched down at Shawbury Field, near Wrexham, and for the first time, I couldn't keep my hope from flagging.

We'd spent the past few days combing the sea for any sign of Marcus and the Blue Flyer. Hundreds of times, I'd expelled from my mind the disheartening cliche about needles and haystacks.

While the goggles occasionally identified whisper trails of bluish light, they ebbed and faded, and I learned to identify the pattern in what I was beginning to regard as trace magic.

None of it looked like the signal that marked the empty rowboat. We must have missed him by minutes.

Since our narrow escape from Ghent, a sneaking feeling of invincibility had lodged itself in my subconscious. Against all odds, we'd found one another there, despite him driving off in a car with a German soldier. I supposed nothing could separate us in earnest for any real stretch of time.

And yet, after our divergent perspectives in Dublin, our drifting priorities, he was snatched away. Perhaps I'd driven him away. And despite all my strength and willpower, there was nothing I could do to bring him back.

If we hadn't found him by now...

"Any luck?" asked Dupont. He'd traveled straight here from Dublin after we deemed it a more suitable location for our searches. We'd done so not for its proximity to the sea, as I'd have preferred, but for its proximity to a prison full of Irish political leaders—a sign that we'd given up hope of finding Marcus by combing the water and would instead commit our efforts to digging up new intelligence.

Still, I'd been warmed and surprised to find genuine concern and pain in Dupont's attitude. He even went as far as assisting with the more mundane preparations and maintenance on our aircraft. It helped maintain the secrecy about me, a woman, flying up in the gunner's bay. I couldn't care less about that precious confidentiality, but Atkins still insisted I changed in and out of my flight gear in private, paying special attention to wrap my hair away from sight under my helmet.

"Nothing, Dupont," Smith said as he climbed out of our Bristol. The news hit the Frenchman with a pang of disappointment.

I pulled my goggles down.

"Aw, well. There's still hope," he said with a forced smile. "And at least you get a proper machine to search in."

I scowled as I fought off creeping hesitations that a machine like this was being wasted on our fruitless pursuit. Dupont reached a hand up to help me out of the plane, but I needed another minute to collect myself.

"Doe," Smith turned back to the plane when he noticed I had not yet disembarked. "Get out of there. We've got reports to make."

He was making appearances. There was no report. The report was "No Marcus Found. Enemy in possession of both marbles. No leads."

Dupont approached the side of the fuselage.

"Jane," he spoke quietly, "doubt kills all magic."

I jerked my head up to take him in. He didn't force a smile now. Genuine concern etched his features. This version of Dupont surprised me. I'd grown used to his disinterested attitude and playful, detached teasing.

"I lost him," I said. "What's worse, I think I—it's stupid, but I feel as though I chased him away."

Dupont clicked his tongue and reached inside the cockpit to take my hand.

"And what about you could chase him away? There's nothing. I've been at war now a long time. You and Marcus scare me—not in a bad way. You scare me into feeling again."

His words were soft. But though he intended comfort, they stoked the growing darkness that had been gaining ground for weeks. It stirred even now, a latent desire to get back out into the fight, that I could achieve progress only by more action. It was a nonsensical belief that if only I shot down more planes, we could find him. If I could win the war, I could keep him safe.

I was a killer, deep down. I'd been to the edge of my soul and peered over. Marcus and I were different, fundamentally.

"Private Doe, let's get a move on," called Smith again.

I twisted back toward the inside of the gunner's bay and tried to hide the tears welling in my eyes.

"He is still alive, and we will find him," said Dupont.

"How do you know?" I asked.

"I see it in you. There is a magnet that pulls the two of you together. Love is a strong magic, no?" he asked.

Love. The word conjured up scenes from a life I wouldn't recognize now even if it splayed out all around me. Mothers loved. Fathers loved. Husbands and wives loved. Young lovers. Children. Even family pets.

Love was the first casualty of war. And now that the war was in me, love slipped through my fingers like clouds.

"Doe!"

"Thank you," I whispered while wiping my eyes. I squeezed Dupont's hand and hoisted myself out of the plane before hurrying across the tarmac to catch up to Smith.

"All right?" Smith asked bluntly.

"Fine," I replied. We headed toward a small building near squadron headquarters that Atkins had requisitioned for our private efforts.

"Good, because despite our bad luck, I've got good news," he said. "Turns out Atkins tracked down one of those Sinn Fein prisoners for us to talk to."

"It's about time," I grumbled, reaching up to take off my helmet. Smith put an inconspicuous hand on my forearm. It could not come off yet, not until I was out of sight. "It's been days."

"Well, no offense, but you English folk don't always put a hurry into things, do you?"

"That hardly seems fair. If I recall, it was me demanding that we get up in the air to look for Marcus. You were still dawdling."

Smith shrugged.

"I'm in a foreign land dealing with a language barrier and Lieutenant Atkins. Talk about an impassible trench. "

I scoffed and shook my head. He was trying to keep my spirits up. I'd have none of it.

"I'm sorry," he said with a surprising degree of sincerity. "I shouldn't go after Atkins that way. It's just—" He stopped.

My interest piqued.

"Just what? You can't start a thing like that and simply trail off without finishing."

"Oh, I can," he said. "Frankly, although we've been through a lot together, I have to assume you're on the other team."

I stopped walking.

"We're on the same team, Smith."

He turned back to address me.

"If you mean the team shooting at the Germans, yes. But there are teams inside of teams, aren't there? Hell, we've got some Germans on our little team right now, and when one game ends, you never know how the players get shook up."

I resumed walking slowly.

"You and Atkins aren't getting along, then?"

"You might say we have different mission parameters, handed down by different commanding officers. And what can soldiers do but follow orders?"

"What kind of parameters?" I asked.

"Parameters others may not understand. Things you don't understand yourself," he replied as I stared at the ground. Suddenly, he put an arm around my shoulders.

"Jane, you were never meant to be a soldier," he started. "Soldiers get a lot of different kinds of training. Some of it's structured and some of it happens on the job. But some of the most important skills get absorbed from the attitude of other soldiers. You didn't get the benefit of that, and we've asked you to go right into combat, time and again now."

His voice was low and raspy, not quite a whisper, but filled with a sense of conspiratorial mischief, as though he were sharing a principle of magic with me that I'd not yet understood.

"You're going to do things in war that you'd never do on the outside. Some of it may stick with you your whole life. I've seen hospitals and asylums full of soldiers who can't escape that."

I swallowed and tried not to look at him when I asked my next question.

"And if one can't seem to conjure terror or remorse about the things they've done?"

He laughed.

"That's preferable," he looked around. "My first time killing a man changed me forever. There's a devil inside each of us that wonders how we'll react. Some of us have more of a devil than others. There are lines to cross, of course. But from all I've seen, for the sake of the soldier, what happens in the war ground has to stay in the war ground."

"And you? How much of a devil is in you?" I asked.

His eyes darkened.

"Enough to keep looking for war grounds," he said.

Even more than the echo of my machine guns, I knew Smith's words would haunt me. I'd often wondered about where he'd come from. His moniker, Smith, was exactly that—a false name to protect his true identity, the same as Atkins, or Dupont, or Private Jane Doe. But while his advice gave me comfort, after all if soldiers allowed the atrocities of war to incapacitate them they had little hope to return to a normal life, his attitude and the far-off longing in his eyes forecasted a terrible future.

The thrill of war should not have thrilled me. I used to put my passion and my faith in magic. Now? How could I?

I changed out of my flight gear and tried to smooth away the effects of flying for hours. The flush in my cheeks would not subside, and my chapping lips begged for more ointment.

When I emerged, Smith smiled as he waited for me beside the mess.

"Pretty as a pin," he said when I got near enough. I scowled.

For one, I doubted that was true. But what was more, I hardly saw how it mattered.

He ushered me to the other side of the aerodrome where Atkins awaited us in a Crossley open-top car.

"What did you find for us, Atkins?" Smith asked. "A singing bird?"

"A canary, indeed," he replied as he held the door open for me. "Shall we?"

"Where is it we are going exactly?" I asked.

"Into Wrexham," Atkins said. He closed the door and walked around to the driver's seat. "A lieutenant at Hightown Barracks has been kind enough to hold our songbird there for questioning."

We made our way through green country northwest from Shawbury Field. Although I knew the stress of war had pervaded every part of the world, the land here seemed pure, removed somehow from the violence that raged far off across the channel in France.

Our drive was mostly quiet. Marcus's absence lingered heavily between us, and what I now suspected to be a palpable distrust between Smith and Atkins dampened any other exchanges between them. What once was a playful rivalry had transformed into political maneuvering, and it had happened right under my nose.

"Who will we be speaking with?" I asked, breaking the humming sound of the motor.

"Her name is Bridget O'Clearey," he replied. I froze.

"Bridget?" That was the name of the woman who had dropped off the ammo drum in Howth. I'd shot at her. She saw me kill Cillian. "Not the Bridget from Dublin."

Atkins nodded.

"Our sources say that she is a well connected middle level

coordinator of the Sinn Fein movement. We suspect that she is also an unofficial member of the Irish Republican Brotherhood."

"Atkins, I don't want to see her again. She swore she would hurt my family if she could find them."

"Well, then it's a good thing she's locked up in Frongoch."

I slumped back on my seat.

"For how long?" I asked.

"We'll make sure she doesn't know who you are," Atkins said. "And if needs be, we will protect your family."

"I didn't think women were interned at Frongoch," I muttered.

"Usually, they're not," he said. "But we've made an exception. At first, we hoped one of the other detainees would speak up, but when they remained slack lipped, I figured we needed someone a little more volatile. I suspect that when she sees you, she will say something to hurt you. And it's that very thing that may give us the information we seek."

"Hardly seems right interning British subjects for their political convictions," Smith said. He could tell how much the identity of our prisoner bothered me. "And if you're worried about them gaining influence, is it a good idea to throw them all into the same prison where they can chit chat?"

Atkins scowled at the road.

"Oh, now you think you understand military detainment, do you?" he asked sourly.

Smith didn't bother hiding his laughter.

A twisting knot started in my stomach as soon as Atkins parked the car. I'd witnessed the questioning of a prisoner months ago near Nancy, at the beginning of our covert assignments. It was an experience I did not want to replicate.

But I steeled myself. If she knew anything that might help me find Marcus, I would take the opportunity.

The jail was old and built of weathered brick

A man in uniform saluted Atkins and ushered us through the

door before escorting us down a hallway to a dark room without windows. Two military guards stood at attention outside the door. They eyed me cautiously, but Atkins dismissed them before we stepped inside.

I hesitated. Smith turned back to me.

"You coming?" he asked. "We won't let her bite." His delivery was dry but warm, in his own way.

I nodded and stepped inside.

Bridget sat on a bench against one wall. Her clothes were shockingly dirty compared to how I'd seem them a few days prior. Her hair matted in knots, and there was a wild gleam in her eyes. If incarceration was meant to break her spirit, the plan had failed so far.

Her pupils flicked up at me and the recognition set in.

"Murderer," she whispered to herself. Then she spoke much louder. "You've brought a murdering witch with you, have you?"

"Your insults will get you nowhere," Atkins said. "Don't look at her. Look at me."

She didn't look at him. She eyed me like a wild dog. Atkins began the questioning, but I soon realized he had nothing with which to threaten this woman. The lieutenant was slow, placid, condescending in a mildly irritating fashion, and altogether bothersome. He barely managed to voice his questions through his veil of contempt for the Irish cause.

After going in circles for a half hour, I needed to end the encounter. I could suffer under that stare no longer.

"Might I just—"

Atkins hissed at me and held up a hand. I scowled and was doubly disappointed to find the prisoner grinning at the display of haphazard command.

"Look how he treats you like a dog," she said.

"Eyes up here, miss," Atkins replied.

I leaned against the wall next to Smith. His arms rested comfortably folded across his chest.

"Shame on you," he whispered to me. It was a jest, but it didn't sit well. With each of his critiques about my commanding officer, for I supposed Atkins was my commanding officer, I appreciated with greater clarity what Smith attempted to do. If he could turn my confidence in the British military, I might end up finding a home for my sympathies somewhere other than I should.

Still, it was hard resisting Smith's playful charm when Atkins was busy treating me like a child.

I paused. How must have Marcus when all of us had treated him like a child?

I stuffed my hands into my pockets, where I discovered Boelcke's goggles. I had stuffed them there after our flight. Neither Smith nor Atkins had requested that I hand them over since Marcus's capture.

"Now, Miss O'Clearey, I've had enough with games," Atkins said. "We know that Joseph Dowling washed ashore with a mind to connect the IRB with the German government."

"If that's true, why does old Dowling still have his head?" Bridget said. "That's treason, isn't it? Unless your government is concerned it's not all that black and white, after all."

"Oh, Dowling will be executed," Atkins said. "You'll have my word on that."

"I don't believe you. Word is that some lofty type made him a promise he wouldn't be killed," Bridget's eyes shone brightly, cheery as a spring day.

"Whoever told you that is mistaken," Atkins replied. "Dowling will die, as will all Irish who try to overthrow His majesty's government."

"Please," Bridget said. "No one is trying to overthrow His majesty's government. Not even the Kaiser wants that. Ireland wants nothing more than what it's rightly owed!"

"And what's that?" Atkins asked.

She smiled mischievously and put a finger to his nose.

"You'd like to keep me talking. I'm sure you'd like an excuse to take my head or keep me penned up here until I've got no head worth taking. But I've got plans."

Her eyes shifted to me again on the word *plans*, plunging me back into the fear for my family's welfare. I'd joined the service to protect them, not bring danger to their door. I panicked. My blood boiled.

"Oh, enough already!" I shouted. I could not endure any more of Atkins's political bickering. He told me this encounter was to find Marcus's whereabouts—or at least find a lead to start our search beyond the fruitless flights combing the sea.

"Private Doe," Atkins started.

"No, Atkins, enough. Marcus is getting farther from us every insult you trade with her."

Bridget laughed, causing Atkins to turn bright red.

"Maybe you do have some Irish in you, Private Doe," she said.

I strode across the room and let the back of my hand fly. The strength of my hands and forearms, honed from my mechanical service, put enough weight into the slap to wipe the smile from her face.

She spat blood and a flurry of curses.

"Too much Irish blood," she muttered. "Aren't English women more submissive than that?"

I raised my arm again.

"Ask Cillian."

My own words shocked me for their coldness. But they worked. She scowled and held her tongue.

From the corner of my eye, I noticed Atkins's face had shifted from red to white. I didn't dare turn to gauge Smith's reaction to my outburst. Doubtless, he'd be proud. That made me queasy.

"Joseph Dowling brought the ammo drum to Ireland. You and a man named Harry brought it to Dublin," I said.

Bridget screwed up her face in a rehearsed expression of disbelief.

"A magical device?" she repeated. "You must be crazy."

"Bridget, you've threatened my family. You've threatened me. I have seen and heard enough to testify in any trial against you—enough to cost your life. Marcus, who did not betray Cillian's trust, who despised me for what I did, is missing. He's missing, and I fear for his life. You know what that's like, don't you, to hold the lives of your friends in your hands? Take a look at mine."

I held my hands up in front of her face.

"You, who would pull a trigger to defend your cause, look and note. These hands are the same. I have no qualms about doing what must be done to protect what must be protected. We are no different, you and I."

She stared up at me before spitting out more blood, but her gaze had softened. I pressed on.

"It was my cousin, Ben. He was a Sherwood Forester. And I want to blame you for what happened to him, and I know I can't because you didn't pull the trigger. I cried for weeks. I didn't think I carried prejudice, but when I got to Dublin, I wrestled with it every day."

I hadn't planned on sharing that with Atkins or Smith, but it pushed the fury out of her. In its place, I found a professional diplomacy.

"He leaves," she said, nodding at Atkins.

"That's outrageous! You are in no position to negotiate—"

"Done," said Smith behind me. I turned to see the American walk across the room and grab Atkins by the arms.

"Don't you touch me," Atkins growled.

"I'm leaving, too," said Smith with a smile. "These ladies need some privacy. Come on. I'll buy you a cupper or whatever it's called."

Out-maneuvered, Atkins submitted to a retreat.

"If she gets rowdy, you just holler," Smith said before closing the door.

I should have been afraid, standing alone in a room with Bridget, but the fear had subsided. She could hate me for what I did to her comrade, but we were both soldiers. We appreciated what must be done for our causes.

"When Margaret, that foolish scrap of a woman, vouched for you, I knew she'd lost it," she said. "It was as obvious as the sea, to me. You had the stink of England fifty miles off."

"We are all products of our upbringing," I replied. "If you've seen what I have, maybe you'd have other priorities as well."

"You're in love, aren't you?" she asked.

"Talk," I said.

She took a deep breath.

"What do you know about magic devices?" she asked.

"Enough."

"Do you believe in them?"

"Some do. That's all that matters," I said.

She wrung her hands and spit out a fresh trail of blood.

"Joseph Dowling's been stirring up trouble for a long time. He was one of the Irish Brigade. Do you know what I'm referring to?"

I shook my head.

"Roger Casement was the founder. They were a group of Irish soldiers going to war for the King. The Germans took them prisoner, and in their captivity, they came together over the idea of an Ireland that could choose whether to send its young men to die or not. But to split from Kingdom? That's a bloody question. And even with the war raging, what chance does an island as small as Ireland have against the British Empire? That's when they started entertaining an alliance with Germany."

"Is any of this important?" I asked. She snorted.

"You're asking the wrong questions," she replied.

"How do you mean?"

"You're asking after a device when you should be asking after a plan," she said.

"Very well, what's the plan?"

"What if the proposed alliance with Germany was a ruse designed to cover something more important?"

I crouched beside her.

"There's no German alliance," she went on. "That plan failed. But something is brewing in Ireland. Powerful, unique weapons with loyal suppliers that might make all the difference. And by now, it'll be too late to stop it."

I knit my eyebrows.

I'd taken the device, and it was a fraud. But what if the ammo drum wasn't the great magical object Joseph Dowling heralded as the promise of a new future for Ireland?

"Are you saying the device was proof he'd secured a relation-ship with someone who could supply more magic items?"

She nodded giddily.

"The same way a baker might give you a small taste of bread to make you buy more."

"What do you know about the suppliers, then? What makes them so special?" I asked. My heart started hammering. Did she know that Harry was the very person that Joseph Dowling may have partnered with to secure such devices? What did she know about the Blue Flyer?

"Only the rumors," she whispered. "Mysterious whispers. Some say they can vanish in front of your eyes, or that the natural world doesn't affect them like it does you and me. I've heard they're ferocious, unfeeling, and all but wraiths. They say they can move freely across the front lines unscathed, and that they know things regular folk like you and I can't know, that they can speak with the wind and water, read the grass and wood."

A chilling recollection stirred from my encounter in St. Bavo's. What had the Flyer said?

I do not enjoy taking the lives of human women.

"You know what they are," she said with a smile. "You've seen them, haven't you? And you know how long they've wandered the lands everyone's fighting over. Ireland, England, France, Germany... We're all visitors here."

"Fair folk," I whispered.

She shrugged.

"The rest of the world wants to pretend magic doesn't exist. The rest of the world wants order and empire. But Ireland? All we want is for the green hills to sing."

Suddenly, the goggles in my pocket seemed very heavy.

"And what would they want with an American pilot?" I asked.

Bridget started laughing, quiet and vicious.

"If you're afraid he's been taken, then you best kiss his memory goodbye. He'll either be dead or so enamored by them you'll never get him back."

My throat clamped.

"Why take him?" I screamed. She only laughed the more.

"I suspect he's a servant now. He'll go about collecting more magical weapons. The Brotherhood has a long list of needs."

My mind raced. I traced my memory back to our own efforts in claiming the artifacts. The Museum of Antiquities had been reticent enough to give up Albert Ball's violin strings, but Baron von Richthofen's scarf was all but under lock and key. If Marcus and I hadn't enticed Oliver LeBoutillier to take it out of its secret hiding spot to show us, I wondered if the Blue Flyer would have been able to make off with it so easily. Yes. Boelcke's goggles identified magic, and he'd told me that the trinkets sang to him, called to him, but short of a gunfight, Marcus could be quite useful as an Allied pilot to find and even steal the devices from Allied aerodromes.

That is, if he cooperated with the Flyer's requests. But even if he didn't, he could be forced to at gunpoint or similar threat.

And if the Flyer was one of the fair folk, there were also magical means of persuasion available.

It made terrible sense. He'd been glamoured already. That would explain his quick attachment to Cillian, perhaps even to Harry. But if the Flyer had taken Marcus to help steal artifacts, that meant he would surface sooner or later. And we'd be ready.

"Thank you, Bridget," I said as I stood up and made for the door.

"Eyes up, lass," she called after me. "You face a whole new monster, now."

She didn't need to tell me.

I swept through the door and found Smith and Atkins waiting for me.

"Well?" Atkins asked.

"I know how to find him."

Chapter 14
The Minefield
Marcus

I held my breath as the ship went under the waves again. The battery didn't have time to charge, but with the appearance of a heavy ship silhouetted on the horizon, we'd have to take our chances. I only prayed that they hadn't seen us before we started going under. After spending so many hours diving through the air in a biplane, waiting for the ship's slow hydraulics to fight against our natural buoyancy was agonizing.

They were pretty far off, though. How quickly did big ships like that move? If they saw us, could they close in enough to fire something our way?

Those were the questions that had me clutching my marble and Luf's machine gun round as though they made up a rosary.

I didn't know why I was so eager to get under the water. It wasn't as though any lesser evil waited for me below. Dieter would have to navigate an underwater minefield from inside a submarine with a dubiously charged battery.

Harry insisted they had done as much on the way to Dublin. He'd said it without any humor, and I knew they had some magical artifact to help them. But I'd had magic on my side before, too, and I still almost got shot down.

We plunged. This time, Dieter controlled the dive himself, ordering me instead to keep a steady eye on our battery, engine performance, bilge pumps, and pressure gauges. I didn't waste time. I didn't want his focus anywhere but on whatever it was he had to do to know where the mines were.

Despite our cool respite above the waves, the oppressive heat didn't have time to vacate the chambers of the submarine. I dripped with sweat within minutes as I unconsciously recited a displaced version of the alphabet to calm myself down. Our alphabet, I called it. It was a letter shift cipher based on the code word Jane and I received at Clairmarais.

Harry felt his way across the ship in my direction, stepping deftly against the angle of the floor. He must have noticed my incoherent muttering.

"It occurs to me that you may be nervous," he said.

"Nervous?" I laughed sarcastically. "Never. Why? What would make me nervous about blindly navigating our way through a minefield?"

"We're not blindly navigating our way through."

"Oh, is there some window in the control station I don't know about? Maybe a big 'ole light so we can see underwater?"

"Well, no—"

"It doesn't matter. Even if you knew where the mines were, I don't think we can maneuver the boat easily enough to wind our way through!"

"It's not easy, no."

"Then why are we doing it?"

He put his hands out as though to calm a thrashing animal.

"It will be fine."

"How do you know?"

"Because we've done it before."

"Yeah, so you've said." I buried my face in my hands. Suddenly, the floor shifted its angle, and we steadied out. Whatever depth Dieter wanted, we'd reached it.

"Where are we going, Harry? What are you planning on doing with me?"

He paused for a moment, considering his answer.

"Would it make you feel better if you could watch?"

I scowled and brought my face out of my hands.

"Watch the mines?" I asked.

"No, if you could watch Dieter pilot us through the field."

"What about my orders to keep an eye on things?"

Harry sighed.

"I think he just wanted to keep you busy. He will need every ounce of concentration."

I had not expected any gesture to calm my anxiety. Harry's offer caught me off guard. He was trying to look after me. He didn't have to. It was pure goodwill.

"If I'm watching him, how will he concentrate?" I asked, eliciting a mischievous smile.

"Do you promise not to cause any trouble?"

I nodded quickly but didn't have full confidence in my word. Death scared me. That was animalistic, instinctive, and basic. Death by explosion on the bottom of the sea floor sounded particularly nasty.

"Very well, then. Let's go," Harry said. He turned and strode out of the chamber as casually as though he were headed to play cards at a mess hall. I followed one shaky step at a time.

We climbed to the central station quietly, reverently even. I was surprised to find Dieter's eyes were closed. He wore around his head an apparatus similar to the ones I'd seen at Clairmarais for detecting far-off aircraft by sound. It had a head strap fastened around his forehead and under his chin, and two large parabolic seashells extending out from where his ears should be.

I snorted in an attempt not to laugh. Harry hit me immediately.

"You were wrong to bring him," said Dieter.

"He was getting too nervous—"

"I heard it all. I understand. But it was still wrong."

"We will discuss it later," Harry said. "Besides, we agreed it was time to show him a little more."

"Typical of you to end a debate by postponing it and taking a parting shot," Dieter said. A small smile crept into the corners of his mouth, and I realized that whatever he was doing had put him in an altogether different mood. The tone of his voice was almost playful.

I hadn't meant to laugh, but with the tension so thick in the submarine, and the sight of Dieter in such a bizarre headdress, it just came out. Now, as I examined it more closely, awe overtook me.

"You told me you didn't have a magical device on the ship that let you navigate minefields," I whispered to Harry.

"I never said such a thing," he replied.

"No more talking," Dieter said. "Unless you want to die."

All the magical devices I'd seen so far were cast offs—ordinary items that had taken on some extra power from the brave men that had owned them. This looked entirely different, as though some mermaid had done its best to imitate a piece of military technology.

I stooped against the wall beside Harry, and let the spectacle of it distract me from all the evil things I imagined outside the submarine. Dieter gripped the helm firmly but calmly, and in a few minutes, I was piquing my own ears to hear past the thrum of the engine and groaning of the ship's metal joints.

I glanced at Harry. He nodded and put an arm around my shoulders.

There it was again. He wanted to comfort me. He didn't assume he knew what was best for me. He didn't want to keep me in the dark.

Time crept by, and as the silence grew heavy, even imagining some false reality for us to pilot our submarine through was better than waiting in a void.

Dieter never faltered. He stood tall with his eyes closed and listened intently. Occasionally, I sensed the shimmy of the ship change as he altered our speed or made delicate adjustments to our heading. But other than these sensations and his insistence that we remain silent, I might never have known we were traveling through mines if they hadn't told me first.

Suddenly, I heard a great scraping beneath us.

"What's that?" I whispered. Harry's back stretched tight and rigid against the wall. Dieter winced.

"Dialythe?" Harry asked. His concern shot my heart rate sky high. He'd yet to demonstrate an ounce of worry, at least outwardly. But even in my panic, I noticed Harry had not used the name Dieter.

"Your questions aren't helping," Dieter said through gritted teeth. My hands groped along the floor until they found a lip of iron to grasp onto. The scraping sound continued.

"Are we hitting the bottom?" I gasped. "I didn't think U-boats could dive so low."

"They can't," Harry said.

"It would appear the bottom is hitting us," Dieter replied in a cool, measured monotone. "There are some abnormalities in the sea floor where we are. A rare elevated shelf is not impossible. I should have been watching for it more closely."

I shuddered. The scraping lessened but the passing of sand on the bottom of our hull sent chills down my spine.

"We can't go on like this," I started. "What if we hit rock and tear a hole wide open?"

Dieter sighed and twisted a number of valves from the twisted mess of pipes behind him before turning on me. The scraping slowed, as did any feeling of forward thrust.

"Take him back down," he said to Harry.

"You're a madman," I interjected. "It doesn't matter where I am, you can't drag a submarine along the bottom of the ocean! If you bump into a stony outcropping, you'll puncture a hole in the bow. How do you plan to get back up to the surface if we can't vent our diving tanks or our bilge tanks or all these rooms are underwater?"

Dieter peered at me calmly.

"There is no rocky outcrop in front of us," he said.

"Like hell. How do you know that?" I asked.

He cocked his head to the side and folded his hands behind him.

"Strange. I was under the impression you were a believer by now," he said.

"Yes. I know. Magic is crazy and amazing but—"

"Have you seen anything that might preclude the possibility that I might possess adequate tools for what I'm trying to do?"

I blushed.

"You haven't told me anything," I said. "How do you expect me to have any faith in you?"

He gestured to his headset.

"Do I wear this to amuse myself?" he asked. I didn't have an answer, and that pleased him. "Do you know how they set the mines around us? They measure the necessary depth to reach the bottom of the sea. They drop an anchor with a chain, and on the other end is an iron ball filled with explosive energy. Then, they hide."

He turned around and studied the wall of hand valves that made up the controls. I appreciated their complexity again. I'd worked on cars and aircraft, but even to my mechanic's eyes, the controls looked like an engineer had a fever dream—like King Midas, but instead of turning everything to gold he turned everything to valves.

If they didn't dictate whether I lived or died, I might have laughed at the thought.

"Tell me this," he went on. This was the most he'd spoken to me since I'd joined them. "You call me a madman. Who in their sound mind would leave behind so much latent destruction with nothing but a discarded hope that it blows the correct thing up? Do you think we navigate waters of sanity?"

He twisted a valve, and the engine reconnected to our propellor. The scraping started again.

"We are hugging a shelf of soft sand," Dieter went on. "The waters in this straight are not deep, but there are pockets that are uncommonly shallow. The mines are anchored in the deeper sections around us, which means that the mine now sitting fifty feet to our starboard side is an impending threat. On the other hand, the mine a hundred yards directly in front of our bow is a secondary threat. Given that our ability to turn while this close to the sea floor will be inhibited, I must take this portion slowly so we can veer to port and evade the mine ahead, or we must clear this shelf and dive again so we will do nothing but scrape the mine's chain as we go by."

The scraping sound stopped.

"Which do you suggest?" Dieter asked. I stuttered.

"How would I know?"

He smiled.

"Finally, you're understanding."

We dove as we continued forward and, as if on cue, a sound that curdled my blood rattled just inches from us. An iron chain clanged against the hull.

"You believe you've joined a revolution, perhaps," Dieter said. "But in reality, you've been rescued. We do not want to spend your life in the name of Ireland. We've seen commendable courage in you but something greater as well. You choose not to dive into the hatred that has stoked the fires of war for so long. There is tremendous power in that."

I'd heard this before, but from kinder lips, more caring and sweet. Jane had spoken to me like this before the war infected her. The reminder made my limbs hang heavy from my shoulders.

"Not all soldiers are filled with hate," I said.

"Hate has many names," he replied. "And surrender may be one of them."

"Surrender?"

"When they've given in to the orders, stopped asking questions. When they shirk the responsibility for their actions and dig themselves into a guiltless trench. It's easy on the conscience to drop a mine when you never see a mine explode."

Dieter worked with a different intensity now. Where before he demanded silence, his philosophizing put him in a type of trance. His hands worked deftly over the valves without pause.

"It's easy on the conscience to pull a lever on an artillery machine and fire into the open air at some target far, far away where it can't be seen. It's easy on the conscience, in a burst of helplessness, to fire a machine gun into the blinding sun where you can be held accountable only for recklessness and luck."

My blood ran cold. Was he confirming that I'd shot him down on our escape from Ghent? On that flight, when I'd heard Jane cry out in pain, something inside of me snapped, and I fired my guns into the sun.

It had been a miracle. Taking down an enemy plane at the

range I did was incredibly difficult, and I'd done it nearly by accident.

"We don't want you to surrender to that, even if the party you fight for is noble," Harry said. "We want you to make choices. We want you to own consequences. We want you to give us a chance to say our part, then use your heart to decide."

Dieter stopped operating the valves and held a hand out to me.

"Come here," he said.

"Why?" I asked.

"It's time for you to know the real magic."

I stood up, reluctantly, and crossed to the mess of valves.

"In another few hundred yards, we will be through. I have us slowly rising now. But our course intersects directly with one of the last remaining mines before we reach the other side. If we don't adjust our heading, we will collide with it."

He touched a valve with his index finger.

"I need to know that you trust us. So I'm going to put you here. Turn the valve this way, and we will avoid the mine. This I assure you. Do nothing, or turn the valve the opposite way, and our paths will intersect. You have only to demonstrate whether your trust me and believe in magic, or you don't."

He took several steps backward to show that he would not physically interfere with my choice.

"That doesn't make sense," I said.

"No?" he replied. "I think it makes sense. Do you trust me or—"

"—or what? Trust that you're saying the opposite? What's this really about?"

He smiled.

"I think you know. We have air to clear. And just like this minefield, if we're going to work together, I must know where the issues are."

I scowled.

"You stole Jane's marble," I said. "Why?"

"You stole Albert Ball's violin strings," he retorted. I shook my head defiantly.

"We didn't. They belonged to the Allies."

A pernicious smile spread across Harry's mouth.

"Is that right? Did the Allies harvest the metal to make the wires? Did they purchase the music for Albert? Did they imbue the strings with magic?" he asked.

"Taking your friend's marble was regrettable but necessary," Dieter said.

"Why?"

He pinched his lips between two fingers to signal that he would not say more on it.

"We can't share all of our secrets with you before we understand your heart," he said.

"By the sounds of it, you two claim to know it better than I do." Dieter shrugged.

"That may be true. But you must know it, as well. Why does it bother you so much that we took her marble?"

"Because it didn't belong to you!"

"No, think more deeply," Dieter said.

"Because it's magic, and it's kept me alive."

"Concentrate," Harry urged.

"Because it was ours!" I cried in frustration. Embarrassment came in quick, and I tried to talk my way out of it. "She made it for us, not for you. You scared her when you took it. You wronged her."

"We've wronged a lot of people," said Dieter. "You're not guiltless in that regard, either."

"Yeah but this is Jane," I said.

Harry and Dieter looked at one another and nodded gravely. Something I'd said seemed to confirm a suspicion they had.

"Go on, then," said Dieter. "Twist the valve and let's go up."

I wondered about the valve. If they had a device to navigate through the minefield, maybe they had magical protection in case we blew up. They might kill me and float up to the surface unharmed. I didn't know. I couldn't know anything anymore. Even Jane had changed, and if she changed, the sun might not rise tomorrow.

Questions tormented me. Was this a test? Did the valve do anything? Could I trust that turning to the left would put us out of harm's way, or did Dieter expect me to leave it alone?

Or maybe we'd already cleared the minefield.

I wiped my sweating palms on my pants, but there was no escaping the perspiration. Between the heat in the sub, the fear, the pressure, and the sinking understanding that what they said was right, sweat beaded on my brow and under my clothes. When I came to the war, that was a choice I made.

When I accepted the mission to accompany Jane, even that was a choice. But now? Jane had shot Cillian because she'd been told he was the enemy. She'd have never done that before. She made that choice. Was she accountable for it in full?

Luf chose to go up after that recon plane. He knew he was going up in someone else's machine.

I chose to follow Harry out of Howth.

I put my hand on the valve, but before I could do a thing, a muted strike against an enormous drum, the sound of underwater detonation, spread through the sea like an earthquake.

Chapter 15
Pledge of Allegiance
Jane

But this she knows, through days of anxious care,
Wherever he may be, her flag is there
Through days of hope, and days of dreadful chance,
Her loyal heart is there, "Somewhere in France."
-Emma Cowan Barber-

"It's out of the question," Atkins stammered.

"Then what would you have us do?" I asked. Both my hands were planted firmly on his desk, allowing me to lean over and muster every ounce of persuasion in my young frame. "Wait here?"

"It was one thing flying you around the Northern Sea to look for boats. It's completely different to have you so close to the fiercest warfare of the front lines."

He sat tall in his seat behind the desk in this borrowed office. But the unfamiliarity of the room had him slightly unsettled. In the corner, Smith sat with his feet propped up on a small side table. Dupont worked on a cigarette beside him.

"You instructed me to fly missions with Marcus near Paris to investigate allegedly enchanted devices," I said. "Was that not also close to the action?"

"One, no. Flying near Paris is nothing like inserting yourself near Amiens. Second, you were sitting behind a man who would rather have poked his eyes out than purposefully put you in any real danger."

I slapped my hands on his desk.

"Oh, I see. Before, Marcus was a childish shellshocked soldier. Now, when it suits you, he's my valiant bodyguard?"

He bristled and harrumphed.

"He's the reason we need to be near Amiens," I insisted. "Smith and I have worked it out already."

Atkins narrowed his eyes and leaned back in his chair.

"You have, have you?" he muttered.

I ignored him and rolled out a map on the desk.

"We have confirmed only a few devices. Boelcke's goggles. That's one. Richthofen's scarf. That's a second. Albert Ball's violin strings. That's a third. What do these men have in common?"

"They're all dead," Atkins said in a flat tone.

"They're all national heroes," Smith chimed in. "Look, I understand you Brits don't like making celebrities out of your top pilots, but from what I understand, you gave Albert Ball the Victoria Cross after he died."

"And even before he died," I continued, "the nation considered him a hero, anyway. The Royal Flying Corps may have succeeded in avoiding official publication of tallies, but you couldn't keep the pilots, or the women they frequented, from gossiping"

Atkins cleared his throat.

"And, it goes without saying what Boelcke and Richthofen meant to the Germans," I said.

"What are you implying, Jane?" Atkins asked me. His use of my first name startled me.

"I believe there is a connection. At first, I considered that these pilots gained access to a magical device that allowed them to rise above their peers. But Ball's violin strings would not have given him a significant edge in combat against enemy aircraft. Instead, what if something happens when a pilot of a certain prestige is killed?"

I grabbed several items sitting on the desk to illustrate my idea.

"Magic follows patterns. We can access magic, or manipulate it, or at least recognize it, when certain unexplained phenomena intersect. My plane repairs are one example."

I smiled, recalling how Marcus had asked me to explain my methods to him as we trekked through Belgium. I'd needed some way to come to grips with my fear, and he knew exactly what to ask to distract me.

He knew how to bring the best out of me.

"What do you mean?" Smith asked.

"I fix defects in planes by exploiting the paradox of their bad design."

"What paradox is there in bad design?" Atkins asked.

"Simply that a country relying on military success might send out faultily designed and haphazardly assembled machines to accomplish the purpose. It's not a powerful paradox in terms of magic, but it has cost how many young lives?"

Smith took his feet off the side table and leaned forward.

"What does that have to do with the devices?" asked DuPont.

"Flying is a new field of existence for the human race," I said, pulling a mug to a central position on the desk. "Meanwhile, the necessity of war has demanded that men take to the sky with violence. However, instead of facing the atrocity of warfare in the way the rest of the military has, the most prominent pilots started out with a mantle of chivalry. While the technology marches them forward, they've moved backward socially."

I dragged a pencil cup toward the mug and tipped it over.

"Finally, despite the astounding danger of aerial combat, some few individuals have managed to be very good at it. They shine above the rest. While most pilots might down a few planes before dying in some self-inflicted crash, Richthofen shot down eighty Allied fighters. It boggles the mind."

I snatched a piece of paper, folded it, and draped it over the mug and pencil holder.

Smith grunted in understanding.

"What's the life expectancy of a British combat pilot?" he asked Atkins. "Do you measure in weeks or months?"

Atkins pursed his lips.

"When one of these aces dies, I think something happens. I don't know exactly how it works, but it's as though they've exceeded the potential of what a mortal should be capable of in our time. Their proficiency, their defiance of natural laws, leaves a trace."

DuPont joined me at the table and cleared the items to reveal the map beneath.

"And you think we need to be in Amiens, in case another hero falls to the Earth?" DuPont smiled, but it was tainted with a painful, ghostly pall. He looked at Atkins. "It makes sense, no? If our top pilots die, it will happen somewhere near Amiens. If a top German pilot dies, it will be close to Amiens."

"Then we can swoop in, find it first, and wait for Marcus and his Irish-loving captor to show up," said Smith. He took his place by my side, too. Atkins stared up at the three of us, a strange trio making our appeal. We were in England, and he was the English officer in our company. I supposed with DuPont and Smith's support, we might override Atkins's opinion, but that was not our way. At least, it had not been so far.

"Will you excuse Jane and me for a moment," Atkins said after a moment's thought.

"Surely they can hear whatever you have to say—"

"A moment alone with the private," he repeated more firmly.

They turned and left, but Smith winked at me on his way out. When the door had closed behind them, Atkins stood.

"This is good work," he said. I leaned back in surprise. I'd expected a reprimand.

"Thank you, sir."

"I know that Marcus's capture has weighed on you heavily," he went on, slowly making his way from out behind the desk. "You two were very close. Where did you meet again?"

I straightened and put my hands behind my back.

"We were both stationed at Villeneuve-les-vertus, near Marne."

"Yes. If I remember correctly, the Americans were using the aerodrome to train their first official squadrons. Is that right?"

I nodded.

"Was it exciting?" he asked.

I knit my brows.

"Was what exciting, sir?"

"Oh, you know, the game! The holiday. I'm not implying that you weren't busy working, but you know how it is. Not many women have such an opportunity to go out and see the world, learn such skills, fraternize—if that is the correct word when a woman is involved—with citizens of other countries."

I rubbed my fingers together as I tried to understand what he was getting at.

"Are you asking if I was excited to meet Americans?"

He looked at me flatly and shrugged his shoulders.

"To be honest, sir, mostly I was concerned about the war effort. I have a mother and father at home near Gloucester, and

I've always been preoccupied with their safety." I dropped my hands awkwardly by my sides.

"And a cousin, apparently, who fell in Dublin during the Rising," he added in tone balanced between sympathy and disappointment. He was right. I should have told him about that before the mission.

"Might I ask what you are getting at?"

He turned and studied a plaque on the wall.

"You and Smith are getting close, aren't you?"

I stifled a laugh.

"Are you joking? Smith shares my concern for Marcus, and I should point out, he's exhibited a surprising degree of compassion. Why? Are you jealous I'm spending too much time listening to another commander?"

He whirled on me.

"I'm looking out for you."

"What are you talking about?"

"You are a British citizen," he said.

"Of course, I am. And I believe I've demonstrated my loyalty first in Ghent, then again Dublin."

"Oh, it's easy to be patriotic when it comes down to a question of overthrowing the government. But your oath is to the King and that government. It is not to finding an American pilot, and it is certainly not to advancing post-war American military interests."

"I'm doing no such thing!"

"Can you say that with the utmost confidence?" He closed the gap between us and hissed out the words.

"They're our allies, Atkins," I stammered. "We're all under command of General Foch now, anyway."

He placed his hands on my shoulders in a fatherly sort of way. It was overly familiar and caught me off guard once again.

"You're young. The war has lasted three of those young years already. It will not go on indefinitely. And the Americans will not be required to live next door to a nation that caused so much devastation to the world over. It's an opportunity for them. From across an ocean, they've come to our aid, just as Germany starts to crumble. They've paid so much less than the rest of us, and they will take full advantage of the harms they have not suffered."

I pulled his hands off my shoulders.

"I only want to save my friend," I said.

"That may be. But the road to your friend lies through dangerous magic. What will you be willing to pay to get him back? For me, duty dictates that I put the interest of my country over the interests of my heart."

I searched for words, but it was hard to find any rebuttal. Of course, he was right. Already, I battled a convention that, because I was a woman, I might act emotionally, rashly. I'd heard these slights muttered by other mechanics and even pilots as I walked by them on base. The whole military success hinged on its members sacrificing all for the greater good.

And yet, I had to believe there was room to maneuver within such a paradigm, that strict military interest and human interest coincided on some level.

"You may be right, Atkins. But as we stand now, I'd have thought you considered King and country much better off with magical devices in the hands of Americans than in the hands of Germans or Irish radicals. As you have put up nothing but stumbling blocks for my pursuit of the Blue Flyer as of late, it's small wonder I've been drawn to Smith."

He stroked his mustache in thought and went back to his seat behind the desk.

"You've forgotten a hero or two," he said at last.

"Sir?"

"Georges Guynemer. I'm surprised Dupont didn't bring him

up immediately. If there was a hero on par with Richthofen and Ball, it's Guynemer."

"Of course," I said, searching my memory for details of the ace. The French had not shied away from lauding its pilots, and Guynemer was a hero. When he died, France and the Allied world mourned for weeks. It helped that he was not only skilled, but poetic, and indeed, handsome. "But he died—"

"Last September," Atkins said and placed a finger on the map. "Just northeast of Ypres, in one of the most hellishly battered areas of the war. If you're right about the magic, he will have left a device for certain."

"But who knows where it is by now?" I said. "Ball's violin strings were picked up and guarded by faithful Ghent resistance."

"And we've no idea how they got there. But if he died in September, it won't be easy to find."

"If it's not found already," I gasped. "The Blue Flyer might have acquired it months ago."

"I'll talk with Dupont to see if we can't discover where Guynemer's remains, and possessions, ended up. The other is Werner Voss, who many pilots consider Richthofen's better. He went down in September as well, also near Ypres. I wonder if Mustermann has had any luck on that front."

"When was the last we heard from Mustermann?" I asked.

"Since your trip to Ghent." He frowned.

"Well, at the very least, perhaps Dupont can question Guynemer's companions and start there, but I'm not confident we'll find anything. If our enemy has known the theory behind the magic all this time, it's most likely they've already snatched up any existing devices. We're stuck waiting for a new one to come about, which means, unfortunately—"

"That we're waiting for another hero to die," he said. Suddenly, Atkins looked so very tired and old. I knew little about him, but the weight of his responsibility and war time experience could not have been kind to his nerves. All at once, his concern for my loyalty did not seem so harsh and unwelcome. He was my countryman, and though we might disagree, we did so in a common language.

"To Amiens, then?" I asked softy.

He lit his pipe.

"To Amiens."

Chapter 16
Spruce Cones
Marcus

Lay desolate the forest.
Memory from severed roots drains.
Taste the brine of progress and decay.
-Widlus-

The ship heaved.

I lost my balance as the floor shifted beneath my feet, a common enough sensation above the waves, but more rare below them.

As a reflex, I grasped at the closest thing to me to steady myself —the wall of valves in front of me. They turned under my grip in indiscriminate ways, doing who knew what to the ship. The engine still ran, but I couldn't make any directional sense out of what was happening.

Dieter clambered over to relieve me.

"What was that?" Harry asked, splayed against the wall where he sat.

"Detonation," Dieter said grimly.

"But we're still alive," I muttered.

"For now," Dieter said. He grabbed my wrist firmly and helped me back to my spot on the floor against the wall beside Harry. He worked the valves like a piano maestro to level us out. "Someone else hit a mine. Far off. We're bobbing in the wake."

"That's not so bad, right?" I asked. I'd battled with the wind in my plane almost every day. Managing the elements was just part of piloting any machine.

"It is if the mines around us bob and bump into the hull."

I froze and hugged my torso tightly, uselessly bracing for an impact. I pictured us as a toy boat swirling underwater in a bubble bath, if the bubble bath had explosive iron balloons swaying with the swells.

"Do I need to make other arrangements?" Harry asked his companion quietly.

"Stop distracting me."

I didn't have the stomach to worry about what "other arrangements" meant. Fear took me. I wanted to be far away from here. My bright idea of playing master spy was running out my ears. I should never have left Jane.

But maybe it was more than that.

Clarity came with the panic. Maybe I was lying to myself if I thought their idealistic fervor hadn't rubbed off on me. The ideals they represented scratched an itch I'd been looking for since long before Luf died. I wanted honor. I reached for dreams of perfection. I did this because it was a way to cope with a world that was everything but simple. At one point, Jane knew how to remove the burden of painting everything in black and white. I missed and needed that from her. When she'd left, the black and white came back in the form of an Irish idealist.

I wanted to see Jane again, or even my mom and dad. Just thinking about them slowed my pulse and steadied my shaking hands. I didn't think about my parents much. I'd learned a long time ago to keep that door in my memory shut tight. But, at times like this, my mother's face waited for me when I closed my eyes.

I smiled amidst the fear.

I wanted to survive, and wanting to survive meant a lot.

"Dialythe," Harry murmured in anticipation.

"Watch your words," Dieter hissed. He had calmed his hands and now focused on only a few valves. We listened and waited for the creaking, clicking, and popping from outside the boat.

Finally, Dieter put down his hands and expelled a large breath from his chest.

"We're through," he said as he tossed the apparatus he'd been wearing to the side without ceremony. He sunk to the floor, limbs weighed down by fatigue and exhaustion. The lines on his face, invisible before, creased and folded into weary strokes of heavy years.

I wondered, for the first time, how old he was.

Harry extended an arm and patted his shoulder.

"Well done," he said.

"Remind me why we're doing this," Dieter replied. His companion smiled and stood up.

"*Hold the standard high aloft,*" he replied with a pat on the shoulder. "I'll make a sweep and assess the state of things. We're alive. That's something." He nodded before leaving the compartment.

I didn't move. Dieter and I slumped like two figures in a mirror, both crumpled with exhaustion on opposite sides of the cramped compartment. Suddenly, I was freezing cold, despite the stifling temperatures, as though a fever broke.

Dieter stared at me and did not look away. At first, I fought it, awkwardly casting my eyes into my lap or at the wall of valves he'd used to navigate the minefield. But he was persistent, and I met his gaze.

"Why are you here?" he asked at length.

I shrugged and scrounged up a believable answer.

"I guess I want to help."

He shook his head.

"You don't belong in a war. Why are you here?"

I bit my tongue.

"That's none of your business," I said.

"It is my business. I need to understand you."

"Why?"

He nodded toward the door.

"Harry insists you can help us. But I have little faith in your kind."

"My kind?" I scoffed.

"Pilots. Soldiers. All the boys who came to war because it sounded exciting and found only bitterness and pain and hate—or worse, boys who still treat it all like a game."

His words reminded me of that day at Gengault, when we heard the Baron had been shot down. I'd been surrounded by happy cheers, as if his death meant something great. But I couldn't celebrate. Nor could Jane. Nor could Luf.

Dieter leaned closer to me.

"Do you know the truth about war magic?" he whispered. His fatigue peeled away the safeguards he'd used to mask his emotions. In his eyes now, I saw fury and fear.

I shook my head.

"It's all hate."

The word made me tremble, but something in my heart fought it. Jane was magic. She believed in magic, used magic, treated it like a rare animal we'd discovered in the wild.

How could Jane be so attracted to it if it was all hate?

But then, she had changed. I'd seen how it had turned her views of violence on their head.

"Where are you from?" I asked.

He leaned back against the wall.

"Ireland," he said.

"You don't sound Irish to me."

"Close to Ireland," he amended with a shrug.

"And that's why you're working with the Brotherhood?"

"The devices you and your partner sought have great power, more power still for those who know how to use them effectively. A tyrant might wield them irresponsibly."

I nearly laughed.

"So it's less about helping the Brotherhood and more about making sure they stay out of English hands?"

"I did not single out England."

"Or Germany, then? Or France? What about the United States? Do only you and the Brotherhood have the wisdom to wield them responsibly?"

He leaned his head against the wall in frustration. Then, Harry poked his head back in the compartment.

"I'm afraid we have a problem," he said to his companion.

"Are we hit?" asked Dieter.

"No. The ship is a mess, but that's no matter. It's the tree. Come see. You as well," Harry said nodding in my direction. Dieter halted.

"It's time, Dieter," Harry's tone was plaintive and decided. "We'll need him sooner than we thought."

Dieter set his jaw but nodded his assent before climbing out of the compartment. I followed, eager to be included in this ring of trust, so eager in fact that I hadn't second guessed what he'd just told me.

A tree?

The word hit me just as I banged my shin on the bottom of a metal door frame. That was impossible. Who in their right mind would bring a tree onto a submarine? There was no light, and with precious little fresh water onboard, why waste it on a plant?

I followed behind them toward the front of the ship into

Dieter's cramped sleeping quarters near the empty torpedo tubes. I'd never stepped foot in Dieter's personal space before. If some rare mechanical issue required attention to any of the valves in this room, I instinctively deferred to him or Harry to get it fixed.

I was disappointed when I breached the veil of secrecy. There was a rolled-up blanket and pillow stowed in one area of the room. Other than that, there was no sign anyone lived there at all. While sacks of rations hid in corners of the submarine through the rest of the ship, I didn't notice any food here except for a small half-emptied bag of sugar rolled neatly on the top.

"Is the tree still working?" Dieter asked as we crawled our way in.

"I have to assume it is, despite the conditions. That's the problem."

A wire ran inside one of the torpedo tubes. When Harry cracked the door open, light spilled out. He reached deep inside and came back with his prize. I doubted my own eyes.

In his hands, he cradled a miniature tree set in a simple, glazed ceramic. I couldn't help taking a step forward to look at it more closely. It resembled one of the large Spruces near my home in California. I used to collect the cones as a kid and throw them back and forth with some of the other boys in my neighborhood. But this tree, from its roots to its bark to its needles, were all there in miniature.

"How did you do this?" I asked in wonder, extending a hand to touch the bristles of a tiny bough. Harry slapped my hand away, but evidently the question pleased him.

"Actually, much more easily than I thought. The temperature and humidity in the submarine have lent itself quite well to its maintenance. Light is the main problem, but for a couple of weeks, he's managed fine, thanks to this bright bulb in here."

The soil at the base of the tree looked moist and mottled with green moss. The surprise of seeing such a thing, and the tree's inherent beauty, tickled childhood memories and innocent wonder. I beamed, and the weight of our circumstance lifted from my shoulders.

With a deft movement of his thin fingers, Dieter plucked a tiny pinecone from the soil at the foot of the tree. Several other cones budded or clung to the Spruce's branches, but this was the only one that had broken free.

He examined it closely before narrowing his eyes in concentration.

"Where did it fall from?" he asked.

Harry delicately pushed aside a couple of branches to point at a severed budding bough.

"Little?" Dieter asked in surprise.

"It's tiny," I confirmed.

"No. Robert Little."

I knit my brows.

"Robert Little? He's a pilot, flies for the English," I said, remembering the name passed around the mess of the aerodrome. The English did not practice the celebration of their living combat aces the way France, Germany, or the United States did, but when a pilot earned enough of a name for himself, it couldn't be kept secret. "He came up from Australia, if I remember right. What does he have to do with anything?"

They shared a solemn exchange before turning to me.

"Robert Little is dead," said Dieter.

Dead.

The word was so familiar. It chased out the childlike feelings the tree had inspired only moments before.

Dead. It wasn't crazy. Even the best birds fell, eventually. When it was your time, it was your time, even if your name was Richthofen or Lufbery or Rockwell or Campbell or Prince or Little.

But I couldn't accept "dead" from Dieter while he held what looked like a child's toy in this cramped, isolated submarine.

"What do you mean *dead*?" I sputtered. "How the hell would you know that?"

"We know. His squadron may not know it yet, but we do," said Dieter.

"Because of this pine cone? This tiny baby pine cone?" I clenched my fists. More details about Little trickled back into my memory. "The man was married. He had a kid. What do you mean he's dead?"

"We only know he was killed in action," said Harry. His tone was more gentle than his partner's, but both of them regarded me with marked curiosity. It made me feel foreign, an animal in a zoo exhibit. I was an ape, taken from home, put in a cage somewhere, with only vague memories of what a natural life should have been.

I think it was Harry's tone of voice that triggered the breakdown. It sounded too much like Smith's soft pity after Luf jumped from his plane. And the anger I fought now may not have had much to do with Little.

"Sooner or later, you'll hear him whispering to you," Smith had said. The words brought me comfort then. But I knew now that death was silent.

I leaned against the door well, let my knees slowly take me back to the floor of the submarine, and tried to bury my face in my arms. Protected in the cave of my elbows, they couldn't see the pain. I could not let them see my pain. Only Jane was allowed to see such a thing.

I felt a body settle beside mine.

"You would call it a magic tree," said Harry quietly. "We've been tending it for a long time. And it wasn't easy to sprout."

He put his hand on my shoulder, and I looked up. He'd handed the miniature Spruce off to Dieter, and his eyes brimmed with melancholy.

"Do you know the first time a piloted aircraft shot down another?" he asked. "A Frenchman named Joseph Frantz piloted a two-seat Voisin biplane. Compared to the planes now, it looked like it was made of toothpicks. His gunner, Louis Quenault, sat on the front with a Hotchkiss machine gun. They flew into the sky and found a German Aviatik plane whose pilot tried to drop handheld bombs on a French town. Quenault fired his gun. His bullets struck the pilot and the fuel tank. The pilot died from the gunshot, his ride-along mechanic died in the crash. Their names were Wilhelm Schilchting and Fritz von Zangen."

He reached for the tree.

"That was the first time we heard the song of the sky as it is sung now. We followed the tune all the way to the crash site into a swamp, and we found a scrap of wood, charred and black, left behind from the wreckage of the plane. We took that wood, and we combed through German administrative files to discover what company had felled the wood for the lumber required for that Aviatik. We ventured deep into Germany, and saw the ravaged woods, and asked their remains if they'd seen the scrap we carried before, until finally, we came to the place where the Spruce had stood. We knelt on the ground where we might have been shaded by its branches, and in the dirt, discarded as naught, we found a cone."

I stared at the tree in Dieter's hands and tried to disbelieve what they told me. How could they have found the very tree? What did they mean they followed the song or asked the wood?

"This tree is special," Dieter said. "We have used it to track the pilots who have changed the song in the sky."

I shook my head.

"What are you talking about?"

"When a pilot reaches a certain level of renown, when the sky and the world below know him for what he is, a new cone forms. And when the pilot dies, it falls."

"There is no song in the sky," I said, voice elevated and sharp. But in the silence that met my outburst, I knew that was not true. I'd heard the song myself, maybe not with my ears, or in the way these two claimed to hear it, but just as the sirens of old lured men to the sea, so did this song take pilots like me. I'd watched them succumb to its allure time and time again. And in the end, it claimed them.

"And when a cone falls, the pilot leaves a device behind," I said quietly.

Harry nodded.

"You had a cone for Boelcke and Richthofen and Ball, who else?"

They looked carefully at one another, but didn't answer.

"What about Lufbery?" I asked. I slipped my hand in my pocket to finger the metal casing of his old bullet. Luf scoffed at the importance of the almighty scorecard. Pilots like me recognized him for what he was, a legend in the air, but his renown had not blossomed like the names I'd just mentioned. Still, in my heart, I wanted him to have a damned Spruce cone on some magic tree. I wanted magic, at least, in all its cosmic wisdom to remember him how I did.

But Dieter and Harry shook their heads side to side.

"A cone fell for Werner Voss and Georges Guynemer," said Harry.

I squinted, trying to remember. The names hit home. Many of us considered Werner Voss to be the best pilot in the world. He lagged behind Richthofen by the numbers, but the Baron was a stalk and kill hunter. Many of his victories came from downing inexperienced pilots from attacks within his well-defended formations.

Voss, on the other hand, was supposed to be a flying god, an ace killer.

"But they went down last year, in September, I think."

"Yes. We managed to collect one of the devices they left behind," Dieter said.

"Whose?"

"Voss."

"And Guynemer? That was eight months ago. You were on top of the Baron's scarf a week after he bit the dust. What's taking so long?"

Harry threw up his hands in surrender.

"We swooped in to commandeer the scarf so quickly because we've discovered it's easiest to acquire these devices immediately after a pilot dies, before his things have been haggled over, memorialized, and safely guarded. Captain Brown tried to keep his trophy a secret, and for that, it was as easy as finding where he hid it away. Boelcke's goggles eluded us because someone guarded them carefully, despite our best efforts."

I smiled. Lina, one of our German contacts, had found the goggles and given them to her husband, a German pilot named Earnst. He told us the Blue Flyer, likely Dieter, had attacked him. Now, I understood why.

"We secured Voss's device at great cost, and we hoped to persuade you to help us acquire Guynemer's. That was until now. Robert Little has just been killed in action, which means we have to change plans."

I laughed to myself.

"And how do you think I can help with that? And why?"

Dieter smiled.

"For one, I believe you're too curious not to sit out," he said. "But second, if you help us acquire the objects, we won't make you give us your glass marble."

I put a hand to the marble around my neck. Dieter had stolen Jane's. The thought seemed foreign, now that I had come to know him. He had chased us back to our aerodrome, and according to

Jane, he wasn't coming for the violin strings. I had something they wanted.

"If I help you get Little's device, may I return to Jane and my unit if I choose?" I asked.

"Yes," said Harry quickly, without consulting his companion. "If that is what you wish. You're not our prisoner. But consider, by then you may see greater value in our mission. You may not choose to go back."

"And what is your mission? Free Ireland?"

"Right now?" He stood and offered me a hand. "To retrieve whatever device Robert Little left behind."

Chapter 17
Amiens
Jane

Then you, for you are cleverest of all
Who have slim fingers and are pitiful,
Brimming your lap with bloom that you may cull,
Will sit apart, and weave for every head
A garland of the flow'rs you gathered.
-James Stephens-

I thought I knew war.

My time serving with Marcus and Lufbery in an active combat zone had shown me the realities of violence. There, far south on the Western Front, the action got quite hot from time to time. But we all knew that it paled when compared to the salient north above the Somme, into Ypres, closer to the sea where England and Belgium lay in a stretch of land stained by millions of casualties.

At Clairmarais, I was humbled by a fresh perspective of yet another hub of the great military machine. Marcus and I marveled at the size of the Handley Bombers and the racket of incessant shelling to the east, the never-ending conveyor belt of attacks, bombings, and aerial movements, to say nothing of the ominous comings and goings of the medic trucks.

But nothing could have ever prepared me for Amiens.

The city bore the weight of its proximity to the front lines. And that proximity had lasted the full duration of the conflict. Both sides had advanced and retreated through its surrounding country, both leaving a mark in their own way. The German Spring Offensive had reached its greedy fingers forward faster than their military infrastructure could maintain. The Allies fought them back, but the Germans had not retreated far past the eastern side of the Amiens's borders.

At Amiens, I saw the impersonal, brutal abattoir in action. The very air had been sapped of any vitality. It was tomb air, a soil sucked dry of its life-giving nutrients.

I had nothing inconspicuous to do there.

We settled into an aerodrome under firm British control. Officer Smith's influence was limited, which was unfortunate because the active lieutenants continually waylaid Atkins with urgent questions or managerial tasks. Smith, Dupont, and I did our best to get comfortable in a makeshift canvas tent near head-quarters under the guise that we had a special intelligence assignment.

I supposed that was true since we constantly badgered the aerodrome's intelligence team, scouring reports, telegrams, and even public radio broadcasts for any news that a notable pilot from either side of the war might have met his unfortunate end.

As it turned out, our timing was dreadfully perfect.

I'd fallen asleep at my table, exhausted from a night's sleep interrupted by the constant chaos of nearby shelling and night raid alarms. Smith, ever presentable in the face of wartime inconve-nience, bounded through the flap of our tent.

"Morning, sunshine," he said. "I've got news."

"Good news or bad?" I asked, groggily.

"Hard to call it good, but it'll help find your boy." I wiped my eyes.

"He's not my boy," I said, but I hardly cared what Smith called Marcus if he had information to share.

"A citizen patrol discovered the remains of an Allied plane over by Noeux-les-Mines."

"The pilot?" I asked.

"Dead. There's reason to believe it's the remains of Robert Little."

I held my breath. Smith smiled grimly.

"If you wanted a war hero to die, you may have got it, and spookily fast."

A man had died, and my heart was soaring. I swallowed it down. It was wrong.

"How will we know?"

"They've got a buddy of his going over today to identify the remains. You up for seeing some more of the lovely sights in Amiens's countryside?"

"When do we leave?"

Dupont had already seen to the requisition of a car. Atkins, despite all his protestations, could not be spared from an important officer's meeting about an upcoming attack. Smith's eyes gleamed with mischief, but I warned him off goading my superior officer. He didn't need to. Frustration distorted Atkins's features as he watched us drive north, leaving him behind to explain, again, to the airfield's commanding office that he, too, had an operation to oversee and couldn't be bothered with coordinating air support for an infantry charge.

The irony would have kept Smith smiling all the way to Noeux, had the landscape been even slightly more pleasant. But the scars left from years of battle sobered even his mood.

If Smith was right, Robert Little's death would reverberate through the ranks as more than that of a deeply qualified combat ace. It wasn't unheard of for pilots to be married, but the vast majority of them were young men, unattached to more than their squad mates and perhaps their parents.

I winced as I ruminated, alone in thought with only the hum of our motor to distract me. I hadn't written to my own parents more than once since we had returned from our mission in Ghent. And even that note was nothing more than a quick scribble to mention that we were taking leave for a couple of weeks so I might not write for some time.

And this after I had hounded Marcus for so long about his neglect in corresponding with his family.

Now, I understood his reluctance. It was like writers' block. Soldiers' block, I supposed? The very idea of putting pen to paper froze my thoughts. How could I begin to describe what happened —who I was now?

No. I was Jane. I was no different, despite how Marcus recoiled from me as he had. Despite how differently I saw myself in the mirror. But now, I would find him, and I'd show him that I was still Jane, his Jane, who had been there for him through his darkness.

Even if he wasn't there for mine.

Our car came to a stop in the starved town of Noeux. Occupation had stolen its charm. The streets did not bustle as a French town should. The village wept one surviving tear at a time, its remaining residents pushing mostly empty wheelbarrows down the street.

Smith and I waited, parked by a vacant flower shop while Dupont entered the local gendarmerie to inquire about the downed British pilot.

"You brought the goggles, right?" Smith asked.

In a panic, I reached for where I'd hung them around my neck. They were there, in Smith's plain sight. I stared at him in bothered disbelief.

"I'm joking," he replied flatly. "You've hardly moved for a half hour. Just wanted to loosen you up a little."

His attitude irked me, and my annoyance was only exacerbated in my state of self-reflection, but he wasn't wrong to worry about me. I took a deep steadying breath.

"Smith," I said, "you should know better than to call a woman loose."

He laughed. The noise sounded irreverent in that quiet broken courtyard.

"I was saying you weren't loose."

"I'm fine, thank you, simply focusing on what we need to do here."

"Excellent. Poker face. I like that. And look, our love-loving Frenchie is back already."

Dupont sauntered across the street, hands in his pockets. I watched him and poked a hole in the upholstery of my seat. I had dragged them to the most hellish side of the war based on a hunch about magic. But I didn't have any plan beyond sitting and waiting once we had found Little's device.

Dupont cracked the car door and hopped in beside us.

"What's the situation?" asked Smith.

"Little's friend, Major Booker Dawson, arrived an hour ago. He confirmed the body."

A heavy silence filled the car. One of the Allies' great aces had gone the way of the world.

"Well, damn," said Smith. "His poor wife."

"And child," muttered Dupont soberly.

"Hell of a thing, this war," said Smith. Dupont raised a pack of cigarettes.

"Share one with me for the fallen hero," he said. I scrunched my nose and shook my head, but Smith accepted. I tried to remember if I'd ever seen him smoke before. Dupont lit up, and in a moment, the car filled with heavy tobacco fumes.

"Little was a star in our skies," he said, as the smoke worked to calm his nerves. "It is rare to see such success."

"Nearly fifty victories," said Smith. "Talented kid."

"They say he was determined to get the kill. He flew so close to his enemies before pulling the trigger. They say, more than once, he came so close that he crashed into an enemy plane."

Smith shook his head in reverence.

"Can't miss at that distance," he said. "I guess your luck only lasts so long, though."

I folded my hands, at war with myself. Smith and Dupont took no issue with pausing for a moment to honor this great fallen pilot, but all I could conjure within myself was impatience, anxiety, and even irritation. We came here for a purpose, and I was not interested in wasting time. As far as I was concerned, we were on the battlefield right now, and there would be time to mourn the fallen later.

At the same time, my disinterest disgusted me. Did Smith's sensitivity bother me? He told me that war had hardened him, as it was hardening me. Yet, here he was, comfortably wading into deep felt sorrow, while I could not summon any similar humanity.

What was happening to me?

"So what next?" I blurted out at length. Dupont stared at me, cigarette raised halfway to his mouth. Smith hurried to smooth away my awkward outburst.

"She's right. Little was an exceptionally fine man, but we've still got a job to do. He'd appreciate that." He turned to me. "Jane, despite the difference in our ranks, we're looking to you for next steps here."

He flicked the remains of his cigarette out the window. Dupont didn't seem as eager to part with his. He took another drag and peered at me curiously.

"Well," I stuttered. "The first thing will be to find his device, if there is one."

"Right." Smith nodded. "Where would that be?"

I pursed my lips. We never needed to find a device ourselves before. Lina had found the goggles. Albert Ball's violin strings waited for us at the Museum of Antiquities in Ghent. But Captain Roy had described to us how he'd found Baron Richthofen's scarf. The Baron had been wearing it when he died.

I swallowed.

"We will need to go through his things," I said, "and examine the body."

Neither of them seemed to relish much in that idea, but they didn't voice their hesitation. I spoke on to soften the blow.

"Boelcke's goggles should make quick work of the job."

"Better get to it then," said Smith. "The whole damn Triple Entente will be here to mourn the man before we can take two blinks."

Little's body was being held at a military hospital adapted from a small church in Noeux. His friend, Major Dawson, still lingered about the building. Dawson was a respected ace in his own right. He'd been out for two years, in active service for the duration. Often, pilots *cracked up*, as Marcus and Lufbery put it, after no more than six months. The stress of constant flying day in and out wore on the nerves. To meet someone with so much experience under his flight cap who still maintained such an enthusiasm was both inspiring and off-putting. His innate capabilities were admirable, but to have such passion after this long... He didn't support the war. He must have loved it.

And while I'd met many soldiers and pilots who appeared to love the game, I'd never seen myself in them before.

Dupont had no appetite for rifling through the possessions of a fallen hero, so I insisted he take on the duty of distracting Dawson while Smith and I poked around.

It took him no time to light Dawson a cigarette and set to swapping war stories.

The nurse on duty required no great convincing to let us through. Smith flashed a smile and mentioned rank, and she left us alone. To think that once I'd fallen for the lie that he was nothing more than a sergeant. His true rank, position, and experience were still a mystery to me.

But it didn't matter. He'd opened doors, and now I had to go through them.

Even though I put on a brave face for the two men traveling with me, the thought of examining a corpse made my hands tremble. It was true that many pilots at our base had lost their lives—even as frequently as several men a week, but examining, in close quarters, a man shot in battle was not the same as attending a hasty funeral.

"You going to be all right?" asked Smith quietly. His ongoing concern for my sensibilities inflamed my irritation. "Could be rough in here. The doc said Little took a round through both thighs. Died from blood loss."

"I'll be fine."

Little's body lay covered on a rickety cot across the tiled room. We approached, and Smith took hold of the edge of the sheet covering the pilot's face.

"You sure about this?" he asked again. I wasn't. I was making this all up as I went along.

"Oh, on with it already," I hissed. Smith smiled.

"All right. Goggles on, Jane."

I slid Boelcke's goggles over my eyes, and he pulled back the fabric.

I didn't know what to expect. We thought we understood how the goggles worked, but the sensations had shifted over time. The traces of magic I'd seen over the Irish Sea had only grown more prominent, as if the goggles identified more magic than they had before. One explanation was the inherent magical heredity of the land itself. But another explanation, one that disturbed me, was that the magic was getting stronger.

Robert Little had a kindly face, even in death. Although he'd been dead for at least twelve hours, he still appeared vibrant to me, like magic coursed through his veins now in place of his blood. His countenance radiated with a power that I shrank from. My mind filled with all the details that Smith and Dupont had just recounted, how bravely and viciously he'd closed in on his prey, how he must have written to his wife with great care. This man had been a father, a protector. When he took to the skies, what motivation fueled him?

"Cover him back up," I muttered.

"What? We came all the way here to look at him for two minutes?"

"The magic hasn't left him yet," I said.

"Hasn't left him?"

"I don't know how to explain it." I took off the goggles. "See for yourself."

Smith took them and looked Little over. I turned around. I didn't want to see the body any more than necessary.

"What are you talking about, Jane? I don't see a thing."

"Oh, come off it, Smith. His face is practically glowing."

"I'm looking right at him, and I'm telling you, I don't know what you are talking about."

I turned and snatched the goggles back, but when I put them on, I found the same ghostly counterfeit of the man I had before. To my eyes, his face appeared to take on the blueish sheen indicative of an enchantment. The impression of power was undeniable.

"You didn't notice anything?" I asked. Smith stuck out his chin and shook his head.

"I've seen a lot of dead soldiers," he said. "I wish I could say this one looked special."

"Smith, wait." As we spoke, something changed. The magic undulated, draining and dripping from under the sheet. For lack of any better description, it appeared to melt off Little's body.

"Are you seeing this?" I asked.

"Seeing what? Jane, have you lost your damn mind?"

"It's incredible!"

The magic split into rivulets streaming through the air. It cut its way around the room in a serpentine pattern, before gathering again into a bright and glittering river of energy, creeping its way out the door we came through, toward Dupont and Dawson.

I followed like a moth to the glow. The stream straightened its path and headed toward a canvas bag propped up against the wall. It seeped through the fabric and disappeared inside. I had the bag in my hands when a sharp pull on my forearm stopped me.

"Excuse me. What do you think you're doing with my bag?"

It was Major Dawson's voice. When he saw my wondrous expression framed by Boelcke's goggles, he let go of my arm and his eyes stretched in alarm.

I dumped the bag's contents out on the floor, and Dawson protested again.

"Easy, major," said Smith as he grabbed his shoulder to restrain him. "There's a point to this."

"Like hell there is," Dawson replied.

I spread Dawson's things apart, giving no heed to what objects he'd been storing, save one.

The magic river had an end. A simple gold ring.

I watched until the stream of energy had completed its transfer, and there was no more magic dancing in the air, before delicately scooping up the ring and cradling it in my hand.

Robert Little had indeed left behind an artifact, and I had just witnessed its creation.

Chapter 18
Double Operative
Marcus

Then suddenly I shudder as I see
A young man stand before them wearily,
Cadaverous as one already dead;
With arms outstretched and drooping thorn-crowned head,
The nail-marks glowing in his feet and hands.
-Wilfrid Wilson Gibson-

I had to hand it to them. They'd planned for just about everything.

We surfaced just north of a small port off a charming coastal town. They told me they had planned to get my help retrieving Guynemer's device, but Little's death called for a change of plans. I'd have thought that, like the tree, they'd have some method of knowing where Little may have fallen, but if they had a device for such a purpose, they didn't share it with me.

Instead, they simply told me we were headed into a particularly dangerous area of France. It made sense. Robert Little was one of Britain's great aces, and the front had been heating up since Germany's big push toward Paris and Amiens. But I couldn't for the life of me remember which squadron Little flew for or which salient he flew in. Since Jane and I started our first mission together, I hadn't kept up with those details as closely as before. Luf and I used to spend countless hours chatting about the great pilots of the war. Though I hadn't met most of them, many of those names seemed like family to me, relatives who lived far away so we didn't get to visit often.

Family. I blinked away the thought.

"I hope you know how to swim," said Harry.

The shore was close, only a quarter mile off. As a teenager, I used to swim out to a rock off the coast near our house that was much further. I nodded.

"What about the submarine?" I asked.

"I'll spring a leak and set her off to the northeast," said Dieter as he carefully placed the miniature Spruce tree on top of the ship.

"You're just going to sink it?" I asked, gaping.

"They're not easy to hide while unmanned," he replied.

"And once we get ashore?"

"According to our last intelligence," said Harry, "Little was stationed near Amiens. But as you know, his aircraft may have gone down anywhere around that part of the front, depending on where his assignment took him. Our best guess is that he was shot down just north of the city. The war has raged quite hot there, and I can't imagine he would have flown too far past that area."

"Enough talking," said Dieter. "We need to rid ourselves of the ship before we're noticed."

"What about the headgear?" I asked. They looked at me blankly. "The headgear you used to pilot the submarine. You can't be scuttling that, too."

"Right," said Harry. He glanced at Dieter with a knowing smile. "That settles it. Better bring it along."

They must have debated leaving the headgear onboard the ship. But if that were true, why did they look at me so confused when I brought it up? Dieter appeared to be resisting the urge to roll his eyes.

"Choices must be made," he said, but he hurried back into the ship to retrieve it. I didn't blame him for not wanting to swim to shore toting so much gear along. I didn't have the energy to appreciate how silly he looked bobbing along with an otherworldly seashell helmet and pulling a miniature tree on a small makeshift raft behind him. The water was too frigid for that. It sucked the breath right out of my lungs, and I swam uncomfortably to shore. When I finally pulled myself up on the rocks, my skin burned from the cold, and we all gulped for air, lungs eager to be free of the all-encompassing pressure of being submerged.

"Quick. To the shed up there," said Dieter, nodding toward the top of the craggy cliff above us.

We hadn't dared shore ourselves along the beach where the soft sand was easily visible. It made the task of climbing up in the dark treacherous. We were fortunate the tide wasn't too low because at least we had something of a head start.

We navigated the rocks well enough, though, and picked a pathway that only cut my hands and banged my knees a moderate amount. My skin was soft from the swim, it hardly resisted the edges of the cliff. I don't know how Harry managed to get the tree up with us.

When we got to the top, we found the shack empty, which surprised me. I'd have thought a lookout like this would be manned for certain. It was small, sure, no more than a fishing hut, but any high point would have military value for sentries.

Harry fiddled with the lock, and soon he'd cracked the door to let us through.

It was as cold as it was dark inside.

"You see any blankets or anything?" I asked, breathing hot air into my hands through chattering teeth. They ignored me and busily got to work. Harry pulled blinds over all the windows, and

Dieter had already lit a curious blue-flamed candle. He'd set down the headgear and the tree to pry up a corner of the floorboards.

"You've been here before," I muttered.

"We have little hideaways all over the countryside," Harry replied as he knelt to assist his companion. They unearthed an excavated chamber beneath. Inside lay a mismatch hobble of bundles and boxes.

"They're not disturbed by the locals or the Navy?"

"You'd be shocked by what you can hide in a war zone. And, we have methods of deterring interest from passersby," said Dieter. He threw a blanket to me.

"Dry off before you suit up," he said.

I looked down. I hadn't thought about my clothes in days, other than stripping an item or two to cope with the heat inside the submarine. I still had my getup from when we'd met with Bridget in Dublin.

A corner of my shirt still had Cillian's blood on it.

"Suit up how?"

"This should be familiar to you," said Harry as he held up an American pilot's dress uniform. We'd worn these on special occasions—going out to restaurants in villages near the aerodrome or at medal ceremonies. The last time I'd worn one was at Luf's funeral.

The outfit was familiar but certainly not comfortable.

"Is it the wrong size?" Harry asked.

"It'll work fine."

"Are you bashful, then? Do you need privacy? We won't watch you."

"I said it's fine. It's all fine." I blushed. Privacy was a luxury I'd all but forgotten. For him to assume I needed it made me feel prudish.

I peeled off my sticking, wet clothes and changed. The dry wool fit snugly and warmly around my legs, but the weight of the jacket settled like a mantle on my shoulders. I didn't want to know how they'd acquired such a uniform.

When I looked up, Harry was just finishing the buttons on a shirt that looked like mine, but Dieter had changed into much more modest fare.

"The clothes suggest a plan," I said.

"We're heading to an Allied aerodrome to gather some more information, and, hopefully, collect Little's device," said Harry.

"Is he coming, too?"

Dieter shook his head.

"No. I have some other business to attend. Once you've retrieved the device, you will steal a plane and join me at our station in Holland."

I had suspected Holland as a perfect home base for the Blue Flyers when we first learned about them. It was a neutral country that bordered the war's combatant nations, so naturally, it was a crawling hub of spies from both sides.

"Let me get this straight. You want me to break into one of my own aerodromes, steal an enchanted artifact from underneath the Allies' noses, and commandeer a plane to make our way to Holland, all so we can help Ireland win its independence?"

Harry stopped fiddling with his collar, and Dieter froze. They both stared at me.

"Is there a problem?" asked Harry.

I scoffed.

"It just sounds kind of crazy. How do you know I won't simply rejoin the ranks and rat you out as soon as we get to the aerodrome?"

"You might," said Dieter. "But you won't."

"How do you know?"

"For one, we've competed with you to retrieve these devices, so it's much more likely you try to break back to your lines after you've taken advantage of our knowledge to find Little's artifact," said Dieter, simply. That made sense. But he was also right that I wouldn't do even that.

My gamble in joining them had already yielded so much information. The Irish were just the beginning. These two had big plans, and I wanted to learn whatever they were. Our mission in Dublin was to investigate and retrieve one of the enchanted devices. But I'd had that mission in Clairmarais, and again in Ghent. It always led to more missions. This was progress we'd never had.

But beyond that, if I was honest with myself, there was something about these two that attracted me to their purpose, their essence even.

"You won't run," said Harry. "You want what we want."

"And what's that again?" I asked.

"To end the war." He looked at me intently, the blue candle cast shadows across his face. "It can be ended, you know."

"End the war?" I asked. "I thought you were kidding when you said that on the submarine."

My throat tightened when I heard myself say it out loud. I swallowed hard. In my gut, it felt like the US joining the Allies might be the tipping point, but to imagine the war ended—I was afraid to let myself believe it.

"This is about stopping the war?" I stuttered. "How do you plan on doing that?"

"One step at a time," he replied. "And this step requires Little's device. Come now, Marcus. Isn't that what you want, to end the war?"

"I want the Allies to win the war," I replied staunchly.

"Is that true?" Dieter asked. "Does it matter to you so much if Germany wrestles some meager territorial possession from France or Belgium? If that's how it ended tomorrow, would your life in peace-time change so much?"

"So you're on the German's side?" I asked with a shake of the head. I didn't have a good answer to his question, and I hated how it made me think.

"We're on the side of peace," Harry replied, "lasting peace. And the idea intrigues you. I know that already. You chose to come with us, rather than return to your comrades. They want to kill their way through their problems. But you?"

'You don't know me like you claim to," I said. But it was a lie, a pathetic defense against their probing questions. I'd been going back and forth for days about why I'd left Jane. Part of me wanted to believe I had a master plan, that deep down I'd gone with the Flyer so I could collect information about him and report back to Smith.

Maybe the truth was too uncomfortable to face. I'd chosen to leave Jane behind. I was scared.

And the way they talked about peace kindled a fire in me. So long, I'd been flying and fighting against the immovable line. I was fighting for victory.

That road led to heartache. That road turned beautiful people into monsters or piles of ash. It was one I'd been all but ready to abandon, even at the risk of prosecution, court martial, and even execution.

But peace? Maybe I could fight for peace.

"You won't leave us yet," Dieter said after smugly scrutinizing my vacant stare.

I straightened my coat and met Harry's eyes. A phrase I'd heard them exchange came to mind.

"Shrink from no great work today."

Before long we were driving through the black of night in a stolen car toward Bruay, a village north of Amiens. That was enough to get me righted in terms of navigation. We must have come ashore in the seaside town of Outreau or maybe Calais, on the Allied side of the line. Bruay would be a bit of a drive, but Harry was inhumanly tireless. Despite all my resolve and the bumpy road, I fell asleep slouched against the side of my seat. The consistent nerves being aboard the submarine, our trek through the minefield, and the swim to shore had pushed me past the point of exhaustion.

I dreamt of Jane and Luf and my mother and father. All of us were at a park near the ocean in California. I could smell the sea and the wild sage and oak that grew in the hills. We were happy. My father tried to impress Jane with stories from his time at war. My mother fussed over Luf relentlessly, and he handled it with all the grace of a diplomat. But then, we heard the blare of a Klaxon, and Jane, Lufbery, and I had to go. There were planes waiting on the cliff. Luf rolled off, but his propellor never started, and he plunged toward the ocean. I took off, but my parents didn't let me go. They hung off either side of my tail wing, dangling perilously from the frame as I climbed into the sky.

When I looked back to see Jane starting the engine on her own single-seater, I woke.

It was still dark, but dawn promised on the horizon. Harry drove steadily onward, eyes bright and unbothered.

"Did you sleep well?" he asked.

"No. Awful," I muttered.

"That sounds right. Bumpy roads and all."

"Yeah," I grumbled, trying to tuck as much of my head into the jacket of my uniform as I could. It was a cold morning. "Where are we?"

"Nearly there," Harry replied. "I'm trying to decide if I want to stow the car so we can creep in or drive up boldly and rely on our uniforms to justify our appearance."

I yawned.

"This close to the action, at this time of day, I doubt anyone would look twice—especially at an aerodrome full of these British flyers. They kind of have a reputation."

"Oh?"

"Don't make me say it," I said. "I'm sure you know."

"Pretend I don't."

"They just get squirrelly is all. Rowdy. They get drinking then roughhousing and breaking things. I think it's just their way of dealing with the weight of what they're doing. There will be a few guys waking up for patrol, but I'd bet you the rest of the aerodrome will cling to whatever sleep they can get."

Harry smiled wryly, but kept watching the road.

"Thankfully, the Americans are much better behaved," he said.

I blushed. I didn't want to think about how Americans behaved. Here I was skewering the British, when I'd heard stories about American pilots and soldiers that would curl their mothers' fingernails.

"I think we'll be fine stopping the car somewhere near base and finding the mess. If anyone knows about Little going down, they'll talk over breakfast."

"Excellent," said Harry. "It's unlikely that Little's device will be in the aerodrome. He died only last night. The pilots here won't know yet."

"You don't think?" I asked. "Word will go around fast if anyone saw what happened."

"Exactly, if you situate yourself correctly, I suspect you'll be there when the tidings fall. In the grief or surprise, you could learn much."

"Take advantage of their sorrow?" I asked.

Harry shrugged.

"Is sorrow sacred?" he replied. "Imagine. The whole war zone would be a cathedral."

"What will you be doing?"

Harry quirked his head to the side.

"I'm not particularly well suited to blending in, socially, with Allied pilots. I'll be inspecting the hangars or waiting near the car."

I shrugged. He was right. I couldn't nail down what it was about him that came across so strangely, but there was an edge to his voice or a lilt to his posture. He was too aloof, congenial in the wrong way. It also made me suspect he wasn't completely right in the head.

I chuckled to myself.

Knowing what he and Dieter were trying to accomplish, I was sure he wasn't right in the head. Maybe I wasn't either.

"Coming up on it, now. From here on, we behave exactly as Allied pilots would."

"I am an Allied pilot," I muttered.

"For now," he said.

We drove up the main road through a bomb-shelled town. Any village this close to the front was bound to bear the scars of the thousands of artillery shells that routinely sailed through the air.

At the moment, the line was far enough off to give war-beaten Bruay a reprieve. But there was no telling how long that would last.

I didn't mind the plan. It sounded like I'd finally have a quiet moment alone for the first time since before Dublin. I'd plant myself in the mess, explain that I was there because my plane was shot down nearby, and relax until news about Little broke through the ranks.

That was practically a vacation.

Harry parked the car a ways off from the aerodrome, and we walked in, all the better to verify my story about my plane going down.

"Remember," said Harry before he strayed off to investigate the hangars—a term that he obviously intended to mean steal a plane. "Gather what information you can about Little, and I'll find you later."

"And if I run off?" I asked.

"I'll still find you later," he said, pulling Jane's marble from around his neck. My hand groped immediately for mine. My heart turned seeing Jane's talisman on him. They'd never told me which of them had chased us through Ghent or through the air all the way back to Gengoult. Dieter must have given it to him after the minefield.

"You can use the marble to track me?" I asked. Harry smiled conspiratorially.

"You wouldn't believe the things we can use this marble for." He clapped my shoulder. "I'll tell you more later. Good luck."

Whether we had actually developed some degree of trust or he was dangling a promise like that out there to make sure I didn't desert them, it didn't matter. I'd grown attached to Harry, despite his flaws, and anxiety filled me as I watched him pick his way through Bruay toward the big canvas hangars.

Hopefully, he wouldn't get arrested or shot.

I shook my head and followed my nose. The morning air beckoned with trails of weak bacon from a tent that would most assuredly be the mess.

I rehearsed my story in my head, wishing I had better answers to the questions I knew would come. I didn't even know which squadrons were stationed nearby, let alone any specific pilots or mechanics they were bound to ask me about.

Maybe something like the truth would be my best approach. I was flying a special assignment, the details of which were classified. That'd help explain my dress uniform as well. Classified. What a flexible word.

I patted my magic marble, rubbed Luf's machine gun round with my thumb in my pocket, and ducked into the mess to join a crowd of hungry pilots, orderlies, mechanics, and officers.

Chapter 19
Cover Story
Jane

The poets, since the War began,
Have written lots of things
About our gallant soldier lads
Which no one ever sings.
-Fredrick Wheeler-

"I don't like the whole business," said Dawson as he shouldered his pack reluctantly.

"I appreciate your discretion," said Smith. He stood up straight, stiffened his lip and offered a hand to the pilot. Dawson didn't take it.

"I'll stay quiet, but not for you. I simply don't believe the man was having an affair. Not Little. Why you're trying to convince me he did is beyond me, but I'm not about to give weight to a lie that would devastate his widow."

Smith shrugged, as though to admit a draw. In a moment of panic, I had told Dawson that I'd been having an affair with Little, that he'd purchased the ring I held as a gift for me, his mistress. Smith did not hesitate to back me up.

"You'd rather risk taking a ring he bought for my betrothed back to her? Imagine, if word ever got out," said Smith.

Dawson threw his hands in the air.

"It's not a good cover story," he blurted out. "I'm not an idiot. If you two—" he thrust a finger at Smith and me, "—are engaged, why is he so unbothered by your affair with Little?"

I worked my jaw, hoping that if I opened my mouth, a convincing answer might come out. Smith replied for both of us.

"Love is complicated during war," he said with a fond shake of his head. "Isn't that right, honeybunch?"

I'd never wanted to punch Smith more, but I had little with which to blame him. The stupid, degrading cover story had been my desperate idea. I tried to soften things .

"A man has needs," I said without emotion. Dawson buried his face in both hands.

"This is why I steer clear of women. I don't know what that ring is, or why Little had it in the first place, but please don't taint his memory with some half-baked rumor that hardly makes sense. I don't want you anywhere near the funeral!"

"I didn't plan on it," I said. "It would be disrespectful to his late wife."

"Oh, shut up," Dawson retorted. With a final disgusted look in my direction, he turned on his heel and walked out the door.

As soon as he was gone, Dupont whirled on me.

"You were having an affair with Little?" he asked.

"Of course not," Smith barked.

"Thank goodness." Dupont sighed. "Imagine how Marcus would take it."

"I don't see what that has to do with anything," I shot back. Smith put his face in his hand.

"Jane, what's the matter with you? An affair? How could you go and try to ruin a man's reputation like that?"

"It was the best I could come up with on the spot. I panicked!"

I said. "Do you have any better explanations as to why I may have emptied Dawson's bag like a woman possessed to retrieve this ring?"

"What if he had believed you and shared the story? Little's wife would have been devastated," said Smith.

I shrugged.

"She'd recover."

"She may not have," Smith argued.

"Do I need to remind you that soldiers abroad aren't always well behaved. It's very possible Little was having an affair."

"I sincerely doubt it," Dupont said. "Especially after hearing how Dawson reacted to the idea. Little was an exceptional man. His affection as a loving father and husband was well known. We can't judge all soldiers the same."

"Even so," I said, "I stand by it. It was believable."

Smith studied me coldly.

"I guess you'd know. After all, love is complicated during war, isn't it, Jane?"

He lowered his eyes at me. I flustered immediately. I knew full well how my hell-bent, never-tiring crusade to save Marcus must come across. But I wasn't about to explain myself to Smith, or Dupont for that matter.

"It's Private Doe to you," I said, finally.

We walked outside and returned to our car.

"Do you think he'll stay quiet?" Dupont asked.

"If he knows what's good for him," I said as I shuffled in beside him.

"I always underestimate the innate understanding our veterans have," said Smith. He stood beside the car, one arm resting on the open door. "Maybe we ought to trust them a little more. All that affair nonsense was unnecessary, Private Doe. If we'd told him it was confidential, I think the man would've understood."

Dupont snorted.

"Does that bother you?" Smith asked.

"Does it bother me that the war can teach a man to accept two strangers stealing a ring his best friend bought for his wife because a ranking officer says it's confidential?" He lit another cigarette and blew the smoke out the window. "I don't know. What's so special about the ring?"

"It's Little's artifact," I replied.

"Yes, but what is special about it?"

"Don't know that, yet," said Smith. "We'll have to take into the air to figure it out. Right, Private Doe?"

"We're doing no such thing," I replied.

"What do you mean?" asked Dupont.

"The mission was to find the artifact. We've got it. Now we keep it."

They stared at me, but I shook my head and bit my lip.

"To reveal its effect would require us to fly it into active combat," I said. "It's not like as soon as a device is airborne it turns to you to explain what it does. We can't risk losing it in a sortie. The ring might be our only way to Marcus."

Smith and Dupont exchanged an uneasy glance.

"You wanna run that by me one more time," said Smith.

I swallowed. I had guessed that they weren't going to like this plan.

"It's the only way to get—"

"You mean magically, right? The ring might magically point us in Marcus's direction. Because I know you're not about to suggest that we use this thing as bait to lure the Blue Flyer into the open and then as a bargaining chip to get Marcus back."

"We've never watched an artifact's creation before. That means we beat the Flyer to it. He might not know that we have it. If we can plant it in the right location, he will come sniffing around and then we can catch him."

"And then if we catch him…" started Dupont.

"We can find Marcus."

Smith whistled.

"We cannot trade a magical artifact to get Marcus back," he said.

I shut my eyes. His life or the ring. I'd trade the magic in a moment.

"I know that," I said. "But the Blue Flyer doesn't. We need information. The Flyer is collecting these objects, presumably for the Irish. Don't you think we should find out what the plan is? If Ireland implodes, how do you think that would affect the Allied war effort?"

I could tell this point was persuasive because they both cocked their heads to the side to turn over the idea. But Dupont sighed.

"I am a supporter of love," he started. "But war is about more than—"

"How dare you, Dupont?" Something vicious reared up inside of me. He spoke to me as if I were a little girl with a crush, as if I hadn't already risked my life time and time again while he and the others sat back in a command center.

But my anger stretched more deeply than that. I'd been demeaned because of my sex on many occasions. This was different. His off-handed remark diluted what I had with Marcus to pathetic terms, reduced it into some burnt, goopy, sour appendage.

Dupont shrank in his seat.

"I'm sorry, Jane," he said humbly.

"We don't even know what the thing does," said Smith after a moment of quiet. He massaged his jaw. "What if that ring supercharges rounds or—"

"I doubt it. Richthofen's scarf seems to do that and we have no reason to assume the artifact would perform the same way."

"—or what if it makes an enemy super accurate or identifies hidden positions or can make a plane invisible… The possibilities are endless, and you know it. If that ring ends up in the wrong hands, it could bring unholy devastation down on Allied soldiers."

I wrung my hands. I'd been working on a theory to bring some order to the magic, but this was the first time I'd shared it out loud.

"I don't think it will do that," I started. "I believe the effect of the artifacts is linked to the pilot that made them."

"How do you mean?" asked Dupont, his voice still cowed from my outbreak.

"Well, what was Richthofen known for? He was the most efficient and prolific killer in the skies. It makes sense to me that his scarf would make machine gun rounds more deadly. And that's what it did. Smith, you didn't see the plane at Clairmarais when the Flyer shot us to pieces, scarf in tow. The bullet patterns made no sense. Some looked like a standard round, others looked as though we'd been hit with artillery."

"All right, what about Boelcke?" Smith asked.

"Boelcke was a visionary," I said. "Pilots on both sides of the war consider him the father of air combat. What could be more natural than goggles that see things others can't, see jammed guns and the magic of the air?"

Suddenly, the hair rose on my neck. The theory was proving itself in the explanation.

"And Ball?" asked Dupont.

"I admit that Albert Ball's violin strings were the reason I didn't bring this up earlier. His doesn't seem to fit the same way."

Smith shook his head and slapped the side of the car.

"You're wrong, Jane," he said. "His strings prove it. You flew a German plane over our lines and used them to tie a French flag to your tail wing. Right?"

"Yes. So what?"

"We talked with a lot of the anti-air battery operators that saw you. They didn't shoot. You know why? They said you *didn't look German.*"

"Well, we were flying a French flag," I said.

"Yeah, but you weren't when you were spotted. After talking with those gunners, I rang up the flight commanders of the squadrons that should have scrambled planes to intercept you. I asked them if they'd seen you and why they hadn't sent up fighters. They said the same thing. You didn't look German. At a half-mile, they got a gut feeling."

He hopped into the car.

"And what did you tell me about the man who was keeping the strings in Ghent?"

Thomas, the museum curator and keeper of Albert Ball's violin strings had left a similar impression on me. He'd gone to the trouble of playing me a song on a violin tuned with Ball's strings.

The memory of that song whispered in my ear. As he had drawn his bow across the instrument, it was as if I'd known the very essence of him—not just details about his life, but his uncompromising identity.

"You think the strings are identifiers," I said.

"Albert Ball was a recluse. He flew on his own terms. He didn't cut his hair the way other Tommies did. He kept a garden beside the little yurt he lived in by himself on the aerodrome. That man never allowed anyone to change who he was."

"That's it, then," I said. "The strings inspired the gunners to hold their fire because they understood who we were, even flying that high above them, even if we were in a German aircraft."

"You're a combat gunner now, kid," said Smith. "How valuable do you think a power like that could be?"

"I owe it my life," I replied.

"And Little," asked Dupont. "The ring?"

"Robert Little was a caring father, a loving husband, and a deadly pilot. Beyond that, I don't know much about him," said Smith.

"The ring was for his wife," I whispered. "What if it had something to do with loyalty?"

"It may be," said Smith. He smiled at me, now, as though our joint venture at understanding the magic had endeared me to him and canceled out my indiscretion about claiming an affair. "All right, Jane. You convinced me. That ring probably won't mow down hundreds of troops at a time. And besides, it's small enough that we ought to keep it from getting stolen without too much trouble. What's your plan to lure the Flyer out into the open?"

We set to work immediately. Little's body was to be buried in the local cemetery at Noeux-les-Mines, and we spent several hours debating whether leaving his ring in the town would be more believable than moving it to wherever Dawson was stationed.

"Dawson's with the 201," said Dupont. "They used to be No. 1 Royal Naval Air Service, before they combined to form the RAF. That squadron moved all over."

"Where are they now?" asked Smith.

Dupont shrugged. "Atkins would know."

Mention of Atkins made me uneasy. I managed to persuade these two, but something suggested that Atkins would need another kind of convincing. He could not be left in the dark for this. Besides, if he found out we'd made such a decision without so much as asking his opinion, it might create an international issue.

So we made the drive back to Amiens.

He was shaving beneath the cover of a bombed out building when we found him. Although we hadn't been gone long, driving back into the war-torn city filled me with a feeling of apocalyptic doom. Something about passing through a shell of what was once such a prominent, populous place made me second guess the permanence of my reality.

"Well," he said when we approached. He flicked the shaving cream from his razor. "What did you find?"

I held out the ring for him to see.

"An artifact?" he asked.

"I watched it happen," I said.

He squinted and dried his face with a towel. "What do you mean?"

"I was wearing the goggles, and I saw the magic leave Little's body and enter the ring."

Atkins gaped and swallowed. His freshly shaved Adam's apple dipped like the bobber on a fishing line.

"Its effect?" he asked.

"Mostly harmless," Smith replied before I could open my mouth. I looked at him in surprise.

"Like Ball's strings," Smith added.

Atkins assessed him for a moment before looking at me for confirmation. Smith was trying to help me. If Atkins believed the artifact had little military application, he'd be much more likely to agree to my plan of using it as bait.

I tried not to swallow, and nodded.

"Damn," Atkins said. "Nothing then that will help us locate the Blue Flyer, either?"

"Well, we had a thought about that," I said.

"You want to use it as bait, don't you?" asked Atkins.

"Now, how in the world did you know that?" replied Smith as he plopped down on a large chunk of stone debris.

"It's only natural. The Blue Flyer has tracked all the other objects. Why not this one?"

"And you agree to the plan?" asked Dupont.

"Why shouldn't I?"

I folded my arms. This had been too easy. And perhaps I'd been out at war too long, but I distrusted anything that was too easy.

But I would manage the consequences later. Marcus was still missing, and this was the only route I had to find him.

"Do you have any conditions?" I asked.

"Yes, and they're the same as before. If your plan goes awry, then I will not hesitate to kill the Blue Flyer myself," he said as he grabbed his jacket from a chair. "I can't trust you to make the right choice if Marcus is involved. Understand that."

I nodded.

"Fine," I said.

"Splendid. How will we go about it?"

"Can you be spared from your services here?" I asked.

Atkins scoffed.

"The damnable field commander thinks he can order me about like a private enlisted man because of 'necessity.' I'm an officer with my own commission, and our mission is paramount."

"Good," I said. "Then perhaps you can tell us where the 201 is stationed."

Chapter 20
Bruay
Marcus

Sleep, drums and trumpets, yet a little time;
All ends and all begins, and there is chime
At last where discord was, and joy at last
Where woe wept out her eyes: be not downcast,
Here is prosperity and goodly cheer,
For life does follow death, and death is here.
-James Stephens-

It was a sober time for Bruay's mess hall.

Most aerodromes were pretty quiet in the morning, and here the early hours had yet to mature into amiable chatter. Even with the innovations of night bombing raids, there weren't many pilots too eager to go up without daylight, and the majority of patrols still happened under the sun.

In the early morning, on a typical air base, a few pilots would be sitting around on alert duty. Others would mount the sky for patrols. The rest of the place would get the chance to sleep off whatever late-night bend of rousing trouble-making the pilots had gotten up to.

But, I'd never served in a squadron this close to the heaviest action.

The scattered men in the mess huddled over their soup bowls, mechanically bringing their spoons to their mouths. Their eyes were vacant, exhausted from overwork. Some had severely chapped lips from repeated hours of open cockpit flying under harsh daylight. Others broke out in pimples from the repeated applications of grease that high-altitude pilots spread on their faces to guard against wind chill and frostbite.

A piano sat dirty and dusting in a corner of the room. Several keys had gone missing.

I'd worried about sticking out as an outsider, but I wasn't sure that these men had enough energy to care either way at this time of the morning.

I walked over to the cook.

"Hi, I'm new here. I—"

"Help yourself," he said gruffly before getting back to cutting onions for lunch and paying me no mind at all.

I did. The food was modest, but my stomach ached from hunger. I hadn't been in the submarine too long, but I got sick of tinned rations stashed in sacks real quick. Now, the dull-colored eggs and thin bacon had me salivating. I took some and put it beside a bowl of soup made of onions and some unidentifiable root vegetable. It smelled bitter and greasy.

When I sat down a yard or two away from an unshaven pilot with dark hair, he didn't bother to look at me.

My food went down quickly, and it strengthened my resolve. I was here for information.

"I'm new here," I said to the pilot beside me.

He grunted and took a sip of his coffee.

"I was just wondering where your squadron commander is?"

His eyes slid lazily over to peek at me from the side of his face.

"American?"

I nodded.

"You a replacement?" he asked.

"No, I uh—" Suddenly, my story about my plane going down seemed really weak. I scrambled to come up with another idea. "I'm here with news."

"I'm all ears," he replied.

"It's for your squad commander."

"Captain will be around later," he looked at my uniform. "You a pilot?"

"Yes, usually."

"I didn't hear anyone fly in."

"I crash landed south and had to crawl my way over. Smashed my plane right up. They gave me this uniform and put me to work until I can get back."

"Which squadron are you in?"

I blinked. Apparently, our conversation was waking up this man's capacity and curiosity.

"No. 124. American," I said. That was my old squadron, the one Luf had commanded. They weren't stationed anywhere near here, though. It'd have been better to name one with an assignment plausibly close, but I'd just spit it out. If this guy had any clue about the 124, he might have some really interesting questions.

I'd be caught.

But then, this was my side. If I got caught, I could just get back to Smith and Jane. Would getting caught be all that bad?

He sniffed.

"Canadian myself. You're at RAF No. 41. You went down south, you said, by Amiens?"

I raked my memory for any semblance of northern France's geography. We'd always flown south, and I knew that area like the back of my hand.

We were right near the line. That explained the rolling artillery thunder.

"That's right."

"How'd it happen?"

I raised my eyebrows and was about to improvise a daring, but not too daring, story about how I was forced out of the air when a man called out.

"Elliott," the voice said. "Who are you talking to?"

The pilot beside me sat up straighter.

"Captain Bowman, this man has come with news."

The Captain had a full mustache and hairline that reached up into the two corners of his forehead. He was dressed for flying, minus his cold weather gear. His silk scarf hung untied around his neck like a mechanic's rag.

He walked over officiously and put a foot on the chair across from me.

"What news? Why not just telegraph? Seems like an awful waste to send someone to tell us what could be done over the lines."

"You're Captain Bowman." I gaped.

He nodded.

"And you are?"

"I'm—well, I mean, I'm Marcus. Sorry. You are Captain Geoffrey Hilton Bowman?" I stuttered. The name shot like a thunderbolt through my memory. Once, Luf and I had spent days talking about Lieutenant Geoffrey Bowman amidst a list of seven other pilots. He had a special place among Allied legends.

"What about it?" he asked.

"You shot down Werner Voss." My breath caught. I must have looked like a little kid meeting a ball player. Luf would have been mortified. Bowman scoffed.

"I didn't shoot him down."

"Well, right. But, you were one of them. One of the eight."

We heard the news the previous September. Luf and I were at work replacing the cylinders on a Nieuport machine when the gossip came in.

Werner Voss was, to many, the best pilot in the war. Although he didn't have the same scorecard as Manfred von Richthofen, many considered the Red Baron a gamester. He preyed mostly on inexperienced pilots and attacked out of the strength of his own squadron, backed up by his allies around him. He got kills the way you might go fishing.

But if Richthofen was a fisherman, Voss was Germany's version of a bull fighter.

"Will you tell me how it happened?" I asked.

A bemused grimace pulled at the corners of Bowman's mouth. For a moment, I forgot all about Harry and Dieter, the plan, the magic, or even Jane.

Hearing the story from Bowman's mouth would answer all kinds of debates Luf and I had about that famous dogfight. We'd argued endlessly about the amount of skill, talent, or dumb luck Voss must have had to fight eight skilled Allied pilots at once, many of whom were already aces at the time.

Voss's final flight was practically a myth, and the pilot in me would not be denied hearing it from a primary source.

"You came all the way out here to deliver a message just to convince me to tell it, didn't you?" Bowman asked as he folded his arms.

"Sure," I said. It was a plausible reason for being there, and I took it. Besides, I could tell he wanted to share the story. He could aggrandize the other pilots as well as himself.

Bowman looked around the mess hall. A few other pilots had filed in, and everyone perked up at the mention of Voss's name.

The captain did not strike me as a braggart. But there was something in the air that morning, a drooping morale, that he recognized as surely as I did. There was nothing like a good sortie story to get pilots energized.

"We're going to need more coffee. Elliott get me a cup will you?" said the captain as he sat down.

The pilot beside me nodded and stalked off. Another took his place at once. The others in the room leaned our direction subconsciously.

"What do you know already?" Bowman asked.

"Just what's gone through the ranks. That Voss fought eight of you at once and got a bullet in everyone's plane."

Bowman put a finger on the table.

"Voss was the best I've ever seen, and I've seen a lot. Fighting him was like fighting a ghost."

Hearing him, I was a kid again, ready for a bedtime story. I must have had a silly grin on my face because he smiled at my enthusiasm in a sly, knowing sort of way and kept going.

"I was flying in the 56 then. McCudden, Muspratt, and Rhys-Davids took off from that field over there. Cronyn flew up from B Flight. I flew up with Hoidge and Maybery for C Flight. All of us were flying SE 5s."

I nodded my head to encourage him along.

"The SE 5 is a great machine," I muttered.

"I was sure as hell glad to be flying one that day," said Bowman. "We were running a patrol over a battle in Ypres."

"Passiondale," I said.

"Yes."

Elliott returned and placed the cup of coffee at Bowman's elbow. He edged his way angrily back into his seat, elbowing out a new pilot over that had taken it in his absence. Bowman went on, heedless of them.

"McCudden split us up, and he landed a victory shooting down a German recon plane. And then we saw a sortie going on in the distance so we closed in. That's when I got my first look at him."

A glaze came over Bowman's eyes, as he recalled the scene. The chummy tall tale took on a very different mood as its teller traveled back in time.

"He came straight at us. Eight planes and he didn't even hesitate. Fear never knew him. What are you supposed to do when an opponent doesn't fear you?"

He swallowed. The mess hall had grown very quiet. The cook stopped chopping vegetables, the clink of cutlery lay mute.

"He was flying some Fokker triplane. It was painted blue and silver. It was the first turn that sent a chill down my spine. He just flicked his plane around. No Immelman, no renversement, it didn't look like a maneuver at all, it just flicked around. And suddenly he was into our formation, like a wolf trapped in a pack of hounds."

Unconsciously, I reached for the marble hanging around my neck.

"The accuracy shocked us. He kept spinning his machine around, flicking into rolls and flat turns, but they weren't evasive maneuvers. Every movement had more than one purpose. He threatened us with machine gun rounds the whole time. Incendiaries, tracers, and heavies that zipped through the air, his own pattern, a trademark signature. We circled around him, and bullets kept buzzing by like hot stingers. I think most of us were paralyzed just watching because we'd never seen such a show before, never known that planes could be pushed to move the way he moved his.

"He got to Cronyn first. Shot him up right nice, and forced him out of the fight. When Cronyn turned and glided for home, I think it lit a new urgency in us. Before then, it never occurred that we might lose against him. Eight against one. Sure, he might try some fancy maneuvers, but after Cronyn..."

He shook his head, and I saw fear and admiration in his

features. Now, as he spoke, he stared forward as if he could see Voss in front of him in the mess.

"It was like shooting a kite in the hands of a child on a blustering day. Every move was so unpredictable, so jolting, that getting a line on him proved impossible. At one point, I was sure we had him when five of us all fired down at once from different directions. But nothing happened. He just slipped away unharmed.

"He hit Muspratt, forcing him down, and suddenly there were only six of us left. To my amazement, he gave me a burst while skidding sideways. By now, I thought something was wrong with us or our rounds. Two more Germans, a Pfalz and an Albatross joined the fight, but Hoidge shot the Pfalz down quickly and climbed back up to join us, and we managed to scare off the Albatross just fine. So I knew our guns were working. For the rest, we saw our tracers hit Voss, but they didn't seem to do anything."

I crept forward on my seat. I was there, too. I could picture the scene in my mind. And this next part was what Luf and I had always debated because people said different things about it.

"That's when McCudden proved why he's worth every bit of fame he's earned. You need your experienced pilots to step up and show off courage in these types of situations. I think Voss understood who he was dealing with by then."

McCudden was one of England's top aces, just as celebrated as Albert Ball and Ace of Aces Mick Mannock. Seeing him joust Voss would have been one of the greatest spectacles in military history.

"They started doing these headlong passes at each other, exchanging shots. McCudden engaged him in a way Voss couldn't ignore. Then, as he was distracted by McCudden, Hoidge came broadside and rattled off a burst of rounds right into his flank.

"It changed after that. No more maneuvers. No more flicks or turns. No more brilliance. He started streaking off in a straight line. Davids went after him, but I think it was already done. I saw him stall, and jerk downward. When his plane hit the ground, a cloud of dust and smoke went up so forcefully that I didn't think there'd be much left of the man."

He paused, staring at one of the wooden stakes holding up the mess tent, his cup of coffee paused halfway to his mouth.

I wished Luf could have heard him tell it. I'd always insisted McCudden must have put some bullets in Voss. After all, he was the highest scoring Allied ace on the sortie. But Luf just smiled to himself as he always did when my boyishness showed. I always wanted heroes. I wanted the war to be full of bedtime stories where the bravest knight won the honors and saved the day.

Luf would have been happy to know that it was Hoidge who got the broadside. But then, if Davids went after him, then perhaps he should have been credited with the victory.

I shuffled my feet in the dirt and hoped they all split it up as partials. It seemed the most fair.

Bowman shook his head slowly.

"They buried that German in a shell crater without ceremony," he muttered. "All that talent and bravery."

He raised his eyebrows and assessed the group around him. I'd hardly noticed, but we were surrounded now. A whole pack of pilots, some half-dressed. The men didn't appear bleary eyed now. A strange reverence rendered the mess hall a chapel. There was more than excitement in Bowman's story. The way the captain told it, Voss was a real embodiment of the skill all of us dreamed to have. This dogfight made him more than a pilot. It made him a demigod that no mortal alone could kill. It took eight of our best, and even then, it wasn't a sure thing.

"And let that be a lesson to all of you lot," said Bowman. "When it's your time—"

"It's your time," echoed the voices around me in muddled unison.

My thoughts drifted back to the submarine, to the little spruce tree with its budding cones. Did Bowman have a cone growing? What about McCudden? What about any of the pilots bumping my elbows whose names I did not know? There were hundreds of us flying aircraft, but that tree wasn't laden with more than a handful of cones.

Voss had been one of them. When I'd asked about him, Harry and Dieter kept quiet. I wondered what would have survived the crash Bowman described, and what effect might his artifact have on the world?

Maybe his was the one that had enabled them to transform their plane mid-flight.

"Story time is over. Planes need repairing, skies need patrolling," said Bowman. "But first, this man's come with a message for us."

I blushed as all eyes turned on me.

"Really, it was just for you, captain," I stuttered.

"Whatever it is, they can hear it."

I wrung my hands but had no excuse to refuse him. I only had one bit of news, and that was based on a magic tree I saw in a submarine. It could be total hogwash.

But I believed it.

"Go on, then," Bowman said. "We've got work to do."

"It's Captain Robert Little." I swallowed. "He's been killed in action."

Chapter 21
One Step Behind
Jane

When you soar into the air on a Sopwith Scout,
And you're scrapping with a Hun and your gun cuts out,
Well, you stuff down your nose til your plugs fall out,
'Cos you haven't got a hope in the morning.
-RFC Mess Song-

"Why did he agree to the plan so easy?" asked Smith. We walked along a paved pathway in Nouex-les-Auxi, north of Amiens about thirty miles. The RAF 201st requisitioned the quiet town for its operations. The aerodrome stretched across what was once farmers' fields.

Before the war, the scene may have inspired painters for its idyllic landscapes. But like so many other French villages, violence and industry had ravaged its charm.

"I'm sure he has his reasons," I said, quickening my pace. There was no outpacing Smith. Whenever his mind raced, so did his feet.

Our plan was simple, rudimentary, even. I'd based it off of what Marcus and I had experienced in Clairmarais when the

Flyer stole Richthofen's scarf from under our noses. I'd hide the ring in a chest inside the barracks. Then, we'd simply wait for the Flyer to come sniffing around. It might take days. It might take weeks. If time stretched on, we'd have to start gossip going around to sell it.

"Come on, Jane," Smith hissed in my ear. "It's weird isn't it? All three of us thought he'd be against it, and he didn't even bat an eye."

"What are you implying?"

I had my own doubts about the plan. At the top of my mind was the disinterested regard the Blue Flyer had for Albert Ball's violin strings. And although he did come to collect them, they didn't seem all that important to him. He expressed much more interest in the glass marbles.

Unless Marcus had tossed his marble into the sea, the Flyer likely had both of those now.

But if he was working for the Irish, he'd need more, especially if it looked like easy pickings. Why not come for Little's ring?

"What isn't he telling you?" Smith asked. I stopped and pulled off the road under the shelter of a crumbling brick facade.

"He's not obligated to tell me anything. He is my commanding officer, and I'm here to accomplish the missions he gives me."

Smith smirked.

"Unless it's about Marcus, right? You were all too keen to throw Atkins's directions out the window if it meant saving Marcus."

"Well, maybe I need Marcus in order to complete the greater mission assigned me," I said, leaning forward into his face. "Have you considered that?"

"And has Atkins told you what the larger mission is?" he asked.

I smarted when I realized I didn't have an answer. Smith took advantage of my silence.

"You've turned into a soldier, now, Jane. You follow orders. You do what you're told. You don't even mind if it requires doing things you don't want mom and dad finding out about. But you're not in the same war as the rest of us. Holding a line? Taking a ridge? All that makes brutal sense because it's easy to understand. That's why we demand obedience from soldiers on the front. We only need them to reason in a limited capacity. If we can march toward Germany, that's winning."

"You don't think I should exhibit such obedience to my superiors?" I asked.

"What is your Berlin? I know Atkins might have one for you, but I'd think he would need your judgment, not just compliance, to get there."

Some days, I considered Smith a friend. On others, he played devil's advocate, and despite his apparently well-meant intentions, I'd never found believing him totally comfortable.

"Why are you so eager to sow doubt about Atkins?" I asked. "Are you trying to alter my allegiance? You think my closeness with Marcus, combined with some foul play by the lieutenant, is enough to make me all but American, don't you?"

Smith leaned his head back to rest on the wall.

"Aw, come on, Jane. Can't you just see yourself in a nice house on the California coast? It's come a long way out there. Beautiful climate. Motion pictures. Walks on the beach."

I peered at him. He was mocking me. I had thrust my sword, and found nothing but air.

"What do you really want, then, Smith?"

He sobered to display his rare sincerity. Was it performative or sincere?

"I don't know, Jane. But when Dupont, Atkins, and I first got together, it wasn't like this."

"What was it like?"

We paused and watched a motorbike drive by before he continued.

"We were all just sniffing out a lead. Mustermann contacted us. We'd heard something about magic, and we all pretended we didn't believe it. But our objective was simple. Learn more, like Lewis and Clark on the magical wartime frontier."

I knit my eyebrows.

"But you don't think Atkins is doing that anymore?" I asked.

Smith smiled.

"It's not hard to spot a man with an agenda. Trouble is, if he's escalating things, I have to as well. I'm under orders."

"What orders?"

"Orders that change whether I'm willing to wager a magical artifact to get back a young pilot. That's my whole point. Atkins should not be comfortable with that wager, but he's playing like he is, which means he knows something we don't."

"What's that?"

Smith sighed, and his shoulders sunk.

"I was hoping you could tell me." He turned and kept walking toward the barracks.

I hurried to catch up to him.

"How am I supposed to know anything about Atkins's intentions?" I stammered.

"He didn't clue you in on anything? I'm sure he talks to you differently than he does to me. Come on. Let's talk our way through it and see if we can't get to the bottom of something."

I scrunched my nose and remembered our conversation in Baldonnel. He'd been so worried about my camaraderie with Smith, that I'd hardly thought to examine what he said.

"He's worried about the Irish," I said.

"That's a start," Smith replied as he stepped over a wet pot hole in the cobblestone road. "And he's connected the Irish with the artifacts...."

"Because the Brotherhood is working with Dowling and the Blue Flyer to smuggle them into the country."

Smith grunted.

"So we assume. But we've only seen the Irish with one such device—the one that you confiscated. And the magic in that one died away faster than a hangover."

We were getting close to the barracks now. I stuffed my hand into my pocket and gripped the ring tightly in my fist the way I used to do with my glass marble. It didn't have the same calming effect. If anything, it reminded me of how little I knew about magic, and how large and dangerous a thing it could be.

"But surely they could have more." I thought of all the wisps of magic trailing over the Irish Sea when I wore Boelcke's goggles. "There are other magical objects in the world."

"That may be," he replied, "but no one seems to be fighting over the other ones right now."

We had reached the barracks. Smith reached his hand out to receive the ring.

"What? You think I'm just going to give it to you?" I asked.

"You're a woman. You going to just waltz into the men's barracks and start rifling through their things?"

"Given that I'm certain I cannot fully trust you, it beats the alternative. But, wait. Let me explore your hypothetical. If the Irish don't have any artifacts, then what is to connect Atkins's assignment to track down the Blue Flyer with the Brotherhood?"

Smith stuck his hands in his pockets and stepped back to allow a pilot exiting the barracks to walk through our conversation.

"You mean other than the fact that the Flyer had some sort of relationship with them?" Smith asked.

"So either the Flyer is a lead he can use to track down the Brotherhood, or the Brotherhood is a lead to track down the Flyer."

"And seeing that Atkins has told us, repeatedly, he wants to kill the man, I think we can make some assumptions. You want to know my personal theory?" I had a feeling that Smith wasn't really asking, and I was about to hear it whether I wanted to or not. So, I nodded.

"I don't think Atkins really cares about the devices. I think he's trying to do exactly what you're doing. Bait the Flyer. And I think he's willing to sacrifice anything to get him."

"Sacrifice anything?" I asked.

"I know that's rich coming from me. After all, when you two first started out on this thing, I threatened you with execution if you spilled the secret behind our operation."

"So that's it? After all this talk you've settled back on, 'pick me because I care about Marcus and Atkins doesn't'?" I folded my arms in front of my chest.

"I'm not talking about Marcus," he replied.

"Then what?"

Smith just laughed.

"We've got a representative from a new era of German political leadership, who speaks for a group that may all but certainly take some form of power if Germany doesn't win the war. I know us Americans don't really understand the workings of European politics, but I'd think that's a relationship worth nurturing, don't you?"

"Mustermann," I muttered. "Have you heard from him?"

"No," said Smith, shaking his head. "Or Earnst. Or Lina. And I'm starting to worry. But what worries me more is that Atkins is not worried. He's too concerned about catching a single man who, so far, has had little impact on the big picture of the war."

My mind was fuzzing at the edges as I chased motives and evidentiary behavior around in circles. So what if Atkins was hell-bent on finding the Blue Flyer? Surely, that objective did not run so contrary to international diplomacy as Smith insinuated.

But I had to admit that I worried for Earnst and Lina, too. If they'd gone quiet, then they'd either been suspected, discovered, or worse.

"You think we should go find them?" I asked.

"What can I say? Maybe it's just my soft spot for democracy. But if there's a Democratic Party budding in Germany, I think my country has an interest in starting that relationship on a good footing. And anyway, it can only help the war effort. But, I'm not doing anything until we find Marcus."

Suspicion, doubt, and uncertainty swirled around in my gut. Smith's resolve to find Marcus still stirred my emotions.

"Why?"

"I made a promise to Lufbery. And though I can be a devil, my word means something to me."

I frowned.

"What about when you promised Marcus you would keep us safe? Did your word mean something then?

Smith smiled.

"I never promised him I'd protect him. I promised him I'd protect you. And when he was around, making sure you two didn't split up did just that. Since he's left... Well, you're still here aren't you?"

He held out his hand again, and haltingly, I handed the ring over. He nodded and ducked inside the barracks.

"Is our trap set, then?" asked Atkins when we returned to the aerodrome's intelligence office. We were tucked in a room branching off the base's main reconnaissance operations so as not to interfere with crucial war correspondence. Dupont leaned back in his chair behind a small desk in the room.

"Sure is," said Smith. "Now, we wait."

"Wait for what?" Dupont asked with a sigh. "You really expect the Flyer will waltz into camp and try to steal it?"

They all looked at me.

I shrugged.

"That's what happened last time. It was a larger aerodrome, granted, but if the Flyer wants the device, I don't see how else he would plan on getting it. In any event, he shouldn't be expecting a trap. That's why we chose to hide the ring in Dawson's barracks. What could be more natural than Little's good friend taking custody of his property?"

"And how long do you think it will take?" Atkins asked.

"That's impossible to say. We will need to give it at least enough time for the Flyer to find the trail and follow it here. Little only died a couple of days ago," I said.

"And you British folk don't announce things about your pilots in the paper very well, so we have to let the gossip wagon make its slow progress," said Smith.

"Has Dawson seen you yet?" Atkins asked.

"Fortunately not," Dupont replied. "But it's only a matter of time. Neoux-les-Auxi is not very large."

"Well, at least one of us will have to stay here on base at all times, in case the Flyer comes calling. There is an old inn nearby the rest of us can use to stay out of sight," said Atkins.

"I'll keep first watch," I said. "We can rotate every 12 hours."

Atkins picked at a bit of congealed grime on the desk. It seemed as though he was making careful, silent calculations, or was that just Smith's mistrust informing my judgment?

"Yes, I'll take second watch," he replied.

"Why not go by twos?" Smith asked. "I'll stay with her first."

"Twos?" asked Atkins sharply.

"Yeah. Come on. These types of things are always done better in twos. What if something happens to one of us? Besides, what good are three of us twiddling our thumbs in an inn down the road?"

"I suppose you're right. But then why don't I stay with Private Doe, and you and Dupont relieve us next?"

"What? And forfeit a British presence at all times? Now you've truly lost it, old boy," said Smith, mocking Atkins's pronounced accent.

Smith had maneuvered well, and Atkins had no real grounds to object other than outright suspicion.

"Come on, Atkins," Dupont said, standing up. "That means we get first choice of whatever is left of the inn's wine cellar."

By the time they left, it was early afternoon, and without much better to do than comb through incoming telegraphs and phone calls, we resorted to playing cards, second-guessing our plan, and trying not to think about what had happened to Marcus.

After a particularly boring round of whist, Smith looked out the window and whistled.

"Dawson's back. And he's angry."

"What?" I scurried to the window. Dawson stomped in the direction of the aerodrome headquarters. "It looks like he's coming from the barracks. Did you hide the ring in his things?"

"I'm not a moron," Smith shot back. "We didn't want him to find it. I left it in a drawer across the room."

"Well, what if he found it?"

He disappeared into the headquarters, but reemerged quickly to stalk in our direction.

"Those idiots!" I shouted. "Did they tell him we were here?"

"There goes any authority Atkins had. Quick, is there a place to hide in here?"

We glanced around the room. It had a pair of chairs. A table that doubled as a desk and a few bookshelves standing against the walls.

"We can't exactly run for it, either. He's too close," I said.

"Yeah, these lightweights would tell him where we went, anyway. Damn it. We're on his turf now. Strap in. This'll be fun."

It was not fun.

"What in hell's name do you think you're doing?" Dawson was shouting before he'd even entered the room. Sheepishly, Smith and I stood behind the table.

"Captain Dawson," Smith started.

"What is this doing here?"

He held up the ring.

I yammered inaudibly as I tried to invent some excuse. Suddenly, I wished we had let Atkins take first watch.

"Are you two having a go at me? Does Command think I'm unfit to fly? Trying to make me looney?"

"No. It's not like that, Dawson,"said Smith.

He stuck his finger in Smith's chest.

"I knew that rubbish you spewed about an affair was tripe. Unless you're trying to implicate me in it now. What kind of sadistic bums are you? I want nothing to do with this. You insisted on having it—"

"We can't tell you what it's all about," I cut in. "We should have said that in the first place. It's secret. That ring must be kept secret."

"What national importance could this ring have?" he asked with a hard slant on his mouth.

"You don't understand the word secret very well, do you?" I countered. "Really? In this complex, confusing war, you can't imagine a single reason military command, an organization with its fingers in everything from air combat to espionage, might have plans for a ring carried by one of its leading aces?"

Dawson stepped back in confusion. I could tell he hadn't expected me to go after him like that. What had he said? He didn't involve himself much with women? I wondered if I could use my gender to my advantage. I stepped closer.

"You might be a good pilot, but you lack cleverness, don't you?

We need this ring. We needed this ring where we left it. And you have interfered with our mission."

He didn't like my scolding or my proximity.

"Well why do I have to be involved?" he complained.

"You didn't," said Smith, cutting in. "We were trying to keep you well in the dark."

"I don't like it," he said, finding courage again when he turned to Smith. "And I don't like how you're already spreading news about Robert's death. Don't pretend it's not you saying it. It's already all over the line, and nothing has been announced yet. His widow will find out through the gossip train first at this rate heaven knows it travels faster than the mail."

"Well," Smith took a big breath and puffed his chest up, "if you'd have just left the ring alone and not gone rummaging around in the—"

I held up a hand.

"What did you say?"

"Nothing," said Smith. "I was about to give this man a tongue lashing he wouldn't—"

"Not you, Smith. Dawson."

Dawson stared at me dumbly. The ring hung in his hand by his side.

"I said I don't like you gossiping about my friend's death."

"We've done no such thing," I said. I peered at his hand. "Where did you find that, may I ask?"

He knit his eyebrows again, trying to rouse his discontent amidst my disarming questions.

"Sitting out right on my pillow, taunting me the way you planned. Now, you both say you wanted to keep me out of whatever it is you're doing, but—"

"Jane," Smith cut him off and whirled toward me. "The goggles."

I jolted for my bag in the corner of the room and pulled out

Boelcke's goggles. Smith grabbed the ring from Dawson and put it down carefully on the table for me to examine it. I had the goggles on before I'd even turned back around.

The ring was matte and dull, not a glow to be found. But that was no surprise. The ring on the table looked only vaguely like it had before.

"It's not the ring," I gasped.

"How is that possible? We only planted it a couple of hours ago!"

I picked it up and ran my fingernail across it. Cheap metallic paint scraped off in chips, revealing wood beneath.

"It's not even metal. You couldn't tell it was a different ring?" I cried at Dawson.

"I hardly had a chance to look at the thing before you stole it from my bag!" he protested.

"But if that's a duplicate, the other must still be in the chest," said Smith.

"He's already got it," I gasped. The air was rushing out of my lungs. My legs were losing strength. That ring was my only path to Marcus. Our plan was slipping through my fingers. "The Flyer is here."

I raced out of the building, searching everywhere through the goggles. But I didn't need them.

Across the aerodrome the propellor on a old single-seater buzzed to life on the long grass field. The pilot and mechanic chasing after it only confirmed my suspicions that it was being stolen.

This was Clairmarias all over again. And the last time we'd chased him, it nearly killed us. I swallowed a tightening knot in my throat.

"Smith," I shouted. "We're going to need a plane."

Chapter 22
Bound by Violence
Marcus

The other men had questions. I had very few answers.

Truth be told, I didn't know anything about Little's death except that it had happened some time in the night, and apparently they hadn't discovered the body yet.

Bowman took the news stoically, but I recognized a brave face at work. Hearing about our heroes going down was different from hearing about our friends. It punched us right in the gut, or wherever the last vestiges of hope lived within us. Hope that our boys could get the job done, and we'd win the war. But deeper, in a more careful hiding place, it punched the hope that we might outlive the odds stacked against us and one day go home.

As the men peppered me for details, I noticed Bowman narrow his eyes in my direction. Maybe he'd started to question why he found me in his mess. I was, after all, a total stranger, wearing a dress uniform, asking to hear stories without invitation, bearing sensational news, and possessing very few details about what I'd proclaimed to come to share.

He likely suspected me a spy.

After a few minutes, when it was clear I had no further information, he chased the men off to perform their daily duties of checking planes, getting sleep, manning alerts, loading their ammo drums, or testing sight adjustments on their machine guns.

The mechanical repetition of the squadron bewildered me. The men here walked differently, as if exhaustion were a part of their bones now.

They looked more like the men I'd known in the trenches.

I hadn't forgotten my assignment, but Bowman's story about Werner Voss had distracted me easily. I relived the tale in my mind over and over again. Dieter and Harry had hinted that they'd already tracked down a magical device linked to the German ace. I wondered what it might be.

When it came to magic, Boelcke's goggles were very useful. Richthofen's scarf was deadly. I wondered, what magical effect would Germany's third great aviator leave behind?

If I wanted to know, I'd have to show them I could be trusted.

Bowman sat a few tables over from me, and he appeared to be sizing me up out of the corner of his eye. I approached him carefully.

"Sir," I started. He grunted. "I was wondering if you could tell me more about Little."

If he'd suspected me to be a spy before, this would really push the envelope.

"I hardly knew him," he said with a shrug and went back to his breakfast.

"But do you know where his unit was stationed?" I asked.

He put down a piece of bread and squinted at me.

"Shouldn't you know that already?"

I took in a deep breath.

"No, sir. I'm all turned around. You know how things happen out there, sometimes. My plane went down near the front, and I managed to crawl to an infantry post. The man there sheltered me for a day or two until we got the news about Little. They put me a in a uniform and told me to hurry the information along back up the lines."

"Why didn't they just call it in?" Bowman asked.

I bit my lip.

"Phone lines were destroyed by an artillery barrage." The crease between his eyebrows softened ever so slightly, so I decided to push there. "Have you ever been in an artillery barrage before, Captain?"

He shook his head and looked at the table solemnly.

"I have not. Only heard the stories."

Once, near the beginning of the war, when I was still driving ambulances, an artillery barrage had claimed my entire unit at the front. I'd blamed myself for their fate because I'd shown mercy to a lost German spotter the night before.

It took one well-aimed shell to annihilate those men. One. They had fired millions of shells since then, a never-ending downpour, thousands at a time, over and over for hours on end.

"It's hell, sir," I said before blinking the dark thoughts away. "I'm trying to collect information so I can keep moving this news down the line and find my way back to my squadron."

Bowman put his elbows on the table and breathed deeply.

"Of the man, I don't know much. They said he had a family and a wife back in Australia. He was with the 203 over by Beaupré-sur-la-Lys. They've been flying missions across the lines here all month, just as we have. The only reason his death is a surprise is because he was so good. You think we'd stop being surprised by now."

His platitude hit me hard, but not because of Little. I shouldn't have been surprised Luf went down. I shouldn't be angry at him for something out of his control either.

But with him went a piece of a secret future I'd imagined, one where we worked together still, fixing up planes and flying them without fear of machine gun fire. His death brought out the stupidity of that dream.

Was I mad at him or mad at myself for believing we'd both make it home?

I shook my head and racked my brain trying to figure out what other type of information Dieter and Harry might want to know.

"Do you know what he flew?"

"Not for sure, but I imagine a Camel. All those RNAS men brought them over when they combined with the RAF."

I nodded.

"And do you know what his score was, by chance?"

Bowman's eyebrows went up as he considered.

"More than me," he said. "And I have more than a handful."

"Can you give me a number, though?" I asked.

"At least forty," said the captain.

Suddenly, movement at the corner of the tent caught my attention. Harry stood outside the mess motioning to me. He wore a mechanic's uniform and grease covered a good portion of his face.

"I appreciate it, captain. I'll leave you to it."

Bowman swiveled on his seat as I started to leave.

"Where are you going?" he asked.

"Just thought I'd stretch my legs before checking with your intelligence office to see if I could get in contact with my flight leader."

"And your flight leader is?"

"Smith. Sergeant Smith. American, sir."

I didn't wait to be dismissed, and I could feel Bowman's gaze burning a hole in my back. He hadn't lived this long out here by being gullible.

Harry paced nervously outside.

"What is it?" I asked, as I pulled him away from Bowman's view.

"Ready to leave?" he asked. Suddenly, I noticed his eyes darting about, alert, and excited.

"Sure. Sooner the better. I think the captain in there is on to me."

"Did you learn anything?"

"Not much," I admitted.

"Well, don't worry. Dieter has found Little's artifact."

I screwed up my face in surprise.

"What? How? I thought he was heading back to—well, wherever it is you guys live."

Dieter waved me off.

"We had to tell you that so you'd come along without asking too many questions."

"But if you didn't think Little's device would be found here, why come here at all?"

"Because," he said grabbing me by the arm and ushering me across the aerodrome toward the hangars. "We needed something different, and it would have made too much of a splash had we taken them all from one place."

My heart started pounding.

"Harry, please tell me we're not stealing a plane."

We weren't stealing a plane. We were stealing two of them. Harry grinned his way to the far side of the furthest structure in a line of Bessonneau hangars. The hangars were made of canvas, like large domed tunnels that made for easy ingress and egress of aircraft.

The hangar we reached appeared to be sparsely trafficked, maybe used more for storage and planes that were being dissembled or in line for repairs.

In the corner sat two well-used poorly maintained DH 5s.

I gaped. The DH 5 was a workhorse for the RAF for a long time. But as often happened in the war, better German planes came along to render it all but obsolete. Now, the DH 5s were being phased out, and quickly, because the SE 5as that I'd already seen flying on and off the airfield that morning were vastly superior.

It didn't look like the planes in front of me had seen action in months, and they were both still pocked with bullet holes no one bothered to patch up.

"You've got to be kidding," I said. "Will these things even fly?"

"Don't worry about that. I've checked them out," he said.

"You're a mechanic now?" I asked as I walked forward to inspect the machines myself. A can of oil stood on a crate nearby, still dripping. Harry had applied it liberally under the hood, evidently in great haste, given how it dripped out the front of the rotary engine. But flying planes wasn't a tidy business, anyway. I'd inhaled my fair share of oil during my hours airborne.

"I've fixed up a plane or two." He folded his arms and smirked, and I couldn't help but give him the benefit of the doubt. I had no reason to believe that Dieter and Harry worked with anybody else. And if that were the case, they'd be the ones maintaining the various planes that soldiers up and down the Western Front had reported engaging with their aircraft.

Given that those mysterious planes came from both sides of the war, he was probably a better mechanic than I was.

Maybe that was part of the secret of their transforming aircraft—some magical component to the mechanical structure.

"So what? We just hop in these DH 5s and fly away?"

Harry nodded fervently.

"Yes, and quickly."

"What's the rush?" I ran my hand along the slanted wing struts.

"It is very possible that Dieter may have pursuers. He had to act quickly, and our usual stealth was not possible."

I dropped my hand.

"Wait. You want to intercept planes with these old birds?"

"Well—I'm not saying—"

"We're definitely not outrunning anything with them! So that leads me to believe that you intend to fly up into the air, wait for Dieter to come back and then intercept any Allied planes that are chasing him."

Harry crossed to me quickly.

"You're an excellent pilot. It will be fine."

"Yeah, except that I've never shot down a plane before!"

"You shot *one* down."

"That was different. For one, it was a desperate shot into the blinding sun. Second, I went animalistic because Jane was wounded in the gunner's bay. It's a totally different thing to engage Allied planes for your sake. I'm not going to turn my guns on British, French, or American pilots."

"Oh, come on." Harry pursed his lips and kicked the plane's wheel. "What difference does it make?"

"All the difference in the world," I said.

"You're lying to yourself about this."

"I'm not. I made a promise to fight for the French. Then when the US entered the war, I promised to fight for my own nation. My allegiance is to the alliance."

"But you broke your promise and left. Is it because I'm not as beautiful as Jane? Is that why you have qualms now? I could put on some lipstick if that would help."

I set my jaw. He had struck the wrong chord.

"You can shut your mouth now."

But despite my tone of voice, he merely rolled his eyes.

"Is your commitment to your nation or to peace? I know where mine is. And frankly, the Triple Entente, so poetically self-titled, has done very little peacemaking and very much butchery. If you think that shooting down planes with an Allied cocarde is any different from shooting down the brightly colored German machines, you're simply wrong. It's all war."

I could not fault his point. Although the Germans had started the war, we'd matched them shell for shell. And while I didn't believe Germany would be content with whatever land it had grabbed already, maybe that was partly our fault. Maybe everyone was in too deep now to stop.

Still, shooting down my own boys... I folded my arms.

"You're not going to convince me on this one," I said.

Harry's eyes and shoulders fell together. His smile faded, and I could almost swear that I'd wounded him with my rejection.

"Then we part ways?" he asked.

"If the only way to go with you is to shoot down my own men, then yes."

"And Dieter? What if he's being pursued? What if he is shot down and your armies recover the device? Will they use the magic for peace?"

I twisted my feet in the dirt, trying to forget how quickly Atkins, Smith, and DuPont had rushed Ball's violin strings and Boelcke's goggles away from Jane and me to perform who knew what kinds of experiments on them. If the magic had any military application, I was certain the Allies would take advantage of it.

Since I couldn't refute what Harry said, I stayed silent. After a moment, he sighed and held out his hand. So this was parting. I shook it.

He stared at the handshake in shock.

"Well, that was, quite nice, I suppose. Now the other thing." His hand hung between us in the air.

"What other thing?"

"If we part, I must take your marble."

I froze. Amidst our growing camaraderie, I'd nearly forgotten that behind the smiles and pleasant conversation, I wore something they wanted badly.

"Why?" I asked.

"If we are parting, I owe you no explanations."

Now it was my turn to feel hurt.

"Come on, Harry. Don't be like that."

"I'm no fool," he said. "I know that you didn't come with me in Dublin because you believe whole-heartedly in the Irish cause. You have been collecting information from us. You were playing a little spy game. That's what you thought, but you've been lying to yourself."

I stared hard, wondering how long he'd seen through me. I supposed I hadn't been shy about my allegiance. But he saw through me in a whole different way, too.

"Yes," he went on, "you'd like to think you nobly carried on your mission. You wanted to prove a point, but not for your superiors. You did it for her. You left her to show her that you were worthy of her."

"You don't know what you're talking about," I growled, but his comments made me burn with embarrassment. He sighed.

"I like you, Marcus—a surprising amount. I'll admit that. I like you enough that your duplicitous plans hurt more than I wanted them to. I don't want you to go back. It kills me to force the marble from you like this. But we're trying to do something important, and we need the marble for it."

My throat began to hurt. Tears built up behind my eyes, catching me totally unprepared. I didn't realize how much I'd come to care for him in so little time. I'd mapped a lot of my grief for Luf's loss, then Cillian's, into this man.

But tears aside, how could I hand it over? It'd be like handing over the last piece of Jane I had—the real Jane.

"I can't give it to you."

Harry took a steadying breath.

"Then I will have to take it. Or, you can come with us. But time is running out. So make your decision."

My eyes darted about wildly from the DH 5s to the opening at the front of the hangar. I could go back to Jane, back to Smith, and we could fight again. But if I'd given up the marble, and the Blue Flyers retrieved Little's device, what did that mean? What were they planning? And could I fight against their plans if, deep down, I believed in their purpose of peace?

"What if I go up but don't shoot at anyone?" I stuttered.

Harry cocked his head to the side, pitying my naivety.

"You know it doesn't work that way. As soon as we're engaged, you'll be forced to defend yourself."

"I can pull out of the fight. Pilots do that all the time."

"And where will you go? Back to an Allied airfield leaving us to battle your friends alone? That would be the same as leaving us. And we'd have to chase after you."

Harry's hand hung in the air still, outstretched and final.

"Make no mistake, Marcus. This is a crossroads, and it is time you choose."

I paced away, assessing the planes again, trying to stall for time.

His proposal was fair on the surface, at least more fair than the choices Smith had offered us. I could walk away without further questions, completely safe. It would cost only the marble.

And because of that price tag, it was no decision at all.

But maybe I could hedge my bet somehow. I stared at the oil on my fingers, and a desperate idea struck me. My eyes flicked to the wooden table, and I traced my finger on it as I thought, trying to mask my action from Harry.

"Well?" he asked.

"Flight suits?" I asked, my voice hollow.

"Here." He had pulled two out from an old crate. They looked musty, tattered, and holed. One had a bloodstain on the leg. We suited up in silence, and when we'd finished dressing, Harry slapped me on the shoulders and embraced me.

"I'm glad you're coming with me," he said, putting his forehead to mine. I squeezed him back and tried to grapple with the competing tides of guilt swaying me back and forth. Tears streaked my face.

Harry pulled me back.

"I'm sorry it's hard. I wish we'd met outside of the war where things greater than us would not interfere with our friendship. You understand, don't you?"

I nodded. Oh, I understood all right. That was the burden every warrior carried. That was the real fatigue of war, that at all times, in all things, you had to put your heart in the gunner's seat and let reason fly the plane.

"Tell me it'll be worth it, Harry," I said. He slapped my cheek gently and smiled.

"Come on, pilot."

I climbed into the cockpit of my aircraft, and Harry took me through the startup. He managed his own through some deft maneuvers and rope he'd rigged to his chocks to avoid the plane from rolling out prematurely.

When the engines sputtered on and the props hummed to life, I braced for what must be coming next.

Mechanics. Pilots. Personnel.

From outside, I saw them turn our way in surprise and approach the hangar at a run. Harry yanked his plane free first and started out through the opening.

He rattled off several rounds from his machine gun as he did so, and those headed our way dove for cover.

I followed behind him tightly. Getting into the air would be tricky now, and we would certainly be followed up. We opened the engine early, bumping recklessly across the aerodrome common area, building speed well before we reached the field serving as an airstrip. We sped under communications lines, cables and wires that were deadly for takeoffs and landings.

Finally, amidst shouts from all directions, we reached our straightaway, and in moments we'd built enough speed to get airborne.

My heart plummeted to my feet as my stomach performed its familiar dance to the sound of whooshing air.

We'd hunted the Blue Flyers. We'd found the Blue Flyers.

And now, I was a Blue Flyer.

Chapter 23
Dark Choices
Jane

A lonely impulse of delight
Drove to this tumult in the clouds;
I balanced all; brought all to mind,
The years to come seemed waste of breath,
A waste of breath the years behind
In balance with this life, this death.
-WB Yeats-

My lungs burned, and I liked it. By now, sitting in the gunner's seat of a two-seater aircraft high above the world resonated with a deep, primal, hunting instinct that had lain dormant inside me for a long time. Here, in this seat, I had power, potential, and catastrophic risk. The spirit of women deep in my ancestral line, hunters and warriors, inhabited my movements.

It intoxicated me.

I craned my neck around to see forward. Our Brisfit's design had rectified many of the problems Marcus and I experienced in a Salmson. Namely, my gunner's bay was situated much closer to

Smith than it had been to Marcus, and it made communication significantly easier.

"Anything?" Smith called over the roaring wind. I squinted and found the speck of blue light we'd been following, and pointed.

"Steady on!" I cried.

It had not taken us long to get our plane in the air. Thankfully, Atkins had enough foresight to order the F2B readied at all times in the closest hangar available.

But even though we made good time, the Flyer had already achieved a significant lead. He'd stolen a DH 5. It wasn't the fastest plane in the air. And the Brisfit performed at its best at lower altitudes, so we had a slight advantage. But he was climbing, and if he managed to get up high enough, there was no way we'd catch him.

"Woah," called Smith.

"What is it?"

"He leveled out."

The air velocity pushed against me as I looked forward, but I noticed it as well. We were too far off to gauge the angle of the plane, but our position appeared to be rising relative to his. A dark dread budded in my stomach as I remembered when he'd flipped around to face us at Clairmarais. He'd nearly blown us to bits.

But I had learned much since then and had faced him once more already. This time, I'd be prepared. I wouldn't waste my ammunition, and we were in a superior aircraft to the Salmson.

"We better ease off, too," Smith shouted.

"What? Why? We could get vertical superiority!"

Smith twisted his head to look at me before shaking it back and forth.

"We're not engaging this guy unless absolutely necessary."

"Why not?"

"Because one, he could kill us. But more importantly, if we kill him, we'll never find out where Marcus is."

Mention of Marcus's name cut through my adrenaline like a hot knife. Of course, Smith was right. That was the point of this. Not revenge. We were here for Marcus.

That I'd forgotten that, even for a moment, terrified me.

"We just gotta make sure they know it, too," said Smith as he gestured roughly behind us with his thumb. I turned and noticed two Allied planes to our rear.

"Backup?" I asked.

"Probably Dupont and Atkins, if I were a betting man."

I whipped around again.

"Dupont is a pilot, too?"

Smith's head bobbed from laughter.

"It's 1918. Doesn't take much to be a pilot these days. Whether he's good for anything up here is a different story."

I bit my lip. If Atkins were flying behind us, it was even more important that we not stall the Flyer long enough for an engagement. Although we had the upper hand with three planes, Atkins would almost certainly want to shoot him down. He'd warned me as much.

"Don't let the Flyer see us," I said, reaching over to tap Smith's shoulder to make sure he heard me.

"Great. I'll just hide somewhere," he replied.

I rolled my eyes, but he edged off the throttle slightly, settling ourselves into an awkward position between our enemy running from us and our allies chasing us. We continued this way for some time before Smith interrupted the irregular whooshing of the air around us with another shout.

"Bad news, Jane!"

"What now?" I asked.

"Unexpected visitors," he said pointing ahead. I squinted to see what he was talking about, but then I noticed them as well, two specks against a cloud as they climbed. Two planes headed directly toward the Blue Flyer in what looked like a route to intercept.

I wrung my hands as I considered the possibilities.

"Are those ours?" I asked.

"The flight office probably called in the stolen plane."

"They'll shoot him down, then!" I shouted.

"They'll try," Smith replied. "Can't let a spy take off with Allied aircraft."

"Even if they can't, they'll slow him down enough for Atkins and Dupont to get there."

Smith nodded. "Things are about to get violent whether we like it or not."

I bit my lip as I considered. An awful and exciting thought trickled into my mind.

"Unless, we engage them first."

Smith turned in surprise.

"Atkins and Dupont?"

I shook my head and pointed toward the specks off to our right. They were climbing, but for now we had advantage, and we could intercept them before they could shoot down the Flyer.

"Those are our own boys," Smith called back.

"We don't have to shoot them down. Once we exchange rounds, we can wave it off as a misunderstanding. That happens all the time, doesn't it, taking shots at allies on accident?"

"But this isn't an accident. What if something goes wrong and you kill one of them? One wrong bullet. That's all it takes, Jane. And talk all you want about being numb to shooting Germans, but you'll have to live with that one."

His protests were true and good, and I could not believe I was so ready to discard them.

"Well, what plan do you have to get Marcus back?" I snapped. "If we engage these planes, Atkins and Dupont can follow the

Flyer. They're in SE 5As. They'll catch up quickly enough to see where the Flyer's going, but I'll bet not quickly enough to engage him outright. We can circle round and join them after."

Smith shook his head.

"This is dark, Jane. Even for me."

I remembered. In that farmhouse near Nancy, after Mustermann had murdered his own countryman to keep our mission safe and quiet, I'd all but thrown up. Smith had calmly eaten breakfast the next morning.

"I'm all ears if you have any better ideas, Smith."

He raised his hands in the air frantically to signal to the new planes. But at this distance, there was little to no chance of them seeing him. The angles were all wrong, and they wouldn't get better in time.

"It's sloppy, but it's a chance," I called.

He sighed and let go of the joystick to reach under his flight goggles and massage his eyes.

"I never thought I'd say this," he started, "but try not to hit anything!"

With the conspiracy hatched, our conversation died away. Smith veered our course to starboard to interrupt the vector of the climbing planes. As we got closer, I readied myself. All at once, the idea of purposefully missing another plane seemed infinitely more difficult than hitting one. I was overcome with the sensation that my bullets would strike true no matter what I did. Fate, now that the possibility of great evil waited, seemed to be stacked without compromise against my favor.

I decided it would make the most sense to fire from far off, both because it would pose less of a threat that I actually hit their plane and because it was believable at a distance that we might not recognize their markings.

But as we got closer, the outline of the two DH 5s was unmistakable. After all, we'd been chasing one since we took off.

Recognizing the model compounded the apprehension I'd been ignoring. Perhaps Smith was right. I didn't know if I had the stomach for it.

But already he was maneuvering himself above, trying to cloak our plane in the sun for a convincing dive towards their position. In minutes, we'd engage them.

My heart pounded in my ears—nothing else was audible over the airstream. I turned back toward the Blue Flyer and saw the glow beckoning to me from across the skies. In some ways, now that I'd seen the birth of the artifact, the glow seemed more personal, and it hurt the more to watch it get away. I could only hope that I had judged Atkins rightly, and he would hold course, seeing the distant plane and recognizing it was what we'd been chasing.

As the panic set in, I nearly reached out to Smith to call the whole thing off, but then I remembered.

Without the Flyer, I had no path to Marcus. We'd kept him in the dark. In Dublin, I was the one who started and set off the events leading up to his capture. I'd promised him I wouldn't let the darkness take me.

I loved him. And I let him down. Now, I'd do anything to make it right.

"Guns at the ready," Smith shouted. Then, he turned the plane over, and we dove. My stomach rushed to my throat, but I recalled my plan, and let off a burst early, wild, and wide.

The two planes responded in a flash, symmetrically, splitting formation into two sweeping wide lateral arcs, a move designed to force pursuers to choose one target. Had we been a true enemy, chasing one plane would have opened us to counter fire from the other. But we weren't a real enemy. We were only putting on a show.

Smith pulled up our nose and used the velocity from our dive to climb quickly, before turning us over. I rattled off more rounds, again without any accuracy, but I kept on the trigger as if to communicate we were serious, until finally stopping abruptly.

"You think that was clear enough?" I called to Smith. Hopefully, the rate and frequency of my firing communicated that we thought we'd seen an enemy but recognized now that they were friends.

Either that or I'd made it sound like our gun jammed suddenly.

I stuck a gloved hand in the air and waved it back and forth, trying to signal to the DH 5s that we were, in fact, friendlies. We'd managed to interrupt their climb well enough. It should have given the Flyer enough of a head start to avoid their engagement.

But as we evened out, the worst happened.

One of the DH 5s turned its nose on us, and though my gun lay silent, rounds roared through the air.

Smith jerked us back and forth.

"I told you this was a bad idea!" he shouted before barreling us over into a slip slide.

It had been some time since someone shot at me in the air. That would have been our escape from Ghent, and that seemed a lifetime prior. The zips punctuating the rushing wind around me shredded my bravery. I tucked my head deep into the gunner's bay as we fell, stomach lurching, arms weightless.

Smith rolled us out of the slide and banked into a turn.

"Why are they shooting at us?" I cried.

"You shot at them first," called Smith.

"Yes, but that was a mistake."

"You're damn right it was!"

More pops hammered from behind as one of the DH 5s came up on our tail. Smith flattened out and feigned a roll to our left before climbing upwards in a corkscrew.

My heart raced, but I managed, somehow, to keep from devolving into panic. This was not my first sortie, anymore. And amidst the nerves and fear, I discovered a new equilibrium, a frontier I'd never dared enter—the combat mind.

I waved my hand up again at our pursuers, trying to signal that we were allies, even going so far as to point toward the red-centered cocarde on our wings. But nothing worked.

The staccato rips from their machine guns belched in our direction all the same.

"Any ideas?" I shouted.

"Not many. Are Atkins and Dupont taking the bait?"

I peeked above the edge of the fuselage, trying to get my bearings. Smith's flying had my sense of direction distorted, but after a moment, I caught the magical blue glimmer of the Flyer getting away from us, and from that, I traced backward to our friends.

"No!" I pounded a fist on the fuselage.

"What?"

"They're coming toward us! The Flyer is getting away."

Smith didn't reply, but I sensed a change in the way he handled the plane. He pulled the nose around to point after the Blue Flyer in the distance and tried to climb.

He was going after him.

A zip and rip broke through my surprise with a bullet hole breaking into the wing fabric. Such a hit would not be lethal by any stretch, but it signaled a cold, dreadful truth. These other planes weren't giving up. One of us, if not more, would die today.

My intended distraction had gone horribly wrong.

I slipped my hand around the handle of the Lewis gun, testing its heft against my strength again. It sat mounted on a horizontal ring pointing backward, allowing me a fair range of motion. But our particular Brisfit also had a swiveling Foster-mounted gun above the wing that faced forward, allowing me, if I were brave enough to stand and shoot over the top wing, an option to fire both ways.

I shook my head back and forth violently, trying to clear my mind of what I considered. But as the rounds continued, and Smith's less exuberant maneuvering confirmed that he was prepared to risk chasing after the Blue Flyer at the cost of our lives, I had no other alternative.

I took hold of the gun, braced my feet firmly at the bottom of the bay, pushed down the tears threatening my eyes, and fired on the two English DH 5s.

Chapter 24
Marcus and Jane
Marcus

The two-seater must have noticed the commotion we made when we took off. Either that or it had a radio cable down at the time, and Bowman telegraphed them. We weren't in the air long at all before taking fire.

If I'd felt like a traitor when taking off, nothing freed me of the sensation now. After the first volley from the Allied plane—what now was an enemy plane—my stomach churned the same way it had when I watched Dieter's Albatross transform into a Nieuport on our flight back from Ghent. It was just wrong. Those were my planes. Good guys. Those were the silhouettes I searched for desperately in times of crisis.

Not anymore.

But then, when the gunner waved his arm in the air to signal a misfire, relief shot through my body. They didn't know we'd stolen our aircraft, after all. Maybe we could just slip away to rendezvous with Dieter without incident.

Harry had other ideas.

Maybe he knew something I didn't. Maybe he was buying his friend time, or he was trying to test me to see how committed I was to the decision I'd made on the ground. But by the time I recognized the other plane as a Bristol F2B, he'd opened fire.

All allegiances aside, I was not happy to be fighting against an F2B while I was busy flying a DH 5 for the first time.

Every plane had its nuances, and exploring these nuances was a fabulous way for pilots to get killed. I was the unlucky idiot apparently doomed to face every new treacherous air combat in some brand new machine.

The DH 5 had its top wing set immediately above and behind the cockpit, which gave me a view unlike any other plane I'd flown. But it didn't have the power of the SPAD or the Nieuport 28. I responded to my controls something like the Salmson I'd flown Jane around in, but without the benefit of a backseat gunner.

Harry hardly cared one way or the other. Maybe he was expecting me to jump right into the fray beside him. My molars ground against one another as I stretched into a wide banking turn, splitting the F2B's attention. Despite what Harry told me in the hangar below, I did not plan on firing on an Allied aircraft.

The F2B followed me, leaving Harry plenty of opportunity to plague it from behind. I heard him firing from his tailing position, but for whatever reason, although the gunner of my pursuer rallied off shots, the pilot did not harass me the same way. I knew the plane had a Vickers mounted on the front, but no rounds came, despite my mediocre handling.

Could I live with this, if I played decoy while Harry shot down a two-seater? At least it wouldn't be my bullet to send anyone down. And if I survived and learned more about the magic, there was no telling how many lives I could save later. Harry and Dieter claimed they wanted to end the war, but they didn't seem to believe the pathway to peace was all that peaceful.

But that was combat logic. War logic.

What had Dieter called it? Hate magic.

Was that different from bargaining the lives of a couple of allied pilots in order to bring back information to Jane? Why not just call it a day, turn on Harry now, shoot him down, and fly home?

All at once, the F2B pulled off my tail. I jerked my head around in confusion, preparing for the pilot to spin and give his gunner a shot at me. But that didn't appear to be his plan at all. To my surprise, he looked like he was trying to escape the sortie, but he didn't have enough elevation to dive away effectively. Instead, he appeared to be climbing.

I scrunched up my brows and wondered. That was all but suicide. The F2B had no underside gun, and if it tried to clamber upwards in a fight like this, even the outdated DH 5 would put it away without a problem.

In the confusion, something Luf had told me came whispering through the wind. *Gather information before engaging.* This was especially true when what you saw seemed idiotic. Whenever possible, a wise pilot tried to take in the full picture before committing to a maneuver.

I took as deep a breath as the rushing air allowed me and relied on the trained sight I'd developed from my hours in a cockpit to survey the sky.

There, far off on the F2B's heading, was the small, almost indistinguishable outline of another plane. I couldn't make out the model or country from here. I doubted the F2B pilot could either. Why would it try to disengage us so desperately to head toward that plane?

I looked the other way and was surprised to see two more

machines. One had split off from his partner and headed in our direction. The other? It was crazy, but by the looks of it from my imperfect vantage point, it seemed like it was heading toward the same target the F2B was chasing.

But I couldn't worry too much about that. Harry was still flagging the two-seater, peppering it with shots, demonstrating no awareness that what looked like a Camel headed toward our fight.

And even if we were in English planes, that pilot would have no choice but to engage us if we were firing on a Brisfit.

To make it all worse, it was only a matter of time before Bowman's men mobilized and righted whatever sabotage Harry had inflicted on their machines to buy us time.

If we weren't careful, we'd be outnumbered very quickly, and I'd die a traitor in a stolen, battered clunker.

My hand reached toward my neck to pat the marble, hoping that it had some last magic to save me. But when my hand hit my chest where it lay beneath my flight uniform, pain seared through me. The marble felt hot as a coal. I'd never experienced that before. Did that mean the end was inevitable?

No. This would not be the end if I could do anything to help it. Allied plane or not, it had fired on us first, and we needed to escape.

I barreled over, curled up toward the Brisfit, and tested the guns on this old DH 5 for the first time.

The gun sang to life, and my rounds proved effective quickly. I saw a line of holes along one of the wings. The F2B banked to the left, and I pulled back on my joystick to sail past and find an advantage from above, but as I did, my marble weighed against my chest again, and the searing pain came back.

What was going on?

Harry had predicted the maneuver and let out his own volley against our opponent. A few of his shots struck the fuselage, and I saw the gunner spasm down into his bay. A sickening wave pulsed in my stomach. Was the gunner hit? Had I just contributed to the death of an Allied soldier?

Whatever had happened, it shook the pilot. The F2B started jerking erratically, abandoning course toward the plane in the distance. Its moves were desperate, pushing the plane beyond what I'd normally expect from a bird that large. And not only that, the front gun came to life.

Whatever had held the pilot back before, we'd removed the obstacle. He put himself on the offensive, cutting back, circling down, even slip sliding the big machine sideways to get a shot at us.

It was as though we'd angered a sleeping lion. And it was an awful moment for the Camel to catch up to us.

The Camel's first shots were wide and wild, fired off at a distance, the same way the F2B had done. Even in the heat of the moment, it irked me. It was bad flying, a waste of ammunition. Firing from that far off was a desperate move to be used as a last resort. The Camel must have been adamant about distracting us from the F2B.

And the F2B must have really wanted attention when it fired its first rounds.

That was strange.

I dove and used the speed to zoom climb into a renversement to change direction quickly and get a better angle at the Camel. My marble seared into my neck all the while, maddening my focus.

Then, I took fire from my right side. The F2B's gunner had popped back up and he fired now like an angry devil.

But it wasn't a man.

The gunner's flight cap was gone, and whipping in the airstream was a crop of hair that I knew all too well.

Jane.

My heart stopped. My body went limp. I wanted to vomit.

I'd fired on Jane.

How? This wasn't possible. Who was her pilot? What was she doing here?

But it was her, unmistakable now. I recognized the overly large flight suit, the way she braced herself as she fired. The sluggishness of the gun's swivel. I even marked her face more clearly, now, wearing Boelcke's goggles.

I wanted to cry. I wanted to pilot my plane directly into the ground to cover the shame that swallowed me whole. I had shot a damn Vickers gun right into her plane.

As I pieced it together, my marble cooled instantly. It had been warning me. The magic she'd used to make my marble was offended somehow, and desperately tried to prevent me from killing her.

What a thing magic was.

The Camel opened up its guns on me, and by instinct I slid out of the way. I didn't have the mental capacity to think about the sortie. My mind raced to understand. But there was no time to sort it out. The Camel dogged after me. The Brisfit—no, Jane— fired at me from the Lewis gun. But all I could think about was getting close enough to show her my face. Maybe she'd recognize me and stop.

Or was she mad that I'd left? I never had a chance to consult with her before going with Harry. Had Atkins or Smith or the whole war effort spoiled any sense of forgiveness or understanding I might have hoped for after leaving? That moment in Dublin, after the meeting went south, she was so relieved to learn I wasn't ready to abandon all to join the Irish. But, then I left...

I shuddered to imagine what such doubt could do to her heart when amplified by the soldier's frenzy that had already taken root there.

She fired, and I caught glimpses of her expression as I flew past. Her mouth was slack, her posture rigid, focused, and deadly.

She appeared just as I'd seen her when she was about to shoot up the checkpoint on our way out of Ghent, just as she had been when she'd shot Cillian.

She was the new Jane. Not the one I knew.

Out of the corner of my eye, I noticed Harry found a favorable position on the Camel and opened fire, but the pilot rolled over smoothly and veered off to the right. The Camel's design enabled exceptionally fast right turns, thanks to its rotary engine spinning clockwise. The pilot would favor turning right, and somehow, I was sure Harry counted on that.

The Camel evened out, but had failed to notice Harry changing course mid-maneuver. He slid into his left and was waiting for it—a perfect shot all lined up.

But right before he could release lead into the Camel's cockpit, the F2B came to life again, this time from slightly below. I looked down to see Jane standing in the cockpit, straining to pivot the top-mounted Lewis gun up toward Harry's DH 5. He had to abandon his position and swerve out, but not before taking a few shots in the tail wing.

I ripped off my goggles and flight cap. The airstream stung my eyes, but I refused to believe that Jane would want to shoot me down. If she could only see it was me.

I banked into a climbing corkscrew. It was a predictable movement, but I hoped that Harry would be interested in keeping me alive enough to keep the Camel off my tail for a minute. It took some shots at me as I climbed, but soon I was above it and the Brisfit, and they would have to take a steep angle to get a line on me. I flipped my plane on its back and swooped down on the two-seater, as close as I dared.

I watched as the pilot and Jane ducked low as I passed. On my exit route, Jane shot after me. I dipped my wings back and forth to evade her fire.

I used the momentum from the swoop to climb again,

achieving a higher altitude faster this time, and circling upward tightly, close enough to recognize her, hoping that she'd see me, too. But her attention was flagged by more of Harry's aggressive attack. I waited until he'd completed a pass, praying that her pilot was adept enough to keep them airborne. I swooped again, and the Brisfit broke right, pilot and Jane both ducking down.

It was a deadly and desperate pattern now, and every cycle would have diminishing odds of everyone staying alive. I climbed and swooped again, but this time, Jane was ready for me. Instead of ducking below, she bravely stood at the top-mounted Lewis gun and met me with a stream of fire. She aimed well, leading my charge, allowing me to fly into the rounds rather than chase me with them. I saw the streaking smoke of tracers poke up around me like firework trails. Holes punctured my wings, and a chilling blast shot through my veins.

She hadn't recognized me. My harebrained swooping idea had only hardened her resolve to shoot me down. To let her see me, I'd have to get directly beside her and fly synchronized with their plane.

I pushed my nose forward and dove below them before kicking down on one of my rudder pedals and banking into a wide sweep. This would be dangerous. The Camel would be after me, and Jane would have a perfect kill shot. If she pulled the trigger before she recognized me...

But my luck got only worse. Bowman's men were in the air now—two of them, flying SE 5As, vastly superior aircraft to the pieces of junk that Harry had scrounged up. In minutes, they'd join the fight.

I searched wildly for Harry. The approach of even greater firepower knocked my survival back into my first priority. So what if I got Jane to recognize me? What then? Would the three of us band together to shoot Harry down? Bowman's men would still attack. I had their squadron marking on my fuselage, there was no hiding that I was the pilot that stole one of their aircraft.

And the idea of shooting Harry down hurt me. Setting aside that I still had much to learn about his plan or that Dieter was still out there or that what they said about the Allied military machine had wormed its way into my personal beliefs, I simply liked him.

What would Luf do?

But then, the thought struck me hard.

Luf was gone, and all he'd left behind was a credo, a rapidly dying pool of pupils, and his memory.

I jammed the stick hard and crossed Harry's propellor to signal his attention before attempting a maneuver I hated: playing dead.

I waited for a burst of fire, not caring which plane had volleyed it, and jerked my controls awkwardly before flatlining into a glide.

This was often the telltale sign that a pilot had lost his faculties. Even if he wasn't dead, a plane forced out of a fight like this often counted as a victory if observers watched it go to ground. If we could fake a crash landing in a remote area, we had a chance at ditching our planes and disappearing into the landscape.

To my relief, the Camel did exactly what I'd hoped, and after a moment of gliding off, he pulled up and left me alone. I had an exit.

But I'd miscalculated, and hadn't paid close enough attention to the F2B's latest sweeping turn, and my glide took me right past its broadside.

The world slowed down as Jane came into my view.

Her gun was true, the fierce warrior blazed alive in her eyes, hair streaking behind her like fire in the wind. I had looked over just in time to see the muzzle of her gun light up. It flashed mercilessly. I didn't need to see the path of the tracer rounds. I didn't need to feel the rip of my plane's timber.

I wondered, vaguely, if her marble was searing hot somewhere, if she'd have known it was me if the marble hadn't been stolen. I was surprised to find that I'd reached my hand into my suit and yanked mine free of my neck.

I held it up as the sound of the engine sputtered and failed, smoke billowing and threatening engine fire.

Just as my plane dropped below her sight line, we locked eyes at last. But I saw nothing there. No hint of recognition. It was like staring into a machine.

A machine with one purpose.

Chapter 25
Strands of Fire
Jane

Cover him, cover him soon!
And with thick-set
Masses of memoried flowers—
Hide that red wet
Thing I must somehow forget.
-Ivor Gurney-

The wind stole my scream. It robbed all the air from my lungs. My sight darkened at the edges.

How could it be?

He floated there in my vision, suspended amidst the snakes of black smoke, oil streaking his face and matting his head, holding aloft the marble with my hair inside, a marble I'd begged my aunt Luella to fashion for us. It was meant to be a protection for him.

His face was not desperate or angry. His expression was calm, eyes gentle and at peace.

But I had—I had—

"Smith!" I screamed, finding my voice at last. "We have to go after that plane!"

"Are you crazy? He's down! We need to get out of here and head after that Blue Flyer. Let Dupont deal with the other DH 5."

"Marcus!" I choked out.

"I know! The Blue Flyer is our ticket to finding Marcus."

"No. That was Marcus! I shot down Marcus!" My resolve was failing as the emotional weight came crushing down on me. Every second was another second that Marcus's machine sped toward the Earth.

"What are you talking about, Jane?" Smith shouted as he twisted our plane sideways to evade incoming fire. "You're seeing things."

"I killed him, Smith! I killed him!"

"You're getting lightheaded. We've been doing these acrobatics for too long!"

"Smith! Turn the plane around."

We needed to catch up to him, to save him somehow. Maybe he could jump into our plane, share the gunner's bay with me. Something. Anything. But the weight of what had happened, what I'd done, was washing over me like a vast tide, smothering all. Making Smith understand seemed impossible. Everything seemed impossible. I couldn't even lift my arms.

"I can't do that, Jane," Smith called back to me. Smith banked us into a wide turn to correct our heading and continue our pursuit of the Blue Flyer. "I'll be damned if Atkins gets to the Flyer by himself."

But I hardly paid attention. As we rolled into the turn, I saw Marcus's plane below us. It had plummeted so far already. When a bright flash signaled the start of an engine fire, I didn't want to watch anymore, but I couldn't tear my eyes away. It seared downward through the air in a terrible strand of fire.

After everything we had done to find him, after the promise I'd made to him about keeping the darkness in check, he was gone. My Marcus, gone the way of Lufbery, down to the very same engine fire. I shook my head violently back and forth, trying to dislodge the thought of him burning alive in his cockpit. It was the fate every pilot feared most.

This must be a dream. A nightmare. A waking hallucination. Anything but true.

My mind lashed out against the idea, latching on instead to any other conscious distraction. I'd rather face the other DH 5 one on one. No. The DH 5 was holy to me now. It was Marcus's machine. No. I could not. Please. Anything. Any distraction. Please. It could not be.

"Jane, we've got big problems!" Smith shouted.

I didn't have strength to respond.

"I think the Flyer just shot down Atkins."

This. Was this distraction enough? I'd seen things. Smith was right. It was air sickness. I hallucinated. It could not have been Marcus. I needed the combat mind back. I needed it desperately. I needed the darkness to welcome me home.

I turned around to face our nose. Far in front of us, a plane was diving to the earth.

"How do you know it's not the Flyer?" I asked.

"Look, that's the silhouette of a Camel going down. It's totally different from the old DH 5 the Flyer ran off with. Shouldn't you be able to tell? Where are those goggles?"

I had pulled them down from my face after realizing who piloted the plane I'd just—

I pulled the goggles up now, and just as Smith had suggested, the plane trailing downward had no glow. The other plane, however, shined brighter than I'd yet seen.

A stream of rounds spat through the air to our right. There was still a DH 5 trying to kill us.

I turned and grabbed hold of my gun just in time to see him fly past, Dupont's Camel in pursuit. Below, for the first time, I noticed a group of planes rising to meet us, British models. They looked new and well-cared for.

"Uh, Jane?" Smith called.

"What now, Smith?" I asked.

"We don't need to chase down the Flyer anymore."

"What? Why? Is he falling, as well?" I swiveled again.

"No. He's headed our way."

Smith was right. The DH 5 in the distance was closing the space between us and quickly. The Blue Flyer had noticed us, just as he had in Clairmarais. And here I was quickly running out of ammunition. How long had we been flying now? The sortie had distorted my grasp of time. Our planes only had a maximum flight duration of two to three hours. But the types of maneuvers we relied on in a fight surely required more fuel.

Still, this was different. We had Dupont on our side, and if the planes beneath us had any brains at all, surely they must recognize what was happening and join us. At any rate, it wasn't as though there were many DH 5s in the air this close to the front anymore.

And now that I'd found Marcus, what use did I have for the Blue Flyer?

My rage intensified as I thought about it. It was his fault. Time and again, he'd threatened Marcus's life, and at long last he got what he'd wanted.

Let him come. If I could not be Marcus's protector, I would be his vengeance.

The idea tasted sweet, sickeningly so. Yes. It was his fault, him and his schemes, tricks, and thirst for violence. He had practically pulled my trigger.

He was still a way off, and the DH 5 that had been engaging us thus far, seemed to sense a change in the air. He fired less frequently. At first, I thought his gun might have jammed, but Boelcke's goggles would have shown me that. Perhaps his ammunition stores ran low. In any case, the momentum of the fight had shifted, and all the combatants knew it. The Blue Flyer raced toward us and brought with him the weight of magic.

I looked about and noticed that the SE 5As were circling us carefully, assessing the dogfight before deciding the best course of action. They did not fire on me, though, and surely they'd have noticed that our plane had one victory against an Allied model.

A victory?

The word nearly made me vomit.

"Jane, I know you didn't want to shoot this guy down," Smith called out, "but I need you to reconsider."

I checked the action on the two Lewis guns beside me. I had reconsidered, indeed.

The Blue Flyer was on us now. He had significant altitude, and he took no time taking advantage. He dove with unusually sharp speed, and I braced for the storm.

His guns roared to life. But I was ready. Smith tipped our nose up to face the rush and fired from his Vickers gun. I backed it up with rounds from the top-wing Lewis. The sky was a mess of tracers and hot lead. Neither scored any hits, though, and the Flyer raced straight past us. Dupont barreled and curled under to pursue him from behind, but the first DH 5 came back to life and forced him off.

Suddenly, understanding dawned.

They were allies. The two DH 5s were working together. And Marcus? Had he been one with them as well? Or had he been a prisoner?

My eyes went wide.

What if there were more than one Blue Flyer?

But how could that be? My goggles would have signaled the other, surely. And yet, if they were not in league, why did the DH 5 maneuver to protect the new combatant?

If there were two, there might be three. Four. Who knew how many?

The Blue Flyer flattened his dive and flew directly into the west-setting sun. We were blinded in watching him. I looked away to protect my sight.

The sun was the pilot's greatest friend and worst enemy, a hiding place for friend and foe. I did not want to be seeing spots when aiming our guns.

But the new DH 5 disappeared, then, and from the sun emerged a sparkling and deadly SE 5A.

My heart dropped.

"What just happened?" Smith yelled. "Where'd he go?"

But I knew what had happened. It was the same thing that had happened to Marcus and me when we thought we had safely escaped back to our lines after Ghent. Boelcke's goggles lit the new SE 5A up clearly.

The Blue Flyer had transformed planes again.

"That's him, Smith!" I pointed past his head

"That's not him. He's flying a DH 5!"

I didn't have the energy to argue. Carefully, I removed my goggles, wrapped them around my wrist for safety, and pressed them against Smith's eyes.

I expected Smith to shout, swear, blaspheme, something extreme. Instead, surprising words spilled from his mouth.

"Blessed are those who have not seen yet still believe."

"Smith?" I asked.

He pulled his head away from the goggles.

"I'm sorry, Jane. I'll do my best, but I'm sorry."

"Just get me close."

"I said that I'm sorry!" he repeated furiously.

"For what?" I stammered. He waved me off, and I leaned back in my bay. "For what?"

Now the fight was on in a whole different way. The Flyer had already shot down Atkins, and he entertained no pretense of deceiving the other SE 5As that waited to jump in the battle. He maneuvered like a devil out of hell, twisting to take a shot at the Camel, sliding to evade my volley, then barreling directly behind another SE 5A.

Getting a line on him was like grabbing at handfuls of water. Each time I thought I had a clear shot on him, he slipped from my sights.

And suddenly, we were taking damage. I didn't even notice when it happened, but as I looked out on our wings, irregularly shaped bullet holes bit into our canvas in staggered lines.

Up and down, side to side, bank to loop, the Flyer made a swimming pool of the air. His machine was magically enhanced. If he had magic sufficient to transform the model and intensify the armament, why not also supplement the engine and handling?

And if that were true, we stood very little chance at all.

I glanced about and noticed the other SE 5As shrinking from the attack. I couldn't blame them. I'd have been confused and unmotivated as well. They didn't know on whose side they needed to intervene. After all the DH 5—

Where was the DH 5? I glanced about, and far off I found it, quietly slipping away from the fray. I wanted to go after him, to signal to Smith, but the Blue Flyer made it impossible to do anything but attempt to survive.

Smith swarmed his controls. But just as Marcus had done against this opponent, his evasive maneuvers had cost us altitude. Our machine did not have the nimble turning or speed of climb that the Flyer did. Soon, I found myself serpentining back and forth all over again. Banking left. Banking right.

But the Flyer was right behind us now. And today, I had no marble to hold up and confuse him. I fired back at him, and he barreled loftily around my shots until my gun finally clicked.

My pan had run out. I had others, but not the time or cover to reload.

I saw the Flyer now, noted the aquiline nose. Behind his plane, Dupont's Camel bobbed, trying to catch up.

Then the Flyer's gun came alive, and I watched our tail wing disappear in fragments.

I expected him to continue firing, to annihilate us from the very Earth. That was what many great pilots did, after all. That's what my instincts had told me to do as of late. Ensure the kill. Don't let off until the pilot is dead.

But the Flyer had simply gauged the damage, and knew the job was done.

"Jane! Hang on to something!" Smith was screaming at me. I noticed the difference immediately. We had lost all balance, and the back of the plane pitched forward, tilting us into a terrible careening fall. My stomach lurched into my throat. I planted my feet firmly against the gunner's bay.

The ground rushed up toward us. Dupont flew uselessly nearby, following us to the end, vainly hoping to help.

The ground approached quickly. My thoughts cast about everywhere, and in the rush I didn't understand what should be flashing before my eyes. Why couldn't I think about my parents, remember their faces? Why couldn't I remember anything about my Aunt Luella, or Lufbery, or even Marcus?

The only thing I could see was the Blue Flyer's meditative face.

Smith shouted again, and somehow, he righted our angle.

Then, a wing came off.

Chapter 26
Atkins's Secret
Jane

The tree may grow it over,
The wind may blow away,
The stream smooths all the corners,
The mud cakes dry and flake.
Deny ye not how powerful
Is latent strength of mind,
For when it's scarred or wounded
It remembers for all time.
-Fissha-

We crashed in a field lined sparsely with trees. The impact jolted me so that I believed my leg was broken. The rim of the gunner's bay smashed against my shoulders and the palms of my hands, all of which were bruised awfully. My teeth had clattered together so violently that a tooth or two in the back of my mouth had chipped, and my head throbbed.

But I was alive.

I tried to call out Smith's name, but nothing came from my

mouth but a fit of painful coughs. The cloud of dust our impact had propelled skyward had not yet settled. It clouded my vision in all directions and made breathing a chore—or perhaps that was an injured lung.

My ears didn't work well either. Noise came dampened and muffled. Vaguely, the sound of a whirring propellor buzzed through both ears. Was our propellor still intact? Still on? Smith must have cut the power from the engine.

I moved my head gingerly, testing my neck, and saw a Sopwith Camel touch down roughly a hundred yards from our wreckage. A man scrambled from the cockpit in a fit. He fell to the ground and picked himself up before sprinting over.

"Jane! Smith!" He called to me in a thick French accent. Dupont. Of course it was Dupont. He flew the Camel. He yelled as he ran. "Are you there? Anyone?"

I tried to call out, but again, my voice failed me, so I raised an arm instead. I didn't get it high before the bruising in my shoulder shot rivers of pain through my body, forcing it back to my side, limp and useless.

"Jane!" The sound of relief in Dupont's voice nearly brought tears to my eyes. He rushed to my bay. "You're hurt."

I nodded and winced.

"We need to get you out of this thing. Can you move?"

I looked myself over, and suddenly, exiting the aircraft seemed to be of paramount importance. My mind seized on the idea that until I was free of the wreckage, I would not have survived our crash. I squirmed about, panicked even, as Dupont got hold of my shoulder.

I shouted in pain, clamping my teeth together.

"Sorry!" Dupont said as he adjusted his grip. One limb at a time, he helped me wriggle out of the misshapen seat. We fell to the ground, and rather than allow him to help me to my feet, I crawled away from the plane as though it were a lit bomb.

Then, grasping at his pant leg, I came apart. Painful hiccuping sobs wracked my chest. He put his arms around me and rocked me back and forth. I wished I could find solace in his compassion, but I wanted Marcus's arms. My body was in agony, but it was the broken heart that had torn me to pieces.

"I shot him," I croaked. My throat was aflame, but I needed to say the words aloud, to tell someone. "I shot him to the ground."

"You're in shock," Dupont said with maddening pity. I pushed away from him, gathering enough of myself to protest. They thought I was crazy. Perhaps they were correct.

"I shot him from the air!" I repeated. Then, suddenly, my mind jumped to a new fear. "Smith? Where is Smith?"

Dupont shook his head, and I knew where Smith was.

I turned back to the wreckage.

"Jane, no."

But I had to see for myself. I crawled around to the front of our plane. Our remaining wing had smashed against the earth and splintered half to pieces. Where the other wing ought to have been was just a jagged mess of wooden boards, clean as a bad butcher's apprentice quartering a bird.

At length, I reached the nose of our aircraft. Smith's eyes were not closed, but unblinking. He leaned rigidly against the side of the cockpit, his arms still reaching down toward the plane's controls.

"Smith," I whispered. But he did not respond, and he never would again. The American's light had gone out, and with it, everything paradoxical and beautiful about him.

I lay with my back on the ground and let grief overwhelm me. The combat mind had abandoned me. I had to claim what was mine. I caused Smith's death. It was my idea to go after the two planes to distract them, to protect the Flyer a bit longer. I had wagered other lives for a small possibility of Marcus's safe return.

Fate had made an absolute mockery of my concept of control.

Once, in a dark wood, Marcus had confided in me that the ghosts of his old platoon haunted him. He had blamed himself for their eradication because of his inaction, his mercy, on discovering a German spotter.

I had tried so desperately to comfort him, to speak peace to him, and to my surprise, he trusted me enough to let some comfort in.

But I had not known the first part of his grief, then. I did now. Had he shared that haunting story with me now, I don't know if ever I'd have found the strength to comfort him as I did. Now, I knew what it was.

Guilt. Blame. Regret. Devils with enough weight to bury you alive.

I would carry Marcus's guilt with me. The guilt he had carried for so long, the beautiful shame born from his compassionate act of mercy. I adopted the death of his platoon. I admitted his downfall. I claimed Smith's death.

And I feared what they would make of me.

Dupont did not disturb me as he watched from a safe distance, allowing me space and time to come to grips with what had happened. I never would.

After a time, the hum of an engine neared us, not that of a plane, but a car. A door opened.

"What has happened?" A sharp British voice cut through the air.

"Atkins," Dupont muttered. "You're alive."

"The devil, I am. Where is Smith? Where is Jane? I saw the crash from binoculars on the way here."

"You were forced down," Dupont stammered.

"But not out. I jumped from that ruddy Camel as soon as landing. Now, where are they?"

"Jane is there."

"Alive?"

"Mostly."

"And Smith?" Silence. "Damn it all."

I heard an entirely uncharacteristic shout from Atkins. He roared toward the heavens, without even the dignity of consolidating his emotions to human language.

"Why didn't you come with me?" Atkins's voice was sharp and accusatory.

"They were under attack," Dupont replied.

"Precious good you did to help them, I'd say."

"Jane is still alive."

"Mostly, you said! You let the Flyer get away from me. I was no match to joust with him, and you must have known that. We were this close to having him, Dupont. This close!"

"I was not about to abandon Jane and Smith so you could claim a prize."

"That's rich, isn't it? Yes. Come down on me, Dupont. You've fallen in love with her, haven't you?"

"Don't be ridiculous. She's a child. Was I in love with Smith, too? It's called loyalty. You should try it yourself some time."

"Remind me. At the farmhouse in Nancy. We were all there to investigate Mustermann's claims. What was your assignment? Assassination?"

I picked my head up and looked over. Dupont grabbed Atkins by the lapels.

"Did I shoot anyone? Or have I taken this as seriously as you insisted? This is your war."

"It's our war. It's the world's war. We were here to finish that thing's terrors!"

I could not listen quietly any longer. There was too much pain pent up within me. I needed a release somewhere.

"We were here to get Marcus back," I called. My voice rasped, undercutting the energy I intended, but it silenced Atkins all the same. "But you had other motives."

Smith's death had crystallized the theories he'd shared with me, his inherent distrust of Atkins. I found a peculiar bond between us now that he was gone. I considered it a duty to represent his point of view.

"Jane, you're in no condition to—"

"Did you want Marcus back?" I asked, leveling my gaze at him, dangerously. "Or was he the bait you used to lure me and my knowledge to whatever project you had in mind? Didn't you say it yourself? He had no particularly impressive qualifications."

Atkins appeared to have lost his fury.

"You've had a shock," he started again.

"I've had a clarification. No more lies, Atkins. No more hiding things one from another. You will answer."

Atkins looked dumbly at me, then Dupont and the wreckage. He fixated on Smith's lifeless form for many seconds before responding. When he did, he expelled the truth from his body like he wanted to be far away from it.

"It was never about the devices," he cried.

"What do you mean?" I asked.

"It was never about the devices, Jane. It was about the Flyer. And I think you've discovered why."

I set my jaw, ignoring the pain. I tried to tie it all together—Smith's confusion about Atkins's motivations, how the Flyer managed to do the impossible even when the goggles did not always light up in blue to see him, Bridget's suspicions that Dowling had been meeting with a mysterious provider of magical goods.

How did the Flyer smell the darkness in me? How had he sensed the turmoil in Marcus? Or heard the marbles sing a different song than the devices?

I'd guessed at it once before. My head throbbed.

"Because he is not human."

"No," replied Atkins. "He is not. The uprising in Ireland a

couple of years ago reawakened concerns for the government. We understood, all at once, just how distracted the war has kept us these several years. Can you fathom? An armed uprising in our own back garden? It made us realize just how weak we were, how quickly our grip on the world was slipping. And then, as though from a nightmare, came the Blue Flyer.

"And he wasn't just a weed appearing amidst the vegetables. No. He'd caused enough trouble already so that the Germans came forward to request an audience. Germans that might claim the political future of their country. It was like a knock on the door from tomorrow. But they didn't know what we did."

I scowled.

"You told me on the ride to Nancy," I said. "Months ago, when I asked about the mission, I asked whether it could influence the outcome of the war. You said it might not matter."

"England has long been at war with magic. I trust you know. We have kept records of our exchanges with with the fair folk. We've written down everything we could about their techniques, their means of devising contracts, approaches to violence and trickery. We've ruminated at length about what they want, how their desires have changed over the years. But after a time, the records went silent. There was nothing more to add. The sightings became more and more rare and less and less credible. We'd nearly forgotten about the fair folk. Industry had all but eradicated them. But when the rumors from the front came trickling in, and we weeded out the drunken stories from the fear-induced hallucinations, we found a strand that was all but undeniable."

"So why form a whole committee? Why have us investigate as we did?" I asked.

"Because the world has changed, and so has the Fae. We thought, for example, that iron poisoned them, that its very contact eroded their flesh. But that does not appear to be true at all. We needed more support, so that I could not only find them, but learn more about them all at once."

"You used us as a lure? An experiment?"

"I used you for exactly the purpose I stated. Things turned complicated. Before our meeting with Mustermann, I was under the impression that the faerie left behind the magical devices on purpose, causing mischief to weaken all parties in the war as a type of revenge against us for what we have done to them in the past. I did not expect magical devices to be left behind by our own men."

"And that threw a wrench into the machine," I said. "But things sorted themselves in your favor, didn't they? We did exactly as you'd hoped, two pawns probing the faerie for his capabilities, their motivations, all while you quietly observed and planned to wipe them out. I presume that is your plan, isn't it?"

"It must be," he replied.

I shook my head.

"You want to kill off the last of a magical race."

"It's not a race, Jane. It's a species. And it's not even about that, anymore. The species is gone. It's one creature, now. One avenging angel that will not rest until it wreaks as much havoc as it can. Is such an entity worth preserving?"

I bit my lip. My head ached and Atkins's explanations only worsened the effect. But he was wrong, perhaps in several ways. Marcus had flown beside another DH 5, and the Blue Flyer had flown to their rescue, transforming into a magically enhanced SE 5A. It had already shot down Atkins. Why else come back for us if not to protect one of its own?

Two flyers. Two fair folk. And Marcus mixed up with them both.

But why wouldn't Marcus just fly home if he had control of an aircraft, especially amidst the dog fight we'd all been mixed up in? What had he learned to persuade him to fly beside them?

Or maybe he only believed he knew something.

Bridget's warning sounded in my ears. He might be cursed.

"Are the fair folk as cunning and deceitful as the stories make them out to be?" I asked.

"That is their defining characteristic," Atkins replied.

I debated sharing what I knew, that there was more than the one he had identified, that Marcus had been flying with them, that, to my horror, I'd shot him down.

But something inside me whispered to stay silent. Atkins had not told the whole truth before, and I had no way of verifying that he did now.

Then, like a cracked gas line, hope started leaking through my despair, transmitted through a ludicrous, delusional idea.

"Might the fair folk make someone see something that was not truly there?"

Atkins shrugged.

"It would not surprise me one whit."

I didn't believe it, not really, but the very plausibility eased my breathing. If there were the slimmest chance that I'd imagined Marcus in that plane, or that for some twisted reason, the Blue Flyers wanted me to see Marcus in that plane....

Even if Marcus were dead, knowing that it was not my bullet would spare me a lifetime of torment.

I glanced at Dupont.

"Did you know?" I asked. "About the truth of our mission?"

He nodded.

"Not until after Clairmarias," he said. "I wanted nothing more to do with Atkins and the British plan. But after what you all went through in Ghent, I knew there was no avoiding it."

"Does High Command know?" I asked.

Atkins nodded. Dupont shook his head.

"How can that be? All of us are under the leadership of Grand Commander Foche."

Atkins smiled darkly.

"Foche did not put down the Irish rebellion. And when we brought up concerns about German-Irish cooperation as recently as a couple of weeks ago, he did nothing. Some problems are still uniquely the Empire's."

I was running out of questions. My mind ran in all directions, and a part of me wanted to continue talking in that field; the novelty of the information I received went a long way in distracting me from what would become the inevitable, incessant whirlpool of my mind.

I had shot him down. In waves, it would wrack me with pain. Over and over and over.

One such tide threatened now, even in a brief lull in the conversation.

I groaned. My body revolted against me.

"What will we do with Smith?" I asked.

"He will be buried, appropriately. I'm only glad he fell on our side of the line," said Atkins.

"His family?" I asked.

Dupont and Atkins both remained silent.

"Well? His family?" I said again.

"We don't know if he had one," Dupont replied.

"Part of his cover," said Atkins. I wrung my bruised hands.

"So a nameless death and burial beneath an unimaginative pseudonym," I muttered. I spoke to them of Smith, but the words made me think of Marcus, how he'd been so reluctant to accept the assignment, so afraid of dying in obscurity. Oh, Marcus...

"Don't think of it that way," said Dupont.

"Then how?"

"This is what he'd have wanted. That we know."

I shook my head ruefully.

"Get me away from this field," I begged, voice breaking again. I was a soldier now. I'd faced the violence. I'd experienced the loss. And, as a final christening blow, the war had broken me.

They ushered me carefully to Atkins's car. I collapsed into the back seat and tried to shut my eyes against the pain, inside and out. There was nowhere to hide but sleep.

Atkins had lied and could not be trusted. I needed answers, and the only place to get them was where Marcus had gone. I needed to talk to the Blue Flyers.

Chapter 27
Death of a Hero
Marcus

Take the cylinder out of my kidney,
The connecting rod out of my brain, my brain,
From the small of my back take the camshaft,
And assemble the engine again.
-RFC Mess Song-

When Luf's plane caught fire, I thought he'd escape it, somehow. He tried. He had jumped from the burning wreckage to land in a stream below.

He'd missed, but he'd tried.

And for that, I was grateful because it gave me the strength to try as well.

My plane sped downward in a glide. My engine had failed. Smoke trailed in black snakes from the front, threatening fire. Fire was a pilot's nightmare. Fire was what we all feared more than the devil himself. It was an agonizing killer that stretched the moments before a sudden death into long, painstaking agony.

But I was lucky. My plane had not yet come apart.

I couldn't chase the mechanical look on Jane's face from my

memory. Maybe she hadn't recognized me. Maybe seeing me was too foreign a possibility.

I held my breath and leaned into the smoke to get hold of the joystick and plant my feet down firmly on the rudder pedals again. I could hardly see anything, but at least I could try to level out the plane.

The crash attempt was a race and a gamble all at once. The faster I dove, the more quickly I could try to exit the aircraft. But it also meant bailing out would be more violent.

On the other hand, I could try to glide down and soften the approach, but every moment that passed, the fire spread. It wasn't just the oil in the engine. The dope of the fabric responsible for the wing's tautness and aerodynamics was intensely flammable—the culprit behind many pilots' grisly demises.

I tried to split the difference. Fortunately, we had never taken the fight to outrageous altitudes. After diving down at forty-five degrees for a bit, I stood in my cockpit to catch a breath of air and see where I was. There was not much in the cratered landscape below but sprawling fields, occasional groves of trees, and a polluted stream or two.

Those weren't great options.

But I'd seen men land planes like this before, planes that had no business flying. It was possible.

The first visible spit of fire belched from the engine. It hadn't caught the edge of the doped canvas yet. It was still an intermittent gurgle. But my eyes went wide as the flames grew.

I pushed the nose down further and increased the speed of the dive. Maybe, if I could get enough wind blowing across the flame, it would sputter out. But even in the desperate thought, I knew that was foolish. The wind would only feed it. The fire had fuel and air to breathe, even if I didn't.

More black smoke ran into my face. Splashes of hot oil seared my neck and cheeks as I willed myself to dive faster, not caring if the wings split when I pulled up, not caring what the maneuvers did to the plane at all. It was a loss already. Please, anything, so long as it wasn't the fire.

The spitting flame from the engine finally caught the fuselage, and the heat came in earnest now, an orange, fluttering monster that feasted with a ravenous frenzy.

I yanked back on the stick and leveled out my approach. My velocity was much too high, but I was alarmingly close to the ground, close enough to see wildflowers in the field whipping past me. This was not landing speed, but today it had to be. I touched down, and the wheels bounced off the Earth. My dying bird refused to perch.

I tried again to the same effect. The flames crept closer. The heat stung my face now. I had to make it work. I was out of time, and the plane seemed to be slowing down.

I pushed down dangerously hard this time. It was still too fast, and I overdid it. I heard a ripping sound and a crash, and suddenly the belly of my fuselage was scraping against the rocks and bumps and shrubs. That must have been the wheels. But somehow, I was slowing.

The bottom of my fuselage ripped out and nearly caught my feet with it. I pulled them up and leapt from the cockpit.

But too late.

I hardly noticed the flames on my suit for how relieved I was to touch sweet ground again. But as I rolled painfully over a jagged stretch of stone, the heat did not leave me. I looked aside and saw my sleeve ablaze.

I tried to roll it over, but I'd caught too much oil in my flight suit. So I stood and ran, fiddling with the buttons and as I desperately searching for something, anything to help. The sting of the burn started, and I screamed. But that was good. Isn't that what they said? It was when the pain stopped that the worst damage began, after the nerves had been burnt away?

Finally, I found the stream I'd flown over. The water was not all clear, but I didn't care. I prayed only that it was deep enough to smother the fire.

I held my breath and dove in. My arm screamed, my fingers throbbed, but as the water gently washed over me, I managed, finally, to undo my flight suit.

I crawled out of it and left it behind. When I pulled myself onto the bank, I watched it bob away. The fire still struggled on, furious that it had been cheated a life, but soon went out.

I lay there alone, streaked with soot and oil, ash and blood. Smoke and vapor came up off my arm, and I sank it back into the water. It eased the pain a bit, but even beneath the cool lapping of the current, the pain shot down my spine and up behind my ears like a thousand tiny needles.

My heartbeat slowed, and as my rasping, ruined breath stabilized, dark thoughts found room.

She had shot me down. We locked eyes, and she shot me down. She either did it on purpose or was too caught up in the fight to stop herself from pulling the trigger. In some ways, I hoped for the former. It was basic, childish, naïve, hopeless, or any of the other words I'd been teased with for having a zero on my scorecard. Was it wrong to wish Jane didn't have to be a soldier? Was it wrong to wish she could have a better life than that? I'd hoped that by going with Harry, I could learn something.

I couldn't face her. That's why I hadn't gone back. Maybe it's why I left in the first place. I couldn't come to grips with a world that turned someone like her into something like this.

Why had she attacked Allied planes in the first place?

I let the water wash over me for a long time, wishing it would carry the poisonous thoughts downstream. I came to the war as a child. It raised me with its brutal, straightforward education. We killed others to protect who we loved. The people we shot at did the same. Jane dirtied her hands to protect aspects of me she treasured. I abandoned her and told myself it was to find out how to protect her better.

But I was just scared. Luf died, and I got scared it'd happen to Jane, too. When I couldn't stop the world, I got mad. And now?

Jane had shot me down. I wondered if they would count my plane as one of her victories. Maybe she had more since I'd left. Who knew, perhaps my burns made her an ace.

"Marcus," a voice called. "Can you walk?"

I picked up my head.

Harry stood nearby in the grass, his features painted creased lines of concern.

"Harry?"

"I'm sorry, Marcus. That was—I mean—That was not our plan."

I used my good arm to push myself to a sitting position in the stream. The air stung my wet burn.

"What happened?" I asked.

"I got away and saw the smoke from your crash. We have little time. We're still on Allied land. Can you walk?"

I coughed in disbelief.

"Walk where? We're in the middle of a field somewhere in France. Do you have a burrow around here you use as a hideout?"

Harry snorted but cocked his head as if to consider the idea.

"No, but we do have a ride."

He turned and pointed to the sky. The sortie. I hadn't even bothered to look up to see what had happened. I saw the outlines of some planes making controlled returns to ground. Then a plane headed our way. By the looks of it, a two-seater. A Bristol F2B.

"Jane?" I asked in disbelief.

"No," Harry shook his head. "It's Dieter."

"You mean he stole an F2B?"

"No. We'll explain once we're safe. We will require you to get in to the gunner's bay."

I shook my head. Going back into the air was the last thing I wanted right now.

"Harry, my arm is screaming in pain. The windchill will be unbearable. My suit burned to a crisp."

Harry stepped forward and cradled my arm. For the first time, I braved a look at it. My flesh had scarred and bubbled in long streaks from my shoulder to my hand. It was grotesque and foreign. This was a prop for a silent film or a play. It did not belong to me.

"Take my flight suit," said Harry, quickly disrobing. "I'm sorry. It won't be comfortable, but it's the only way."

His voice wavered with anxiety and urgency. I'd never heard him speak with such a tone, and so I nodded and carefully slipped it on. It didn't fit quite right, but Harry helped me tie off any openings that might allow air whistling into the sleeve.

By the time I'd finished, the Brisfit was on the ground.

"Let's go," Dieter shouted without turning off the propellor.

Silently, Harry helped me clamber into the gunner's bay and retreated back to his parked DH 5. It kicked to life instantly. I shook my head, wondering how a single pilot managed to start his engine without so much as cranking the propellor. Everything moved slowly like a dream.

But my distorted perception of the world couldn't slow our ascent into the air. We carried on. I was too tired to pay attention to our heading. Thoughts of Jane and Luf and my parents danced around one another. They had all disappointed me inevitably, brutally. My parents let me come out here. Luf left me behind. And Jane...

It was strange riding in the back of the plane. A gun rested on a ring mount beside me. I had no intention of using it. If an enemy plane found us, so be it. My arm throbbed, and whenever a trail of air found its way up my wrist, it seared with fresh pain.

But I was alive, and that was something.

Somehow, in the discomfort of that bay, I nodded off to sleep.

I woke upon landing. It was dark already, so dark I thought something was wrong with my eyes. There were no flares lighting up the landing strip, no lights marking hangars or mess halls. I squinted around me trying to make out the landscape and was shocked to find hills dotted with groupings of trees. We had landed on a narrow strip of flat land, a small clearing that looked strange set against the hillside. Dieter taxied us toward a group of trees ahead, and I remembered how ineffectively Jane and I had tried to hide our plane when we flew into the farmland surrounding Ghent.

But I saw no dwellings here. They may have been close, but with the roaming hills surrounding, I got the sense that we were tucked away and invisible in a remote area of the planet.

We taxied deep into the trees. The limbs arched above us, forming a tunnel. Tree branches and shrub boughs kissed the tips of our wings as we rolled past, but as we wound to the right and left on our approach, we encountered no obstacles. Beneath the canopy, the dark intensified, but far above I made out an occasional star or beam of moonlight. The inside of these woods came across more like a cave than a group of trees. I wondered if Harry and Dieter had lopped off branches to create a blind.

At length, we came to a stop, and when the engine powered off, I realized it had been humming much more softly than any engine I had ever heard. I wondered if my hearing had been damaged in the crash somehow.

Dieter hopped out of the cockpit and held up his hand to help me down.

"Are you all right?" he asked. The tone of his voice softer and more compassionate than I'd ever imagined him to be. Still, even amidst my surprise, I shook my head.

"Yeah." But when I tried to swing myself out of the plane, my arm scraped against the metal lining of the gunner's bay and pain shot my nerves to pieces, up my arm and spine and needling into the base of my skull. The sensation knocked me off balance. I stumbled from my seat, and Dieter caught me awkwardly.

"Easy now," he said, taking care to hold me up without touching my arm.

"Thank you, Dieter," I replied. Around his neck, I noticed a stray streak of moonlight shine off a satin fabric. I stared.

"Is that Richthofen's scarf?" I asked.

He nodded.

"What does it do?"

"It's time I answer many of your questions," he said with a gentle smile. "You've proven yourself to me. Let's get you inside, and we'll talk."

As the pain ebbed in my arm, and I stood upright on my own, my mind raced to distrust him. This last statement reminded me of the choice he'd proffered at the helm of our U-boat right as we were about to exit the minefield. Was it a true choice or a trick to confuse me?

"What is your real name?" I asked. He gazed at me. I think he understood that I was testing him, but instead of getting grumpy, his gentle smile returned.

"My name is Dialythe."

That's right. I knew that. I'd heard Harry call him that already in a moment they didn't think I was listening.

"And Harry? What's his name?" Dieter's smile flickered.

"His name is not mine to give you. But I see why you asked me for mine. I admit that I do not open easily to others."

Harry's plane touched down more loudly than ours had. My ears must have been regaining their senses. He taxied carefully into the grove of trees and powered down.

"Home sweet home," he said cheerily as he descended from the cockpit.

"Home?" I asked.

"One of them," said Harry. "Come along."

They ushered me into what looked to me like a crude lean-to. Bearing against the trunks of a close crop of trees was a mess of boards sloppily thrown together around a rough door.

There were no windows, and they opened it carefully, urging me inside before closing it behind us. Once inside, all was dark for a minute until we inched forward. They led me by the hand down a sloping pathway. Then, from behind the silhouette of thick branches criss-crossing and barring our path, a glow came to life. Dieter moved the branches aside and my concerns about my arm, the war, even Jane took a back seat to my wonder.

I could only describe it as a dome or some kind of cathedral. A cavernous room stretched out before me. The ceiling swept high above, made of intricately weaving tree limbs, all rich and alive with leaves and foliage. Amidst the branches hung orbs of soft, bright, warm light. The ground was lush grass, covered in places by rugs or carpets to support an eclectic collection of writing desks, dressers, curio cabinets, tables, couches, and chairs.

It looked like the living room I'd expect to see in some rich estate, if the house were owned by Mother Nature. In the center of it all was a bubbling fountain.

For the first time, I considered that maybe I hadn't survived my plane crash.

"What am I looking at?" I muttered.

"We have a lot to tell you," Harry started. "And it may be best to share one surprise at a time."

I stared at the glowing balls of light suspended from the boughs above.

"Am I dead?" I asked.

"No," said Dieter.

I stepped forward and fell on my knees. I felt the green grass between my fingers, then traced the carved wooden leg of a table. The grass reminded me of home, of peaceful afternoons playing in the park before going home to dinner. The table leg vaguely resembled one we'd had in our kitchen. I used to pick at it with a fork when I was just a kid. My parents scolded me, but it became a sort of game. I tried to make my mark without them noticing. I got so good at it that I could eat dinner with one hand while going to work at carving pictures or letters with the other.

A swell of anger, grief, and confusion swept into me. How did this place feel so much like home?

The question came tumbling out of me, a question I'd been rolling over for a week but had been afraid to ask ever since I'd put Boelcke's goggles on in Clairmarais, when I'd discovered magic was real. If I could put off answering the question, the danger appeared so much thinner. If I didn't ask it, our missions and magic were about nothing more than a new military technology.

But it couldn't be like that. I had known for a long time.

"You're not human beings, are you?" I asked.

They looked at each other with something like pride. They seemed pleased I'd finally puzzled something out.

"No," Dieter said. "We are not."

Chapter 28
Trail of Oil
Jane

Then scanning all the crowded mass,
Should you perceive one face that you loved
It is a spook. None wears the face you knew.
Great death has made all yours forever more.
-Charles Hamilton Sorley-

I refused a trip to the hospital.

Atkins had driven me to a field tent at once. When we arrived, he and Dupont went to their usual pains to obfuscate my gender, procuring me a private compartment to be examined in and having a thorough conversation with the surgeon about discretion.

Apparently, they had no desire to explain how a woman had suffered wounds like mine so close to the front.

They needed to protect their tool, the same way a soldier might clean his gun or polish his spade.

I was bitter and numb. The doctor examined me all over, and though he poked and prodded in sensitive and private areas, amidst a shower of his apologies, I could not muster even the energy to endure a sense of violation.

My heart was drowning, and my mind had caught hold of a rope. Atkins's comment about the Fae had filled me with the most ridiculous hope I'd ever imagined. Perhaps the faerie had wanted me to believe I'd shot Marcus down.

Perhaps what I'd done wasn't real.

But why? Did they expect I would stop trying to get hold of the other devices if my partner and I were separated? Even if I had not shot Marcus down, what hope was there that the Flyers had not killed him themselves—killed him and taken his marble. Isn't that what the Flyer had mentioned in the tomb under St. Bavo's? He'd hardly cared about Ball's violin strings.

I tried to recount all I had learned about the Blue Flyers. Now, I believed there were two, if not more. They had at their disposal several of the magic artifacts that bestowed enchanted effects on their bearers. The scarf. The ring. What else?

We had deduced that such devices came from the top aces in the war, and I'd even seen the ring's magical genesis. But in the end, all of this amounted to little. The breadth and scope of the magic overwhelmed me. My Aunt Luella had warned me as much, so had my mother.

As a child, I had asked them both about the fair folk on several occasions, but for all their propensity to discuss magic at length, their lips sealed quickly and tightly at my questions.

The most I'd ever received from Luella was a brusque confession that the Fae had existed once and must have been truly terrible. Having faced them now on several occasions, I could confirm the sentiment.

Marcus had to be alive.

I had to hold on to that, if only to avoid going to pieces.

"Rest now," said the doctor as he put down a stethoscope. "I'll return shortly. You're quite bashed up."

"I was shot down," I replied numbly.

"Of course you were."

The capacity of men to disbelieve women stopped surprising me. The doctor turned and ducked out of the room, but I overheard his conversation with Atkins and Dupont.

"Some terrible bruising, and not confined to her hands or arms, I'm afraid. There are some chipped teeth as well. Obviously, she should not be at the front in the first place, but given her condition, I recommend you remove her to a hospital in Paris immediately."

I shook my head.

The faeries were not in Paris. The second DH 5 had flown off, feigning a failed engine, and it had been heading toward Marcus's crash site. By now, they could be anywhere.

I needed more information. When we found the two DH 5s, they were still climbing into the air, not yet at any significant altitude, and they were Allied planes. Neither of them had shifted form the way the SE 5A had, either. They must have come from somewhere.

Dupont and Atkins entered the room.

"Thank heavens you are all right," Atkins started.

"Which aerodrome were we nearest?" I asked without preamble.

Atkins and Dupont shared a glance before the English lieutenant took a seat beside my cot.

"Jane, I have pushed you so very hard, to the brink, I'm afraid. Now it is time to rest and regain—"

"Dupont?" I cut him off and directed my inquiry toward the Frenchman.

"We were near Bruay, Arras, Liettres," he admitted. "Could have been from anywhere."

"Will you drive me?" I asked.

"Now, wait one moment—"

I cut Atkins off with a raise of my finger.

"I will take you wherever you want," Dupont replied.

I started, not wanting to lose a second. My body ached. Everything hurt, but the Flyers distanced themselves from us every moment by miles or maneuvers. Dupont and Atkins fell in behind me.

"Those DH 5s hadn't been off the ground long when we found them. There must be an airfield nearby."

"There are several," said Dupont. We ducked out of the medical hut. Atkins's car sat parked nearby in a patch of dirt.

"Then we'll need to search each of them."

"I insist you rest," Atkins said, edging in a grumpy shoulder. We ignored him.

"What are you looking for?" asked Dupont as he climbed into the driver's seat and held out his hand so Atkins could give him the keys. Gingerly, I got in on the other side.

"Anything," I replied. "I don't know. Maybe someone overheard something or noticed Marcus there acting strangely. Anything."

"You think we can still find him?" Dupont asked.

I bit my lip. They had not believed my ravings about how I'd shot him down. I didn't want to push the point. Telling them would make it real, and there was still this fool's hope that things weren't as they seemed.

"I think we're losing time," I replied.

"Very well, we can start near Arras and work our way North."

Atkins put both hands down on the car's bonnet and expelled an exasperated sigh from his lungs.

"Will you not stop?" he asked me.

I piqued my head and acknowledged him at last.

"Shall I remind you what we have before us, Atkins? A mysterious Fae opponent in possession of magical devices of untold power, and who, I've recently learned from you, has some type of grudge against our country. Ireland is biting at your heels. They took Marcus. Smith is dead. And you want me to stop? Why?"

Sheepishly, he ducked his head between his shoulders.

"If you push yourself too far, something may snap," he said. "I worry only about your well being."

I was done rolling my eyes. This was fury, now. He was lying to me, but before I tore into him for it, I realized something worse.

He didn't think he was lying at all. He thought he had my best interests at heart. And somehow, that made him so much more dangerous.

"We are so far past my well being. Hand over the keys and get out of our way. I have aerodromes to search."

Defeated, he fished the keys out of his pocket and walked around the front of the car.

"Move over," he said as he slid into the driver's seat. "You don't need to search all those aerodromes."

"Why not?" asked Dupont.

"Because it's already been called in. We're going to Bruay."

"I should have known he was a spy from the moment I laid eyes on him. Damn kid appealed to my sense of vanity."

Bowman leaned back in a chair behind a table in one of the steel tunnel huts that served as a squadron office. It had taken us only a pair of hours to get here and find Bowman. He was bristling and bothered by the action earlier that afternoon, an action he did not personally engage in.

"Those DH 5s should have been requisitioned and sent back as trainers months ago. But it wasn't considered a priority. How they managed to get them airborne is beyond me."

"He must have been a brilliant mechanic," I said, knowingly. We had yet to disclose our connection with Marcus, the man he considered a foreign agent. Bowman leaned forward and put his elbows on the table, a pen twisting between his fingers.

"Miss, I have brilliant mechanics. I have men who can turn

metal into miracles and wood into wonders. Those planes had no business flying." He dropped the pen to the table with a loud clatter. "We don't even have the time to figure out where he came from or what he wanted. No investigation at all. My whole squadron is already bleeding with exhaustion. The patrols must be flown. The Huns are sure well flying theirs."

Atkins, Dupont, and I stared at one another.

"You'll be happy to have some assistance on the investigation, then," said Atkins.

Bowman grimaced. "This must be the strangest day I've had in the war. First the spies, or deserters, or whichever they were. Now a Frenchie, a lord, and a woman that looks like she's been to hell and back claiming they're here to investigate."

I blushed, Dupont smiled sheepishly, and Atkins tried to mitigate the damage.

"You may say that finding this man is our number one priority. I should also mention, perhaps it goes without saying, but our involvement must remain—"

"Confidential? In some ways, that explains things."

Atkins nodded.

"His Majesty's Royal Air Force thanks you."

Bowman shrugged, as though he expected the devil himself to enter the room next.

"Tell His Majesty He's welcome."

"Can you share what your encounter with the pilot this morning was like?" I asked.

"Of course. I came into the mess and found him dressed in formal uniform, the type of thing we try to convince the men to wear for medal ceremonies. He claimed that he was here with urgent news for me."

"What news?" asked Dupont.

"He told us Robert Little died."

"What time was that?" I asked.

"In the morning."

My pulse quickened. How would Marcus have known so quickly that Little's plane went down?

"Then what happened?" Atkins asked.

"Well, I had my suspicions about him, but he asked me to recount my dogfight with Werner Voss. He looked so sincere about it that I figured him for a true pilot. I shared the story. He shared the news. Then he left the mess to speak with a mechanic I'd never seen before."

"What did the mechanic look like?" I asked, leaning forward on the balls of my feet. Hearing about these concealed moments from Marcus's life kept him alive in my mind.

"I didn't get much of a look at him. Then I was sidetracked. Pilots reporting in after coming back from their patrols, others with questions about assignments. By the time I had another moment, they'd already wandered off. Then, from the far Bessonneau down the line, two DH 5s came out treating our taxi area like a runway. One of them was firing the machine gun already to make sure no one came too close.

"Well, I rallied my boys to go after them, but a fair share of SE 5As had cables cut. They had it all thought after, left me standing like a fool."

"Can you show us the hangar?" I asked.

"If you're interested in discretion, you won't want me showing you around it. It's getting dark enough. Take a torch, it's the furthest on the end. If it's full of packing crates, that's the one."

Atkins thanked him while I turned and strode off. Dupont hurried to my side again as if he were my second in command.

It was already dark, but my eyes adjusted to the dim and we made our way quickly down the line of hangars. Atkins ran to catch up with us, distributing lights to aid our search.

I don't know what I expected to find in that Bessonneau, but when we arrived, it was as uninteresting as Bowman had promised. Stacks of crates, some opened, some empty, some molding, lay strewn about everywhere. From the indentations in the dirt, I could see where the DH 5s had rested. After walking further inside, I turned to face the entrance, and my light found a couple of bullet holes, undoubtedly from a mounted machine gun.

Bowman had said only one pilot had shot his gun.

Dupont tried poking around the crates, shifting lids, hoisting some to check the boxes below.

"Anything interesting?" Atkins asked.

"Just spare tools and parts," Dupont replied as he shoved one away in disappointment. "A can of oil."

"There you are," said Atkins. "Jane, we tried. And I'm sure there is more to learn from the men here, but I must insist you get some rest, that we all get some rest. We'll be no good if we're not sharp."

But I didn't want to give up. I shone my light on the ground near the indentations left by the wheels. There was a puddle of oil, suggesting a hastily performed engine service. But that would be expected, given Bowman's description of the unknown mechanic. Either Marcus had fixed up the plane before entering the mess that morning, or else one of the Blue Flyers was hard at work while Marcus had distracted Bowman. That would explain why he'd asked to hear the story about Werner Voss.

I allowed myself to smile, indulging a memory of Marcus and Lufbery going on for hours about the dogfight in question.

My arms protested as I helped myself up to sit on a table, scooting the tool box that rested on it to one side with my hip. Voss was one of the top scoring pilots in the war. Many considered him the Baron's better.

"He must have been helping them," I muttered.

"Marcus?" Dupont asked. "No. He wouldn't."

"Why else gather information about Werner Voss? If top pilots are leaving behind artifacts, then surely Voss would have left one as well."

Atkins folded his arms.

"But they were on Little's device so quickly. You wouldn't think the Fae would have any need of collecting that type of information. We have only two in our possession, and you said they expressed little interest in the violin strings. Perhaps they have a similar apathy for the goggles because they have no need of its effects."

I bit my lip. We knew so little about the Flyers, and Atkins was right. I had hardly paused to take a breath. I was afraid. A pause might have me coming apart in moments. Even while I busied myself, I had to swallow down sporadic, painful sobs before they escaped my throat. But this hangar, at any rate, appeared to be a dead end.

"Very well, Atkins. Perhaps it is time for a rest. But if I may request it from both of you, I don't want to be alone."

Dupont's posture softened. He cast a sympathetic glance at Atkins.

"Of course," the lieutenant said. "We will watch over you in shifts."

"On your shift, perhaps you can share all you know about the fair folk with me. It could only help."

"So long as you rest," he replied, massaging the bridge of his nose.

I grinned without spirit. I'd never imagined my wartime experience would include Fae stories with someone like Atkins.

I was shifting my weight to get off the table when I lost the grip on my light. It tumbled over and cast a dramatic shadow of the toolbox on the wall.

But as I turned around to pick it up, I stopped.

"Atkins. Dupont. Come quickly."

Under the toolbox, written in shaky streaks of oil on the table's surface were letters.

BRXJIHIO
CNQI HNBDY

"What's that?" Asked Atkins.

"It must be from Marcus" Dupont cried, clapping his hands.

My heart swelled. Another sob threatened to escape me. He'd left us a clue. He was still ours, still mine.

Unless I'd killed him.

I denied the thought.

"It's code," Atkins muttered. "I'll check if I can track down someone trustworthy from the intelligence office here."

"I can work it out," I said as I wiped at the tears escaping the corners of my eyes. "It should be me. I can do it faster."

"I suppose you're retracting the rest you just promised me you would take," Atkins said.

"This counts. Plus, I'll still need you to tell me Fae stories to keep me awake while I work on it."

He coughed, and the hairs of his mustache flared out.

"I'll get a pen and paper," he said as he walked out of the hangar.

Chapter 29
Love and Loss
Marcus

I shall spend brief and idle hours beside
The many lesser loves that still remain,
But find in none my triumph and my pride;
-Vera Brittain-

"We are the last we know of," said Dieter. I sat comfortably on a tufted, moss-covered couch. Harry sat on a chair beside me, taking special care to wrap my wounded arm. It felt better already, and I suspected that, like the water he'd given me on the submarine, there might be more than met the eye with the bandage he used.

"For generations, our kind was hunted by ambitious men, but we considered ourselves the true possessors of the earth, for mankind did not seem to understand her magic," Dieter went on.

"They still don't," said Harry without looking up. Then he added quietly, "Save a unique few."

Dieter, Dialythe, took his friend's comment as an opportunity for a sip of tea. I'd watched him prepare it. The amount of sugar he added made an impression. I recalled our time in the U-boat, how

I'd never noticed them eating, the sacks of sugar in Dieter's sleeping quarters.

It had been a couple of days since we'd arrived, and I'd slept through most of them. Whether they had some device to assist that or I was just plain exhausted enough to catch up on some shut-eye, I couldn't tell.

On the table in the center of the room, the miniature Spruce tree held a place of honor. I eyed its several cones and wondered.

"You were top of the food chain, then?" I asked.

"We don't eat human beings," said Dieter with a laugh.

"No. I just mean, you were apex predator. You were the top dog."

"Some felt that way, yes."

"And what changed?"

"Men changed," he replied. "Over the centuries, mankind has taken one short step after another up a ladder. Occasionally, they have fallen down, and in some aspects of their existence, they have yet to recover. But when it comes to technology..." Dieter trailed off and searched for words. "Science has rendered men deadly to magic."

"That's not completely accurate," Harry said. "Science has emboldened mankind, and the arrogance of man is deadly to magic."

"I don't understand," I said. Harry finished with my arm and stood to pour himself a cup of tea.

"Once, man's exploration confined itself to the physical dimension. They sailed to see lands they hadn't before. They braved climates that threatened their safety. Now, faster than ever, they are pulling up the roots of phenomena they can't explain, and killing them in the process."

Dieter cleared his throat and cast what appeared to be a warning glance at his friend.

"They are exploring magical arenas," said Dieter, "and demystifying them. They reduce the phenomena down until the savor is gone, wasted. They make simple explanations, easily communicable as quickly and efficiently as possible, to pass on their dominion over nature to others. They believe science can answer everything, and so they ask questions only science can answer. Our kind lives from the magic of the world. As the magic runs out, we die off."

"Like flight," I said, recalling Jane's explanations of magic. "We figured out how to get planes in the air."

"And now, the air is governed by principles of man. It will only get worse," said Harry. Dieter cut him off again.

"Long ago, as mankind gained significant ground in its war on magic, our folk held councils in a desperate attempt at self-preservation. But we could not agree on any proper method of coexisting with human ambition. Some factions thought humans must be exterminated. Others argued we should come out of hiding and position ourselves among humans as custodians of the remaining magical realms. Our disagreements turned bitter. It led to war at the worst time possible."

"Faeries killing faeries," said Harry. I nodded grimly.

"You fought a war over the how to go about self-preservation?" I asked.

"Ironic, isn't it? There have been wars fought for sillier reasons. And our kind did not shun war amongst ourselves. It was a cyclical and accepted part of our existence. It resonated with the forces that gave us power in a way it never could for human beings," said Dieter.

"What does that mean?" I asked. "You guys don't have beating hearts, or something?"

Dieter smiled. That was a rare sight.

"We won't get into the anatomy, where our differences are but subtle. Fae magic is different from natural magic, which is different still than what gives humans their greatest strength. Fae magic derives from cunning, artful deception, schemes, and self interest. When we were checked only by the natural forces of the world, and when mankind's grasp on technology left them woefully oppressed by the world's natural forces as well, little threatened us. But our kind were not so bound by natural magic. We delighted in crafting deals with humans to share just enough of our strength to keep them complacent and believing.

"But with the rise of man's ambition and industry, they became less dependent on what we had to offer. Our magical currency, so to speak, lost its value."

I leaned my head back on the couch. The moist moss was cool on my neck, the leather of the upholstery even cooler. I stared at the tree boughs above us, a living ceiling of woven branches.

"Man destroys nature," I said, understanding. Had humans built a structure like this, it'd be all cut lumber and stone, lifeless material, killed for our advantage. "And we destroyed your kind as well."

"Not intentionally," said Harry. "There was no great war of violence between humankind and ours, though there are some humans who believe that. There was no need. The magic that sustained us changed. That scarcity combined with our own selfish fighting did the rest."

Harry put his teacup down and sauntered over to a curio cabinet. I watched him as he avoided eye contact with Dieter. Odd. When I had joined them on the submarine, they came across as lock-step. But more and more, I noticed a divide.

"We need to plant more trees," I said. Harry laughed loudly.

"I would be quite pleased," he said, "but this goes much, much deeper than that. It is not about the physical. We don't need forests. We need the fear of what's inside them. We need the respect and forbearance of mankind. We need humans to embrace their individual ethics and apply them to the dangerous potential of the whole species."

I stood up to stretch my legs. I'd been in this hideout for days, and it was finally taking its toll on me. I wanted air and exercise, but more importantly I wanted something to do. The conversation was stimulating, but my body grew restless.

"That's why you're trying to stop the war. It's pushed us to new technological limits, and all in the name of destruction. We haven't had the luxury to stop and think about why we should or shouldn't build the next big cannon. In the name of survival, we just plough ahead. We don't recognize the value of the individual. Lives are collateral damage."

Harry turned away from the cabinet to look at me. The expression on his face was cold, foreign. I didn't see much of the chummy friendship we'd forged.

"We don't want you to suffer our fate," said Dieter. "The wheels of your war machine have been in motion for so long. And while war pushes men to accomplish incredible feats, it is not where mankind is most powerful. War relies on the cold logic and devious strategy that gave the Fae their strength. But it's self-destructive, even in our hands. The strategies used to win a war do not promote human welfare. Once you subscribe to it, to the game and its rules, to contracts and their structures of words, there is only one end. Unless we can right the ship in time."

"Hate magic," I muttered. "You said war is all hate magic."

Harry's mouth went slack.

"If only there were a record of hateful things done in the name of love," he said. "Every country in this conflict has a story they tell their children at bedtime. Every one of them. The story is the same. The characters are different."

"But that's not true," I pushed back. "There are rights and wrongs. There are people who decided to start the war."

"Do you think the average American parent has a firm grasp on the Baltic political nuance that led to the Black Hand's assassination of Archduke Ferdinand?" Harry asked. "Do you think they could even begin to explain the web of alliances and historical tension building between the nations of Europe for the past hundreds of years? And if they did, do you think they could simplify well enough to explain to their children? No. The widows of warriors tell their children that bad men from other lands killed their fathers. Antagonism and heroism. That's what children can understand. And in the telling, the adults convince themselves of the same."

I rolled the idea over in my head. I felt at home in their philosophy, and I realized that it reminded me of the way Jane used to speak before she'd gotten wrapped up in the mission and become a soldier herself. I wondered what she would make of all this. Really, it should have been her speaking with these two. She understood it all much better than I ever would. But I doubted she'd have any interest in sitting down to talk with the Blue Flyers she feared so much.

"I used to dream of being a combat ace," I said. "I wanted my five kills, but I wanted more than that, too. I wanted ten, fifteen, twenty-five, fifty. I wanted to be a legend. My best friend was a legend. But I could never do it." I shook my head and stared at the miniature spruce tree. "All those pilots, the great aces, the devices they leave behind... You're trying to tell me those devices came from hate magic?"

Harry stood by my side, solemn as an undertaker, and held my hand. His tone was soft but completely resolute.

"We don't get many opportunities to ask someone who will take the question seriously, and we don't ask rhetorically. Attachment and attraction for our kind did not work the same as it appears to work for human beings. Can love ever be the reason to take another human being's life forcibly?"

What a question. And who was I to answer even the first thing about love?

"You mean romantic love?" I asked.

"What other kinds are there?" asked Dieter.

I paused and stared at them. They did the same, faces all earnest and curious.

"You really don't know?" I asked.

"We understand the concept the way a scholar might," said Dieter.

"But every time I think I know what the word means, I discover that I don't," said Harry in tired tones.

I rested my head back on the couch again. This question would send me into some psychological crisis. I was like Harry. I thought I understood what love meant, not just the romantic kind, but the brotherly love that preachers went on about. I'd internalized it, jealously protected it. In the name of love, I spared a German spotter, and it ended in the death of my platoon. In the name of love, I made an idiot of myself in attempts to protect Jane. All I ever got from it were reprimands.

It wasn't that simple. Mercy for the spotter meant death for my platoons. Protection for Jane meant refusing mission objectives. There were competing priorities.

By now, the war had taught me that love, in all its forms, was a weed that would pop up at the most inconvenient times. In spite of the war, maybe because of the war, I couldn't help it sprouting over and over again. Lufbery. Jane. I was on track to considering Cillian like a brother.

Another name flittered into my mind, an addition to the list.

I glanced at Harry, who I'd known for such a brief time. I couldn't go through it again, not while I was still recovering from Jane shooting me out of the air.

"Is it hate magic that lets you change your planes, then?" I asked, changing the subject.

"Of course," Dieter replied. "Though the technical application of it is a little nuanced." He stood and beckoned me over to the curio cabinet.

Inside the cupboards, framed in glass, sat a collection of knick-knacks. I recognized the Baron's scarf, blood stained and dark. Sitting beside it on the shelf was a woman's ring, a cracked pocket mirror, and a well-used wrench. On the shelf above, in a place of honor sitting atop a velvet pillow, lay Jane's glass marble.

The sight of it made me queasy. I knew that Dieter had taken it from her by force, and to imagine Jane scared and alone, confronting him, made my heart ache. But it went beyond that, too. It was as though Jane the mechanic, Jane the civilian, had been taken away with that marble. Maybe part of why seeing the marble made me sick was because I imagined the old Jane trapped inside it somehow, a Jane that would never have shot anyone down, let alone me.

"Every device you have been hunting contains a degree of power. This power may manifest itself in certain ways. For example—"

"Richthofen's scarf enhances ammunition," I finished for him. They both looked at me apologetically. "Am I wrong?"

"No," said Harry carefully. "But the reasons behind the effect are important to note. The scarf replicates the influence of the man who left it behind. In the Baron's case, it makes it easier to shoot down an enemy plane. So in the Baron's case, yes, the guns have more sticking power."

"Have you ever examined a plane on the other end of that scarf?" I asked. "We had bullet holes of every size and shape you could dream up."

Harry shot a bothered glance at Dieter, who continued.

"But the devices are not the only source of power in the world. As we mentioned, there are natural founts of magic, and we have one to draw upon as well. When we combine our powers with what we can draw from the devices, we manage to create some helpful effects."

My shoulders sank.

"You mean only you can do it," I said with disappointment. I had hoped to learn the secret and try it myself. Strangely, the thought that I couldn't do what they could made me feel so very alone.

"We mean that you will need our help to accomplish the same," said Harry, "if you're going to be any use to us."

They smiled at me, but the phrase "use to us" sent a spark through my body.

"You're going to show me how to transform planes?" I asked.

"If you agree to join us," said Dieter.

"Haven't I already proved myself?"

"Not like this," said Harry. "We need assurances. We have withheld the details of our objectives from you. But now we must share enough for you to make a choice, a real choice, about whether you would like to return to the Allies or swear your allegiance to us and our cause."

Harry guided me back to the couch. They sat on either side of me.

"We are going to stop this war once and for all," said Harry.

"How?" I asked, but now I feared the answer. I glanced, instinctively, toward the curio cabinet. They didn't answer, instead encouraging me to puzzle it out, as if they were schoolteachers. "The devices? They each contain power, and you're stockpiling them."

Harry looked pleased with my deductions. I kept going.

"You can transform your plane in the air with the power contained in just a few of those. And if you can collect more..." My hands began to shake, remembering our flight from Ghent, conjuring up the nauseous dread that struck me when the Albatross that pursued us transformed into a Nieuport 28.

"If we can collect more, we can make something strong enough to compel all to put down their weapons and be done with the violence," Dieter said. "That's why we risk our lives for the devices. We are trying to save the human race from itself."

"And you want my help," I muttered. "But why? What can I do that you can't?"

"So many things," said Harry. "For one, we will never understand human emotions and reasoning the way you do. And that can open many doors. Secondly, you, more than any other person alive, are equipped to retrieve the goggles and violin strings."

"No," I whispered. "You can't mean you want me to go back and steal those from the Allies?"

"If you try to persuade her, Jane will give them to you."

"She just shot me out of the sky!" I said.

"Are you certain she recognized you?" Dieter asked.

"I recognized her, well enough. And she looked me right in the eyes as the bullets tore up my engine. I thought if I could get close enough, she'd see me and stop. But—she just—"

"The bloodlust had already taken her," said Dieter.

"Don't call it that. Please don't call it that."

"You may call it whatever you wish, but you know what I'm referring to. In the excitement of combat, she might have gunned down her own mother before realizing what she'd done. And this makes you afraid. Doesn't it? It makes you look at everyone you know differently, makes you wonder how much it would take to push any person over the brink. You thought she was immune, but none are immune."

Harry put a comforting hand on my shoulder.

"You loved her."

There it was. Somehow hearing it in the past tense made it easier to admit. But with it, came the concrete understanding of what I had lost. She hadn't simply shot down my plane. She'd riddled my heart with those rounds. It was the final confirmation that the woman I loved was gone.

"I did."

I bowed my head and wanted to cry.

"I understand," said Dieter. "Some things are all but impossible to forgive. Sometimes, people outgrow us. Or, as may be the case here, we outgrow others. But that doesn't make the loss hurt any less. Accept the loss. Accept the grief. You are mortal, and time will heal you if you fill it with good things."

He was right, and I wanted to believe he'd be right about the future as well. As the pain swelled in my gut, so did a sweeping sense of relief, as strong and nurturing as the safety I'd surrendered to in Jane when I'd shared my darkest secrets with her.

"Do we have to steal those devices right now?" I asked.

"Soon," said Dieter. "We thought that would be the biggest request, so we started there. We are missing three devices at present. The goggles, the strings, and the artifact left behind by George Guynemer. First, we can focus on retrieving Guynemer's, and we can use that as a schooling ground to teach you about your new abilities. Then, we will send you back to get the others."

I nodded. I could do that. First we did Little, next would be Guynemer. I had committed to that much already.

"All right," I said. "Do we know where Guynemer's artifact is?"

"There's one last thing," said Harry carefully. "Forgive us our Fae nature, but we still need the assurance we mentioned."

"What kind of assurance?"

"An important bit of collateral. Your marble."

My stomach sank. Even in the days after my crash, I had not removed Jane's marble from my neck. It was the very last bit of her I had.

"Come on," I said. "Anything else."

They looked at one another as though to consider it. I took their hesitation and improvised. I felt in my pockets and found Lufbery's round. It had survived the crash with me, but it was not shiny and polished anymore. I didn't want to give it up. It was the last I had of him.

"Here. This was my best friend's round. Lufbery. You two must know Lufbery. He didn't have a cone, but he was a great man. A great pilot. This is all I have left of him. Come on. This would be enough. This round has to have some magic to it."

"It does not," said Dieter.

"You're lying. It has to. Luf was our best. I'd have put him against Richthofen or Voss, or if not one of those, definitely Little or Ball or—"

"We kept an eye on Raoul Lufbery," said Harry. "He was the United States' Ace of Aces, after all. But your emotion clouds your opinion of him. He ran away from home to see the world and search for his absent father. He served as a rifleman in the US Army. His mentor, who he was rumored to talk about the same way you talk about him, died flying reconnaissance missions for the Escadrille N 23. He was a courageous pilot, a thoughtful man, and a reluctant leader. But you don't carry that machine gun round for any of those reasons. Yes, he likely had more kills than were attributed to him, but he was no Werner Voss. You looked up to him like an older brother, like a hero. That's enough, you know. He doesn't need to be a legend for you to mourn him like one."

I stared at the round sitting in my palm. Harry's hand squeezed my shoulder again, gentle and understanding.

"The marble is different, and it's the difficulty in giving it up that makes it a trust-earning gesture," he said. "But what's more, I think it might help you heal faster from the wound we can't treat."

He meant that it was time to let her go, to admit that Atkins and the great military complex had her now. And maybe he was right. Maybe, if I took it off, I could shed some of the weight and guilt and longing I carried with me all the time.

I glanced at the curio cabinet, and saw Jane's marble on the shelf, in its own spot, isolated from the others. My hair rested in the glass drop.

It had been taken from her forcibly, yes, but then a dark, uncomfortable idea popped up. She'd had the marbles made to protect us from the war. Then she'd pushed us headlong into one dangerous scenario after another. How had she expected to keep it safe? You cannot pray for peace and then go looking for a fight.

Can love ever be the source of taking another person's life?

I looked at Dieter, then at Harry. Neither had their hands out in expectation.

My hands moved on their own, unclasping the marble before dropping it on the small table in front of the couch. It landed without ceremony, chain draping over the glass.

The world did not end. I did not die.

"Do you feel lighter?" Harry asked.

I smiled, genuinely.

"I do."

Chapter 30
Shifting Lines
Jane

We didn't stay long at Bruay. After transcribing the message Marcus had left for us and interviewing a few of the other pilots and mechanics stationed there during the excitement, there wasn't much more the aerodrome had to offer. After all, Marcus and the Flyer got airborne, Dupont and I knew the rest.

Back in the relative safety of Amiens I managed to get a full night's sleep, and this despite grief about killing Marcus and hope that I had been seeing a faerie-induced illusion bouncing around in my head.

The human mind is capable of incredible things.

I dreamed of him, though. We were in the air. I was standing in my gunner's bay. His plane, a DH 5, flying adjacent—but instead of shooting and darting about, we flew side by side, calmly looking at one another as war went on around us.

When I woke and had a bite to eat, the solution to the Marcus's message came to me at once.

"Nun yunu wi," I said to myself over my coffee cup.

"What's that?" Dupont asked.

"The code word you sent Marcus and me when we were at Clairmarais. One of the pilots there said it was a word from an indigenous North American tribe."

Atkins was sitting down reading a newspaper. He glanced up over it.

"The message is with my intelligence agents now. I'm sure they'll have it cracked soon."

"Atkins, sometimes the desire to slap you is so overwhelming the only solution left to me is to leave the room."

I retired to the mess. The memory of decoding messages with Marcus in Clairmarais came back to me. We'd used the mess there as well, and I'd had to hide it quickly under the table when Oliver LeBoutillier introduced himself. Later, he would save our lives.

Dupont followed me out. I had scribbled my own copy of the message, and now it was a question of pride to have it decoded before Atkins's precious intelligence crew.

"It's a letter-shift cypher," I said.

"I know," said Dupont. "If you remember, I came up with a code word for the two of you as well."

I plugged in the letters NUYWI at the front of the alphabet and scratched out the rest of the order with those letters omitted. Then, I scribbled a copy of the alphabet in its proper form beneath.

It took no more than five minutes.

BRXJIHIO
CNQI HNBDY

"Dupont, I've got it." I twisted the scrap of paper around so he could see.

GUYNEMER
HATE MAGIC

Dupont, who had so enthusiastically clapped his hands upon my exclamation of deciphering the code, stopped.

"Guynemer hates magic?" His eyebrows knit together in confusion. "What does it mean?"

I frowned. "It says 'Guynemer hate magic' not 'hates magic.'"

"Isn't it more correct to say he hates magic?" Dupont asked. "At least that makes sense."

"Does it?" I asked. Guynemer was France's top ace, and his country had taken every pain to revel in its pride of him. Every man, woman, and child in France knew his name and famous exploits in the sky.

"When did Guynemer die?" I asked.

"Last September," Dupont replied with a sad cast to his face. "It was all the newspapers could write about for weeks."

I flipped over the piece of paper I'd been working on.

"What are you doing?" Dupont asked.

"What do we know for certain?" I said, drawing a small two-by-two table. On the left side, I jotted down names. "Boelcke. Richthofen. Ball. Little. We know they all left devices behind. The goggles. Scarf. Strings. Ring." I swiveled the paper back around to Dupont. "Does Guynemer's name belong on this list?"

"He'd be the only Frenchman," said Dupont. He couldn't hide the curl of his lip as if to suggest Guynemer's superiority. It made me smile.

"Ignore the country of origin."

"He'd deserve a spot near the top."

"Right," I said. "Which means we must assume that he would have left behind a device."

"We know this. It's why Atkins has been hounding me to track down Guynemer's remains."

"What other names are we missing on this list?"

Dupont stared at the list and closed one eye as he thought.

"From our side, I don't know if I'd group any other pilot with them, except for a few who are still living," he said.

"What about German pilots?" I asked.

"Werner Voss," said Atkins as he walked up behind me. "The Baron's rival. He died last autumn in a sortie fit for the history books. Took eight of our lads to bring him down."

I penciled Voss's name on the list.

"Any others?"

Atkins and Dupont both frowned.

"It's hard to say. There are other names that spring to mind, but I don't believe they inspire the same dread. Immelmann, perhaps. But he was more of an early pioneer than a storied killer."

"Well, let's just settle on those for now," I said. I circled the spots beside their names. Boelcke. Richthofen. Ball. Little. Voss. Guynemer.

I looked up as it hit me. "If they all left something, it'd be quite the collection, wouldn't you say?. We have two of the items. We know they have the scarf and the ring. But these other two?" I underlined Guynemer and Voss. "What if they don't have them yet?"

Atkins pulled the paper closer to himself.

"I see you decoded the message," he said as he eyed my scribbled alphabets. "What does it mean?"

"What if Marcus is trying to tell us where they're going next?" I said. "If they don't have Voss's or Guynemer's devices, then surely one of them would be their next target."

Dupont frowned. "But Guynemer's plane went down months ago."

"As did Albert Ball's," I replied. "But someone recognized the magic and hid it. We didn't go retrieve the strings until long after his death. Why not with Guynemer as well?"

Dupont frowned.

"That poses a big problem," he said.

"Why is that?"

"The front line has shifted significantly since then. The region Guynemer last flew was north near Ypres, well behind the current German line. Even back then, he crashed in contested territory. We couldn't confirm his death until a captured German pilot claimed to have identified his body. He said he was shot through the head."

"You mean his device might be in German hands?" Atkins asked.

"I can't see how it would be anywhere else," Dupont said with a shrug. "The Prussians buried him. He had such a stature, I'm sure he was looted. His belongings would be fought over as prizes."

"And still no word from Mustermann?" I asked with a resigned shake of my head. "Why would he take on so much risk to work with us only to vanish like this?"

"He may be dead," said Dupont. I swallowed hard. The

thought had occurred to me already, but I'd rejected it. If he were dead, Earnst and Lina may have come to the same end.

Atkins pushed the piece of paper away from him.

"At the very least, if Guynemer went down in Belgium, our intelligence network might be of some use. Let me see what inquiries can be made. La Dame Blanche may favor us yet again, although, I confess it's a long shot. They're not configured to report this kind of information. They're more concerned with troop movements and the like."

Dupont sat a little taller.

"France shares a border with Belgium. If there's information to be had, it won't be from the papers coming in. It will be from those who brave the border crossing. We have a network as well, it is not named. You asked to investigate. Have faith. Something is bound to come up. I put the request in many days ago."

"And the second part here?" Atkins asked pointing at the phrase below Guynemer's name.

Hate magic.

"It looks like we all have some investigating to do," I replied.

The days were agonizing. My mind split in two directions. Marcus's death plagued, and as time went on, my only protection was denial. Doubt and hope had trenched in, and neither could gain any significant ground in my heart.

Atkins and Dupont had been busy in the intelligence office for days, coming out occasionally to eat or let me know that nothing of value had been discovered yet. Time slipped through my fingers, a rope meant to strangle me.

And through it all, I tortured myself over the meaning of hate magic, sitting against a steel hut, watching the planes on base fly in and take off.

At first, I had discounted at once the meaning Dupont had

suggested. Whether Guynemer liked or disliked magic seemed irrelevant. But then something caught my attention. When we had first met with Earnst in Nancy, he recounted an experience in which the Baron told him to destroy Boelcke's goggles, never to use them, or he'd shoot Earnst from the sky.

I'd never understood why Richthofen would have said such a thing. Was he superstitious? Religious? I recalled nothing from the man's reputation to suggest as much.

Perhaps Guynemer had a similar experience, to make him detest the magic. If that were true, we should be spending our time trying to find overlaps between his life and the Baron's.

But another, simpler, explanation tore at me. What if Marcus had been trying to tell me two different things? One, the location of the Flyers' next target. Second, something about the magic itself. What if hate was a classification?

Hate.

The word was strong enough to provoke an emotional reaction of its own, a word reserved for the most bitter feelings. To say one hated another was superlative. No sentiment could supersede it.

Could such a concept come with its own inherent magic?

It lined up well enough with the other arcane schools on which my Aunt Luella had instructed me. But to explore the magic of hate, I feared I had not the courage. What dark avenues and threatening tendrils would I tempt in such an expedition? My parents had taught me about hate, not as a magic, but as a poison. Hate twisted the perception of reality. It was a perversion of love, for both were branches of obsession.

To hate something, in the truest sense of the word, meant it was impossible to leave it alone. One must be willing to sacrifice for such a fixation, to give up life for its passionate pursuit.

And yet, at the same time, hate manifested itself in many ways. It sat deep in the heart, pulling strings like a puppeteer until there was no telling which actions were caused by which motivations.

A Nieuport glided through the air ahead of me and set down. Watching it land reminded me of all the hours I'd spent waiting like this in Gengault, praying that Marcus made it back safely, wishing he never had to risk his life in the first place.

I'd embarked on this mission because Atkins had urged, in strong language, that it was of paramount importance. I believed him, and because it validated my clumsy attempts at magic and the gravity of the request made me feel tall, I accepted. And, in so doing, I gave Marcus up.

Tears slid down my cheeks, but I wiped them away quickly, afraid that if I allowed a few, there would be no preventing the deluge I'd been holding at bay these many long hours. But it was hard to face such truths without crying.

I gave up on Marcus the moment I accepted the war.

Hate magic made all too much sense because it had been growing in my chest. The Flyer had smelled it on me in Ghent. The fear of death brought it out of me. Whether it was preparing to kill as many people as necessary from behind the machine gun on my motorbike sidecar, failing to ease off the trigger when I'd clearly already felled a plane, or finding no objection to risking Allied lives to pursue our mission objective, hate had me by the throat.

I hated it all. I hated that I had to leave my wonderful parents. I hated that I'd been surrounded by death for so long. But what was more, I hated that I met Marcus and grew attached to him when I knew so well there was no chance of protecting him. And I hated that when we had thrown away the opinion of the world and committed loyalty to one another, I was too afraid to abandon what made me feel strong.

I should have left with him when he asked.

More tears came, but a drizzle had started as well, the start of one of those lovely and warm spring showers that I had adored as a young girl. I'd gone out to play in them, soaking my dress, infuriating my mother, but making my father smile ear to ear.

Hate magic. Why tell me? I'd seen the power leak out from Little's body and fasten itself to a ring intended for his wife. Could that power really be hate magic? Had Little experienced the same tug and pull in opposite directions as I did now? Protecting one's family could only be an act of love. Yet, killing another person...

Suddenly, the hunger for answers came stronger than ever. I needed to know, not only if by some miracle Marcus was alive, but how the magic factored into the war at all, why the Flyers wanted it, and whether they might be in the right, as everywhere around me it was abundantly clear that humans were not.

"Jane!" Dupont called to me from down the path. I wiped my eyes more in a fury, trying to erase all traces of my breakdown.

"What is it?" I asked as he came to a rest beside me. He ran all the way and huffed a bit.

"We have information," he said. "It's about the Germans. A contact all the way from Berlin."

I bit my lip as I remembered Gervaise and her boundless courage. I hardly had strength to stomach the sacrifices people like her made to provide such information.

"The Germans buried Guynemer with full honors and made great efforts to make sure we knew that. But, the remains of his aircraft, and any personal effects, were not guaranteed to be buried with him. And I think you know a thing or two about Germany's efforts to collect culturally important items."

I nodded. In Ghent, Thomas, who worked at the Museum of Antiquities, was arrested in the name of a search for a painted panel of great value. He had mentioned just how thorough the search had been for such objects throughout the war.

"You think some of Guynemer's possessions were confiscated?"

"Wilhelm von Bode is the man behind gathering cultural items of note for German museums. He is a well-known supporter of Kaiser Wilhelm, and I do not doubt that if there were any objects from Guynemer's crash site giving off an impression of importance, he may want it collected."

I frowned.

"But if that's the case, what are we going to do? Earnst and Lina are out of contact, and I don't expect we can infiltrate Berlin to go poking around their Royal museum."

Dupont grinned.

"Wait a moment. This is where the information comes in. Apparently, there was a discrepancy on the packing description. The batch of artifacts that contained Guynemer's possessions arrived in Berlin with a missing item."

I bit my lip. It wasn't much, but it was a loose strand to pull on.

"Do we know who was in charge of moving that shipment?" I asked.

"We know more than that," said Dupont, teeth splitting his smile in two. "We know where he's stationed."

My mouth fell open.

"You weren't joking when you said the French had their own network."

If we knew where this man was, and he had confiscated Guynemer's device, then we could track him down and either steal it or trade for it. Then, if we had it, we might have another chance of luring the Flyers to us.

My optimism fell as I realized how many hypotheticals I was stringing together.

"Well, it's a start, at least," I muttered.

"Well, you might not be so happy when I tell you where he's stationed."

Chapter 31
Transformaton
Marcus

We used to heed them not,
Little toys for play,
So learned we not to love,
And taught them well to hate.
-Widlus-

"You're absolutely crazy," I said, shaking my head back and forth.

"I agree," said Harry. "It would have been better to raid him while he was in Berlin. German forces would never have expected a heist like that so deep within their own country. And, even if they did, most of their strength is busy fighting at the front."

Dieter waved us off. We stood under the canopy of trees outside our hideout. Three planes were parked there now, all German models, transfigured one at a time by Dieter.

"We had more pressing issues at the time. And the way things are going, it's likely to get even more complicated to retrieve the artifact soon. The Americans are moving in numbers, and the German response is unpredictable. We're not about to fly in while a battle is raging to retrieve an artifact. If we don't go now, we will lose the chance."

"Yeah, but German High Command?" I gawked.

"Oberste Heeresleitung," Dieter corrected. "You'd better practice the accent in case you're shot down."

I threw my hands in the air and turned away.

"That's not helping his confidence," Harry said as a nagging reprimand.

I walked over to my machine, a sterling Albatross triplane, the same model that Dieter had used to pursue us on our flight from Ghent. My first time flying it was exhilarating.

It had been about a week since my crash, and my burn was healing faster than expected. It still looked terrible, but the pain had lessened significantly. The Flyers took that time to train me, including how to transform my aircraft.

It required a significant amount of magical energy from the devices left by the war's top pilots. But even with all that, as a human, I needed a little boost. Around my neck, in place of Jane's glass marble, I now wore a leather strap and a pendant made of compressed ash imbued with some special Fae enhancements.

I didn't understand all the details exactly. The two of them had been rattling off so much information about one important figure in their history after another, how one had bested another in wits, then in violence, and how consolidating the magic of contractual misdirection and powering it with human hate magic had inherent difficulties, and the stabilizing effect of the Fae power was ever so important and on and on for hours.

Who knew that magic could be so boring?

But whatever they did to make it happen, it worked my very first time flying that DH 5 into the air. They sent me up wearing Richthofen's scarf and Little's ring with instructions to relive a moment in which I'd shot down a plane.

I looked at them blankly, wondering if they understood I'd

only shot down one plane in my life, and that being Dieter's plane thanks only to sheer luck and desperation.

But Harry gave me a knowing glance and sent me into the air all the same. Dieter put my flight helmet on himself and whispered to me to remember how badly I wanted to kill the other pilot, that I had to bring back the moment I split that pilot's reality.

"What if the pilot I shot down didn't die?" I asked.

"It's more about the intention than the result," he replied. "Your new amulet will guide you. You will sense how to do the rest."

I was shocked by how simple it was. One moment, I was flying the DH 5. I leveled it out and gave myself an easy sweep of sky before closing my eyes and remembering that awful moment of desperation at hearing Jane's shout of pain, my longing to get home safely, my unbridled anger that someone else could hold my life, her life, in their hands.

My memory floated on its own then, like a raft down the current of a river, and my perspective shifted. I traveled with the rounds I had fired, blazing fast into the blinding sun. I saw Dieter's eyes as he understood his plane had been hit, and could all but feel the workings of his plane, then a Nieuport 28, screeching into failure. The punctured engine. The cracked line. The disrupted cylinders.

And then a jolt rattled me, and my eyes shot open.

Suddenly, my DH 5 was nowhere to be found. I was flying a Nieuport 28, and I nearly cried from the nostalgia and comfort of being in my own plane again. This was the model Luf had taught me in. I knew the cockpit and controls and handling better than my own reflection.

Like greeting an old friend, I flipped into familiar and challenging maneuvers and pretended, for a while, that the last four months never happened.

When I came back down, Dieter and Harry both had wide smiles.

"I can only transform into planes I've shot down myself?" I asked.

"Yes," said Harry. "So make sure you conjure the correct memory. The last thing you want is to turn into an obsolete aircraft when you needed the latest model to avoid dying."

I didn't correct them to say I'd be switching only to Nieuport 28s, but I didn't think it would matter for now. Dieter seemed to have a certain idea in mind when he configured our aircraft for this new mission.

While I was busy practicing magic, they got busy with research and finding another plane. Over the course of a week, they flew in and out, sometimes leaving me alone for hours at a time. After a three-day absence, Dieter returned with a new plane and great news. He had found Guynemer's device. Apparently, when the French ace went down behind German territory, some handsy looter took a liking to some of his property. Now, he was stationed at German High Command in Avesnes, south of Mons.

"Do we even know what we're looking for?" I asked.

"We will know when we see it. It will call to Harry and myself," said Dieter.

"And why do you need me at all? I'm not any good on the ground. I don't speak German, and they'll peg me as a spy for sure."

They both lowered their brows as if I were some dumb animal.

"Why do you think we've gone to the trouble of teaching you how to transfigure your plane? Things may not go well for us on the ground, and having a hidden ally in the sky might be a crucial and deciding advantage to our survival. We are stealing something from within the heart of German High Command, after all."

"So I'll just be flying around waiting for you to come back up and hoping we don't get into a huge sortie right above German High Command?"

"That's it," said Dieter. "You'll be fine. You have the Baron's scarf, so your shots should be more deadly, and you have Little's ring, which should make the German planes more hesitant to fire on you."

I shuddered. Dieter told me he suspected Little's ring was a distillation of his loyalty and devotion to his family. It inspired similar loyalty in its bearer's comrades, or in this case, enemies who believed they were comrades.

So if it came to it, not only would I be firing on German planes from my own German plane, but the pilots would be magically encouraged to believe I was on their side.

Luf would have hated the idea.

"Let's review one more time," said Harry. "I want to make sure everyone understands their assignments." He tried not to look at me, but I knew exactly what he meant when he said *everyone.*

"The device is in the possession of a driver named Albrecht Meier. He is stationed in a shelled estate near Avesnes and the Oberste Heeresleitung. His job is to transport important cultural objects from the war zone to Berlin. And while the Germans are defending the line, he checks in on worthy candidates for the German's increasing wartime collection. He spends his time driving around picking up items and stockpiling them at German command before sending these loads back to Berlin."

"He's a looter," I muttered in distaste.

"As are we," said Harry. "He's a well-educated looter, and if weren't for his work and the work of his companions, many items of worth might have been otherwise destroyed."

"Where do we find him?" I asked.

Dieter continued. "We will fly across the lines and land well behind Avesnes to refuel and prepare. Then, Harry will infiltrate High Command and, if needed, ask about Meier's location."

"If needed?" I asked.

"If we're lucky," said Harry, "he and the device will be there, and I won't need to ask anyone anything. They sing to us, in a way, so that we can find them when we're close enough to hear them."

"And if he is there, how will you get it from him?" I asked as I climbed into my cockpit. My jaw clenched. Part of me did not want to know.

"I'll have to persuade him," said Harry grimly. "And quietly, at that."

He clambered into his own machine.

"While he's doing that," said Dieter, "Marcus and I will patrol the air to make sure there are no surprises for our getaway. Understood?"

"I'll just follow you two, then," I said. Dieter approached.

"You have the amulet?" he asked, hands resting on the edge of the pilot's bay.

"I'll be fine. I just need a little push," I said, nodding at my propellor. Harry's Albatross kicked to life, and I couldn't hold back envy and awe knowing they had some method of starting their engines and propellors so easily. In a pinch, a pilot could do his own propellor start, but it required starting the engine, leaving the plane to kick the prop, then climbing back in, and there was plenty of room for awful things to happen at any point in the process. "Maybe you can teach me that trick next."

Dieter smiled. "Marcus, I'm glad you decided to come on our side," he said.

I stared. Maybe it was the faerie in him, but the warmth he tried to express didn't quite come across. His smile looked forced, and I'd never known him to be soft like this.

But then, maybe Dieter was the type not to open up until he believed he could trust someone. I couldn't flag him for trying.

"Don't make me regret it," I said with a laugh, gently bumping my fist against his fingers.

"No promises!" he cried. I winced as he extend the banter beyond the point two humans might. But he didn't let me sit in this discomfort. Instead, as he stood between our three planes, he shouted over the roar of the engine:

> "Shrink from no great work today,
> Leave no plans or schemes in store.
> Expel from all the ignorance
> Of what you've built behind closed doors.
> Burst the battle horn asunder.
> Ravage stillness. Mark your claim.
> Swear before the great sun sets
> The very hills will know your name.
> The time for planning now is over,
> The day has dawned, the hour here.
> Let eyes from all behold and wonder
> How you bind and master fear.
> Follow now and do not falter
> In unknown paths we bravely go
> Raze with me the stony spires
> Of critic, tyrant, flagging foe.
> And if I fall, charge bravely on.
> Hold the standard high aloft.
> Though closed my eyes and still my lips,
> Still can I hear your song above.
> You thunderous starshine, you climbing dove,
> From ground below to sky above,
> Will shine our work, the host we stay,
> Oh, shrink from no great work today!"

As he repeated the final refrain again and again, he got to work starting my propellor. When my bird came alive, he gave me a hearty thumbs up and climbed into his own machine. I'd heard them repeat portions of this poem to one another on the U-boat and before separating to get Little's ring. After getting over the shock of seeing Dieter shout it with such animation, the words worked their way under my skin and emboldened me.

I would not shrink today.

Soon, we were flying, and after so much time cloistered in a little enchanted wood, it took me a while to get my bearings.

It was still early in the day, and we flew toward the sun as we climbed high and turned to the south. Far below us, the sea stretched like a matte blue painting.

I smiled as I put the pieces together.

We had been in England all that time. Atkins, Smith, and Dupont were exhausting themselves trying to track down vigilantes nested on the King's old island.

But my smile melted as we put the channel to our tail. Now, I could almost feel it below us. The line called up from the earth with its bloodthirsty appetite. I'd flown over it dozens of times, but this time hit me differently. I had elected to step away from the allegiances that governed the war. I'd not yet returned with the information I swore I'd report back. In some ways, entering the war zone struck me as trespassing.

I grasped for the marble around my neck. But there was no marble there. No glass with Jane's hair. Just an amulet made of ash.

Beside me, Dieter tipped his wings, pulling me out of my head. He motioned to look below.

I rolled my wings to get a good look. Beneath us, in a prime position, flew an Albatross C X two-seater. We had pulled up from behind them, and whether they didn't think to look for enemies from the direction we came in, or if the silhouettes of my companions' planes put them at ease, this pilot and his gunner were sitting ducks.

And now, Harry and Dieter expected me to prove I could be trusted.

Shrink from no great work today.

The poem rattled in my mind. This was different now. I didn't fly for glory, and I didn't take human life to earn a score. It was the plane I needed. In case something went wrong, each of us needed the power to transform into a two-seater.

Shrink from no great work today.

I couldn't get the words out of my head. They were empowering, emboldening... Downing this plane would serve a greater purpose.

I righted my wings and glanced to Dieter. He pumped his fist in the air, encouraging me to hurry before I missed the chance. I looked to Harry. He was several plane lengths away, but I could still see him nodding toward me. I gripped the joystick and looked back at the Albatross below.

They hadn't heard me. They hadn't seen me. And with a squeeze of my finger, they'd fall from the sky.

I twisted my hands around the joystick and tried to steady my breathing. This was a German plane. I'd been brought up as an Allied pilot. I'd been squeamish about this in the past. I'd wanted my kills to be honorable, wanted to cling to the notion that honor was important at war. Now, a whole new reservation struck me.

I wasn't even in the game anymore. This kill would not be for the Allies. It'd be for the faeries, and if I believed them, to further their plans to end the war.

What would Lufbery say? What would Jane say?

But Luf was dead, and Jane had shot me down.

Understanding that changed things. I let go of something I'd been holding on to and allowed myself to do whatever I had to.

I would not shrink today.

I dipped my nose down and dove. Faster, faster. My triplane

picked up speed as the C X grew in my sights. This was my victory. Luf was allowed to do it. Jane was allowed to do it.

Just as the gunner looked upward and noticed something was wrong, I mashed the trigger back hard. The Spandau guns roared to life, louder, more ferocious than I remembered. The kickback made the plane shake and quiver. My machine belched out hot fire and lead. I had no idea what variety of rounds came out, but Richthofen's scarf was wildly powerful.

Tracer. Incendiary. Heavy. Hot. Rapid. Tearing. I knew what it was like to be on the receiving end of a round fired by a pilot wearing the Baron's artifact. The gunner and pilot both jolted in their seats, the C X started to tilt. I let off the guns and watched, my stomach sinking with their plane.

They fell from the sky, transitioning at first into a smooth unguided glide. But then they started to spin, faster and faster. There was no recovering from a spiral like that, plummeting and suddenly vanishing into a cloud of smoke and dust so far below us it looked like a drop of blood falling into a bucket of sand.

My breath heaved. My throat seized up, painful and rigid. I wanted to scream. I wanted to sob, but I couldn't do anything at all.

The moment stuck with me like a photograph, imprinted indelibly on my conscience. The nightmarish heat turned the dream I'd been so negligent in preserving into a living terror. I'd killed them. I'd shot down an Albatross two-seater.

I grabbed again at my marble only to find the Fae medallion, and I realized just how alone a man could feel in such an awful world.

It hardly came as a surprise when I looked out at my wing and saw the change.

I'd unknowingly gone through the steps.

My plane had transformed into the Albatross I'd just sent to the Earth.

Chapter 32
A Fool's Prayer
Jane

"Good morning; good morning!" the General said
When we met him last week on our way to the line.
Now the soldiers he smiled at are most of 'em dead,
And we're cursing his staff for incompetent swine.
-Siegfried Sassoon-

"It is too dangerous," said Atkins flatly.

"It's the only way," I replied.

I stood in front of him in the Nissen hut he'd requisitioned for our mission. What mission we had now, I wasn't entirely sure.

"The only way to what?" he asked quietly.

"To find them," I replied, trying to keep a stiff upper lip.

"Like we did last time? If I remember correctly, you wanted to use a magic trinket to lure the Flyer out then as well. That didn't go very well for us."

"Well, we will have to do better this time, then," I said. "Atkins, we're running out of opportunities. Guynemer. Maybe there's a device out there from Werner Voss, but we don't know where it is. We have intelligence that suggests—"

"That suggests what?" Atkins stood, stooping inside the hut to avoid touching the ceiling. "We have nothing. We have a manifest with a missing, undisclosed item on it. And you want to march into German High Command to find the driver! It's a foolhardy risk, and I won't abide it."

"You seemed perfectly ready to use this strategy before," I said.

"Yes and look where it's led us!" He was bristling now. His face was all red, and his mustache twitched.

"You can't tell me you don't want another chance at the Flyer," I continued. "Imagine. You could be a hero for the crown. The man who finally ended the Fae inconvenience. And if you don't, what's to stop him from emboldening Ireland, as you fear? Or worse, what if he works alongside the Germans and aids them in finally bleeding our country dry, one life at a time?"

"Don't pretend that you know how to conduct wartime strategy. I know all about risks, more than you'll ever understand because, believe it or not, a person has more to lose than a boyfriend."

I reddened as anger blossomed in my breast.

"Look around you, Private Doe." He spat my moniker with a snarl. "We are in the business of widow making, and His majesty's armed forces learned long ago that the very impulse you currently let run wild in your personal conduct is the perfect tool to do just that. Can you possibly appreciate what it is like to watch tens of thousands of men die in a matter of hours? You want to hazard the success of my mandate on a high-risk window of opportunity. But the faerie has proven he can best you time and again."

He took a deep breath and straightened. His eyes softened, but mine did not. My fists had balled, and I stuck my chest out at military attention. He sighed and massaged the bridge between his nose.

"I can't lose you, Jane," he said. "We've lost Smith already. We've likely lost Mustermann, and you don't want to hear this, but Marcus is likely dead, as well. We are running out of firepower, and if you throw your life away, I will have next to no chance of success."

At mention of Marcus's likely demise, I stiffened and willed my features to betray no evidence of my suspicions, fears, hopes, or doubts on that front. A small part of me wished I could tell him what had happened during our last sortie in the air. I had tried in the immediate aftermath, but everyone I told assumed I was in shock. Perhaps I had been. I was counting on it.

But I'd reached the end of the road with Atkins. Smith had planted seeds of mistrust in my mind, and one surprise discovery after another had done their work at making trust impossible.

We had different motives. This was what Marcus was trying to tell me. I would always have different motives than the men who commanded me unless I gave my life over to them. To give a life to someone required either great fear or great love, and I did not fear Atkins any longer.

My hands relaxed as I bowed my head toward the dirt.

"I understand," I said.

"Thank heavens for that," he said, coming round to wrap an arm across my shoulders. "Now, I promise, we will conduct this properly. I have not given up on Marcus, even though I know the odds are long. And, like you, I eagerly look forward to the day we can make the faerie pay for how it has meddled in English affairs."

He led me gently toward the entrance of his hut.

"I'm sorry, Atkins. I'm just so eager," I said blankly.

"Well, you've hardly slept since your crash. Go by the mess, get a bite, then catch a wink. We will get about making a proper plan tomorrow."

I took one long last look at Atkins before gently cupping his cheek. He reminded me of home in so many ways: his manner of speaking, his unhurried nature, his methodical dedication to the proper state of things.

He was a little startled by my gesture, but removed my hand from his face gently with a nod.

"You'll be another person tomorrow," he said and sent me on my way.

I made it about twenty steps before Dupont rushed to my side.

"What did he say?" he asked.

"He'll be no help," I replied. "Did you mean what you said when you promised you would take me anywhere?"

Dupont grinned. "Where are we going?"

I t was easy to discount the resourcefulness of my French companion. At our first meeting, Dupont had come across as something of a caricature. He spoke as though half drunk at all times, and his enthusiasm for skirting boundaries and procedure cut starkly against Smith's cold efficiency and Atkins's rigid formality.

But as we'd gone on together, I understood the mask he wore. Whether the unique obstacles of our mission pushed him to grow or reveal his true nature, I didn't know. But now, when the occasion called, and he believed in the cause with his heart, he demonstrated just how much influence he had.

Atkins's and Smith's equal in the French infrastructure, he did not lack for resources. As I walked away from my chain of command, I stepped into his world of passionate war making.

"One of Bode's drivers is stationed near German High Command at Avesnes," he said conspiratorially as we watched pilots check their sights at a munitions testing field. We spoke quietly. "The closest aerodromes are northwest of Avesnes-sur-Helpe, and the entire airspace is contested. But, we can fly by night and drop into a field quietly. I won't be able to stay. Hiding a plane so close will be impossible. But I can return to the same spot a night or two following."

"How will I find the man we're looking for?" I asked.

"According to our sources, he is often seen at a train station on the east of the city. Beyond that, you will have to rely on the goggles," he said. "Will they not identify the object? Perhaps the location? Geographically, the town will not be so large that it is unnavigable. You will need to find some way to look busy while you search. Steal some clothes. Dress as a laundress or baker."

"I'll figure something out," I replied.

"Jane, this is not like Ghent," he said severely.

"I know. For one, I won't have Marcus."

"No," he turned to me, breaking the air of affected nonchalance. "Sending you into an occupied city well behind the lines to make contact with a group of people friendly to us was one thing. This is different. You are headed into one of the most carefully guarded outposts in the world. You may not trust anyone. You must be a ghost. Your safest approach is never to be seen, and if you are seen, to be nothing but paint on the plaster. Study how the women move, so if you have to go into the open, you can mimic their actions. You will have no support. If you're caught—"

"Then I'm dead," I replied. Germany had no sympathy for spies, especially now that they were so wary of intelligence networks. I remembered well how Gervaise had declared the names of women who had become martyrs for the military cause.

Dupont turned back to the field just as a Nieuport 27 swooped low and shot a large boulder. Few, if any, fragments chipped off the stone. The mechanics would need to rectify the sights on those Vickers guns.

"Do you want one day or two?" he asked.

"One," I replied. There was no telling how long it might take me to find the device, if it were there at all, but I'd much rather have a quick exit available than be stuck waiting around.

Dupont nodded.

"If you're not there, I'll return the next night as well."

"You'll do no such thing, Dupont. It's too dangerous, as you've said."

He grinned again. "But you cannot stop me."

"Dupont," I warned.

"How does it feel, when someone does it to you?" His smile faded quickly as the severity of our mission settled in. "We leave tonight."

That night, Dupont and I got quietly into a car and drove to a neighboring airfield. We wore oversized military jackets we'd found sitting in a storage crate. The jacket was used, and I harbored no illusions about what that meant for its previous owner.

When we arrived at our new aerodrome, the sun was setting, but a two-seater waited for us. Dupont went ahead to dismiss the small group of mechanics that had readied it. After some enthusiastic salutes, they cleared and Dupont motioned for me to join him. I hopped into the pilot seat while he got the propellor started, and briefly, as I eyed the joystick, I wondered what it would be like to pilot one of these machines myself.

It wasn't entirely unheard of. There were a couple of women who flew as exhibition pilots before the war. Perhaps one day, I could join them.

But I banished the thought as it came. Wishing and dreaming of future lives did me no good now.

"Here," said Dupont as I crawled to the gunner's bay. He handed me a Star pistol and climbed into the pilot's seat. "Just in case you need it." He called back.

I tucked it away quickly, attempting to stave off thoughts of just how badly things would need to go for me to use the gun.

We took to the air in a hurry. Dupont would require at least some light to find the valley we'd identified on a map. He'd put me down northeast of Avesnes with the hope that trying to get into the city would be easier coming from a direction that was not the front. I doubted it would matter much.

We didn't have time to climb much, but our luck held as a stretch of low-hanging clouds masked our position from Archie fire on the ground. Normally, these clouds would make it significantly easier to spot the black speck of our plane against them, but with night falling quickly, the sorties were dissipating and making room in the sky for the infamous night bombing raids both sides of the conflict had increasingly relied upon.

We flew above the clouds by compass until Dupont signaled to me that we'd be going below. I gripped the handles of the gun in my bay, but when my palms made contact, the flash of Marcus's wounded expression as he plummeted toward the Earth jolted me off it. A flash of pain went through the bruise on my arm, and I prayed I wouldn't have to touch it again.

Dupont's navigation served us well, though. I saw a city behind and to the right. Our luck held, and no enemy planes patrolled near the field we had circled.

"Do you see anything?" called Dupont. Through Boelcke's goggles, I squinted to get a better view of the city. There were faint traces of the magical blue snaking through the sky at a distance and close to the front lines. There were hums from the city behind us as well, but since Ireland, these stray signals had only grown. I'd learned to be judicious of them.

"Nothing is standing out," I said. "But it's possible."

"I hope our contact was right," said Dupont. "Or else you might have a disappointing holiday."

Dupont cut the engine, and we descended in a quiet glide. He set us down on the ground without many corrective belches of power, either, but it came at a cost.

As we rolled across the field, a snap and a jolt brought bad news. By the sudden lopsided tilt of the engine, I knew at once we'd damaged a landing strut. When we came to a stop, I hopped out to take a look. Light was fading quickly, and the field would soon be dark as pitch.

"Is it the wheel?" asked Dupont.

There was a sharp crack down the strut that attached to the two wheels beneath the plane. We must have hit a rock on entry.

"We may be lucky," I said. "It hasn't snapped off. It is only fractured a bit. Do you have anything we might use to reinforce it?" I asked.

"Some radio cable," he replied after a quick search inside the gunner's bay.

"That will have to do. Come down and help me set it."

We worked together, fumbling about in the dark carefully to wrap telegram wire around the damaged strut. We twisted the ends together; but by only the feel of it, we both knew it wouldn't take much to come apart again.

I sighed.

"Well, you might get airborne, but I doubt that will hold much on landing," I said.

Dupont snuffed.

"Well, it's a good thing pilots never die while attempting to land," he said with an attempt at British sarcasm. He looked around. "I suppose I'll have to come with you after all."

"No. It will increase our risk. And we can't leave a plane here." I shook my head. "Something told me to bring this along. I might as well use it for a good purpose."

From a pocket on my flight suit, I produced Albert Ball's violin strings.

"Are those what I think they are?" asked Dupont.

"Yes," I said. My arm ached as I tied it tightly atop the other cable. Between the strings and the telegram cable, we had enough to make a few passes. The strut felt more secure than it did before, but it wasn't going to replace an earnest repair anytime soon. "The strings held a French flag to the back of a Rumpler. I imagine they'll work well enough for one landing. If it's a soft one."

Dupont clapped me on the back.

"I will make it soft," he said. "Thank you. I expected one of your witch fixes."

I laughed. With the devices taking so much of my attention, I'd hardly given any thought to my old primitive attempts at magic.

"Go," I said, waving him on. "I have work to do."

Chapter 33
Forgiveness
Marcus

Even serving love, are our mortalities,
And cling to what they own in mortal fears:—
But oh, let end what will, I hold you fast
By immortal love, which has no first or last.
-Eleanor Farjeon-

I put down the Albatross two-seater without any hiccups. Dieter and Harry had set down before me in a field close to a tiny agricultural village. As soon as I powered down, they rushed over to me.

"Well done!" Dieter said, clapping. "He didn't even see you coming. You stalked him masterfully!"

Harry's congratulations were slightly more subdued, but he put a hand on my shoulder and squeezed it like a proud father.

"Now you'll have a German two-seater in your transformation repertoire. It may just save one of our lives," he said.

"Yeah." I had to admit that their cheers made it a little easier to swallow the misgivings I had over shooting the Germans down. "Though, I don't have a gunner, and that looks awfully suspicious, doesn't it? Maybe I should change back to the fighter?"

"We could make a dummy out of a bale of hay," Harry suggested, eyeing a shelled out cottage nearby.

"Yeah, that's exactly what I need," I murmured. "Bits of straw floating out in bunches behind my tail wing."

"A melon, then." Harry smiled.

"Where are we going to find a melon?" I asked, allowing myself a laugh.

Meanwhile Dieter scurried off to the farmhouse nearby.

"You guys have little hideouts all over the place, don't you?" I asked.

He pushed a small cart back toward us with what looked like large milk pails piled on it.

"It is shocking how many hiding places are available," he replied. "So many villages and buildings that used to be cared for and looked after now sit without custodians."

Dieter made it back, and we set ourselves to task, filling up our fuel tanks. It took us over a hundred gallons and a couple trips back to the cottage, but soon we were fueled up and ready again. Before we sealed the tanks, Dieter stuffed something that looked like paper into each.

"What's that?" I asked Harry.

"You two will be patrolling in the air," he replied as he helped me back into my cockpit. "It's some encouragement to make the fuel stretch farther."

Dieter scrunched his nose as he finished closing the tanks, giving me the impression he did not like the smell of the fuel, but he didn't make a fuss of it.

"We had just enough stashed here for these refills," he said to us. "We can't come back this way should we need more."

"Then I'll be quick about our business," said Harry. "Does everyone remember the plan?"

"What's there to forget?" I asked. "We fly around waiting for you to get the device, ready in case we have trouble on the escape."

Dieter frowned.

"Your tone makes it sounds as though you think such precautions are unnecessary ."

I shrugged.

"I know. Part of me does. But then, I got shot down on the last flight didn't I? So what do I know?"

"Thank you for humoring us, then," Dieter replied. He got my propellor started. When the engine was on, I gave him a thumbs up. He scurried into his Albatross.

"You be careful in there," I shouted to Harry. "Don't leave me stranded with Dialythe!"

Harry's smile twisted. He put his hands behind his back.

"I should have never let his name slip that way," Harry said.

"He told it to me, as a gesture of good faith," I replied. "My marble had to be worth something."

"He told it to you?" asked Harry in surprise.

I nodded. "Still don't know yours, though." I smiled. This was the type of good-hearted chiding I used to engage in with my old squad mates. But Harry didn't look amused. In fact, he stared long and hard at Dieter, who, sensing the eyes of his comrade on him, met his gaze and shrank.

"Perhaps if we make it through this mission, I'll reward you with it," Harry said at last.

"I don't even care!" I said. Clearly, I'd hit a nerve, and I didn't want to prod any sensitive issues between my two companions, especially right before heading into a mission. "Honest, Harry. Forget I mentioned it."

Harry's smile returned, but it came across as rehearsed this time. He was still bothered, not by me, but by Dieter. He must have sensed my unease.

"Relax," he said. "It's nothing. Dieter and I have spent a very long time together. We're both bound to have oddities that drive the other a little mad."

That I could relate to. I learned during my time with the Lafayette Escadrille that there were times I wanted to fight with even the brothers I held closest. A pang of regret stung my conscience as I remembered each time I'd been annoyed with Luf.

"All right. We'll let you two wrestle it out when we get back," I said. I gave him a thumbs up, and he helped me get my plane started.

As my plane gathered speed for take off, he stared at me in a strange, unsettling way. If I didn't know better it looked like fear, or even regret.

The bumps of the ground rattled up with the joystick on my big Albatross C X. Without an observer in the rear, the plane handled more responsively than other two seaters I'd flown. It had a little bit more power as well. When I pulled back on the stick and brought her into the air, the mechanics felt strange—empty and dreamlike.

I swooped into a slow upward cycle and saw Dieter following in my trail. I took a deep breath and reminded myself that though we were in German territory, I was in a German machine. But, should any of the numerous Allied patrols that swept through this sector come by, I could always transform into a Nieuport.

The freedom this power of transformation offered the Fae pilots was astonishing.

I peered over the cockpit and looked earthward back at Harry.

The town of Avesnes-sur-Helpe lay to the west, but for some reason, he headed back into the farmhouse. Maybe they had some more supplies he wanted to collect before heading into town to find the device. He'd have to get a move on, though. I didn't know how much more efficient the fuel consumption would be with Dieter's added bit of magic, but he had ground to cover.

My wingman cut in front of me to lead us through our holding pattern. He had shared his planned patrol route back at their hideout in England. It was a sweeping oblong oval for many miles north and south of Harry's plane. It'd take us a few hours and change.

I wondered what device Harry might be picking up in that hut to help him out in Avesnes. Despite all the danger and trauma it had caused, the magic continued to excite me. From the first time Boelcke's goggles had lit up the Flyer's plane in Clairmarais, it hit me that magic was as true a force as any in nature and every new discovery ignited my imagination.

Why not, especially now that I was one of them? With the magic, we would stop the war. That belief sustained me, cancelled out so much of the pain I'd experienced. If the magic could do that, maybe everything I'd gone through had been for something.

First the goggles. Then, how could I forget the sensations that coursed through me the first time I handled Richthofen's scarf? Ball's violin strings. The apparatus Dieter wore to navigate the mine field...

I paused.

That strange headgear had been the start of a whole new variety of magic for me. They had never bothered to connect that headwear to a pilot. It was my introduction to Fae magic. Or was it hate magic? Or was that the same?

I wished I could share it all with Jane. She'd have found it all fascinating. Pushing the difficult emotions aside, I missed her, plain and simple. She'd been my foundation for so long.

Alone in the cockpit, I finally had a chance to come to grips with how real my feelings for her had been, and how much it hurt to lose them.

I recalled hundreds of our exchanges, scenes from times we'd spent together as if they were formed like sculptures in the clouds around me. And once I started remembering, I couldn't stop. What an idiot I was, not to have recognized her earlier.

A warmth blossomed from my chest as I indulged in the memories I'd been restraining. The sensation contrasted sharply with the cold air rushing by. A smile split my face. Tears welled behind my flight goggles.

In some ways, I despised myself for admitting it, but even though she shot me down, I wanted to find an excuse for it. I wanted her to be sick or crazy or blind, any label I could blame for what she'd done because I wanted to see her and hug her again and tell her it was all right, and it had only burned my arm, anyway.

I wanted to forgive her. The desire consumed me, and now that Harry and Dieter weren't there to guide me carefully away from this pathway in my heart, I indulged. Even if it were just for a moment, I let myself believe that I could forgive her and that together we could get the hate magic out of her. If I loved her enough, maybe that would chase it out.

With my imaginations, the memory of her standing in that Bristol F2B lost its sting. I could give her the benefit of the doubt. I'd been in air combat. Things got confusing. I'd even been in the gunner's bay of a Brisfit, just like she had.

In fact, I'd done it right after she shot me down, after Dieter had rescued me in a Brisfit.

I frowned as I put those pieces together for the first time. I never asked what had happened after I left that sortie. I'd been so caught up in my own misery that I never bothered to wonder if Jane was all right.

And Dieter came and picked me up in a Brisfit...

The ring around my finger burned, and I let out a shout in surprise.

Little's ring. The fairies called it a ring of loyalty, but they hadn't possessed it for long enough to understand its effects. The horror of it gripped me. We relied on the ring's power to help me change my plane. As they explained it, I would need to channel the cumulative power behind both the scarf and the ring into the ash amulet they'd given me to trigger a transformation.

But though we siphoned magic from the devices, Dieter still predicted they would exhibit their latent abilities—the scarf enhancing my rounds, and the ring...

I didn't know what the ring did other than burn my finger.

I was scared to take it off, though. What if removing it broke the enchantment and my plane reverted to its DH 5 model? I'd be a sitting duck back here behind German lines wedged between German High Command and a handful of aerodromes.

Maybe it'd be best to park my plane by Harry's and just hide until he came back. Dieter could manage the patrol fine himself.

I looked up from the dull burn in my finger.

Dieter wasn't in front of me.

As my thoughts occupied my attention, I'd lost track of him. I swiveled my head from side to side, then behind me. He wasn't there.

I leaned over my bay to check the sky below but saw only European countryside dotted with an occasional village or patch of woods.

The ring burned again. It hurt enough to make me wince. It reminded me of how my marble heated up before...

A chilling thought struck me. It dragged my head and neck around, craned it upward.

I found Dieter.

He was flying above and behind me, trying to cloak himself in the sun.

Suddenly, a rush of understanding flooded my brain. Humiliation, desperation, and disbelief all rolled up into a wad of gum in my throat.

But it was far too late to work out the details of why.

He dived on me and opened fire.

Chapter 34
The Collector
Jane

They ask me where I've been.
And what I've done and seen.
But what can I reply?
Who knows it wasn't I.
-Wilfrid Wilson Gibson-

I crept through the woods bordering the field Dupont left me in. We were wise to approach from this side of the city. The fields I traversed were not heavily patrolled. The few soldiers that did wander about didn't bother being too thorough in their searches.

It was dark, and I moved quietly. They were content to travel the roads with their guns draped across their body hoping not to find anything amiss.

I snuck through the shadows, daring occasionally to cross a clearing to the dark side of a crumbling wall or shelled cottage. I didn't approach the main road, as occasionally I saw trucks bouncing down it, their headlights shining through the night. Far in the distance, I heard the heaving and chugging of a cargo train.

A flight of bombers and their escorts flew overhead, embarking on a mission to unleash their payload on an unsuspecting Allied target.

The German machine of war, in its most impersonal nature, was hard at work. Before I'd yet arrived at the city walls, the overwhelming automaton of the war effort was undeniable, fearsome, and humbling.

The goggles bounced around my neck. Every few hundred yards or so, if I had a good hiding place, I'd slip them over my eyes and glance about to see if any blue sheen would guide my way. But I couldn't leave them on. They fogged up quickly, making my pathway arduous at best.

I hadn't had adequate time to study the map of Avesnes that Dupont provided before we took off, and it was too dark to see the copy I'd brought along. But if I remembered correctly, walking into the city through any of the main entrances would be challenging. The outline of Avesnes's buildings inspired an anachronistic nostalgia in me. The architecture harkened back to the type of town one might read about in a medieval story. Everything was carved in gray stone, and the age of the settlement explained the layers of styles in how the stone was laid.

It was old and storied, built as a fortress a long, long time ago, and although modern artillery made its historic defensive work obsolete, I was not an artillery cannon.

But I wouldn't need to get into the true heart of German High Command anyway. I sought a man tasked with transporting cultural artifacts to Berlin. I doubted he would be housed with the army's top generals and strategists. Or so I hoped.

In any event, if transportation was his assignment, I planned on investigating transportation hubs first and foremost. That meant making my way toward the truck depot and the train yards on the eastern side of the city. And according to Dupont's map, they were accessible without trying to sneak past the formidable stone walls.

I continued on, trying to calm my anxiety about my limited time. But surplus hours were a luxury only if I were not captured. If I hurried and got myself shot as a spy, all the hours in the world would not help me.

I kept moving, appreciating and cursing at once the lights erected on posts and buildings that illuminated the city for nighttime war logistics and to prevent people like me from creeping about.

A railway ran from far over the visible horizon on my left across to the right. I followed it carefully as it carved its way through stretches of dense trees. I was grateful that these pockets of wood had not been laid bare, as so many others had. It made for easy hiding. As I ducked behind a shrub beneath one such canopy, I had to take a moment to wait for what seemed like a never-ending parade of train cars. After a few minutes, I recognized I had no chance to cross the railway anytime soon, so decided to follow it further south. Eventually, it would lead me to the station.

But just as I turned to continue, I noticed a car full of German soldiers, sitting at an intersection, waiting for the train to go by themselves. The clanking rattle of the locomotive had covered the sound of their engine.

I fell back quickly, snapping a branch on the way. But thankfully the train clambered on, and the soldiers were none the wiser.

I was too afraid to move, and so I waited, after all. Long minutes stretched on and on. The train did not end, and after what must have been an hour, the soldiers in the car got fed up as well. They exited the vehicle and stretched their legs before lighting up cigarettes and prattling on loudly as if they were on a forced lunch break.

I took a deep breath, settled in, and put on my goggles, just in case something decided to light up for me.

Nothing did. Another German car had arrived, and the pace of the train slowed, but after half an hour, the caboose finally came, and a big rush of empty air revealed the road and country beyond. The Germans applauded and started their engines again.

With the cars out of the way, I crossed the railway to reach more trees on the other side and continued onward. Finally, after miles of slowly sneaking through difficult terrain, the platforms lining the train station came into view.

They were not vacant. Even at this hour, German sentries stood watch as their companions set to work unloading supplies.

My shoulders slumped. The gun Dupont gave me had seemed light at first, but one slow mile after another, it grew heavier. My abdominal muscles protested against the slow-building fatigue.

Finding a way into the station at night would be risky. If I was to pose as a washer woman, I'd have no explanation whatsoever if I were caught after hours. It might be better to approach during the day when surely there would be more people about.

But if I were going to hide until morning, I would need a better place to rest than this. This close to the station, I would be discovered as the sun rose. I backtracked. About a mile back I'd passed a small hut. It was all dark inside, and half the roof had gone missing so that I doubted anyone would be using it.

The idea of walking another mile ached me, but I had little choice, and I started back toward it.

It took me nearly half an hour to stumble through trees to get there, but eventually, the wood gave out, and I stood exposed in an open stretch of field before the shack. I willed myself on, breathing heavily, and sprinted to duck behind its walls.

Inside, an owl had roosted, taking one of the few covered nooks left of the roof. A plank of wooden shingles leaned against one wall askew. That would have to do for my purposes.

Exhausted, I lay down, and despite my best intentions, sleep overtook me in no time at all.

. . .

I woke up with a start and cursed myself for falling asleep. The minutes ticked away before Dupont would be back, and I prayed that I hadn't wasted too many of them.

It was still cool, and the sun appeared to be mid-rise. More importantly, there were no German guards leveling rifles in my direction. The muted heartbeat of artillery fire thumped from the west. But despite that ever-present reminder of the war, and the sounds of the bustling train, the atmosphere was relatively peaceful.

I needed to rise quickly and make my plan to get into the train yard and find the collector, as I'd started calling him in my head. But though the daylight, ironically, gave me more cover, I'd need to make some adjustments to take advantage of the opportunity. My clothes, at present, marked me for certain as a British soldier. Fortunately, half buried in the collapsing stone wall, I found the remains of a dresser. It took me more exertion than I expected to clear enough space to crack one of the drawers open, but to my relief, there was an old, linen skirt crumpled up inside. I yanked it free and slipped it over my trousers. It was filthy, two cuts too large for me, and the fabric was pocked with holes from moths and other vermin, but it would have to do. I abandoned my jacket as well, undressing down to my blouse, and covered my shoulders with a ripped shawl that hid deeper in the drawer.

I had no mirror to check myself, but the disguise had to be better than my previous outfit. I shoved my old clothes back into the dresser, replaced the rubble to prevent their discovery, and stuffed my Starr pistol and Boelcke's goggles under my shirt before heading back toward the station.

The landscape appeared altogether changed in the daylight. The fields were smaller, the woods less cavernous. There was more activity on the road around Avesnes as well. There wouldn't be much hiding like I had done the night before.

Half buried in the grass in front of me was an old garden rake and a holed woven basket. I picked them up and tried to give the impression of purpose.

Glancing about, I didn't find many farmers tilling the land, but I did see pedestrians on some of the main roads. There were women and soldiers hoisting loads, tasked with responsibilities too menial to afford them vehicles.

I kept my distance from these others but followed their path toward the city until I walked into groupings of structures tight enough to allow for a nook and cranny here and there to make myself scarce if needed.

Like this, I made my way back to the station.

I arrived on the city side of the entrance, opposite where I'd been the night before, and hid across the street in a window well beside a stack of apple crates to survey the area. For the moment, there was a lull of activity near the entrance, and I imagined I could walk inside and find a closet to hole up in. I abandoned my basket and rake, picked up an apple crate, and started across the road.

But just as I did, I heard elevated voices shouting in German.

I shrank to my spot just in time to see two soldiers emerging from the front.

The German in lead had a pair of keys in his hand. His partner shouted from the top of the station steps and gestured to his watch, but the first man hopped into a car and called back an excuse of some kind, waving his arm to suggest the other was being too dramatic.

Something about the way he spoke to the other soldiers, and some particularities about his uniform, persuaded me to put on the goggles.

He had a different insignia on his jacket, and his posture didn't suggest a military background. The car he sat in was elegant, far too elegant for a standard working car.

I fumbled with the buttons on my blouse to reach Boelcke's artifact just as the engine turned over. The German soldier on the steps waved a dismissive hand at the driver and turned to go back inside.

I held them up to my eyes cautiously and sucked in a sharp gulp of air.

The driver and the car lit up in blue.

I couldn't believe my luck. Perhaps that was an omen that I'd been right, that Marcus was not dead, and there was still a chance of finding him.

But a new problem arose instantly as the car rode off down the street. It was getting away, and I was stuck on foot hiding in an alcove behind some crates.

I stuffed the goggles back in my shirt, leaving a button undone for ease of access, and started after it, not at a run, but certainly at a brisk walk. The car might be headed in any direction, but if I could manage to keep its heading up to date, perhaps I could cut through alleys to keep up. If only I knew the city better.

With the apple crate in my arms to hide the bulge of the gun and the goggles, I hurried on the side of the road. Ahead of me, the car hit an intersection and took a right turn. I turned as well, and to my relief, found an alleyway to snake across just in time to see the car heading northeast. The driver had been forced to stop and wait for a train passing by. But unlike the endless cargo train I'd encountered the night before, this caboose was already visible on the horizon.

A woman bumped into me as I stood gaping after the car.

"*Entschuldigung*," she muttered before continuing on. The bump woke me anew to the very active world around me. My disguise worked well enough. At least, the people going about their business did not think to look my way twice. That was a blessing.

But the end of the train was coming closer, and I needed a way to follow.

There was a military car parked nearby. It tempted me, but I didn't dream of trying to steal it in broad daylight.

If only there were something a little less conspicuous, something easier to misplace.

I hurried toward the intersection casting my eyes all around until they settled on something. Discarded beside an old shoe shop lay a bent and damaged bicycle. The wheels needed mending. The metal frame needed righting. But I had no time.

I hurried toward it and set it right side up. The handlebars were crooked and half the seat had been ripped off, but the main components appeared to be in working order.

Even if they weren't, I was getting desperate. The train had just about passed the intersection. I hopped on with my crate and started off on the street just as the car picked up its journey again.

Even in my hurry, I couldn't help but notice embittered looks from other women carrying loads of laundry and hand-pulled carts. But if a woman riding a bicycle was uncommon, it didn't appear to be so rare as to cause a witch hunt. I imagined it helped that we weren't in the city proper, nor were we headed in that direction. The car pulled onto a road that headed toward the country, again to the northeast, and I wondered in dismay whether this man might not be planning on driving all the way back to Berlin.

I followed on my bicycle and kept my head down. The handful of cars that went by in the opposite direction were mostly silent, although one carriage of younger soldiers shouted and whistled at me, raucously. I ignored them.

When I'd gone several minutes without seeing another car coming in, I stopped and pulled the goggles out again. The man with the strange uniform had put so much distance between us, it was nothing but a small speck, similar to an enemy plane a mile off flying against a white cloud.

But I could still see it. I propped the eyewear on my head and continued on.

A few more minutes passed, and to my surprise, I appeared to be gaining ground on the driver. Then I reached a fork in the road, with a dirt path stretching off behind the blue light marking the vehicle.

So he was not going to Berlin.

The dirt pathway made the already uncomfortable ride nearly unbearable. But thankfully, it wouldn't continue long. Another ways off the road, the car appeared to have stopped beside a small farmhouse.

The grasses around the path had grown tall, making them inaccessible to a faulty bicycle, but the road curved around ahead of me to reach the farmhouse entrance. The carriage of the car was just visible protruding from the corner. I could save time cutting across the field by foot, so I ditched the bicycle in the weeds, crouched low, and traversed the grass.

I pulled out my gun as I neared the building, and when I heard no sound, I sprinted to lay my back flat against its stone walls right between two windows. I adjusted my head ever so slightly to catch a sliver of what was inside the building. In front of a table, a man stood with his back to me. He was illuminated in blue. Or perhaps, more correctly, he was silhouetted by the arcane glow. I tiptoed to the front corner of the house and froze.

Parked near the car was an aircraft—an Albatross, to be exact. Single seater. Fighter.

Did this driver know how to fly as well? Or was he meeting someone?

I wished now more than ever that Marcus had taught me how to be a pilot. It would be so convenient to steal this aircraft and fly back home, should I manage to get the device from this man's hands.

Instead, should things go well, I'd have to steal the conspicuously extravagant car and wait around until Dupont came back for me.

And the German would have to cooperate. I shifted the grip on my gun. There was a small feeling inside of me that itched to pull the trigger, to take control again, but I stamped it out. This temptation had little power over me since I'd shot down Marcus.

No. Since I was made to believe I had shot down Marcus.

Slowly, as my heart hammered violently in my chest, I pushed the front door open. It creaked loudly.

The collector whirled around and stared at me with wide eyes. Time froze as I took in the scene. His gaze darted to the gun in my hand, and fear spilled over him from head to toe.

"Please, I don't want to hurt you," I said.

But he had already fixated on his vehicle out the window, a desperate chance at escaping. He made a break for it without giving me a second chance to speak.

He couldn't escape. He'd seen me, for one. And he had a magical artifact, the only lead I had to lure the Flyers out of hiding.

I'd had these thoughts before, though. This was the reasoning that I used to justify Cillian's death in Dublin. They were excuses to feed an evil thing that grew inside me. I'd been ready to use any and all of them.

Now, even in a split second, I hated that they were true.

I fired the gun once. My shot found its mark. The man didn't make it out the door. He stumbled and lay still.

I dropped the gun, leaned against a doorframe, and started sobbing.

I hadn't wanted to do it. I wanted to threaten and persuade him and run away before he could raise the alarm. I had no quarrel with the man, personally. The remorse flushed in like a tidal wave. Sweet, sweet remorse.

What had the war done to me? What more might it require?

I sank to my knees and let the grief overwhelm me. For the first time, I was alone with a body, a corpse of my making. There was no speeding away in a motorcycle or airplane. There were no Irish nationalists shouting at me to go away. There was only me and this man, whose name I didn't know. He wasn't even a soldier. He collected pieces for his museum.

A box beside him glowed blue in the goggles, but I ripped them from my eyes. I needed to see clearly for once. I crawled closer. He wasn't breathing. His blood pooled underneath him on the rough wooden floor. My mind raced, unexpectedly, to my mother and father. My family waited for me at home. They prayed every day that I would be kept from danger. I imagined my father waiting impatiently for the mail for any news from me.

Who waited for this man?

Awkwardly, I searched him for identification. He didn't carry much on him, and some small bills, identification papers, and a photograph of a beautiful young woman. She looked to be in her teenage years. The corner of the photograph was stained in blood, but I picked it up and studied the woman. She looked like the man on the ground. They shared the same nose, the same cheekbones, and dark brown hair.

Not a wife, then. A relative. A sister? No. The ages were too disparate. A niece?

But my conjecture was only a pathetic attempt at circling the truth.

He was a father.

My hand trembled, softly at first, then with increasing violence. I'd killed her father. I tried to push swarming memories, but I didn't have the strength. They were happy scenes of interactions with my dad at his restaurant or among friends, the sensation of his arms swooping me up as a child, the hum of his deep voice. Robbed. All gone.

The girl's picture stared at me now, with poignant brown eyes.

Her dad was not a soldier, but the war had taken him. I had taken him for following his orders.

The pain I felt was physical and wracking, and I could not stop it until the crunching sound of a footstep shook me back into primordial fear. It was not the collector. Someone else. A pilot. The collector wasn't alone.

"Well," said a voice, coldly familiar. "If it isn't Private Jane Doe."

I looked up and gaped. Standing across the room was the Blue Flyer.

Chapter 35
Hate Magic
Marcus

I banked left and pulled up as Dieter's guns roared by me.

Thank goodness I'd looked skyward when I did, otherwise, he'd have shot my plane so full of lead that I'd be nothing but a streaming comet heading toward the ground by now.

But I couldn't make sense of it.

I hadn't dreamed Dieter would turn on me like this. It didn't make sense. Did Harry know?

My mind flashed back to that awkward exchange before I'd taken off, when I'd told him that Dieter shared his real name with me. Was that some kind of signal?

Dieter used the speed from his dive to climb up and turn over, before unleashing a new hellish volley in my direction.

By reflex, I corkscrewed down, maneuvering into the space behind him. He was flying a single seat fighter, and the space behind him would be the safest spot in the sky.

But why? I had the devices with me. I had Richthofen's scarf even, which gave me more firepower. If he planned to betray me, why give me the gear first? Was he so confident of getting that first shot off successfully?

And why nurse me back to health? Why go out of his way to connect with me the past week? Was it all just to throw me off the scent? If so, that meant he'd planned this all out. It was strategized.

And here I'd been asking why it was necessary to have me in the air.

I shook my head in disappointment. It was necessary to have me in the air so he could kill me in the air.

But even that conclusion started a whole new circle of questions. Why now? What had changed? He had so many opportunities this whole time. Was it because Harry was securing Guynemer's device on the ground? They completed the collection and now had no use for me?

I set my jaw, refusing to believe that Harry was complicit. The ring on my finger burned like crazy, sending a shock through the damaged nerves of my arm.

Dieter slipped by again, guns ablaze, and I reacted by weaving into a vrille, spiraling over and evading fire. But even absent the weight of a gunner, my machine was sluggish for maneuvers better suited to fighters.

Suddenly, the pieces started sliding together. The necklace hanging on my chest seemed heavy. I had traded it for Jane's marble. That was what they wanted this whole time. It had all been for the marble. And they must have needed me to give it willingly.

My mind raced like engine cylinders activating. Each revelation led to greater output. They had needed my help to get the rest of the devices. They got the best of all worlds. My absence must surely have been a distraction to our team. And then I'd personally assisted with their getaway once Dieter acquired Little's ring.

They needed the magic for something—who knew for what. Was peace a lie? Was Ireland a pawn? They needed all of it together.

Including the marbles.

The marbles were different. They hadn't been created because of a kill count or the death of a pilot. The marbles were made from something far more pure.

I grimaced as castor oil struck me in the face. I was pushing my engine through a lot. Dieter headed my way again, a frontal assault this time. I feigned right with the angle of my wings, but slid the other direction with my tail wing. He bit on the deception and gave me a shot on him. I took it happily, glad to get my own guns active and in the fight. All my rounds went harmlessly wide, though.

As my plane righted, and I shifted into a serpentine figure eight to engage again, I noticed that the betrayal did not sting as I might have expected. In fact, I was hardly angry or hurt at all. I was just disappointed—both that they turned out to be just as mischievous as the Fae stories suggested their kind might be and that the hopeful vision of the future I'd allowed them to sell me was misinformation after all. They told me what I wanted to hear.

But if their plan was to shoot me down and recollect the devices they'd dressed me with, I had other ideas.

And once I got away... Well, I'd figure something out.

I looked around and saw Dieter circling up to win altitude. At this rate, he would outmaneuver me easily. And, now I wondered what he'd really done to my fuel supply, because it certainly wasn't something to keep me in the air longer.

I closed my eyes and breathed in the magic they'd shown me,

remembered the desperation and wild intent of firing into the sun after Jane had been hit on our flight back from Ghent.

It took less concentration to transform into the Nieuport 28 this time around.

My engine roared anew with fresh life. I loved the sound of that Gnome rotary engine, even if it had given us all sorts of problems when the 94th first picked it up. Once we'd gotten the kinks worked out, this aircraft had proven to be powerful, strong, and maneuverable.

Suddenly, I could climb faster, my turns were more responsive, and as Dieter came through on his next pass, I barreled over him, reduced my speed, and happily lit him up.

The overpowered ammunition hurtling out of my double Vickers guns made me scrunch up my face in horrified appreciation, as though I'd heard an incredible melody on one of the aerodrome pianos from a replacement conscripted man back in Gengault.

Dieter scrambled out of the way, but I think I'd landed something on one of his wings.

We had a fight on our hands. I smiled. For the first time in a long time, I stopped worrying about the morality in each of my decisions. This was life or death. I had nothing to fear by defending myself from a would-be assassin. And because of that situation, it felt almost like it had when Luf were still alive, before we'd started on this damned magic mission.

The sky was a game. The pilots players. The planes, points to be earned.

Suddenly, before my eyes, Dieter's Albatross D III flashed, and its shape winked from one existence to another. Now, he piloted a Pfalz. I smiled. That was a sturdy, formidable machine that had given me no shortage of trouble around our base at Gengault. But it was a machine I knew well, and it was not as powerful as the 28.

We continued our dance to the song of the sky. Dieter tried the Pfalz for several minutes before getting frustrated with its climb and speed against my Nieuport. He flashed again and transformed to an Albatross D VA.

I took a deep breath. Now here was a matchup.

It was much showier than the D III he'd chosen for our mission. It was more powerful, but not all that much better than its previous models. For that, I thought it was a nice dancing partner for the Nieuport 28, a plane that itself drew significant criticism for its tendency to shed wing fabric.

The dogfight marched onward, and its movements filled me with a subdued euphoria. I had only two planes available for transformation, but Dieter had appeared to shoot down everything imaginable, and thus had a multi-national selection at his disposal.

The devices he and Harry had lent me radiated with power, and even though my ring continued to burn, the scarf gave me unbridled confidence. Every viable shot I got on his plane counted for three of his passes on mine. So even though he continued to shift models, from the Albatross back to the Pfalz, then to a British Camel and an SE 5A, until finally he morphed into his tri-wing Fokker DR I, he could not disrupt my flow. The DR I was the plane he'd chased us with when we flew the Rumpler. It was the plane the Red Baron had died in.

It was a very special design.

The three wings gave it incredible maneuverability, and Dieter put it on full display in front of me. For the first time, as he flitted like a kite in the wind, forward and over, rolling and sliding, turning on a dime, fear entered into my mind.

Fear.

He dropped on me from above and rifled off a long volley. I banked vertically on my wing, giving him a narrow profile to shoot at, and allowed myself to fall so I could pick up momentum before looping upward.

Fear was everything. Fear is what drove the whole war. Every soldier lived in fear, though they all handled it differently. I'd come to know its ugly face so very well.

And that's when it hit me—the most important lie the Fae pilots had sold me. Hate magic.

I had known men with high kill counts. But though they professed to hate the Huns, they didn't. Not really.

I leveled out my plane in a luxuriously wide turn.

Rockwell and Chapman and Prince and Lufbery. They didn't hate the men they killed. They hated the war itself. They hated the hate. If anything, they respected the hell out of the pilots they went up against. We'd have gladly treated with an enemy pilot downed behind our lines, given him a royal, respectful treatment—exchanged gifts, games of cards, rich meals... all in the name of the aerial fraternity.

Yes, there was plenty of hate in the war. But not nearly so much hate as there was fear.

And though I didn't know much about magic, fear magic seemed to me to be an altogether different beast than hate magic.

Dieter took a straight line on me, trying to take advantage of the time it took to complete my turn. He fired again. The shots came zipping by my head.

All this time, I was afraid that hate had crept into Jane's heart, that she'd become hardened and cruel. But it was fear that had infected her. She had been a lovely girl, turned war-time mechanic who met me and cared so much that she tried to forge a magical necklace to keep me safe. That's all she wanted to do, keep the people she cared about safe. Discovering the Blue Flyer and the magical devices must have flipped the only safe part of her world, a zone that was exclusively hers, completely on its head.

Hate makes people do awful things, but they're intentional and purposeful. Hate sat and fermented and took strength from time. Fear was reactionary. It made people do things they'd never dream themselves capable of.

But that was never the measure of a person. It was the cleanup that mattered.

I'd left Jane because I was afraid, not for some spy mission. I was afraid of what she was becoming, but also what we were becoming. I was afraid that my weakness would get her killed.

I was afraid because I loved her, and losing her would tear me up more than losing Luf did.

Raoul Lufbery. The brother I'd always wanted, the mentor I never deserved.

And finally, I knew what Smith meant when he said I'd hear him whisper to me.

The wings of my plane were riddled in a series of holes as Dieter passed by at near point blank range. I cut my engine and slammed on my foot pedals, allowing my tail to spin and my plane to drop.

This was the fear move. It was the move that Luf used to take down the Gotha in Nancy. It required faith in your plane and faith in yourself that though you allowed a fall, you could right it again.

Dieter looped over me in a victorious flip and watched.

The world spun like I was a wheel on a peg. The horizon blurred together, and my stomach lurched as gravity opened its maw to swallow me up. I heard Dieter dive past me, eager to witness my demise and collect the magic artifacts.

Just as he passed, I seized the controls again, pulling and stomping with all my strength to retake control. My death spiral stopped abruptly just as Dieter was making a broadside pass in front of me. The moment could not have been better.

I saw his face staring in surprise. I didn't hate him.

But he was going to kill me, and it was time to make good on my promises to Jane.

Chapter 36
No Choice At All
Jane

The lonely road no longer I roam.
We met, and were one in the heart's desire.
Together we came, through the wintry gloom,
To the little old house by the cross-ways home;
And crossed the threshold, and kindled the fire.
-Wilfrid Wilson Gibson-

"**Y**ou're really alive," said the Flyer in surprise.

I grabbed the pistol off the ground and aimed at him with shaking arms. He didn't seem to notice. His posture was frozen. The only movements about him were the machinations of his brain visible in his eyes.

"You're not human," I replied.

My retort seemed to bring him back to the present, and slowly he stepped beside the collector's body.

"You killed him," said the Flyer. "You've become quite the soldier."

"Is he alive?"

"No, he's dead. I just said that."

"Not him. Marcus."

The Flyer sighed.

"You're alive. And if I may be frank, that complicates everything."

"You're not answering me," I said. Relief swelled in my breast, and I tried to push it down. Hope was one thing. I couldn't believe it until I saw him. "Which makes me think he is."

"Jane, you keep surprising me. I didn't expect you to act the way you did after Marcus left you in Dublin," the Flyer said quietly. "I hoped that we could persuade you to come over, as well. But I was afraid of the hate magic in you. There's something in there that is altogether too inhuman to rely on."

"That's rich," I replied, "coming from a faerie."

"You shot him out of the sky, Jane. I thought you loved him. The marbles were built on that. We're relying on that. But you shot him."

I swallowed, blinking furiously to stem more tears. I didn't want to show weakness. He was Fae. He would turn my words, my desires, against me if I were not about my wits. That was why he poked me where it hurt most.

"I didn't mean to," I said.

"No. I know that. You never mean to. And that's the great problem isn't it? Humans never intend to hurt anyone, do they? You only prepare yourselves to do so, just in case the need arises. And when the opportunity comes calling, suddenly it's a need, and you abandon what makes you human because you're afraid or greedy. Then, it takes you. The dark magic takes you, and it is so very hard to unravel."

"That's not fair," I said. "I didn't have control of myself."

"Then why were you behind a machine gun?" he asked. He sat down on a chair beside the body on the floor. I had to force myself to keep looking his way. This man's death had been necessary. Had he been armed he would have—

"You're justifying it now," the Flyer said. "You need to craft a story that makes sense of the nightmare, something that will excuse you in shooting me should it come to it. But I'm not wearing a German uniform."

He looked down and cleared his throat. At present, in fact, he was in a stolen uniform.

"Well, I don't normally wear a German uniform. This was for mission purposes, you understand. I mean, you're dressed in what look like dirty rags, and I can only presume you don't normally wear that."

"He would have raised an alarm. He may have had a weapon in his car and used it to kill me."

"You're the one that hunted him. And you know what raises an alarm?" the Flyer asked. "A loud gunshot from a field on the wrong side of the city."

I shook my head.

"No. That won't scare me. Who hears single, far-off gunshots anymore? You're not in a hurry. I'm not in a hurry."

"Perhaps I'm not in a hurry because I look forward to the Germans coming. Perhaps I've made a deal with them, brokered something for Ireland."

"If that's the case why are you wearing that ill-fitting mission-purposed uniform?" I caught myself asking the question. Why was he wearing that? Why wasn't he aligned with the Germans? "You're not brokering anything for Ireland, are you?"

"No. Please, don't tell them, that, though," he said.

"Then what were you doing in Ireland?"

"Marcus was there. We needed him."

I tightened the grip on my gun as my friend's name fell from the Flyer's lips.

"Where is he now?" I asked.

The Flyer pointed to the sky.

"No," I said. "You're lying."

"I don't lie," he said.

"No?" I asked. "Incapable?"

He rolled his eyes.

"All right. That's fair. It's more accurate to say I find the direct presentation of falsehood distasteful. It's part of our charm. We twist appearances. We can misrepresent things. But there's not magic in blatantly misrepresenting facts."

"Why are you here?"

He shook his head.

"That's business talk. If this is personal, I understand the firearm. The desire for vengeance is so very Fae. But if we're going to talk business, I insist on doing so without a gun in my face."

I was grateful for an excuse to lower the weapon. I did not want to pull the trigger. I was done. I was past done with shooting. I darted my eyes at the collector's body.

"Then I insist on speaking somewhere else."

He grinned and stood up.

"Fair is fair."

He scooped up the small box from beside the corpse and led me to a room attached, a rough kitchen by the looks of it. There were counters and cupboards and a heavy, rustic table in the center.

He placed the box on the table and stood on the other side.

"You've tried to lure us to you before," he said. "Why?"

"I wanted Marcus back," I said in disbelief. "Why else? You took him."

"We didn't take him. He came willingly," said the Flyer. He cocked his head to the side. "But was that what everyone in your party wanted?"

I looked down. He claimed he didn't like lying, but he also appeared to be very adept at sniffing out unrepresented truths.

"I didn't know Atkins wanted to kill you," I said.

"Nonsense. What did you think they were going to do once you'd found us? Invite us to dinner?"

"You've shot down their planes! What do you expect?"

"Exactly. We shot down their planes. And you say that you didn't know they wanted to kill me."

I balled my fists, feeling like a child.

"I meant I didn't know—I didn't understand—"

"That we are Fae," he said. I nodded. "You didn't know there was another war going on."

"I didn't know your kind existed," I whispered.

"We don't, really. Not anymore," he replied as he leaned back against a cabinet. "For a long time, I believed I was the last one left. Then I found another. This leads me to believe there may be more scattered throughout the world, but we are mere remnants."

"We killed you off, then?" I said. "Atkins said you'd been at war with England for hundreds of years."

He waved a dismissive hand in the air.

"Maybe once upon a time, there was some type of formal conflict," he said, "one recognized by both sides. But I can't remember any instance in which two armies took to a battlefield and had it out. No. It was the people that killed us. The people who stopped believing and carved out bleeding chunks from what was once a very rich and magical world. That was the start of it. We managed to do ourselves in after that."

"So why are you shooting down planes?" I asked. "Do you have a vendetta? A score to settle? Are you trying to prolong the war so as many human beings die as possible?"

To my surprise, he looked wounded by my accusation.

"We are trying to stop the war, once and for all," he said. "It may be folly, but I don't want to see the human race suffer the same fate we did. If the war continues, even what remains of human magic will diminish and decay. And when the magic is gone, you will have nothing to preserve yourselves."

"And what is human magic?" I asked.

"Do you not know?" he asked with a sad smile.

As he posed his question, it dawned on me. Marcus had scrawled it in oil on a table. As a girl, my mother had always told me that love was more powerful than any magic. My Aunt Luella reiterated the same as she trained me in her odd lessons on enchantments and hexes. It was to this I appealed when I requested she craft the glass marbles.

The faerie must have noticed me piecing it together.

"There will never be a scientific explanation for how human love can create life, extend life, beautify life..."

"And war is hate," I said, remembering Marcus's finger-scrawled note. "Hate magic. The artifacts are not powerful magic devices are they? They're memorials."

"A remembrance and a regret that the traits of men which rendered them so lethal might have made them into something great, instead." The Flyer shook his head, sadly. "Boelcke's vision, Richthofen's leadership and strength of will, Ball's uncompromising sense of personal identity... Do you think war was the only furnace in which these attributes might have shown through? And what might they have done for the world?"

I'd been thinking about the magic all wrong. I shut my eyes tight.

"I watched the magic leave Little's body and enter his ring," I said dumbly.

"You saw magic desperately cling to Little's loyalty, torn apart by hate magic at the intersection of human flight."

Suddenly, his comments about my marble rushed to the forefront of my mind.

"You stole my marble," I asked. "It was you. I remember your face. You said it interested you more than Albert Ball's violin strings. Why?"

"It's a more powerful magic," he said plainly. "Your marble

was living magic. The devices are, as you so aptly named them, memorials."

"Did you steal Marcus's as well?"

The Flyer's smile dipped, but there was no sincerity in the sympathy.

"He gave it to us."

A bitter swill of disbelief climbed up my throat. Against my will, I collapsed to my elbows against the wooden table.

"You lie."

He grimaced like a child tasting sour milk.

"Not unless absolutely necessary," he said.

Marcus had promised me he would never take it off. Even when I begged him to remove it, when I feared that the Flyers could use it to track us or gain some sort of intelligence on him. He refused.

For him to have handed it over to them, after knowing they'd stolen mine forcefully. What was he thinking?

"What did you tell him?" I asked.

"The truth."

"Which truth?" I asked. Atkins's warning that the fair folk's defining characteristic was misrepresentation blazed in my mind. "Does he know you're Fae?"

"He does."

"Then how did you get him to give it to you?"

The Flyer crossed his arms.

"He put it up as collateral. It was a gift to signify trust."

"Trust?" I scoffed. I wanted to bring the gun level again, but I resisted. "Why would he want your trust?"

"He wanted to demonstrate that he was one of us now, you know, that he'd left the Allies behind him."

I took a step away from the table, fingernails biting into my palms, teeth clenched, as I fought the impulse to hit something. This was the answer I could not refute. He had asked me to leave with him. He had asked me to go, and I refused, so he found someone else to care for him the way I would not.

"You believe me now, don't you? We gave him a purpose. The Allies left him desolate. And you know what? Turning him against his military was not all that difficult, but convincing him to join our team over yours, the team of Jane, took much more gentle persuasion. Do you think he made the wrong decision?"

I leaned my forehead against a cabinet, desperately holding back the painful knot in my throat.

"I don't know."

"Let me rephrase. Do you think he made the right choice in departing from a team that did not have his best interest at the forefront?"

There was no holding them back. Hot, stinging tears trailed down my face. This was my great judgment, and he would have my confession. I needed to say it out loud to stop the pain increasing any more. I'd been carrying it since he left in Dublin, wondering why he'd leave if he trusted I was on his side, if he knew that he came first, if he knew I loved him.

"Yes. He made the right choice." I wanted to melt into the ground. I started to sink to my knees, but the Flyer had already rounded the table and put an arm around me to keep me standing.

"I need to tell you something important now," he said. "The whispers in your heart are correct. You did not kill Marcus, yet."

The destructive expanding hope in my chest went off like a bomb. But the Flyer's cool statement turned it all sour in an instant. What game did he want with me? How much more could I take? I sobbed. I gripped his arms firmly to keep from falling over. He had my heart and my intellect wrapped in his mercy. He dangled my most ardent desires this way and that.

"Please," I begged. "No. I don't want to play."

"You wish for me to take the choice from you?" he asked.

I nodded eagerly. I couldn't take more blame. I could practically feel the blood on my hands.

"That may be your wish, but before you surrender your choice, you must hear the options."

He picked up the small box from the table, and led me outside to stand between the car and the plane. The world was blurry from tears, but he pointed to the sky.

Two planes glided through gentle banking turns.

"You have a decision to make. We both came here under the pretense of hunting Guynemer's device. Meier had it. I lured Meier here by letter, hinting that I'd found a once-in-a-lifetime treasure to take back to his superiors in Berlin. My companion, Dieter, believed that if you were still alive, you would not be far from Guynemer's device."

My world was spinning. I wanted to disbelieve what he said, to insist no one could be so pervasive and calculating. But here I was, and here he was, and I was in a panic and he was not.

"You still have a chance to return with this device." He nodded to the small box on the table. "You are armed, and I am not. If you insist on taking it, I cannot stop you. You will have to kill me to get it. And, if you allow me to keep it, I can assure you that our plans for it will cost many, many lives."

The planes flew in easy formation. One in front and below, the other sitting just behind.

"What's the other choice?" I asked. "How do I save Marcus?"

"You may have already predicted that Marcus is one of the pilots you are watching now. If you allow me to leave with the device, I will signal to my companion to let Marcus live and disengage immediately. We will leave, and the two of you will be reunited. If not, any moment now, my companion will open fire on your unsuspecting friend, and send him to the Earth. He will not survive this time."

"You'd betray him after earning his trust as you did?" I asked, choking.

To my surprise, his voice broke as he responded.

"Without hesitation, but not without sorrow."

"So that's the choice? Save Marcus's life at the cost of losing the device?"

"Essentially." The Flyer put a hand to his eyes to shield the sun while he watched the planes. "Serve your country by killing me and taking a powerful magical item, but do so at the cost of your friend. Or, save him, and sacrifice the lives of others to do so because I must represent to you the facts. We will use the devices to harm people. There is no other way. Be sure that people will die through our plans."

He patted my shoulder gently.

"Which does love permit? Can you live on knowing the high price of your bond? Could Marcus forgive you for it? Or will you live knowing you sacrificed the man you owed so much for the greater good?"

The planes looked so peaceful at this distance. They looked like sparrows sailing through the breeze. It might be a trick. Marcus might already be dead. But if the Fae despised bald-faced lies as much as he said, at any moment Marcus would have to fight for his life, and I knew how hard it was to fly against a Fae pilot.

But if he didn't know the attack was coming, what chance did he have?

"What if I refuse?" I asked.

"Then my companion will shoot him down, anyway. You may choose not to choose, but that will be a choice of its own."

My eyes shot about. There was no telling how much longer I had. I wanted to scream, to curse the ground and the sky. How could this be? Who would force such a choice, and why?

I froze.

Why would they make me choose this? It was an ugly, complicated, contrived choice. It begged explanation.

I turned away from the sky to stare at the faerie.

"There's no right choice," I said.

"Then there is no wrong choice, either."

"Why give me a choice at all?" I asked.

"A courtesy."

"No, you said yourself. You lured me here. If you wanted the device, you could have just got it on your own. You wanted me. You wanted Marcus. You needed us."

"You're running out of time," the Flyer said. "Any moment, he will be shot down."

"Because of the marbles?" I wondered aloud. "Living magic. Not hate magic. The marble was made and powered by something beautiful, and you're trying to corrupt it, aren't you? You didn't want to steal the marble from Marcus. You needed him to give it to you of his own accord, to weaken the bond."

"I'm begging you to make a choice before something happens that you will regret."

"You wanted me to shoot Marcus down." My confidence grew as I talked it out. "You want me to choose more violence in the name of love. But why? What are you planning with it?"

Before he could give me a response, the sound of a distant machine gun crackled through the air. I whirled around to watch.

"I didn't want this, Jane," muttered the Flyer. "I care for him, too."

Chapter 37
You Fly, I Fire
Marcus

Dieter's plane spiraled downward through patchy clouds. My shots had ripped a hole right into his fuselage, but they hadn't killed him. Maybe they wounded him, but he was frantic on the way down.

I fired and hit a Fokker triplane, but I watched his aircraft transform five or six times before it struck the ground. The transformations told a story. He shifted to a Nieuport 27, then a SPAD XIII, back to the Pfalz he'd engaged me with, an Albatross DIII, a

Sopwith Camel, and Brisfit, a cross-section of all the missions he'd flown. The lives of those pilots were flashing through his mind.

The plane hit the ground hard. The cloud of smoke went up high into the air, dirt dispersed in a dense bank of fog, but I flew down to check my work. Many of my heroes would advise against something like that, saying you never knew what other planes or anti-air batteries were in the area, but I had to ensure he was dead.

Reluctantly, I strafed the crash site with a line of machine gun fire.

After two more passes, I eased my plane down next to the wreckage. It was one of the many empty fields in that part of the country. The plane was broken to bits. I disconnected my cylinders but kept the engine running. I didn't want to be down here for long.

The burns on my arm sang hotly when I neared the patches of fire eating up the wings, but I clambered to the remains of the cockpit. It had collapsed on itself, and Dieter was pinned, disfigured, and still. I wasn't sure if the Fae had a heartbeat to begin with, but I couldn't find one on him, and the expression on his face was demure and peaceful, as though relieved from some great burden.

For all I could tell, Dieter was dead.

Quickly, I took my marble from around his neck and put it beside the Fae amulet.

It was odd. Although he'd betrayed me, I still grieved for the kinship we'd shared. I'd have thought it would be easy to look back and write off all of our positive interactions. But, I couldn't do it. By the end, I felt like Dieter, Dialythe, had actually come to like me, and I him.

I took a last look, gave him a quick salute, and scurried back to my Nieuport before it had a chance to roll off on me. But before I put her back in the air, I paused. My dogfight with Dieter had lasted all of five minutes. Where did I have to go now? I had with me several devices that I'm sure the Allies would be thrilled to possess, but I didn't know if I could trust them with such magic. Despite the betrayal, all the philosophy the fairies had shared with me held water.

I needed answers, and even if Harry had been a part of the attempt on my life, he was the only source I had for them.

I set off down the field, pulled the plane into the air and transformed into the triplane I'd just shot down. It'd take me no time at all to get back to the farmhouse, so I could be waiting for Harry when he got there. I wouldn't exit my plane. I had an advantage in the air now, given all the devices I carried. Then again, I didn't know what Guynemer's device would do.

I pushed the engine of the Fokker as fast it could go, not bothering to gain too much altitude. I saw Harry's plane parked beside the farmhouse in minutes and noted, with marked surprise, a German car parked beside it.

Between the car, two figures faced off.

I squinted, trying to make out the identity of the people. It was hard even from my low altitude. Had Harry run into bad company?

I passed over low and blinked. It appeared that he stood over a woman, kneeling on the ground in torn rags. I banked around and looked closer, shocked to see that this woman had a pair of flight goggles around her neck.

I shook my head and looked again.

No. Could it really be Jane?

As soon as the hunch came to mind, her identity grew more and more obvious. Jane supported herself with two hands, wracked by some torment, while Harry stood awkwardly beside her and looked up at my plane.

She must have come to retrieve Guynemer's device. She must have seen my message on the hangar table and puzzled it out. But if that were true, what was she doing out here? Had Harry already gone into the city, retrieved the artifact, and returned? There was no way. We hadn't been airborne that long.

If the goggles had led Jane here, it meant that Harry had the artifact already. It meant he was lying about why we were there in the first place. Maybe he had some great answer that didn't implicate him in a plan to kill me, but if so, he'd have a lot of explaining to do. Why they'd dragged me out here? Why did they take such great troubles to take me in and indoctrinate me on some phony plan to stop the war?

But I didn't care. Whatever flimsy grace I'd been willing to offer Harry, it flagged as I saw the grim resolution on his features as he waited for me to land.

Anger finally boiled to the surface. My muted disappointment did not satisfy me anymore. That was Jane down there, and even though she'd shot me, I needed her to be ok. I loved her.

I barreled over into a strafing line. They were close, but I had the room. I lined up Harry's Albatross and opened fire. The guns were deafening. The shot reverberated through my arms as if I'd just fired an artillery gun.

The plane splintered into a heap. I'd risked flying very low and very steep on my pass, and some of the enhanced rounds made contact at very close range. It only took that moment to make the plane inoperable.

I pulled off, looped, and transformed from the Fokker triplane and into the Albatros C X two-seater I'd shot down only hours earlier, then landed with reckless abandon into the tall grass. My propellor chewed it up as it mowed through, and I hopped out of the cockpit before the plane had even stopped moving.

I was sprinting and stumbling toward them, toward her. Every bit of my heart wanted to wrap her up in my arms and keep her safe.

Jane didn't look up. A Starr pistol lay in the dirt beside her. Harry watched me, though. He didn't run to grab the gun. He didn't move to intercept. In fact, his expression melted into something like regret. When I got close, he put up his hands in surrender.

But these were just more tricks, I knew. I bowled into him at the peak of my stride, colliding my shoulder hard against his jaw, sending both of us tumbling to the dust.

I righted myself first, picked up the gun, and scrambled to Jane to help her. We needed to get back to the plane before Harry could beat us there.

"Jane," I gasped as I took hold of both her shoulders. She blinked up at me as if I were a ghost. "Are you all right?"

"Marcus," her eyes lingered on me for a moment before flicking over my shoulder. The warning came too late. Harry had recovered from the blow faster than I'd anticipated, and instead of running to my plane, he'd come after me.

The jolt from the attack knocked me on my face, and the gun flew from my grasp. Harry jumped on top of me, his hands at my throat. But he wasn't trying to strangle me, he was trying to rip Richthofen's scarf free. I resisted, and we rolled on the ground in a bout of strength.

"You lied to me," I said through my efforts. This angered him more than I'd expected.

"I let you believe certain things," he spat back. "You lied to me, too."

I smashed my head against his, and we both went reeling off one another. Unfortunately, my blinding pain had rolled me away from the gun, and Harry closed in on it now, one hand on his head to stem a streak of discolored blood. I looked over. Jane had already started running for cover, but I wouldn't have time. Harry would have a clear shot on me.

My mind raced. I tore Little's ring off my finger.

"You want these so bad?" I shouted. "Here!" I threw it at him as hard as I could, but didn't wait to see his reaction. I turned and sprinted after Jane. She had just sheltered behind the car. I heard a shout of surprise from behind me and then three gunshots as I dove and slid beside her.

"You're gonna run off on me so soon?" I asked, nodding to the car. "I've got a better ride out of here."

Jane stared at me, tears welling up and spilling down her cheeks.

"I thought I'd killed you," she said in a broken voice. She grabbed my flight suit with both hands. "I thought—I thought—"

I grabbed her fingers to calm their shaking.

"We need to get back to my plane," I said. "Or we'll never get out of here."

She nodded.

"Courage, then," she said. "Hopefully, this will help." She showed me a small wooden box, stood up, and ran. I followed after.

Harry had already started wading into the grass toward the two-seater, but he limped badly, and his pace flagged. When he saw us he lifted the gun.

"Duck, Jane!" I shouted.

But instead of a gunshot, a cry of pain rang out from his direction. He shook his hand violently, as if holding a coal, before throwing something on the ground. His shot came late, and it went wide.

"You couldn't find a Rumpler?" Jane asked as she lay beside me in the brush. Prone as we were, the grass stretched above us, and though it prickled with burrs, it was safer than facing a faerie with a gun and a God complex.

I put a finger to my lips to sign for quiet. I heard movement nearby. Harry walked through the field. His heavy German boots crunched with each step.

"Marcus, I didn't want this," he shouted. "Dieter was convinced it was the only way. But I thought you'd understand, with time. I was sure Jane wouldn't shoot you down, that we could work with both of you. When she did, I lost the high ground, and Dieter had to have his way."

Jane gripped my hand tightly. Her eyes glistened with remorse. I shook my head. We wouldn't talk about it now. We were getting out of this.

The sound of Harry's steps grew closer.

"But I just spoke with her. You're right to love her, Marcus. After she shot you down, I took it as evidence she did not return that affection. But I was wrong. She loves you. It's obvious."

I looked at Jane. Harry was a liar. He'd set me up, and I didn't want to believe anything. But as my eyes rested on her beside me, time slowed.

The grass waved in the breeze. Dirt clumped on her temples by her hairline from perspiration. Her face calmed, and her gaze filled with intention. She stared back at me, framed by errant strands of her hair, and I knew that Harry could not be lying.

She knit her eyebrows, as if the truth of it was a source of great pain to her, as if I held her in my very hand and could crush whatever remnants left of her happiness should I so choose.

I put my finger on her lips, to insist we'd have time for this later, but I wanted to freeze that moment forever.

Instead, we had Harry to deal with.

"Marcus, I—"

His last step was close enough. I sprung up to find him facing the other direction. He turned, but the half second was enough. I connected with his back and got a hand on his wrist. When we hit the ground, I smashed his hand on a rock, and his grip on the Starr relented. I pried it from his fingers as he flipped around, but I had him.

I had a knee on one of his elbows, and I clutched his collar with one fist. The gun waited in my grip.

He blew out a tired breath.

"Marcus."

But that wasn't his voice. It was Jane's.

"He set me up, Jane," I said.

"I know."

"He tried to kill me. He made me an idiot. A fool."

"I know."

"So then why not? Why shouldn't I do this?" My breath raced in and out. Harry's eyes, bloodied at the brow, were locked on mine, unflinching and unafraid. Ready.

"It's not you, Marcus," Jane said. "You fly, I fire. Remember?"

"No, Jane. I thought I could get through the war without dirtying my hands. But all I've done is make a mess of everything. I can't ask others to do what I should."

"You've done enough. Walk slow," she said.

I winced, but she was right. When I shot down the Germans, the regret was nauseating. When I'd shot down Dieter, it was bittersweet. I was already wracking up the numbers, and each one pained me less. That scared me.

Jane's fingers gently closed around the gun, and I let her take it. That was how we worked. She was my gunner.

I braced and waited for the shot. I didn't expect several.

But Harry's face was not distorted. His body didn't convulse. I turned and found that Jane had emptied the rest of the chamber directly into the ground. The pistol clicked ineffectively.

"Jane?" I asked.

She tossed the gun to the side.

"I don't fire anymore, either," she said. "Not like this. He's the last of the Fae, Marcus. The last of his kind."

"But Atkins ordered you to kill him," I said. She shook her head.

"I don't trust Atkins, anymore. He wants extermination. But it's like you told me in Dublin. Killing doesn't feel the same when you're outside the heat of a battle. I should've realized with Cillian, but I was too frantic, and I justified that as an accident.

Look at Harry. He's done. He's got nothing left. I think it's at least worth hearing what he has to say. He still knows more about the magic than we do. We could learn from him."

My grip on Harry's collar slackened, and I was surprised to find myself crying. I was mad at Harry, yes, but not because of his scheme with Dieter. I hurt because our friendship was real, and he'd betrayed me, anyway.

"I thought we were friends," I said. "Real friends." He sat up and put his forehead to mine.

"I'm sorry, Marcus," he said.

"But why, Harry? Why did you do this?"

"My name," he said, "is Hirythe."

Chapter 38
Misfire
Jane

Go, Winter, now unto your own abode,
Your time is done, and Spring is conqueror
Lift up with all your gear and take your road,
For she is here and brings the sun with her.
-James Stephens-

My bruised arm ached, and the gushing air made a mockery of my blouse and shawl. Marcus pushed us high into the air, and before long I was freezing. My teeth chattered, and their chipped surfaces from my crash landing rendered them sharp and uncomfortable against my tongue. I folded my arms across my chest and ducked low in the bay, cradling the device that I'd taken from Meier by force.

Below me, the Blue Flyer, Hirythe, sat in a gunner's bay we had carefully emptied of ammunition. Marcus piloted our aircraft. After a lengthy debate, Marcus and I decided it would be best to keep him close as our prisoner. He was all too content to comply and transformed our aircraft into a three-seated bomber. I'd never flown in such a large plane.

I wasn't sure where we headed. I mentioned all of Dupont's support and expressed that we could rely on him. He planned on returning that night, anyway. If he didn't hear from me he'd presume me dead or risk returning several times behind enemy lines.

The Flyer suggested a few places, as well. But Marcus wasn't ready to take any of his advice, electing to set a heading of his own.

We turned northeast, but our prospects were slim. We were directly in the center of the war zone. If we were short on fuel, there was no refuge in any direction. To the west, we'd fly into some of the most contested airspace of the war. To the east lay occupied Belgium, then Germany. Given that neither of us spoke German or Dutch or even French, that didn't bode well, either. We'd seen how that worked in Ghent already. To the south was more French and German territory, still contested, but perhaps our best option if we wanted to return to Allied land.

But Marcus chose none of those possibilities. He headed toward the North Sea. Even with a full tank of fuel, though, I doubted we had the range to get there.

The time dragged by as I struggled against the cold. Marcus had instructed the Flyer to give me his flight suit, but it was much too large, and air whistled through the gaps at my wrist and neck.

After a pair of hours, I began to worry.

"Marcus, we must be nearly out of fuel. Where are we?" I asked.

"She's holding," he replied. "I think she'll hold a bit longer."

"She'll hold a long while, yet," muttered the Flyer just loud enough for me to hear.

The thought occurred that now we benefitted from whatever enchantments the faerie had used against us. As time passed by, and cities passed beneath us far below, the effects of these enchantments grew more obvious.

Somehow, the engine kept running.

I was too tired, hungry, and cold to digest what had happened on the ground. My conversation with the Flyer repeated itself in fragments in my mind.

There was one thing I repeated to fight off the cold, over and over.

Marcus was alive. We were together.

Every so often, I would reach across the fuselage to touch him.

When my body was numb, I cared less about the cold, and peeked over my seat more regularly. I was surprised to see the towers of Ghent below us. The sight of them sent a chill through me, and I wondered if ever I might have a desire to return to that city, if the war were to end.

I attempted a rough calculation in my head. We must have flown more than a hundred miles, and we flew on still.

We left Ghent behind, and soon the ground beneath us gave way to marshes, then water. We flew directly over the sea. The sun was starting to dip into the west, and I noticed we hadn't changed our heading much at all. But that would mean we had crossed the border between Belgium and Holland. We were officially in neutral territory, at least, if we headed inland.

Finally, Marcus banked to the right.

I wasn't sure what would happen if the Dutch military saw a German bomber setting down in its country, but we had altitude, and Marcus had flown us north across the sea some way before turning to land. By the time we headed eastward, I could just make out two sister cities far off and below either wing. At long last, Marcus pushed our nose down into a suffocating dive.

We plummeted downward at immense speed, canceling, in moments, the altitude we had so sluggishly gained. My stomach lurched in my throat.

"Marcus, it's too fast!" I tried to yell, but the wind stole my voice from me. When I was sure the wings would shed from the plane, he pulled up, leveled us with the ground, and the engine went quiet.

We were quite low now, and beneath us, farmland stretched in each direction, interrupted by intermittent lakes. Very few structures loomed about.

We landed roughly, much too fast. The plane bounced once, twice, and we ran directly into a patch of trees. The impact slammed me against the rim of the gunner's bay, and my bruised arm screamed in protest. The wings of the plane cracked, with one nearly splitting entirely from the fuselage.

But we were on the ground.

Marcus hopped out of the cockpit and quickly helped me down. I wanted to fall into his arms immediately, but his eyes shone with intent.

"Do you have everything that can be salvaged from the bay?" he asked.

"I didn't have much with me," I said. I looked up at the machine gun. "I suppose we could attempt to dismantle the machine gun."

He shook his head.

"No guns." He patted down his flight suit, which he had zipped half open. My eyes rested on his neck.

"Is that Richthofen's scarf?" I asked. He nodded grimly and climbed back up on the plane, reaching across the engine to yank a line of tubing free with a jolt.

"I'm fine as well," said the Flyer as he hopped down beside us. "If anyone was wondering."

"What are you doing?" I asked Marcus.

"Lighting it," he replied. The engine was still very hot after our long flight. The piping from the radiator Marcus had just yanked off was meant to cool it. I didn't ask questions, only climbed beside him to help. The Flyer joined us.

It wasn't easy, but between the engine heat, the leaking oil, and a bit of dangerous manipulation of the machine gun rounds, we had a spark, then a flame, then a blaze.

"With any luck," Marcus said as we watched the fire, "people will assume we were a pilot that lost control after getting shot down. Hopefully they will presume us dead." As though an afterthought, he stripped the flight suit from his body and tossed it into the flames. Beneath, he wore simple clothes, not dissimilar to mine, if mine weren't damaged by age and decay.

I unzipped to do the same, but the Flyer put a hand on my arm.

"One will be enough. You're freezing," he said. I looked to Marcus. He nodded.

An out-of-control plane flying this deep into Holland seemed unlikely, but perhaps not impossible. After all, there were naval air battles over the North Sea.

In any event, it would have to do. We would make do.

We watched the burning plane and scanned the horizon, looking for the inevitable spectators that would come running when they saw the smoke.

"I'll climb that tree there and see what I can about our options," said the Flyer. He didn't wait for our approval, only began climbing, leaving Marcus and me alone on the ground. It was not ideal, but I could wait no longer.

"Marcus?" I asked. Silence. "Marcus, please."

He turned toward me and expelled a large, collected breath of air.

"I thought the war had got you," he said. "I saw it eating you up. The look on your face when you were at the gun on our motorbike in Ghent. The way you wouldn't let off the gun when you'd shot down that plane in Paris. Your willingness to follow orders without question... I thought I'd lost you."

I swallowed. His concern mirrored that of my own. I wished I could soothe those concerns away.

"I shot you," I said. "I couldn't stop shooting until it was too late. I didn't mean. Please believe me, I would never mean to—"

"The fairies tried to tell me that all war magic was hate magic. And I believed them. I was afraid you had let hate overtake you. But that's not you. You're just afraid."

Afraid. The word resonated in my marrow. I'd been afraid since the first declaration of war, and the fear had never shrunk. It only grew and grew, as my heart expanded, as there was more that I couldn't stand losing.

"What scares you most?" he asked.

I took a deep breath, inhaling the smell of burning oil, timber, and canvas.

"You," I replied. My freezing hands shook as the fire made them sting. My heart hammered. "Until you came along, I was perfectly happy pretending that fear was nothing. But now? The world won't stop trying to hurt you, and there's nothing I can do to stop it. But if I lost you, I'd--"

His expression softened.

"Then why didn't we leave when we had the chance?" he asked.

"Because I didn't think we could outrun the magic," I said. "I was afraid, sooner or later, I would be the thing that hurt you."

I didn't have the courage to stare into his eyes. They searched the ground, searched him, until they landed on his arm. Beneath the rolled-up sleeve stretched a line of blisters and burns.

"You're burned," I said, forgetting myself enough to take it gently in my hands. I started to pull back the sleeve to examine it, but he pulled his arm away. I looked back to his face. "It was me?"

He rolled the fabric down to the wrist. My chest tightened painfully. I couldn't avert my eyes from the wound poking out the edge of his sleeve. I'd hurt him, and he wouldn't even let me see how much.

"We'd better get moving," he said.

"Where?"

"Our best option is a farmhouse," replied the Flyer. He dismounted the tree quickly. "Over that way some thousand yards. They might have use for some labor. With any luck, the farmer won't be too skittish about deserting soldiers." He started walking off.

"Is that what we are now?" I asked. Marcus didn't reply.

<hr>

We slept in a barn that night. The next day, when our stomachs could take it no more, we chanced approaching a farmer. He was working his field when Marcus made an attempt at contact. The farmer looked surprised, then scared, then sent us away empty-handed.

A few hours later, we tried again with a man sitting on his porch, trying to find some shade from the afternoon sun. At first, it appeared we would achieve the same result, but just as the man barked at us in Dutch to go away, his wife hurried out of the house and scolded him.

She called after us, with a bright smile on her face, and motioned us inside. We were skeptical at the start, but we could not refuse when she laid out some bread, butter, and milk. We tore into the food without manners. Even Harry dug in. The woman's husband gave her a knowing look, and after the meal we tried to express our thanks repeatedly. She smiled. He frowned. But we were allowed to stay. She even made up a small bed and a sleep roll for us in a spare room upstairs.

Marcus and I would have to bunk up. I smiled as I recalled how I once swore I'd never share a bed with him again. Everything was different now, and I was nervous about it for new reasons.

We lay down that afternoon. The Flyer insisted he would be no trouble, but Marcus and I resolved to rest in shifts just in case.

I woke in the dark and noticed immediately that the cramped room felt more spacious than when I'd fallen asleep. Marcus sat on a stool beside a window. He'd pulled back the wooden shutters and stared at the sky.

"You let me sleep. How long ago was I meant to wake up?" I asked.

"A couple of hours," he replied quietly. "It looks like Harry's finally conked out. Or he's pretending."

He turned on the stool to face me. The moon illuminated the edges of his silhouette, but not much else. "What happened after I left, Jane?"

"Smith is dead," I replied flatly. "We searched Ireland. We searched the sea. Then we worked out everything we could about the devices. We got to Little's body before the magic left him. I saw it attach to his ring. Then, we used it as bait so we could try to get you back. That's what led to the sortie. After we shot you down, one of the Flyers came down on us in an SE 5A. Smith wasn't the pilot you are. We didn't stand a chance."

Marcus shook his head sadly by the window.

"You know what they are?" he asked.

"I do."

"I killed one of them, the one that shot you down. He was the same one who chased us home from Ghent. In Dublin, at the barricade, I went with him because I thought I could be a spy. But they tricked me, Jane. They told me they wanted to stop the war. They told me so many things, and I don't even know what was real and what was illusion to make me look in the wrong direction."

I sat up on the edge of the bed.

"I don't think they lied about everything, Marcus."

"What are you talking about?"

"I've been thinking about what Atkins told me about them, my conversation with him in Ghent and now back in Germany. I'm not sure how to explain it, but I think they do want to end the war. I'm just not sure why or in what way."

He leaned his head back on the window frame.

"I gave them my marble," he said.

"I know."

"I got it back." He pulled the marble out from around his neck. On a separate length of cord, he wore a black amulet as well.

"Can you forgive me for that?" he asked. "I promised you I wouldn't take it off. They tricked me about you, too. I didn't know what was up or down."

I slipped off the bed and knelt by his stool, putting my hands on his knees.

"Can you forgive me for leaving in the first place?" he asked. His voice was thin. I grabbed his hands and kissed them. He bent his forehead to mine and wept like a child.

The next morning, we emerged gratefully. The farmer, through very broken English, managed to communicate that it was time for us to go. We bowed in appreciation and clasped the wife's hands many times before heading out the door. But as we walked out the front, we turned and saw a large gas-engined tractor in a field adjacent, disengaged mid-row.

Marcus tapped the farmer's shoulder and motioned to it. The man waved us off.

"No, we're mechanics. Engineers," he said. "We can help."

I had no experience repairing tractors, nor had Marcus for all I knew. But on the word *engineers,* Marcus put a hand on the back of the Flyer's neck.

The farmer eyed us suspiciously, but after several iterations of the word mechanic, and its cousins in whatever languages we could remember, we took his silence as assent.

He followed us across the field and observed. The tractor was hooked up to a set of ploughs. We took a peek at the motor. It was no more complicated than an airplane engine, and we discovered the issue in no time. It took us all morning to fix it, and much of it was spent requesting specific tools from the farmer. At first, he was very reluctant to go and find them. But before long, he was running back to the house, bringing us wrenches or screwdrivers or whatever he anticipated we might need.

We got the engine running in the early afternoon, and to my surprise, he hugged all three of us with a large toothy smile.

Watching the Dutch farmer squeeze a disgruntled faerie was nearly enough to make me laugh.

We were welcomed back to the house, and that evening, they invited us to their table. After dinner, the man went on and on in Dutch, trying to explain something lofty to us. We nodded along, mostly happy to have a roof above our head. His wife pulled out a photograph of a young man and put it in my hand.

"He's very handsome," I said.

"Zoon, zoon," she repeated.

"He's her son," said the Flyer.

"Oh, your son? You must be so proud. Where is he now?" I asked. "Where?"

Her face grew sullen, and the exuberant energy from the man faded with it. Suddenly, I knew whose room we occupied upstairs.

"I'm so sorry," I said, handing the photo back, fighting back the flashes of the blood-stained photo on Meier's body. The woman smiled and replaced it in its revered spot on the shelf.

That night, she brought us extra blankets for the room. All things considered, it had been one of the most pleasant days I could remember. But just as night had fallen, and we were about to fall asleep, a harsh knock on the front door roused the house.

"Who's that?" I whispered.

"Bad news," replied Harry.

Marcus slipped out of the bed and took a careful peek out the window. He faded back instantly.

"It looks like police," he said. "They must have found our plane. Quick, get your things. We might need a quick escape."

"Escape where?" I asked.

"We can overtake them," replied the Flyer.

"No," whispered Marcus. "We'll figure something out."

We heard the creak of the front door, and the farmer's voice, then a brusque response. We crowded close near the window. It was a drop to the ground, but I doubted we would break a leg.

"We'll leave as soon as they come up," Marcus said.

"Very well," I replied.

But just as we were about to squeeze outdoors, we heard laughter. I froze to listen better, but I'd heard correctly. The farmer and the police laughed heartily together before the familiar tones of congenial farewell. The front door closed, and the sounds of police voices faded into the evening.

We emerged from our room and found the farmer and his wife, breathing heavily, nerves rattled.

I stared, dumbfounded that they would risk such a thing for us.

"Why did you do that?" I asked.

The woman walked forward, a shawl wrapped around her sleeping gown. She touched Marcus's chest with her forefinger.

"Zoon," she said.

Marcus and I sat against a tree on the farmer's land, watching the glow of windows in the scattered cottages across the landscape light up from evening fires.

The Flyer was with our host at a neighboring farm, assessing a piece of machinery for purchase. We were reluctant to let him go, but he swore that he'd return that night, and we couldn't very well insist that he not leave our sight without raising suspicion from the farmer and his wife. But I trusted that he would come back. He liked Marcus too much not to.

And besides, we had the devices with us. Marcus wore his marble beside the Fae amulet. I wore mine. The rest were stored in a sack that never left our sight—Boelcke's goggles, Richthofen's scarf, Little's ring, and Guynemer's box. Ball's violin strings had gone back to the allies with Dupont.

On the flight out of Germany, I'd inspected Guynemer's box. It was empty, but the box itself glowed. It was a puzzle I hadn't mustered the energy to unravel yet.

I wasn't in a hurry, either. They were all parts of a life we wanted to leave behind. We wanted to pretend we had always lived on this farm and the war had never existed.

With the Flyer on an errand, it was the first stretch of time alone Marcus and I had together since Dublin. And everything had changed since then. We'd made our emotions clear to one another. We'd discovered them ourselves. And what was more, we sat together in a country not wrapped up in the war.

I rested my head on Marcus's chest. He held my hand gently. I touched the burns on his arm with my finger with all the delicacy of a feather.

From a nearby tree, an owl hooted. There was no sound of cannon fire. Somewhere far beyond the horizon, Dupont would assume me dead. He would take the news to Atkins, and Marcus and I would be free.

I shifted and lay down sideways, my head on his lap.

The Flyer had wanted me to do terrible things in the name of love. I had done them. But he had not counted on forgiveness. He had not understood that as destructive as fear and hate could be, something greater than either of them could heal things as well, and render it more beautiful than even before.

Gentle smoke rose from chimneys in the valley.

"I had a cousin in Ireland," I said quietly. "I should have told you."

"Are you part Irish?"

"No, I mean, he was stationed in Ireland. He was killed in the Rising. I didn't tell you because I didn't want you to think my judgment was distorted."

He squeezed my hand more tightly and nodded.

"So why are you telling me now?" he asked.

"Because I want you to know it was."

He smiled at the play on words.

"I'm so sorry. You never told me about him. Were you close?"

"No," I replied. "His parents and my mother didn't get on well. But his death came as a shock to all of us. I think my mother took it hard because she'd allowed some petty disagreements to get in the way of family. Grief is its own kind of magic, you know."

"Magic," Marcus repeated. He stared at the bag. "You said Guynemer's box was empty?."

"That's right. But it still lit up in the goggles. I'm not sure I have the energy to figure why yet," I said.

"The curiosity will kill me," Marcus replied, "after all we did to get it."

"Very well," I replied with a sigh. I reached for the sack and pulled it closer.

He pulled out Guynemer's box. It was made of a beautiful gold-hued wood. Its hinges were of dark iron, and it was no larger than what might hold a necklace or even a ring.

Marcus eased it open gently, lid facing me.

"Still empty," he said.

"Did you expect otherwise?"

"I don't know what to expect, anymore," he laughed.

I took it from him to inspect it over.

"I don't understand. Did the Flyer steal what was in it before he gave it to me?" I asked.

"Maybe there's a secret compartment," Marcus suggested.

"I'm telling you, Marcus. There's nothing here. Guynemer left nothing in this box."

Marcus paused, as though struck by an idea, then laughed.

"That son of a gun."

"What?" I asked.

"It's Guynemer. Before he died, the papers got hold of something he said and republished it so many times it made all of us vomit. But, maybe it wasn't just propaganda."

He smiled broadly before reciting the quote by heart.

"If one has not given everything, one has given nothing."

I pondered on this. Guynemer died at the age of twenty-three. He had claimed, officially, fifty-four victories. He was rumored to have applied for military service several times, after at first being rejected because he was considered too weak. The Flyer's words came to my mind. Had there been no war, what would have become of Georges Guynemer?

He had given everything, and left us a box with nothing in it.

"Marcus, sometimes I forget how terribly clever you can be."

"No one has ever called me clever," he replied as his eyes rested intently on mine.

Suddenly, in the sunset, I realized that the two of us had another puzzle to solve. He must have sensed it as well.

"How do we go forward?" he asked softly.

"Perhaps we need not go anywhere," I said.

"Something has to go somewhere, Jane. Do you believe anything can stand still, really?" he asked.

I tilted my head and softened my eyes to look up at him.

"There is a way I've heard to stop the time from passing," I said, "to make it stand still."

He swallowed nervously, but grinned.

"I don't know how to do this part," he said.

"Nor do I." But our faces were nearing.

In Dublin, we'd posed as husband and wife, but I had never kissed him on the lips. I'd drawn that line, intuitively, in my heart. Now, we stormed the trenches.

I leaned into the kiss, putting all my intention, all my love, behind it. I shut my eyes tightly, closing out everything but what and how we were, tried to feel his beating heart through his motions.

Something inside me wanted to be closer to him. It searched for that connection between us desperately, grappling and grasping for the life line promised deep inside his heart. This kiss would be a bridge burned forever, never to go backward again.

At length, we pulled apart and looked deeply into one another's eyes again.

"Jane," he said.

"Yes?"

"We just kissed."

I nodded. He let out a deeply held sigh.

"Can I ask you something important?" he continued.

"You may."

"When we were kissing just now, what did you feel?"

I wanted to lie to him, but this was too important.

"Nothing," I said. "Nothing at all."

He studied me for a moment, longing and pain etched into his features. I wanted to tell him it was a fluke, that I was clearly still traumatized by our experiences, that if we kissed again, or again and again and again, that butterflies and stomach knots and fireworks and everything wonderful promised by love would come. But he spoke before I had the chance.

"Me neither," he said. I blinked.

"What do you think it means?" I asked.

"It means we're not in love."

Chapter 39
Sand Castle
Marcus

And who loves joy as he
That dwells in shadows?
Do not forget me quite,
O Severn meadows.
-Ivor Gurney-

We sat for a while longer on the hill wading through the disbelief, then the relief, and finally the humor in the situation.

"But I'm sure that I love you," Jane said.

I laughed.

"Don't go mushy on me now, Jane." She hit me in the arm.

"I'm not kidding."

"I love you, too. You mean everything to me," I replied. "But come on. When have you ever craved any kind of romance with me?"

She pursed her lips. I continued.

"I tried to point out how weird it was in Dublin. You held my hand, sat on my lap, kissed my cheek, played with my hair... It was always distracting, but not because I wanted you. It was because I was worried. Hell, Jane, part of the reason I left was because I knew our relationship was changing, and it scared me to death."

She bit her nail.

"If you only knew how many men, and women for that matter, tried to force the idea on me," she said. "I couldn't so much as mention your name without Dupont making kissy faces."

"Harry and Dieter pushed it on me, too. It was kind of silly. They asked me what love was, like faeries couldn't understand the concept. It's ironic because they claimed to understand hate well enough."

"Hate magic?" Jane asked.

"Yeah. But the devices can't all be hate, right? Emotions aren't tidily boxed up like that. It's murky. Each artifact hints at the virtues of the man who left it behind. Even Richthofen or Voss—"

Suddenly, I froze. We didn't have Voss's artifact in the bag beside us. I had assumed it still sat in a curio cabinet in the faerie's hideout. But that was a foolish assumption.

"Marcus, if the Flyers wanted us to believe we were in love, it would have been for a reason," said Jane.

I stood.

"We need to get back to the house."

Even at a run, we got back to the farmhouse well past dark. By the time we arrived, we both heaved for air. We'd spent the whole afternoon walking to our idyllic spot under the tree on that hill. It must have been at least a mile out.

I thought the kiss would be the start of a new, beautiful road. It wasn't. It was a detour. If Jane and I weren't in love, my understanding of everything about the magic, my situation, and Harry flipped upside down.

And Harry was the part that worried me most.

The farmhouse was dark. No lights shined in the windows. And though we tried to open the door quietly, we might as well have busted it open with a sledgehammer because the faerie waited for us on a chair in the kitchen. He'd got his hands on a revolver, and the farmer and his wife were nowhere to be seen.

I froze just as Jane bumped into the back of me.

The barrel of the gun glinted in the light that came in rays from outside. Its mouth was cold and lifeless. Harry extended his hand. In his lap sat a small cracked mirror. It was the mirror I'd seen him holding when I'd first met him. Voss's mirror.

"Devices, marbles, amulet, in that order," he said. I shook my head.

"Now," he repeated. I should have resisted more, but something in me wanted to obey him, something that wasn't mine.

"No, Marcus, don't!" cried Jane. She put her hands on my arms to keep them from moving.

"Jane, stop," said Harry. "I really don't want to shoot the two of you, but I will. You know I will."

At a glance from me, she eased her grip, and my hands moved of their own accord. First, I dropped the bag at his feet. Then, I slipped my marble off my neck and put it in his hand. I turned to Jane.

"I won't," she said, putting her hands over hers as protection. "I just got it back."

It. She meant me.

"Jane, he'll take it either way." I gently but firmly pulled her hands away and took it from her neck. It found its way to Harry's hand as well. Then, at last, I pulled the amulet off its length of cord and dropped it in with the others.

The moment the amulet left my fingers, a palpable sense of control returned to my limbs.

"Voss's mirror," I said. "I thought you left it back at the hideout."

Harry shook his head.

"Boelcke's vision," he said. "Richthofen's leadership. Ball's individuality. Guynemer's sacrifice. Little's loyalty. Voss's...?" He hung the name out there to see if I knew.

"Influence," I finished.

"Yes," smiled Harry. "You're learning to recognize it without the goggles."

"I felt it when Bowman told me the story of his last dogfight. His influence still carries in a room of pilots." I shifted uneasily on my feet. "How long have you been influencing me? Since Dublin?"

"Only gently," he replied. "You were still reeling from Lufbery's death. With Jane's own grief distracting her, we found you with a void of deep friendship, a vacuum where fraternity and love once was. You required no great persuasion. We leaned on it, admittedly, to speed our bond along, yes. But you unraveling your romantic feelings for Jane, that had to be unassisted."

Jane took my arm.

"You wanted us to believe we were in love," she said. Harry nodded. "But why?"

He calmly held up the two marbles. "Living magic," he said. "Living, corrupted, human magic. I despise blatant falsehood, Jane, as I've told you. I never said the two of you were in love, only that you loved one another. Blame the English language for its ambiguities. You loved one another enough to forgive unspeakable harms. Abandonment. Betrayal. But human love, in such a pure form, was inaccessible to us. We needed to corrupt it to control it. And sometimes, the best way to corrupt a love like yours is to introduce the concept of romance."

My blood boiled.

"You purposefully distorted our friendships," I said.

"I needed you to distort your friendship and your sense of identity, too. At one point, Marcus, you had given up on Jane because you were convinced that the version of her you loved was gone." He laughed darkly. "You lied to yourself about completing some mission no one gave you. But really, you left because she was in her darkest hour. She needed you, and you were too afraid to stand by her side and take the hurt. How loving does that sound? She was never two versions of herself. People aren't gone until they're dead. The one thing you may count on people doing is changing. If that invalidates love, then the concept doesn't exist."

He turned the gun on my friend. I put myself between them.

"And Jane, you let fear get such a hold of you that you shot down your best friend in the world, a man you'd moved mountains to find, a man you would die for."

He stood up and motioned for us to sit as he circled to the door.

"We corrupted your bond many ways over. That you both succumbed to the ambitious, illusory promises of romance, and desire was just the magical sealant necessary to freeze that corruption in time. Now, the love that created these two marbles is volatile and pliable. I have plucked them from you at their ripest. I can build with them at last."

I wanted to pounce on him, wrestle the gun from his grasp and take back the serene life we'd had such a small glimpse of. At the same time I wanted to slap him so he'd come back. He wasn't like this on the submarine. He wasn't like this for the whole time I'd known him. I wished he would break his determined expression and the three of us could laugh it off as one big joke.

But then, that was just me missing Luf.

"Oh, don't be so broken up, Marcus," he said. "I do care about you deeply. When we started, I didn't expect to find such a bold and honorable heart as yours. But I can't untie the knots I've made. Dieter sacrificed himself for our cause. We made sure that you would best him in that sortie. You had to believe you had taken control of the situation, that it was you and Jane against the world again. Only then would you feel the confidence and recklessness to pursue her romance. But I can't give up Dieter's sacrifice for something as worthless as my own emotions."

He swallowed. He wasn't lying. This was hard for him.

"You really are trying to stop the war," I said. "But we're not gonna like how you do it, are we?"

He shook his head with regret and recited the poem Dieter had shared with me before we flew to Avesnes.

"And if I fall march bravely on, hold the standard high aloft. Though closed my eyes, and still my lips, still can I hear your song above."

"There are other ways to end the war," Jane offered. "With your help, and with Voss's mirror, Mustermann could leverage support for peace in Germany and—"

"You have not seen what we've seen," he said. "I'm sorry, my friends. I wish we lived in the luxury of a world where our concurring views amounted to no great disturbance. But I have restitution to make. I care for humanity, and I must preserve it if I can. The police will be here soon to take you. As soldiers crossing into neutral territory, they will imprison you to maintain Holland's neutrality, and I will finish what Dieter and I started."

"The farmer and his wife?" Jane asked. "Did you kill them?"

"No, of course not," he said. "But I explained to them that you two are wanted and dangerous and the police will be coming tonight. They'll return tomorrow. They were quite upset over it."

He stuffed our marbles in his pocket. A curious breeze swept through the room from the open door. Harry hesitated before continuing, mulling over what he said next.

"May I ask you something?" he asked, lowering the gun. "Not as your opponent, but as a friend and student of human emotion."

I scoffed at the notion he could point a gun at us one moment and treat us with candor the next. But I guessed that him lowering his gun should have comforted me. Maybe he was telling the truth, and our friendship was no more than collateral damage in the business he was honor-bound to pursue.

But it was Harry that told me it was all personal.

"If you understood anything about human emotion, you'd know not to ask," said Jane.

"Alas, I am merely Fae," Harry replied. "It's only—what pulled you to the romance? Why pursue it? Was what you had not enough?"

I turned to Jane in the mostly dark room and wondered the same. We had undergone relentless teasing, poking, and prodding about the state of our friendship. I imagined that everyone who worked with us had assumed, at one point or another, that we were involved and desperate to keep it a secret, everyone except Luf. He understood our great secret—that there was no secret at all.

We were two people trying to navigate our darkest waters, and we saw in one another a hope that we might make it through to a happier time. We didn't have the bravery to consider what that happier time would look like.

"Perhaps you don't know yourselves. I only thought I'd—"

"It's because we won't last," I replied. "We know we won't. Either we will die, or the war will end, and then what? We're a sand castle. That's all. And the tide is coming in. Maybe if it were romantic, we could survive tomorrow's waves. If it were romantic, there'd be a script to follow. But you can't take home a sand castle."

A sparkling tear came down Jane's face, lit up by the shaft of moonlight coming through the door. But she didn't lower her brave face.

"Rocks to trouble. Trouble to sand. Sand to fire. Fire to glass," said Harry quietly. He studied our faces as though to commit them to memory. "Farewell, Marcus. Farewell, Jane. If only the generals of the world reasoned as you do."

He picked up the bag of arcane devices and closed the door swiftly, shutting us into the dark inside. It clicked with the sound of a heavy lock closing. I sprang forward to try the handle. It rattled, but did not move. I peered at the hinges.

"Can you find any tools?" I asked.

But Harry had been thorough. He knew we were mechanics. He left us nothing to work with.

"We could try the windows upstairs," Jane suggested quietly.

"We both know they're boarded up. He'd have thought about it."

"Still, we should try."

I nodded, and without hurry, we walked up the steps to check. Just as suspected, they were sealed tight.

He had closed us in well.

"I've never made a castle in the sand before," said Jane. "I'd always wanted to. Tell me. Does it hurt much when the waves knock it over?"

"Enough," I replied. "Enough that the hurt sticks with you longer than the castle was there."

We stepped carefully down the stairs in the dark. She took my arm.

"Does that mean they're not worth building?" she asked.

I patted her hand.

"You know, I've seen a lot of castles since I got to Europe," I said. "Few of them are left standing."

We sat on the couch and waited in silence.

At length, Jane spoke up.

"Well, now that we know we're not in love, we have to get the marbles back, don't we?"

"Obviously. They're ours," I replied. "I'm not about to let a faerie use them for who knows what."

She put her arm around my shoulders.

"I missed you, Marcus."

"I missed you, too, Jane."

It took no more than an hour before they started banging on the door.

END OF BOOK TWO

Review

Dear reader,

Thanks for continuing the Marcus and Jane's magical journey.

If you enjoyed the book, I humbly request that you take a moment to leave a review. A simple review or rating on Goodreads, BookBub, Amazon, or any other book outlet goes a long way in helping the series gain greater success. I'm so grateful for every review and rating, and I appreciate it in advance.

Thanks again. I hope to see you again in the final installment of The Shards of Lafayette.

Sincerely,

Kenny

About the Author

Kenneth A. Baldwin writes stories that blur the lines between history, magic, and reality. He loves finding oddities in history books with unbelievable tales or unexplained phenomena.

Before writing novels, Kenny paid his way through law school by performing and teaching humor. e. You can still catch him on stage or in corners of the Internet that feature sketch and improv comedy. Now, he lives nestled under the Wasatch Mountains with his wonderful wife, sons, and dogs.

f facebook.com/kennethabaldwin

instagram.com/kennethabaldwin